Praise for *Exiles*

'Once again, Harper proves that she is peerless in creating an avalanche of suspense with intimate, character-driven set pieces that are as exquisitely engineered as the inner workings of a Steinway. Harper's legions of fans will exult in reading *Exiles*'
David Baldacci

'A truly wonderful read. Rich in detail, landscape and character, and deeply satisfying on all levels'
Sarah Hilary

'Harper skilfully ratchets up the tension in this powerful, slow-burning portrait of small-town life . . . high-quality, atmospheric crime fiction'
The Mail on Sunday

'Exceptional in every way'
Jane Casey

'This is a softer, gentler Harper, but with the same fine writing and addictive storytelling'
Ann Cleeves

'Atmospheric, beautifully observed and fluently written, this is Harper back at her very best'
Daily Mail

'A murky, unsolved crime in the past; an Australian setting so dramatic it's almost a character in itself'
The Washington Post

'This is another must-read, one that you'll reluctantly leave'
Belfast Telegraph

What readers say about *Exiles*

'The embodiment of literature at its best. Love it and highly recommend'

'I couldn't put the book down and now I have finished it I feel somewhat bereft! Please don't make us wait so long for the next one Jane!'

'Absolutely beautiful, well-written, great storyline, great characters. Satisfying ending. Can't recommend it highly enough. If I could give it ten stars I would'

'One of my favourite authors!'

'A brilliant, slow-burning, tension-building, mystery'

'Wowsers. Jane Harper is (I think) the best crime writer in the business, the queen of outback noir and *Exiles* is a stunning book'

'Such a clever and thoroughly enjoyable book'

'BRILLIANT! One of the best books I've read in ages. This author just keeps raising the bar'

EXILES

Jane Harper is the author of four internationally bestselling Australian mysteries, including *The Dry*. Her books are published in forty territories and have sold more than 3 million copies worldwide. Jane has won numerous top awards including the CWA Gold Dagger, the British Book Awards Crime and Thriller Book of the Year and the Australian Book Industry Awards Book of the Year. The 2021 movie adaptation of *The Dry*, starring Eric Bana, is one of the highest-grossing Australian films of all time.

Jane worked as a print journalist for thirteen years in both Australia and the UK, and now lives in Melbourne with her husband, daughter and son.

JANE HARPER

EXILES

PAN BOOKS

First published 2022 by Pan Macmillan Australia Pty Ltd

First published in the UK 2023 by Macmillan

This paperback edition first published 2023 by Pan Books
an imprint of Pan Macmillan
The Smithson, 6 Briset Street, London EC1M 5NR
EU representative: Macmillan Publishers Ireland Ltd, 1st Floor,
The Liffey Trust Centre, 117–126 Sheriff Street Upper,
Dublin 1, D01 YC43
Associated companies throughout the world
www.panmacmillan.com

ISBN 978-1-5290-9846-4

1 3 5 7 9 8 6 4 2

A CIP catalogue record for this book is available from the British Library.

Typeset by Palimpsest Book Production Ltd, Falkirk, Stirlingshire
Printed and bound by CPI Group (UK) Ltd, Croydon, CR0 4YY

Visit **www.panmacmillan.com** to read more about all our books
and to buy them. You will also find features, author interviews and
news of any author events, and you can sign up for e-newsletters
so that you're always first to hear about our new releases.

For the readers, who make these books what they are.

Prologue

Think back. The signs were there. What were they?

They all asked themselves the same questions afterwards.

How did it come to this? Could we have stopped it?

That was the key one, Aaron Falk knew. And the answer was probably yes. Even with no warning – and there were warnings – the answer was almost always yes. A million decisions paved the road to a single act, and a single act could be derailed in any one of a million ways. But choices had been made – some conscious and considered, some less so – and of all the million paths that had lain ahead, this was the one they found themselves on.

The baby was asleep when she was discovered. She was just short of six weeks old, a good weight for her age, healthy and well, other than being completely alone. She would have been warm enough deep inside her bassinet pram. She was swaddled carefully in a clean wrap purchased from the state's leading baby-wares retailer, and tucked in with an artisan wool blanket, thick enough to have the effect of flattening out the bundle of her shape if placed in the right way. It had been placed in

1

exactly that way. A casual glance towards the pram would inevitably first see the blanket rather than the baby.

It was a spring night and the South Australian sky was clear and starry with no rain forecast, but the weatherproof hood had been pulled over to full stretch. A linen square normally used as a sunshield was draped over the opening between the hood and the pram. A casual glance would now not see the sleeping girl at all.

The pram was parked alongside a few dozen others in the Marralee Valley Annual Food and Wine Festival's designated pram bay, fighting for space in the shadow of the ferris wheel with a tangle of bikes and scooters and a lone tricycle. It had been left in the far corner, the foot brake firmly on.

The contents of the bay were collected one by one over the next couple of hours, as families who'd been mixing wine, cheese and carnival rides decided they'd celebrated local produce enough for one night. By a little after 10.30 pm, only the pram and the assistant electrical technician's bike were left.

The technician paused as he undid his combination lock. He looked around. The festival had officially closed half an hour earlier and the site was mostly clear now, with only staff still around. The technician put his lock in his backpack, swept his eyes once more over the rapidly darkening grounds, then walked over to the pram. He bent and peered under the hood, then straightened and pushed it all the way down. The swaddled bundle stirred at the rush of cool air as the technician pulled out his phone and made a call.

The baby's name was written on the label of her onesie. *Zoe Gillespie.* Her family wasn't local – not anymore, at least – but the festival director and the responding on-duty officer knew both her parents by name.

Zoe's mother's phone rang from the nappy bag stowed in the shopping holder underneath the pram. The tone trilled loudly in the night air. The zipped bag also held a set of car keys and a purse complete with ID, cards and cash. The technician ran out to the visitors' car park. A family sedan matching the make on the key ring was one of the few remaining vehicles.

Zoe's father's phone rang a couple of kilometres away, in the foyer of the Marralee Valley's better Italian restaurant. He'd waved off his own parents in a taxi and was now paying the meal bill while chatting to the owner and her husband, who both remembered him from school. He was showing them pictures of Zoe – his firstborn, and already six weeks old on Sunday; he could hardly believe it – and the owner was insisting he accept a celebratory bottle of sparkling wine on the house, when his screen lit up with the call.

The restaurant was a fifteen-minute walk from the festival grounds. The restaurant owner broke the speed limit that she herself had campaigned for to drive him there in just over three, slamming on the brakes right outside the main gate. He ran from there past the closed and darkened stalls, all the way to his daughter's side.

The site was searched. Zoe's mother, thirty-nine-year-old Kim Gillespie, was not found.

Volunteers were assembled and the area was combed again. Then the car park, then the vineyards on either side. The pram had been parked facing east, towards the back of the festival site and the overflow exit. Beyond the exit lay bushland and a small track that led only one way. The search moved along that track, following it all the way down to the reservoir. Then along the broad leisure trail that circled the water – empty at that time of night of walkers and service vehicles – to the highest point along the rugged embankment: a steep rocky ledge known locally as the Drop. Far below, the reservoir stretched deep and wide.

Two days later, they found a shoe. Kim Gillespie's white trainer, waterlogged and streaked with sediment, was recovered more than a kilometre to the east, jammed in the dam's filters.

Specialist divers were called to broach the crack in the base at the centre of the natural reservoir. They went as deep into the cavernous void as they could, while searchers swept the perimeter on foot and in ranger vehicles, and volunteers combed the shallows in their weekend boats. The search continued for another week, then two, then slowed and finally stopped altogether, with promises to return when the water level dropped. Spring turned into summer and autumn. Zoe grew out of her pram, took her first steps, needed shoes of her own. Her first birthday came and went.

What did I see? Those who knew and loved the family were left with their questions. They asked themselves and each other. *What did I miss?*

But Zoe's mother did not come back for her.

Chapter 1

One Year Later

Someone else was already there.

Aaron Falk felt faintly, if unreasonably, annoyed as he pulled up next to the other car. The turn-off had been as hard to spot as he remembered, almost swallowed by the bushland towering over both sides of the road. It was so well concealed, in fact, that Falk had blithely assumed that what was waiting at the other end of the track would be his alone. Not so, he could see now as he touched the brake and suppressed a sigh.

Falk hadn't been alone there last year either. Greg Raco had been in the passenger seat then, Falk following his friend's directions as they neared the end of their eight-hour drive. Raco had ignored the sat nav, especially after they'd crossed the Victorian border into South Australia. His high spirits had been infectious and they'd chewed through the kilometres, taking turns trading news and picking the music. Raco's newborn son was being christened that weekend, in the same church where Raco and his brothers had been themselves

5

several decades earlier. His wife and two kids had already made the trip and were waiting at the other end, but Raco's sergeant duties had held him back. He was clearly keen to be reunited with them, so Falk had been surprised when he'd suddenly leaned forward in the passenger seat, peering at the empty road and pointing to a patch of trees. 'You see that break ahead? Turn there.'

They had still been a good thirty minutes out of town and Falk could see nothing. The stretch of bushland had looked identical to the rest lining the route. 'Where?'

'There, mate.'

Falk had still missed it, and had had to illegally reverse several metres before he saw the single-lane track. He'd eyed the unpaved surface and mentally assessed his car's suspension.

'What's at the other end?'

'Quick detour.' Raco had grinned. 'Trust me. It's worth it.'

He'd been right. It had been worth the stop, both then and now.

With no Raco beside him this year, Falk had slowed to an almost crawl and still managed to slide past the turn-off. He'd caught it in his rear-view mirror and, again reversing further than ideal even on a clear road, had bumped up the track that looked like it led exactly nowhere. At the end was a small clearing and one other car.

Falk came to a stop and switched off the engine. He sat for a moment, staring ahead to where the heavy bushland parted. The sky was a bright dome, glowing with the vibrant blue of spring. Nestled below was an intricate patchwork of greens that made up the Marralee Valley. Falk had felt last year that the view had been all the more beautiful for being so unexpected. But now, lit up by the late-afternoon sun, it was even better than he remembered, if anything.

He climbed out of his car and stretched, the movement stirring the owner of the other vehicle. The man was standing a sensible distance from the lookout's wooden safety rail. He was also staring out at the view, but his arms were crossed in a way that suggested he was taking in none of it. A child's sippy cup dangled from one hand and, behind him, a sturdy toddler sat straight-legged on the wooden picnic table, scattering a box of sultanas across the battered surface. At the sound of Falk's car door slamming, the man unfolded his arms and rubbed a hand over his eyes. He turned and handed the cup to the toddler.

It was the husband.

The recognition came to Falk all at once, followed by a jolt as he realised the little girl now smashing a fistful of dried fruit towards her mouth must be Zoe Gillespie, who up until this moment had remained frozen in his mind at six weeks old.

The man nodded at Falk and as his daughter swallowed her last mouthful, he hoisted her up and carried her to their car. He seemed to sense he'd been recognised, and his body language didn't invite questions or conversation. Fair enough, really, Falk thought. The bloke would have had plenty of questions thrown his way at the time. The husbands always did.

'You're here for the christening.' The man spoke suddenly, catching Falk by surprise. He'd stopped between the two cars and looked a little relieved, like he'd worked something out. 'Is that right? For the Racos' son?'

'Yeah.'

Kim Gillespie had been part of the extended Raco family for close to twenty-five years, Falk knew. Since that long-ago

7

autumn afternoon when she'd first ridden her bike past the Racos' house, teenage ponytail swinging, until the night last year when she'd disappeared under the bright festival lights. The christening had been immediately cancelled after Kim went missing. It had taken the Raco family a full twelve months to reschedule.

Falk took a step towards Kim's husband and child and held out his hand. 'Aaron Falk.'

'Rohan Gillespie. Did we meet?'

'Only briefly.'

Rohan was nearly as tall as Falk and while he would only be forty-two now, he looked to have aged a fair bit over the past year.

'You here for the christening too?' Falk asked.

'Yeah. Well, no, the appeal actually.' Rohan looked tired as he fastened his daughter into her car seat. 'But we'll go to the christening as well.'

'When's the appeal happening?'

'This evening. Festival grounds.'

'Festival opens tonight?'

'Yeah.'

'Good time to do it.'

'I hope so.' Rohan clicked the seat buckles and patted his daughter's leg. He turned back to Falk. 'I thought you looked familiar when you pulled up. Greg Raco's mate? You were on the witness list?'

'Yeah.'

Rohan tilted his head, trying to remember. 'Remind me. Near the entrance?'

'The ferris wheel.'

Rohan nodded as he thought back. 'Yeah. That's right.'

Falk was surprised the man remembered him after a year, but only a little. Falk had been a visitor in town, one of hundreds, but still worth following up. Rohan had probably flagged Falk's presence to officers himself – *There was another bloke there, tall, forty-something, short hair, grey-blond maybe. Friend of the Racos but on his own, kind of hanging around* – dredging up whatever information he could hours after the fact.

'You're police too, aren't you?' Rohan tucked the sippy cup in next to Zoe before shutting the car door. 'That how you know Greg?'

'Yeah, but we don't work together. I'm AFP, financial division. He's with the State Police, back in Victoria.'

'Right.' There was a muffled wail of complaint from inside the car and Rohan sighed. 'Anyway. Better keep this one moving. Good to see you. You're staying at the Racos' place?'

'Yeah.'

'Then I'll probably see you at the appeal. They'll all be there.'

'Probably. I hope it goes well.'

'Thank you.' The reply was reflexive and Falk recognised the apprehension. It was exhausting to keep hope alive. How well could a missing person's appeal really go after twelve whole months? There were no good answers left out there.

Falk watched Rohan reverse and disappear down the track, then walked over to the barrier. He leaned both hands on the railing and let himself relax for a minute, soaking up the sight in front of him. Light wisps of cloud moved across the sky, throwing delicate patterns of shadow below. From that height, the town looked small, its surrounds vivid and lush. Long rows of grapevines stretched out, their man-made perfection drawing the eye. Far in the distance, he could make out the aggressively imperfect crack where part of the giant Murray River carved its way through the land.

Rohan had the look of a man who did not sleep well, Falk thought as he let his gaze settle. That wasn't surprising, given the circumstances, plus the demands of parenting a one-year-old. But still, Falk wondered what specifically was keeping the guy awake at night, in those hours when he could be snatching some precious rest.

A few things, probably. The statement from that young bloke who'd been manning the first-aid station, for one. What the kid reckoned he had or, more crucially, hadn't seen. A couple of the alleged sightings, almost certainly. The drunk woman at the bar, maybe. The crying heard from the toilets. Confirmed or not, those were the kinds of things that played on your mind.

Falk took one last look at the view, then dragged his eyes away and walked back across the clearing. He climbed into his car and checked the directions for the last leg of the journey.

Most likely, Falk guessed as he started the engine and reversed carefully, Rohan Gillespie spent those dark early hours trawling through the choices he himself had made that night. That short stretch of time in which his movements remained uncorroborated, definitely. How long had the gap been? Falk tried to remember. Not huge. Eight minutes? Seven? Either way, long enough to cause headaches for the spouse of a missing woman.

The decision Rohan had taken to leave the festival. That moment when he'd waved goodbye to his wife and child and turned alone in the direction of town, heading into the night. The hours leading up to that moment. The days and months leading up to that night. Those things that you didn't even notice at the time. Little decisions that ultimately added up to something so much bigger.

Falk edged his car along the narrow trail, emerging from the trees and back onto the road. He turned the wheels west and pressed down on the accelerator.

Those were the decisions that lingered, he thought, glancing over as he flashed past a temporary billboard, its colours bright against the green bushland. The Marralee Valley Annual Food and Wine Festival, it told him, just thirty minutes ahead.

The little things you could have done differently, that was the stuff that haunted you.

Chapter 2

The déjà vu that had been hovering all journey really kicked into full gear as Falk pulled up the long dirt driveway and came to a stop outside the bluestone cottage.

The town of Marralee had looked much as he'd remembered, and he'd kept an eye out for the local landmarks Raco had pointed out a year earlier. That pub the Raco brothers and their various mates had drunk in when they were old enough; the park bench they'd drunk on when they weren't. A row of shops, much more gentrified these days, apparently, with painted heritage awnings and handmade soaps and organic vegetables on display. The tree-lined road that led to the school. The cricket pitch. The turn-off to the festival grounds.

Even driving at a tour-guide pace via the scenic route, it had only taken Falk and Raco a handful of minutes last year to travel right through the town and out the other side. The main street had not long disappeared behind them and the land opened up again when Raco had pointed to the dirt driveway with a painted sign on the fence.

Penvale Vineyard. Tastings by appointment.

At the other end of the driveway, they'd ignored the arrow directing visitors to the office and instead pulled around to the front of the cottage and parked up outside Raco's brother's front door.

A year on, Falk stood on the step of that same front door and knocked. It always felt to him like trauma should mark surroundings in the same way it could mark people, but that didn't often happen. Depended what the trauma was, he supposed. Here, anyway, all appeared well. Better than well. The vineyard glowed in the late-afternoon sun with the same fresh vibrancy as it had twelve months earlier. The welcome sign had been recently repainted, and carefully cultivated rows of vines stretched out in pleasing symmetry. Their leaves shimmered bold and green, and from that distance had the illusion of almost breathing, alive in the light of the warm spring day.

From inside the house, Falk heard a clatter of fast footsteps down the hall, followed by the tread of heavier ones. The door opened, and there stood Raco, a little girl at his feet and a one-year-old in his arms.

'You made it. Welcome.' Raco grinned. He didn't have a free hand so settled for gesturing with a jerk of his head. 'Come in, mate. Rita's out the back. Mind your step, here,' he added as his five-year-old daughter, Eva, clung to his jeans, entangling herself in his legs. Raco's toddler son rested against his shoulder and fixed Falk with a glassy, accusing gaze.

The kids looked older than Falk had expected, but they always did. Rita texted him photos, but Falk had last seen them in person a good six months ago, when they'd brought Eva to Melbourne to see a musical.

Raco was also looking older these days, Falk couldn't help but notice. His dark curly hair had definite flecks of grey now, and his boyish face had lines that had never been there before. He was younger than Falk, not even forty yet. But after the past year, for the first time ever, Falk thought he was starting to look his age.

'Beer? Water?' Raco called over his son's head as Falk followed them down the hall. 'Or there's heaps of wine, obviously.'

'A beer would be great, thanks.'

'No worries.' Raco gently kicked a stray toy out of the way. It may have been his brother's place, but Raco was as at home there as Falk had ever seen him.

In some ways, Raco had barely changed over the six years Falk had known him. He was still quick with a smile and had an invaluable ability to make people feel that he understood exactly where they were coming from, and actually cared about it as well. But he'd shed the green rawness he'd had when Falk had first met him, out in a barn that had once belonged to a friend of Falk's. The heat had been blazing then, the property still bearing the bloodied telltale signs of death.

Raco now wore the quiet solid confidence of a man who had come face to face with the worst and had proven himself. He had leaned into his role as sergeant of a small country town and was liked and respected by the locals back in Kiewarra. As a former Kiewarra local himself, Falk thought it was impossible to overstate what an achievement that was.

'He's here,' Raco called as they came into a large bright kitchen which in turn opened onto a raised verandah with a spectacular view of the vineyard below. A small woman in a patterned dress was leaning with one hip against the wooden post, her cloud of dark hair shining in the sun. She was ignoring the scenery, instead frowning at a printed flier in her hand.

As Falk stepped out, she put the flier down on the outdoor table, trapping the corner under her water glass.

'Aaron.' Her face broke into a smile as she came to him and rested her hands on his forearms. Rita Raco looked up at him for a moment before enveloping him in a hug. 'Hello. So good to see you.'

She meant it, Falk could tell, and he felt a rush of pure warmth towards them both. That was the thing about Rita and Raco. Their friendship was as close to unconditional as Falk had ever found.

'How long have they let us have you for, in the end?' Rita said as she took Henry and settled him into his highchair with a banana in his hand.

'A week.' Falk had tried for two and got a flat no, which he'd pretty much expected given the current workload. 'If that's okay?'

'Of course.' Rita smiled and didn't add anything – *You really can't stay longer?* – and Falk loved her a little bit more. That was the other thing about the Racos. They never made him feel like what he was offering fell short.

'Thanks for driving all the way out,' Raco called as he disappeared back into the kitchen and reappeared a moment later with three beers. 'For a second time.' His smile dipped a little as he passed one each to Falk and Rita.

'Of course. Couldn't miss this.'

Falk had been surprised and touched on that evening a few months before their son's birth, when Raco and Rita had come down to Melbourne to take him out for dinner. Falk had suggested a restaurant he knew they'd like, and after they'd ordered, the couple had asked Falk if he'd consider being their baby's godfather. Also, if it was all right by him, they'd like to name their son Henry Aaron Raco.

'Really? You don't want to ask someone in the family or –'

'No, mate. We want to ask you,' Raco had said, as matter-of-fact as he ever was. 'So what do you reckon?'

'Well, yeah. Thank you.' Falk's answer came automatically. 'What do I have to do?'

'Not too much. Be a good influence.'

'We wanted someone we trusted.' Rita had smiled at him. 'So who better?'

Later, when Raco had gone to the bathroom, Rita had scraped her dessert bowl empty, then pushed it aside.

'So, the thing is,' she'd leaned in a little, 'his parents and grandparents were quite religious. He might be lapsed, but you can never totally get rid of it. Runs quite deep, you know? He'll play down this godparent thing but it actually means something to him.'

'I know. I'm honoured. Genuinely. I didn't expect this.'

Rita had looked at Falk across the empty plates, her face a little sad. 'You really didn't, did you? Even after everything.'

'Well, it's just that you have so many people –'

'That's true. But we wanted you.' She'd taken his hand, placing it on her stomach. 'It's not like the movies, I'm afraid. And fair warning, it's more church than I find ideal, personally.'

'Noted. But still up for it.' Under his palm, Falk could sense the future Henry Aaron Raco stirring, and felt a protective surge. 'Thanks, Rita. I'll do my best for you all.'

'We know you will.'

Had he really done his best? Falk wondered now, as thirteen-month-old Henry regarded him with nothing warmer than suspicion. He'd had good intentions. He'd driven out to the Marralee Valley last year for the christening, fully ready to play his part, but then everything had been derailed. When he'd got back home to Melbourne, work had been manic and sometimes he'd blink and find whole months had gone by and he hadn't once spoken to the Racos.

Okay, he thought, smiling at Henry. Starting now.

Henry slid his dark little eyes away, as though embarrassed on Falk's behalf.

'Ignore him.' Raco laughed and plonked a sunhat on his child's head. 'Grab a seat.'

Falk pulled up the chair next to Rita, while Eva lolled against the table beside him, fiddling with a glittery hairclip. Eva was big for five, with her mum's curly hair but her dad's eyes. She kept stealing glances at Falk, a little overwhelmed by his presence. Her parents had once mentioned that it had been Falk who'd given her the doll which had been her constant companion for the past few years. That, coupled with the fact that she only saw Falk in person on rare occasions, had given him something of a Santa Claus allure.

'Watch the table, sweetheart,' Rita said as Eva leaned in to slip Falk the glittered hairclip and nearly knocked over Rita's water glass.

'Thanks very much, Eva.' Falk took the clip and moved the glass. Beneath it was the printed flier Rita had been looking at. Kim Gillespie's face smiled up from the paper.

The photo had been taken in sunlight and the woman's dark brown hair had a sheen to it. She had slightly rounded features that made her appear a little younger than her thirty-nine years, and she looked happy in the photo. Falk wondered when it had been taken.

'He's been out there for a while,' Rita murmured suddenly, and Falk glanced up in time to see Raco nod.

The pair both had their eyes trained on the vines stretching

17

out below. At first the space appeared empty but, following their gaze, Falk could now see the shape of a man moving along the rows. He was alone and walking at a slow pace. He stopped at a fence post, something unseen catching his attention, then after a long moment continued on.

'How is your brother?' Falk said, and Raco and Rita exchanged a glance.

'Charlie?' Raco rubbed his chin. 'Yeah. He's not bad. Considering.'

Falk nodded. If there was one person likely to attract even more questions than the spouse of a missing person, it had to be the ex-partner. However amicable the parting of ways was said to have been.

Charlie Raco and Kim Gillespie had shared a seventeen-year-old daughter and an on-again, off-again relationship, which had sparked to life with a teenage infatuation, bumped along for two decades and finally fizzled out for good five years ago. A co-parenting arrangement and division of assets had been mutually agreed without the need for either party to engage a lawyer. Falk knew this, because everyone knew it now. The details of the relationship had been rehashed and picked over at length after last year.

Falk turned back to the vines, but the rows once again appeared empty. He couldn't see where Charlie Raco had gone. He reached out instead and picked up the flier from beside Rita's glass.

'Zara got them made up,' Rita said.

Falk nodded. The seventeen-year-old. He cast his eye over the information. All the important stuff was there. She'd done a good job. 'And what's the plan tonight?'

'The festival's agreed to do a minute's silence for the anniversary,' Raco said. 'Plus an appeal on the main stage.'

'Appealing for what exactly?' The question came out more
bluntly than Falk had intended, and he rephrased. 'I mean, are
there doubts? I thought after they found her shoe it was pretty
much –'

'Not doubts,' Rita said quickly. 'But questions, I suppose.
About Kim's state of mind on the night.' She glanced towards
the house and Falk guessed that Kim's older daughter was
inside somewhere. 'But we're trying to manage Zara's expect-
ations.'

'She's struggling?' Falk said.

Rita flashed a reassuring smile as her own daughter looked
up, and waited until Eva wandered off in search of more gifts
for Falk before she spoke again.

'To be fair, it's not only Zara pushing for this; we'd all like
to know. I mean, I still think about it a lot,' she said, and Raco
nodded in agreement. 'What Kim must have been thinking to
leave her baby like that.'

Falk looked down at the caption below the woman's photo.
*Kim Gillespie, age thirty-nine. Last seen at the opening night of
the Marralee Valley Annual Food and Wine Festival. Brown hair,
brown eyes, medium build, 168 cm. Wearing a dark grey jacket,
white or cream t-shirt, black jeans or leggings, white trainers.* Falk
had never met Kim and as far as he knew had seen her alive
only twice – once on a phone screen and once from a distance.

'I reckon the locals have probably said all they can say by
now, but the opening night's always mostly tourists.' Raco took
a long pull on his beer. 'They'll probably get maybe a thousand
of them tonight. Lot of the same families come every year. So
it'll jog a few memories, at least.' His frown returned. 'Like it
or not.'

Falk nodded. He'd been involved in all kinds of witness

statements over the years, and among the least helpful – worse than those who refused to speak, worse than those who straight-up lied – were the well-meaning bystanders who reckoned they'd seen plenty. It was rarely deliberate, most people simply wanted to help. Falk didn't blame them; there was something in human nature that compelled people to fill in the gaps. But what they'd seen and what they thought they'd seen were not necessarily one and the same.

Falk looked out to the empty vines again and thought back to his own statement last year. The local cop had been young and his questions a little leading at times. He should have known better and if they'd been in the same chain of command, Falk would have pulled him up on it.

How did Kim seem?

Falk couldn't say. He couldn't even begin to say.

He suspected he probably wouldn't have remembered anything much about those minutes at all if Kim hadn't gone missing, but that was life. Insignificant things became significant unexpectedly. He'd tried to pick out only what he could recall for certain.

The time. It had been 8 pm, and he knew that because the children's fireworks had started. Night had crept in and he remembered the lights and music had suddenly felt brighter and louder, the way they always did in the dark.

It had been busy. There were lots of people around but Falk had been alone. He had been making his way back across the grounds from the east end of the site towards the main entrance on the western edge. He'd been returning from the festival's head office to the Penvale Vineyard stall, where Raco and Rita were waiting for him. He had weaved through families who were parking or collecting prams and bikes from the bay near the ferris wheel, and was just past the ride itself when he'd suddenly slowed on the path, and then stopped.

The young cop should have asked the reason why, but he hadn't, and so Falk hadn't offered. It had had nothing to do with anything that night, anyway.

And that's when you saw Kim Gillespie?

No. Here's what had happened: a burst of static screeching from the speakers by the ferris wheel had snatched Falk's attention away from the path and, still distracted, he'd glanced towards the ride. A man nearby had also flinched at the noise and their eyes had briefly caught in mutual irritation. Falk hadn't really known the man at the time, but was later able to confirm that it was Rohan Gillespie. Rohan had been chatting to a couple with a tired-looking toddler, who were eventually tracked down and positively identified as tourists from Queensland.

Above them all, the ferris wheel had been continuing its slow rotation. The carriages on the wheel were the enclosed kind, like gondolas or cages, designed to seat family or friendship groups together. Perhaps designed also to stop falls, Falk reflected later, of both the accidental and deliberate kind.

By this point – Falk had leaned in to make sure the young officer was clear on this – he had already been losing interest in anything happening in the area around the ride. Falk's focus had been slipping elsewhere, even as he and Rohan Gillespie broke eye contact. Rohan had turned to say something to the tourists and then pointed, upwards to the dark-haired woman and baby at the very top of the wheel. The movement had been enough to snag Falk's gaze and, driven by some animal survival instinct rather than any real curiosity, he'd looked up himself. He'd sensed rather than seen Rohan wave from the ground. For a beat there had been no response and then a

JANE HARPER

small movement from the gondola at the top of the ride. Falk
had already been turning away as she'd waved back.

Now, a year later, Falk sat on Raco's brother's verandah with
the printed picture of Kim on the table.

Last seen.

There was contention over the exact timings of many events
that night, but the children's fireworks had at least pinned that
one to a point on the clock. Falk's statement had become one
of several used to map Rohan's movements, which – other
than those missing eight minutes or so – had eventually been
independently confirmed from the time he'd waved goodbye
to his wife and daughter on the ferris wheel until the moment
two and a half hours later when his phone had buzzed in the
Italian restaurant with the news that his child had been discovered alone in her pram.

How long Kim had lingered after her husband had left the
festival grounds was still a matter of debate. As was exactly
what had happened over those two and a half hours.

Maybe she had wandered. Maybe she was the woman who
had joined the increasingly boisterous festivities outside the
ale tent with a group of people who had never come forward,
spirits soaring to a point where the overworked barman had
been forced to cut her off.

Or maybe she had gone to try her luck on the carnival
games, winning a blue stuffed toy kangaroo similar to one later
found dumped in a bin. Or maybe she was across the field
talking to a man in a beanie. Or crying in the toilets. Or leaning
into the open window of a white or grey car in the car park,
speaking to the driver. Or maybe she'd done none of those
things. Maybe she'd parked the pram, turned away from her
baby sleeping inside and walked alone to the reservoir.

'Hopefully something useful will come out of tonight, anyway,' Rita said now, looking at Kim's face on the appeal flier.

Falk nodded. He would love to be able to tell Rita and Raco more about that moment at the ride. It wouldn't be an answer, but he knew the family would welcome any insight, however small. He couldn't, though. Most of what Falk could remember now had almost certainly been fabricated after the fact, he knew. Memories were fragile and fluid and prone to error and embellishment. No matter how many times he thought back to that night, how many details he tried to conjure up and how crystal clear they might seem, it didn't change reality. And in reality, Falk knew, he had barely glanced up.

Chapter 3

Raco walked Falk across the drive to the vineyard's small guesthouse. It was just as Falk remembered from last year: a tidy, white-painted weatherboard studio, set a short way from the main cottage and complete with a bathroom and basic kitchen facilities, plus a bonus postcard view of the vines.

'Rita keeps threatening to move in here herself,' Raco said with a smile as he unlocked the door and handed Falk the key. 'Bloody kids always find you, though.'

There was fresh linen on the bed and a mini-fridge stocked with cold drinks. A stack of paperback novels lay in a shaft of light on the shelf above the bedside table. Falk put his bag down and had the overwhelming urge to pour a large glass of chilled water, collapse into one of the outdoor chairs on the front porch and close his eyes, and just sit as the golden evening sun grew heavy and low. Raco was leaning against the door-frame and from the tired stoop in his shoulders, Falk suspected he was thinking the same. Instead, Falk rinsed his hands, splashed some water on his face and they both made their way back to the house.

Raco's brother Charlie was in the kitchen, chatting with Rita as they set the table for an early dinner. He grinned as Falk came in.

'Welcome back, mate,' he said, leaning over the placemats to shake Falk's hand. 'Good to see you again.'

Charlie, the middle sibling of three, was Raco's bigger brother in every way. He was stockier than his younger sibling, with a thicker and more solid version of the family's facial features. But both brothers had the same easy smile, and although Charlie had only met Falk for the first time a year ago, he had the Raco gift of always seeming genuinely pleased to see him.

He looked a little rougher around the edges this year than Falk remembered, though. Under the kitchen lights, his shave was patchy, and the fit of his checked shirt suggested he'd gained a bit of weight.

'We thought we'd better eat now.' Charlie leaned over to peer at a bubbling casserole dish in the oven. 'I'm not sure we'll get much chance later.' He straightened and glanced in the direction of what Falk guessed were the bedrooms.

'You want me to get Zara?' Rita said, following his gaze.

'It's all right.' Charlie opened a drawer and dumped a handful of silverware on the table. 'I'll go.'

He disappeared down the hall and Falk heard a knock on a door, followed by a muffled conversation. The tone was calm and a few minutes later, Charlie re-emerged, a silent teenage girl in his wake.

Zara was striking rather than pretty. She looked more like a feminine version of Charlie and Raco than like her mother, especially around the eyes. They were the giveaway. Falk felt fairly sure that if he'd passed her on the street without context, he would have recognised her as a Raco.

'You remember our friend Aaron, from last year?' Raco said, strapping his son into a highchair.

'Oh. Yeah,' Zara said politely, glancing up from her phone as she pulled out a kitchen chair. 'Hi.'

She sat, but didn't return to her screen immediately, instead running her eyes over Falk's face. She had been crying and didn't try to hide it, and there was a familiar but mildly uncomfortable element to her scrutiny. Falk couldn't immediately put his finger on it, until he realised he'd already been subjected to it once that day. It reminded him of the way Rohan Gillespie had considered him earlier, as they'd stood beside their cars at the lookout. Not suspicion – or not exactly – but a distant cousin perhaps. A kind of keen and very specific interest those left behind had in anyone who might be able to shed a ray of fresh light. *What do you know?*

'You want to run through anything before tonight?' Charlie asked his daughter. 'Practise your speech on us?'

Zara finally dragged her eyes away from Falk. 'No, it's okay.'

Charlie seemed tempted to press her, but didn't. Instead, he nodded and passed her a plate.

Even before Kim went missing, Zara had been living at the vineyard with her dad. Continuity of schooling and friends, Falk had heard someone explain last year, but he would have been surprised if the fresh dynamics of her mother's new marriage and baby hadn't had something to do with things.

Charlie and Kim had never been married, Raco had told him, even after Zara came along in their early twenties. Looking at Charlie now, Falk wondered if the two decades he and Kim had spent together in some form or another would have lasted that long if they hadn't had a daughter together. Falk didn't know him well enough to guess.

Either way, Kim, Charlie and their daughter had lived together as a family on the vineyard until Zara was twelve, but from what Raco had said, the deterioration of their relationship had been slow but steady. Eventually they'd concluded they'd be happier if the off-again status became permanent. Kim had taken a job in Adelaide and married Rohan a couple of years later. Zara had been a bridesmaid and Charlie had not only attended but supplied the wine for the reception as a wedding gift.

Now, Charlie and Zara mirrored each other's miserable expressions at the kitchen table, heads bowed as they pushed their forks around their plates.

It had barely been possible to get a word in edgeways over that same table on Falk's first night last year. Music had been playing from a speaker on the counter and Falk remembered that Rita had been sitting next to him, her mobile tucked between her shoulder and chin, arranging a catch-up with someone as she breastfed newborn Henry and popped olives into her mouth with her free hand. Charlie had been circling the kitchen, refilling glasses as he and Raco engaged in an animated sledging of their oldest brother, Ben, who was a detective sergeant up in Brisbane.

'. . . and then tries to make out he's offended by the suggestion, the way he does, like: "I am an officer of the court, I would never tow a trailer without the appropriate registration." And I'm –'

'Bullshit.' Raco had laughed and torn off a hunk of bread from the bowl beside the pasta. 'It *is* bloody registered, because he was moaning about the hassle a few months ago, so why's he pretending –'

'I know! I said, Ben, mate, look. Greg reckons it's legit. I mean, you might not *want* to lend out your trailer, but don't pretend you don't *have* a trailer –'

Charlie had broken off from the argument suddenly, Falk remembered, turning as Zara had wandered into the kitchen. She had been different last year, her expression light and soft and a half-smile curling as she read a message on her phone.

'Hey,' Charlie had called across the room. 'What did your mum say about tonight? Did you fix another time?'

Zara had looked up at her dad in genuine surprise. 'I don't know. I thought you called her.'

'What? Why –?'

'I told you. She didn't answer. And you said "Okay".'

Charlie blinked at his daughter. 'Because I assumed you'd try again.'

'Oh. I thought you were going to.'

'No, hey.' Charlie was already fishing out his phone. 'You were supposed to get back to her, as you bloody well know.'

'Yeah. I tried. She didn't pick up. I'll text –'

'Yeah, well, that might have to do at this rate.'

Rita had finished her own call and was patting Henry's back. His eyes were closed in satisfaction and his tiny milk-drunk head lolled on her shoulder as she reached for another olive. 'Everything all right?'

'Yeah.' A note of frustration had crept into Charlie's voice. 'Just Kim. She messaged Zara last night. Wants to come over tonight to drop off her birthday present but she'll be turning up to an empty house.'

Zara had at least appeared shamefaced. 'I tried, okay? She hardly ever answers since she had the baby.'

Charlie had ignored her, tapping the screen. They'd all fallen quiet and Falk had been able to hear the faint ringing from the other end of the phone. Eventually it had stopped.

'See?' Zara had looked mildly triumphant. 'She never picks up.'

Charlie had said nothing as he tried a second time. Again, they'd all listened to the ringtone for what felt like a long time. On the verge of cutting out once more, there had suddenly been a moment or two of nothing and then a rustle. A woman's face had appeared on the screen.

'Kim. Hey.' Charlie himself had sounded a little surprised. He'd propped up his phone on the table against the wine bottle. 'How're you going?'

'Hi, Charlie,' Kim Gillespie said, her voice instantly softening as her daughter had moved closer to see the screen. 'Hello, Zara, sweetheart.'

It was the first and only time Falk ever heard Kim speak. The sound was clear but the phone line lent her voice a flattened, distant quality.

'Where are you?' Charlie had reached out to adjust the angle of the phone and Falk had caught his first real glimpse of the woman. Kim's features had been distorted by the shaky upwards tilt of the camera, but he could see her dark hair. 'Still in the car?'

'Yeah. We're – ah – near the eastern bridge now,' Kim had said, and Falk had been able to picture that stretch of road, about thirty minutes from town. 'Listen, Charlie, what's up? It's not a great time, Zoe's asleep in the back.'

Falk had seen something flicker across Zara's face at the mention of her new sister. It vanished quickly, if not completely. Kim hadn't seemed to notice, turning to focus instead on a murmured voice off-screen.

'That Rohan there?' Charlie had cleared his throat. 'Congratulations on the little one, mate.'

The image blurred momentarily as Kim tilted the phone towards the driver's seat, where Rohan raised a hand in greeting.

'Thanks, mate.' The man's voice was friendly enough but hushed. 'Sorry, we had better keep it down, though, if that's all right.'

'Charlie,' Kim's own tone was brisk as she turned the phone back on herself, 'we'll talk later, okay? I'll see you and Zara soon anyway.'

'Hang on, Kim, it's actually about you coming by tonight.' Charlie had leaned in. 'We're not going to be around, sorry.'

There had been a pause. The only sound from the other end of the phone was the low hum of the car engine.

'Was that tonight?' Rohan asked.

'Yes. Rememb–?' The volume suddenly dropped, like Kim had put her hand over the phone. Another pause, and an indistinct exchange. '– stop in while you're at the restaurant.'

Across the table, Rita had pulled herself up and passed baby Henry to Falk.

'Can you hold him while I go to the toilet?'

'Ah. Sure.' Henry was placed in Falk's arms even as he answered. He'd sat up straighter in his chair and put his hand behind the kid's unsteady little head because he remembered that's what you were supposed to do. He'd tucked Henry to his chest, feeling the lift and fall of the tiny rhythmic breaths against his collar. It had been an unfamiliar experience. Nice, though, with the freshly laundered smell and the small solid weight on his shoulder.

When he'd tuned back in to the phone conversation it seemed to have ramped up a notch, Zara now talking fast.

'– and I've already said I'd meet them. So that's okay, isn't it?'

There had been no answer on the other end of the phone. Charlie was rubbing his chin, eyes on the screen.

'I mean –' Zara had glanced at her father. 'Dad's got to cover the festival stall anyway.'

Charlie had nodded. 'Yeah. You know how it gets. Opening night rush.'

'So neither of you will be home tonight?' Kim said, after what felt like a long silence at the other end. 'You're both going out to the festival?'

'Yeah.' Charlie had nodded. A beat passed. 'Sorry.'

'What about Rita and Greg?'

'All of us are going.'

'Oh.' A pause from the phone. 'Okay –'

'Okay?' Zara had smiled. 'Great, thanks, Mum.'

Falk couldn't see Kim's face but it had been clear enough even to him that that wasn't what she'd meant. Still, Zara had seen her chance and taken it. They all fell silent for a moment.

'Charlie.' There had been a new undercurrent in Kim's voice when she spoke again. Falk didn't know her normal tone well enough to place it, but if he'd had to guess, he would have said she sounded upset. 'You and Zara can't wait for me?'

Charlie was already shaking his head. 'Look, Kim, not really. I'm sorry, but we'll rearrange. I've got to do the stall. And Zara's sixteen, she wants to hang out with her mates tonight. You remember what –'

'Yes, of course, I –' The words abruptly cut short and there was a hush on both ends as the screen went dark. At first Falk thought Kim had again covered the phone with her hand, but as the seconds and silence ticked on he'd wondered if the connection had dropped in a black spot.

Charlie had seemed uncertain too. 'You still there?'

The line had been quiet for another beat, then it had been Rohan's voice that had edged through, louder now.

'Hello? Can you hear us now?' As soon as he heard them respond he dropped his volume again. 'Sorry, guys, this is all a bit hard with Zoe right here. Look, could we just agree Zara should go tonight? Have fun. We'll work something out for another time.'

'Great. Okay.' Zara was more than happy to quit while she was ahead.

'I –' Kim started at the same time as Charlie had sighed and leaned forward in his chair.

'Hey, listen,' he'd said. 'Why don't you stop by the festival instead? We'll all be there.'

'No, Dad, I'm supposed to be meeting –' Zara had started to whisper, and Charlie had motioned for her to pipe down.

'Well –' A pause. Kim had sounded reluctant, but then appeared to change her mind. 'Yes. Okay, then. We'll come to the festival.'

'I'm catching up with my parents tonight.' Rohan had clearly been less keen. 'Dad's got to go in for some more tests for something. But –' Another brief pause. 'Yeah, we could maybe swing by.'

'All right.' There had been the smallest hesitation in Charlie's answer, almost as though he hadn't expected them to agree, but by the time Falk had glanced over he'd been smiling again. 'Good. Well, we'll see you three there.'

'Okay,' Kim said in a way that had made Falk vaguely wonder – even then – if she was already regretting the commitment. 'See you there.'

'Great. Bye, Mum. Love you.' Zara had pushed her chair back to stand, her finger already hovering over the screen.

'Bye, Zara. I love y–'

Zara had tapped the screen once, and the call went dead.

There was no way she could have known at the time what was coming, Falk thought now as he looked across the kitchen at the teenage girl, twelve months on. There was a dark weight behind her eyes that had not been there a year ago, and Zara's gaze was somewhere else as she stared out of the window at the vines.

Falk would bet good money she relived that conversation often. The ending, at least. When she'd leaned forward and reached towards the screen. The single tap of her index finger, the light touch of skin against glass to cut short those last words she would now never hear from her mum. Falk hoped he was wrong, but he doubted he was. Zara looked like she felt that movement in her sleep.

Chapter 4

The sun was lower over the vineyard by the time they'd finished dinner and loaded the boxes of appeal fliers into Charlie's Land Rover. Rita and the kids came to the front door to say goodbye, Henry already wrapped in a bath towel. Raco kissed them, then climbed into the back seat next to Zara as Charlie fired up the engine.

From the passenger seat, Falk watched Rita wave as they pulled away. Her smile didn't dip, but he knew her well enough to spot the hint of stress. He couldn't decide if she was relieved or sorry not to be joining them.

Charlie didn't say anything as he drove. The boxes of fliers slid in the boot with a gentle thump as he turned out of the vineyard and onto the road. Last year they'd driven this same route, but the boot had been clinking instead, loaded with a couple of crates of Charlie's own shiraz.

'I make a few bottles most years,' he'd told Falk back then, as they'd loaded those crates into the boot. 'See how it turns out.'

'It's not a big part of your business?' Falk had asked, and Charlie had laughed.

'Not even a small part. A few of the wineries buy pretty much everything from the vines, but I keep a bit back myself for fun. Bottle it up. Sell it at the festival, couple of the farmers' markets, that kind of thing. Give it to friends, whether they want it or not.'

Falk had reached into a crate and picked up a bottle, turning it over in his hand, looking at the vineyard's logo on the label. He'd tried to imagine creating something like this from scratch, from grapes to crate. 'Does it come up well?'

'It does.' Charlie had grinned. 'If I do say so myself.'

Falk had put the bottle back. 'You didn't fancy following in the family footsteps, then?'

'No, I did not,' Charlie had said with such vigour that Falk had had to smile. The Racos were a police family, and the three brothers had grown up watching their dad oversee this very town as the long-standing local sergeant. Keeping the place firmly shipshape by all accounts, until he'd finally retired fifteen years earlier and moved away with their mum to soak up a bit of Queensland sun. He'd died a couple of years ago, Falk knew, but two of his three sons had continued his legacy with careers in the force.

'Never appealed to me at all,' Charlie had said. 'You've got to be a certain type, I reckon. No offence.'

Falk had laughed. 'None taken.'

'*I'm* a little offended,' Raco had said mildly as he straightened up a crate.

'I know, mate. That's because you're exactly that type,' Charlie had said and grinned back at his brother as he'd slammed the boot.

There was no joking in the car this year as they drove towards the festival site, barely exchanging a word. Marralee's streets were already heavy with tourist traffic and they hit a slow crawl well before they could see the grounds themselves. The site was only a few kilometres from the vineyard, Falk remembered from the previous year. Close enough for them all to walk, had it not been for the boxes of fliers stacked in the boot, but no-one complained. They were edging into the car park when Zara finally broke the silence.

'Do you think this will work?'

Raco shifted in his seat. 'The appeal?'

'Yeah.'

Falk glanced at Zara in the side mirror. She was running her eyes over the cars in the next lane, scanning the occupants carefully. He wasn't sure what she was expecting or hoping to see.

'I think it depends on what you're expecting, mate,' Raco said. 'Will it shake some memories loose, maybe help fill in the timeline a bit more? Yeah, hopefully. Are you going to come away knowing what your mum did, step by step? Unlikely. I'm sorry, I wish –'

'No. I know. It's okay.' Zara's face was still. Only her eyes continued to move, darting from one car to the next.

The approach to the site looked exactly the same as Falk remembered. Even from inside the car he could hear the lilt of a band playing somewhere in the distance, the faint notes mixing with the familiar low, steady hum generated by hundreds of people converging in one place. Parking attendants in sunglasses and high-vis vests directed cars into a single file and herded them past rows of earlier arrivals towards an open field.

Last year, it had been Charlie who had spotted Kim's car.

He'd been a little quiet on the drive then, too, but his face had relaxed a notch as they'd crept along with the traffic.

'Hey,' he'd said then, as he'd eased the car forward. 'Looks like your mum made it.'

'Where?' Zara had raised her head from her phone as Charlie pointed to a silver family sedan parked to their left. A man – Rohan Gillespie, Falk had guessed rightly at the time – was beside the boot, trying to wrestle a pram into shape.

'Oh. Good.' Zara's eyes were already drifting back to her screen.

Charlie had beeped the horn lightly and Rohan had looked up from the pram. Charlie touched the brakes, but another horn had blared from the line of cars behind, and a harried parking attendant had urged them onward with a jerking motion.

'Yeah, all right, mate, I'm moving,' Charlie had muttered and rolled forward. He'd glanced in the rear-view mirror at his daughter, a small frown forming behind his sunglasses. 'Make sure you catch your mum inside, yeah?'

Rohan had been shielding his eyes from the low sun, squinting at their car. Seeming to recognise them suddenly, he'd lifted his hand as they'd trundled past, then put the pram down and leaned around to call something through the sedan's passenger door.

'Zara?' Charlie had said again. 'You heard me? About Mum?'

'Yeah. I will.'

She'd sounded distracted, though, and in the mirror Falk had seen her eyes fixed on the back of her mother's car as they pulled away. Someone had put stickers on the tinted rear window. A chalk-drawing stick family of three – mum, dad and baby. Zara had blinked once, then dropped her gaze back down to her phone. Her thumb moved fast across her screen.

Rohan Gillespie had later told police his family had arrived at the festival site at around 7.15 pm. Zara had pinpointed that moment to 7.19 pm, confirmed by the text she'd sent a friend as they'd driven by: *Here now. Parking.*

The last alleged sighting of Kim fell somewhere between 90 and 130 minutes later, Falk knew, depending on whether you put more weight on the statement from the kids' face-paint artist or the overworked bartender. Or, as some people decided, neither.

Twelve months on and the car park was still as slow-moving as Falk remembered it, and Charlie had to park some distance away from the entrance. They each took a box of fliers from the boot and made their way through the sea of cars. The same wide bright banner Falk had seen the year before swayed gently overhead in the warm evening breeze: *Marralee Valley Annual Food and Wine Festival. Est: 1951.* Strings of lights created a canopy leading up to the entrance which glowed a warm gold in the encroaching twilight. At the turnstiles, a pair of grey-haired officials in matching fleeces kept an eye on crowd numbers, opening the side gate every few seconds to let through a family with a pram or wheelchair. Admission was still free, Falk noted, which he remembered thinking added to the community feel of the event. Beyond the entrance he could see volunteers collecting gold coin donations for a charity.

'Where are we meeting everyone?' Charlie called to Zara as they joined the bottleneck for the turnstiles. 'The main stage?'

'No, our stall.'

'Okay.' Charlie mouthed *thank you* as one of the officials spotted the boxes in their arms and beckoned them through the gate instead.

'I thought you might not do the stall this year?' Raco said to his brother once they were inside.

'Yeah, I could do without it, to be honest,' Charlie said. 'But we'd committed to three years on that spot and in the end Shane agreed we may as well.'

'Is he coming tonight?' Raco asked.

'Should be there now, hopefully. Setting the casuals up.'

Charlie led the way through the crowds, and before long Falk saw the distinctive crimson branding up ahead. The Penvale Vineyard stall had a long table along its front, with several bottles already open for tastings. A friendly young woman who looked like she could be a uni student was pouring small measures for a family group, while another pointed out something printed on the bottle's label.

Behind them in the dim back half of the stall, a large bloke was breaking down empty boxes, his shoulders and chest broad enough to stretch the fabric of his vineyard t-shirt. He'd been there last year too, and although Falk hadn't been formally introduced, he recognised the face.

'G'day, guys.' Charlie nodded to his staff and cleared a space at the end of the table for Zara to put down her fliers.

The stall looked to be more or less in the same spot as last year, Falk thought as he glanced around. He didn't claim to know much about retail exposure sites, but this seemed well positioned for foot traffic. They were right at the top of the main drag between the entrance and the exit, meaning most people had to pass by on their way in or out.

Perfect for crowd-watching too, as it had been last year. Falk had wondered for a while, at the time, if that might end up proving useful. It hadn't, in the end, other than to suggest that on the balance of probabilities, Kim Gillespie hadn't left the grounds by the main exit. Falk supposed that was useful information in its own way.

'Oh, great. Dad, that journalist came,' Zara said, and Charlie put his box on the table and looked to where she was pointing. 'There. Talking to Rohan and Sergeant Dwyer.'

Falk placed his own box down and turned as well.

Rohan Gillespie was on the other side of the wide path, standing beside a tall, grey-haired police sergeant. They were both leaning in a little, straining to hear over the noise as a woman with a notebook asked something. Nearby, a photographer with ill-fitting jeans and an equipment bag near his feet waited patiently. The reporter finished her question and the police officer nodded in response, indicating back towards the entrance at something above the canvas roofs of the stalls. Falk looked up to where he was pointing and saw a CCTV camera fixed high on a pole. That was new. They'd only had cameras on the main exit last year.

Rohan's eyes drifted down from the camera and back to the stall, with a flash of relief as he spotted the Racos there. He murmured something to the journalist, who was scribbling fast, then threaded his way across the busy path towards the stall.

'Hey. Good to see you, guys. Zara, that reporter's very keen to chat to –' He stopped as his gaze landed on the boxes. The lids were unsealed and after a beat, Rohan reached out and took an appeal flier from the top of the pile. He held it in his hand and stared for a long moment at the picture of his wife and the words beneath.

'Thanks again for doing these, Zara.' His voice was tight and he gave a tiny nod. 'They're . . .'

He searched for a word but didn't find it.

'Where's Zoe?' Charlie asked.

'Oh. With my parents,' Rohan said, still distracted by the

picture. A frown flickered across his face. 'Bit of a nightmare drop-off. They're all –' He stopped again. Shook his head. 'Anyway, doesn't matter. I had to be here.'

'You're always welcome to leave her with us,' Raco said. 'We've got all the baby stuff, so it's no extra hassle.'

'Thanks, mate,' Rohan said, but his eyes had fallen back down to his wife.

Raco seemed about to say something else, but stopped as the police sergeant began to weave his way towards them, the reporter and photographer in his wake.

'G'day, all,' the officer said as he reached the stall. 'Good to see you, mate. Welcome home.' He shook Raco's hand, then turned to Zara. 'And how are you?'

'Okay, thanks.'

'Yeah? Then you're doing better than most would be.' The officer gave her a small smile and picked up a flier, pulling a pair of reading glasses from his shirt pocket. He was probably in his late fifties, Falk guessed, but his wiry, outdoorsy build suggested he enjoyed the cholesterol and blood pressure readings of someone ten years younger. The nametag on his pocket read: *Sergeant R. Dwyer.*

'These have come up well, Zara. Good job.' Dwyer peered over his glasses at her. 'Listen, that journo wants a word before you move off, but the volunteers are here and ready so if you and Rohan are right to go, I reckon we get this started?'

Rohan's face automatically firmed into a look of attentive determination. Falk regularly saw that same expression in high-level professional meetings, where it felt crucial that the right decisions were made. It was usually bullshit. Bravado masking fear and self-doubt. He had a version of that expression himself.

Zara was counting the few dozen volunteers milling around

the edges of the stall, talking among themselves. It was a mixed bag, old and young, and one or two families. Falk vaguely recognised a handful of them as friends of the Raco family. They probably all were, in some way or another, and from the tense, eager way they waited for instruction, he could see that the events of last year still cast a shadow.

Falk hadn't been there to witness the aftermath himself; once the shoe was found and the history of antidepressant prescriptions began to seep out, Kim's death had taken the shape of a very intimate family tragedy. He had suddenly felt in the way. No-one had said as much, not at all, but he could tell his bed in the guesthouse would be more useful freed up for the relatives now arriving by the day. Falk had checked in with Raco and, separately, Rita – both already turning inwards to their family pain – and less than seventy-two hours after he'd arrived, they'd waved him off with mutual understanding on both sides.

'All right,' Dwyer said now, raising his voice over the crowd noise. 'If you're here for the appeal, please step in a little there, so we don't block the path. Yep, perfect.'

He gestured for the fliers to be passed around as the crowd formed a loose circle.

'Right. Thanks all for coming out,' Dwyer started. 'I recognise a lot of faces and I know a lot of you knew Kim well. But there'll be plenty of people here tonight at this festival who didn't know her as well, or at all. And it's them – anyone who was here at the opening last year and might have seen her – those are the people we want to talk to.

'We've got leaflets here – yeah, thanks, grab a handful each – and our aim tonight is to get people to have another think about that night. What they might have seen or noticed.

Maybe it didn't seem important at the time, but I'd rather know about it and make that call myself. I'll be around all evening, or can be contacted through the station.

'All right.' He clapped his hands. 'We'll be on the main stage a little later for an appeal and a short tribute from Kim's family, so please encourage people to be there. It's scheduled for –' He looked to Zara and Rohan for confirmation. 'Eight-thirty? Yep, eight-thirty.' He kept his eyes on the family. 'Anything either of you would like to add?'

Rohan glanced at Zara, who blinked. She wavered a moment, and when she shook her head, he cleared his throat. 'Look, we'd like to thank everyone for being here. We –'

'Actually,' Zara cut him off. 'Sorry. Sorry, Rohan. I think I do want to say something.'

'Yeah? Okay. Of course.'

Zara still seemed uncertain as all eyes turned to her, but took a breath.

'I know most of you were here last year and know what happened. So you'll probably have heard that my mum had postnatal depression. And that's true. You've probably also heard how she abandoned my sister in her pram, and went down to the reservoir drop and –' Zara stumbled over the words and stopped. She took a second to gather herself. 'That bit is not true.'

Falk saw a few among the crowd shift their weight and throw a glance to the person next to them. No-one seemed quite sure how to best react to that, and the atmosphere took on an awkward undercurrent. Raco and Charlie exchanged a look, a silent communication passing between them. They both slid their eyes back to Zara, who had also sensed the ripple in the crowd.

Rohan had felt it too, Falk could tell. The man had been listening to Zara with his head bowed, staring at a spot on the ground, but now he glanced up. The professional face had faded and he simply looked disappointed. He ran his gaze lightly over the gathered group, sending several pairs of eyes skittering away, then took a small but distinct half-step towards Zara. It barely closed any distance, but the instant effect was one of solidarity. He gave Zara a little nod of encouragement, and she looked relieved. Charlie, Falk noticed, looked like he wished he'd done the same but the moment had passed. It was too late now and he knew it.

'Yes. So,' Zara recovered her train of thought and her momentum, 'what I'm saying is, my mum would never have left Zoe. Or me. She loved us, and she would hate to see what we've all been through this past year.'

A subtle movement at the back of the crowd caught Falk's eye and he tilted his head to see better. A lone teenage boy was standing a little apart from the group, his arms folded across his chest as he watched Zara speak. He had a flier in one hand and was listening with a hint of a frown on his face.

Falk felt a faint stirring of recognition. He didn't know the kid, though. He didn't really know anyone here other than the Racos. The boy had close-cropped hair and looked about eighteen. He was all angles, with the lean coat-hanger look of a growing body trying to keep up with itself.

'I know what everyone believes happened.' A note of urgency had crept into Zara's voice. 'And actually, I can understand why. But my mum did not go down to the reservoir. Someone – *a witness* – who was working nearby all night has told police that she never went through the reservoir exit.'

The teenage boy barely reacted. He kept his gaze firmly on

Zara as several heads turned his way, but everything about his stance morphed into something instantly defensive.

So that was him. Falk felt the pieces click together now. The one who'd been stuck out at the first-aid post near the back end of the site. Who'd given his statement and – Falk guessed from the mutinous look on his face – presumably stuck to it over the past twelve months.

'Something else happened to my mum that night,' Zara went on. 'Either someone made her leave the festival, or her mental health was so bad that she agreed to go, or got tricked, or, I don't know –'

Raco and Charlie exchanged another look. Zara caught it this time.

'But Mum should still be considered out there somewhere, until we know for certain otherwise.' Her words turned sharp. 'So here are the things we need to know: the timeline of what she did that night –'

Falk glanced at Sergeant Dwyer. He was yet to meet a cop who enjoyed being told how to do their own job, but rather than seeming sceptical or annoyed, the officer's face was determinedly neutral.

'– we need to know who she spoke to and when –'

As Falk watched, Dwyer's head inclined in a near imperceptible nod, almost to himself. That was interesting. Sergeant Dwyer had been on leave last year when Kim left her daughter in the pram bay underneath the ferris wheel. Falk wasn't sure he'd ever known exactly why Dwyer was away – some family reason, maybe? – but he did remember being surprised that the sergeant had been granted time off during what had to be one of the town's busiest weeks. Whatever the reason, Sergeant Dwyer hadn't been around to deal with what happened. Falk wondered if he felt the need to make up for that now.

'I miss my mum and I love her and –' Zara sighed. She suddenly sounded very tired. 'And look, the fact is, someone knows something. That person might be here tonight. We need to find that person, so we can find Mum. So if everyone could please take some fliers, that would be great. Thank you.'

Sergeant Dwyer saw his opening and stepped in. 'Thanks, Zara. Everyone, let's make a move. Get yourselves into pairs, groups, whatever, and we'll head out. See what we can get back.'

A buzz of chatter rose as loose groups formed and began to drift away, fliers in hands and varying degrees of enthusiasm on their faces. Falk looked over to Raco, who was still in the same spot, watching Zara as she shook the journalist's hand.

'You want me to grab some fliers?' Falk said, and Raco nodded slowly.

'Thanks, we should, I suppose.'

Falk walked over to the nearest box, waiting his turn as other volunteers reached in. Nearby, he could hear Rohan being accosted by a couple of older men who were asking about his dad's health.

'– thank you, yeah, so far he's still ignoring pretty much everything the doctors want him to do,' Rohan was saying. 'But Mum's keeping him in line, lots of veggies, no booze. So, fingers crossed.'

Over by the stall, Falk could see the large broad-shouldered employee had come out from behind the table and was now standing with Charlie. They had been joined by a petite blonde woman who was wearing a crisp white shirt that opened low at the neckline and was tucked at her waist into dark skinny jeans. The three of them talked softly while pretending not to watch Zara as she thanked the reporter and photographer, then extracted herself neatly from the crowd and headed directly over to the teenage boy.

The boy straightened as she approached, and she reached up and they hugged briefly. Zara handed him some leaflets and said something Falk couldn't hear but could guess from the body language.

Was that okay?

The boy nodded. *Yeah. Good.*

Neither smiled. Zara pointed somewhere towards the east of the festival site and the boy gave a small shrug of agreement.

Falk reached the front of the line and grabbed a stack of paper from the box, then headed back to Raco, who he could tell had also had his eye on Zara's exchange.

'Here.' Falk passed him a handful of fliers.

'Thanks, mate,' Raco said, without glancing at them. 'Listen –' He was still watching as Zara and the boy walked off together. 'I reckon there are enough people covering the grounds. Let's head down to the reservoir. See what we see.'

'Yeah, okay,' Falk said, a little surprised. He shuffled the fliers straight in his hands, looked once more at Kim's face gazing out, and took half a step towards Raco. He angled his head so Charlie and the others couldn't see what he was saying, and lowered his voice. 'Mate, is something about all this bothering you?'

Raco was still looking past him, his eyes following Zara as she and the boy weaved their way through the festival-goers. 'It's bothering her.'

Not answering the question was sometimes the same as answering it, Falk thought, but he didn't push it.

'All right.' He turned in time to see Zara disappear into the crowd, and nodded to Raco. 'Then let's go and take a look.'

Chapter 5

'She reckons she's spotted her mum a couple of times this past year,' Raco said to Falk as they headed deeper into the festival grounds. The meandering nature of the foot traffic made it difficult to lift their pace much beyond a leisurely stroll. The warm evening air was heavy with the aromas of deep-fried batter and cinnamon.

'Zara has?' Falk took a quick step to one side to dodge a small child on a scooter.

'Yeah.' Up ahead, Raco's niece bobbed in and out of view as she and the boy moved through the crowd. 'Every now and again she gets one of these false glimpses.'

'That's a pretty common response, though,' Falk said. 'Especially when a body isn't found. I suppose they don't feel false at the time.'

'Yeah, that's what I told her.'

'She wasn't convinced?'

'Not really. She doesn't want to be convinced, that's part of the prob– No, thanks, not for me,' Raco said politely as a tray bearing free samples of homemade blue cheese was thrust in front of him. 'One was at the supermarket here in town. Zara said she saw Kim pass by the end of an aisle. Would not let it drop. In the end, the manager let her and Dwyer take the security footage to the station.'

'Did she find who she'd seen?'

'Kind of. It was no-one, just some woman. Apparently she didn't even look much like Kim. No-one you'd normally confuse her with. Then another time, Zara and Charlie were in Adelaide, and Zara made him turn the car around and follow a bus because she thought she'd seen Kim getting on. She hadn't, obviously. After that, Charlie was –' Raco sighed. 'I dunno. More worried. He doesn't know what to do either.'

'Rita said you'd been back here a few times to talk to Zara?'

'Three. Not counting this trip.' Raco looked down at the flier in his hand. 'Charlie thought maybe going through things from a police perspective might help. Talking her through the evidence and statements and things. Doesn't feel like it has, though.'

Raco suddenly slowed on the path, apologising as a distracted couple wandering arm in arm close behind bumped into him. Falk glanced over his own shoulder then stopped too, following Raco's gaze. Zara and the boy had positioned themselves near the beer tent. The same spot where a woman – drunk, emotional and loosely matching the physical description of Kim Gillespie – had been cut off by the bartender towards the end of the evening.

Falk and Raco watched as Zara engaged a young family who were clearly reluctant to stop. Whatever Zara said was good enough to slow the parents' stride and, in a movement swift enough to be choreographed, the boy had stepped out and presented a flier in a way that gave them very little choice but to take it. Zara continued speaking, everything about her manner earnest and urgent, and by the time the family was allowed to walk away, they were all looking at the flier and the man was pointing to it as his partner nodded. A few more people now aware of the appeal, Falk thought, as Zara and the boy quickly homed in on their next targets. The kids were doing a very thorough job. Falk glanced over at Raco, who seemed to be thinking the same.

'Let's keep moving,' Raco said and, perhaps feeling a little guilty, thrust a couple of his own leaflets at a passing group.

'So, that's him, is it?' Falk glanced back at the teenage boy. 'Zara's key witness?'

'Yeah. Joel Tozer.' Raco gestured for them to step off the path and cut down the side of what seemed to be a very popular shiraz tent, and they emerged into a different zone of the grounds, this one a maze of fairground rides. Up ahead, the ferris wheel dominated the darkening skyline. 'Although, I dunno. Are you still technically a key witness if you reckon you didn't see anything at all?'

Falk gave a small smile. 'Where exactly was he stationed?'

'I'll show you. It's up here, we've got to go past it anyway.'

They were nearly at the ferris wheel now. It had stopped to take on passengers and Falk looked up as they walked by. At first glance, the very top carriage looked empty against the last light of the day, but Falk could see it tilting a little to one side so someone must be sitting inside. A moment later, he caught a flash of movement behind the coloured bars as the occupant shifted in their seat. Back on the ground, the pram bay nearby was once again packed with buggies, bikes and scooters. There was an attendant on duty now, though. Something else that was new since last year.

Falk watched the crowd loosely gathered near the base. Some were lining up for a ride, while others waited for friends to come off. A lot were simply chatting and catching up. Either way, it was a busy intersection. Falk tried to pick out the spot where he himself had stopped twelve months earlier as the fireworks had been starting. He couldn't be sure. It all looked a little different a year on.

'Nearly there now,' Raco said as they navigated their way through the rides. It was a younger demographic around here than back at the food and wine tents, Falk noticed. Mainly teenagers or families with kids. Even they started to thin out, though, as he and Raco approached the eastern boundary of the site, and the attractions made way for admin and support tents. The lights and music were mostly behind them, and the track ahead, Falk knew, led nowhere but the reservoir trail. He thought about that for a moment. It was a faintly odd and lonely sensation to leave the bustle and noise behind.

'So if Zara doesn't think Kim went down to the reservoir at all,' he said as they walked on, 'what does she make of the shoe they found in the dam filter?'

Raco shook his head. 'Lots of things. It's not her shoe, someone dumped it, Kim dumped it herself –' He smiled without humour as he saw Falk's expression. 'No, I know. Zara tried arguing for a while that it was a coincidence. That the shoe could be anyone's. It's the most commonly sold women's size in that brand, apparently. Zara told me that herself. Do you know how many of those exact pairs were sold in Australia last year?'

'No.'

'Me neither, but Zara knows. A few thousand, I think, but

52

she could tell you exactly. She contacted the distributor and found out.'

'Enterprising.'

'Yeah.' Raco looked sad. 'That's one word for it. Anyway, it was Kim's shoe. Definitely.'

'Yeah?'

'Yeah. She'd dropped a cooking fork off the outdoor grill a couple of months earlier and scorched the side of her shoe. There are photos of her wearing them and you can see the mark. It's distinctive, not just a smudge. I've seen the images of the shoe they pulled out of the filter. Size, brand, whatever, is one thing – fair enough – but the scorch mark's right there. The shoe's hers.'

'What's Zara's answer for that?'

'She doesn't have one. I mean, there isn't one, really, is there? It's her mum's shoe and on some level Zara knows that. But, at the same time, she's grieving. Makes people selective in what they want to see, don't you reckon?'

'Yeah,' Falk said. 'Sometimes.'

The stalls had completely thinned out as they neared the eastern perimeter and Falk fell quiet now, keeping half an eye out for something he felt pretty sure was around here some-where. He was starting to wonder if he'd lost his bearings when he saw it ahead of them as the path curved around. The headquarters caravan.

It was a large retro van, parked in a secluded spot across a stretch of grass under a huge tree. Falk guessed in the daylight the leaves offered shade, but now its branches glowed with lanterns. A small folding table and chairs had been set up outside.

Falk remembered them from the previous year. He had been

walking alone back then, heading over to find this very caravan with a couple of sheets of signed paperwork in his hand that Charlie had needed to be delivered. Falk had volunteered for the task and Charlie, cheerfully distracted by the demands of the stall and still nearly three hours away from learning that his ex-partner and the mother of his child had gone missing, had been grateful.

Falk had wandered through the festival grounds for the first time then, soaking it all up with fresh eyes, and stopped when he'd found the caravan. As he'd crossed the field he'd already been watching those windows, looking for a hint of movement inside. It hadn't been easy to tell either way, even as he'd got close, ducking under a low-hanging branch and stepping around the table and chairs. He'd had his hand up, poised to knock on the door, when he'd heard a voice behind him.

'I can grab those forms off you, mate.'

Falk had turned to see an older man in an official festival fleece appear from around the side of the caravan, wiping oil from a small spanner with a rag.

'What've you got there?' The man had nodded at the paperwork. 'Safety check all signed off? Great. Leave it with me.'

'I —' Falk had looked back up at the caravan. *Was* that movement in the windows? Or a reflection of the light? In front of him, the man had his oil-stained hand out.

'I'm just giving the generator a once-over,' the bloke had said, misreading Falk's hesitation. He'd twisted his head to read the signature on the paperwork, and smiled reassuringly. 'But tell Charlie that Kev's got them. I'll file 'em straight after.'

Falk had paused. He was here now. The headquarters caravan was right in front of him. He should at least try. 'I'm supposed to give them directly to —'

'She's not in there.'

'Oh.'

'Yeah. Out on site.'

Falk had glanced once more towards the windows. All was still. The light moved on the glass and suddenly he could sense rather than see that the man was telling the truth. There was no-one in there. In front of him, the guy had still been waiting, his friendly expression undercut with a touch of something else now. Falk had got a second sense then, strongly along the lines that this man thought he was a time-waster and was debating whether or not to say as much.

'The kids' fireworks are starting soon,' the man had settled on instead. 'So she'll be out for a while. At least until they're done.'

'Right. Okay.' There hadn't been much else Falk could see to do but hand over the papers. 'Thanks. I'll tell Charlie.'

The man had smiled, clearly relieved the exchange had at last reached its sensible and satisfactory conclusion. He'd returned to his generator and Falk had stepped back from the empty caravan and walked away, carrying nothing but a deep sense of disappointment.

A full year on, and Falk realised that he was once again slowing his pace as they neared the caravan. He frowned and picked up speed to keep in step with Raco. The caravan door was open, though – he looked over, he couldn't stop himself – and there was definitely a light in the small window this time. He thought he could detect movement inside. He slowed again, but no-one came in or out.

'I heard they'd stepped up the security this year,' Raco said, and Falk's attention was dragged back to the present and the path ahead. Raco was squinting up at a camera on a temporary pole near the boundary fence, its red light blinking.

'There was another one near the entrance as well,' Falk said, pulling his focus and thoughts in line.

'I get it, I suppose,' Raco said. 'But it's a bit of a shame. I've been coming to the festival since I was born, and it never felt like something that needed a lot of surveillance. It was always about families and celebrating what we produced here, looking forward to the seasons ahead. It's got a lot bigger, though. Guess you move with the times.' Raco's face hardened. They'd reached the very edge of the site. 'And respond to events.'

They both stopped. Ahead lay the east exit, although Falk wouldn't even necessarily call it an exit, not compared with the main one at the west of the site. This was simply a break in the otherwise solid chain-link fence, with a single rope running across it at waist height. The rope could be unclipped at either end, Falk could see, or easily ducked under.

'Do many people come to the festival this way?'

'No-one really. Or next to no-one. Maybe one or two locals, but no tourists. There's nothing to stop them, but it's a pain in the arse to get in around this side. There's no festival parking. You could stop in the reservoir car park but then you've got to trek along the hiking path, and back again in the dark with a few drinks under your belt. And it's free entry anyway, so there's no good reason not to come in the west entrance.'

'Why have it at all?' Falk said. 'Safety reasons?'

'Yeah, legally there's got to be an alternate exit.' Raco stepped forward and ran a hand along the rope. He sounded tired. 'In case of overcrowding or an emergency or whatever. Same with where they position the first-aid stations.'

Falk followed his gaze along the fence to where a small first-aid tent had been set up with a chair out the front. A middle-aged volunteer was sitting alone, scrolling through her phone, a radio and clipboard on the ground beside her.

'That's where the boy was working last year?' Falk asked.

'Joel? Yeah.'

Falk looked around. This area was very quiet compared with the rest of the grounds. The tent had an unobstructed view of the exit. 'So he would have been able to see who was coming and going.'

'Yeah. I'm not saying he couldn't. But cameras at the front show Kim didn't go out the main exit and there are no real alternatives. So –' Raco shrugged.

'You're pretty sure she came out this way?'

'As sure as I can be.'

Falk nodded. If Raco was satisfied, that was good enough for him. 'How long was the kid's shift?'

'Two and a half hours – 7.45 pm to 10.15 pm.'

'Long time to stay focused, especially if you're not watching for anything special.'

'Yeah,' Raco said. 'And look, in Joel's defence, the fact is he's eighteen years old – was only seventeen then. And we've all done it, haven't we? Stared at your phone for five minutes and when you next look up, twenty have gone.'

Falk looked at the exit and found himself picturing Zara, her face tight and drawn as she'd addressed the volunteers earlier at her dad's stall. He remembered the way Joel had been watching her, his small frown, her reference to his police statement, their brief hug afterwards.

'Are they together?'

'Zara and Joel? No,' Raco said. 'Personally, I reckon it's a factor, though. They were friends as kids, but it's pretty obvious he likes Zara more than that now. So no, they're not together.

And Joel would deny this, but whether he admits it to himself or not, on some level that boy is highly motivated to tell Zara what she wants to hear. Highly.'

'So is he lying?'

'It's possible. I think more likely mistaken, though,' Raco said. 'I can believe he believes what he's saying. Charlie's known him since he was a kid, and he agrees. He's not the type to make something like this up for the sake of it. He's Gemma Tozer's stepson. The festival director?'

Raco nodded back across the wide expanse of grass to the caravan in the distance. The door was still open and the warm glow spilling out from the windows looked brighter in the growing dark. The lanterns in the tree rocked gently as the branches caught the evening breeze.

'I'm not sure if you saw her here last year, but you guys met once in Melbourne a while back, that time when I was –' Raco yawned widely, his palm over his mouth. 'God, bloody baby brain. What was I there for again? A court case or something.'

'You were stuck late on that one-day course.'

'That's right.' Raco turned and lifted the rope guarding the exit. 'Yeah. Anyway. So you remember. Well, that's her.'

'Yeah.' Falk looked back as he ducked under the rope and stepped onto the reservoir track. The light in the caravan windows dimmed a fraction, then glowed bright again. Movement within. Someone was definitely there this time. 'I remember.'

Chapter 6

It had been sixteen months earlier, Falk could have told Raco if he'd wanted to. Back on one of those dark Melbourne evenings that was still technically autumn but felt a whole lot like winter. The rain had come and gone in sharp bursts all day, leaving the pavements slick and shining with reflections of the city at night.

Rita had been five months pregnant up in Kiewarra. Baby Henry was still to be born, still to have his first christening celebration arranged, let alone cancelled. Falk had yet to ever hear of Kim Gillespie, had not yet set foot in the Marralee Valley. He'd recently got a call from Raco, though, who was going to be in Melbourne briefly for a one-day professional development course. They'd arranged to meet for drinks afterwards.

The day had rolled around and it was late afternoon in the AFP offices when Falk's phone had buzzed from the top of a thick stack of battered files that were threatening to take over his desk. Falk welcomed the interruption as an excuse to stand up and get away from them. Grabbing his phone, he moved over to the window. It had started raining again and he watched a tram come to a stop down below, waiting as passengers shook umbrellas and brushed off their jackets before stepping on. They were all dressed differently – jeans, uniforms, one pair of scrubs – but from the body language Falk guessed at least a few had already finished work for the day. He'd felt a faint pang of envy, then turned his phone over in his hand and opened Raco's message.

A friend from SA's here for a conference, the text read. *She might swing by tonight to say hello.*

Raco had followed it almost immediately with another message: *That okay?*

Honestly, it wasn't ideal. Falk leaned against the glass and watched the tram close its doors and pull away. He'd been looking forward to catching up with Raco, but – he glanced back at his desk; the files hadn't gone anywhere, unfortunately – he wasn't sure he had the energy to make small talk with a stranger. He swiped his thumb over his phone and wondered if he could simply say that. He probably could, to Raco. On the other hand, it wasn't Raco's fault he had friends other than Falk.

Falk had stood there for as long as it took for another tram to pull up, then texted back: *No worries*. He'd watched until the tram moved away, then made himself turn from the window and walk back to his desk.

So that was how Falk had come to find himself crammed into a busy bar that overlooked the Yarra River a few hours later, waiting for Raco. They'd arranged to meet at Southbank, which had been convenient but possibly a mistake, on reflection. The Friday night post-work rush was even busier thanks to footy fans stopping for a quick drink on their walk to the ground. To the east, Falk could see the MCG blazing with light ahead of the night's game.

He'd fought his way into the bar and carved out a spot near the door to wait, closer than he liked to a table where three women were sharing a bottle of wine. One of them flicked her eyes up, mildly irritated by his presence in a way that reminded him abstractly of his most recent relationship. He shifted his angle against the wall. He could still feel the woman's eyes on him and fixed his own gaze through the window to the river outside.

This woman in the bar wasn't his ex, obviously – she was still in Sydney as far as he knew, which was probably best all around. They'd met at a mutual colleague's wedding, and for eighteen months it had been good without being great for either of them. His colleague Carmen had swung between frustration and disappointment when she heard they'd split up. *You two had so much in common*, she kept saying, and she'd been right.

Plenty in common, like how they were both with the AFP based out of Melbourne. And how they both had individual workloads that didn't leave much time or space for anything else. There had been other factors as well, though. Like the fact she was at her happiest when they visited her family on the peninsula, where she would swim and play with her nieces and help out for hours in her brother-in-law's bookshop, and have long lazy dinners on the back deck with the scent of jasmine heavy in the evening air. An old high-school boyfriend, now a friendly divorced single dad, seemed to be around often enough to make everyone but the pair of them a little uncomfortable. At night, she'd whisper to Falk across the bedsheets in her sister's spare room. *It's so parochial*, she'd say, in a tone that made it sound both like a joke and something else completely.

But there was no denying she was different there – lighter and softer, her eyes and mouth taking on a new shape. Just as she was always different again on their return to Melbourne and to work. Brittle and brisk for a week as her hard professional edge slowly resurfaced, sharp and painful.

'You're different, too,' she'd thrown back at Falk the one and only time he'd raised it.

When she'd been offered a transfer and promotion in Sydney, it had come as something of a relief for both of them. She'd accepted the opportunity almost defiantly, this new role based right in the urban heart of a different state, a long way from her little nieces and the peninsula swims and the independent bookshop. She'd made the arrangements as if daring Falk to challenge her decision. He'd thought about it – seriously and carefully – and then hadn't, and was very aware that she felt let down by that. So she'd gone, leaving some gaps in his social life and a few more in his living room – why did losing a girlfriend always involve losing furniture? he wondered – and then quickly, very quickly in fact, the gaps had closed over as though they'd never been there. For the past year, whenever Raco or Rita had asked what he'd been up to, Falk always gave the same honest answer: work, mainly.

A gust of cold air blew in straight off the Yarra as the bar's door opened and then closed, and Falk checked the time. Raco was late – unusually for him – and Falk finally, reluctantly, surrendered his spot and fought his way to the counter. He was scrolling through his emails and half-heartedly attempting to get served when his phone buzzed in his hand.

A text from Raco. *Bloody stuck here, will try to call . . .*

A young bartender suddenly materialised in front of Falk, saw him looking at his phone and turned immediately to the woman at the bar next to him, with a snapped: 'Yep?'

'Ah, I'll . . .' The woman paused, also distracted as her own screen lit up in her hand. The bartender didn't attempt to suppress his eye roll. She looked up and caught him at it.

'Sorry,' she said, and he softened a little. 'I'm supposed to be meeting someone but he's just messaged and —' She stopped herself. The bartender clearly could not care less. She gestured to Falk. 'Maybe let this guy go ahead while I . . .'

Her navy-blue coat was dotted with rain, and she'd brought the cold in with her. She put her phone down on the counter-top and wound her damp hair into a quick loose bun on top of her head, frowning at the lit-up screen. As she lowered her arms, she eased her bag off her shoulder and onto the empty stool in front of her. Two wrapped children's gifts were visible inside; the label on the top one read: *Baby Raco*.

Falk twisted to look at her properly now, bumping against a young guy standing too close behind him. 'You're here to meet Greg Raco?' he said. 'His friend from South Australia?'

'Yeah.' She turned in surprise. The bartender threw them both a look of impatience and moved on. 'Are you . . . Adam?'

'Aaron. Falk.' He held out his hand.

'That's right, sorry.' She smiled as she took it, her palm cool from the evening air. 'Gemma Tozer. Hi.' She glanced at her phone. 'Did you just get —'

As if on cue, Falk's own mobile rang. *This is him now*, he gestured as he answered, covering his other ear to drown out the chatter and music.

'Mate, sorry, this is the first chance I've had to step out —' Raco launched straight into a rambling explanation that Falk only half caught. The course instructor had been urgently called away, the replacement was now running well behind. They had to get through it tonight so the officers could all get back to their home turfs before the weekend shifts.

'Listen,' Raco was saying. 'Gemma'll be arriving any minute, I'll call her –'

'She's here now, mate. Hang on, I'll pass you over –' Falk had held out his phone to the woman. 'He's stuck there.'

'Not going to make it?'

'Doesn't sound hopeful.'

'Okay.' She'd undone her coat and underneath was wearing a knee-length patterned dress that gathered at the waist. She dried her damp hands against the hem before taking Falk's phone and listening for a minute, concentrating to hear over the noise.

She fell somewhere between him and Raco in age, Falk guessed. Probably closer to Raco, or maybe she was just religious about applying sunscreen. Her hair was light or dark brown, depending on how it caught the overhead lights.

'No, Greg,' she was saying. 'Don't worry. Absolutely. It happens. It's –'

The reassurances went on for so long that Falk had to smile. Gemma met his eye and grinned as well. She leaned against the bar, picking up a promotional beer mat with her free hand and turning it over idly as Raco continued to apologise.

'I think we can forgive you,' she said finally. 'Give my love to Rita. Okay. Yes. Look, sometimes you've got to do what you've got to do.' She cringed as she spoke and immediately stopped fiddling with the coaster, placing it down firmly on the counter. On the side facing up, Falk could see a slogan for a new craft ale: *Sometimes you gotta do what you gotta do.*

He felt a flutter of amusement and glanced up. Gemma shrugged with her free hand.

Been a long day, she mouthed.

Fair enough, he mouthed back.

She smiled at him then. 'Okay. I'll make sure he knows,' she said into the phone, still looking at Falk. 'No worries. Bye.' She hung up and returned Falk's phone. 'He was being called back in. He's very sorry about tonight.'

Falk laughed. 'Yeah, I got that.'

'He said he'll call you tomorrow.'

'I'm sure he will. He's a good bloke.'

'He really is. Always has been.' Gemma's gaze skimmed the packed room. 'Well –'

'Yeah.' They teetered on the brink of awkward. 'So –'

Stay or go?

Outside, the rain seemed to have passed, at least. Gemma still had her coat on. Falk had some work he needed to catch up on at home. He could put the footy on TV in the background. Raco wasn't going to make it. The bartender pointedly served someone behind them.

'It's a shame.' Gemma fiddled with a button on her coat but didn't do it up. 'I'm sorry not to see him.'

'Me too,' Falk said. 'You've known him a while?'

'Yeah, and his brothers. I don't see him that much these days, but we were all at school together so, I don't know, what's that? Twenty years now? More?' She widened her eyes good-naturedly at the number. 'How about you?'

'Met him and Rita about five years ago,' Falk said. 'So we're not quite close enough yet to be giving each other advice from beer mats, but you know, I'm hopeful we'll reach –'

'Yep, you can stop right there, thanks.' But she was smiling

65

as she flipped the coaster over on the counter. *Sometimes you gotta do what you gotta do*, now hidden against the scratched marble.

'I mean, if we *were* close enough, I'd obviously say –' Falk turned over the beer mat nearest his elbow to reveal: *You regret the things you didn't do more than the things you did.*

'Jesus,' Gemma said. Her sleeve brushed his as she leaned in to read. She smelled nice, he noticed. 'What brand is this?'

'It's not calling to you?'

She wrinkled her nose. 'But I'm probably not the target audience. I guess the "no regrets" thing works for some people.'

'Craft beer marketing teams?'

'Clearly.' She absently turned over Falk's mat too. 'Tattoo enthusiasts?'

'Bungee jumpers.'

'Energy drink companies.'

'Disgruntled employees who've told their boss to shove it,' he said. 'And are now going backpacking through Thailand?'

'Middle-aged executives signing up for a marathon against their doctor's advice.'

'People who've never really had to, you know –' Falk stopped himself. No. Wrong tone. Too heavy. He tried to steer the thought a different way, but she'd already sensed it.

'Reflect bitterly on things they can't change?'

'Exactly.' He made his voice light.

They caught each other's eye. Neither said anything for a moment. Her face was open and relaxed but there was a shadow of something he couldn't quite read.

'Do those people exist?' Gemma said.

'Apparently.' Falk nodded at the coasters.

'Lucky them.' She smiled then, warm and deep, and in that

tiny moment he suddenly felt it, as clear and resonant as a bell.

Stay.

Gemma was already looking past him, though, outside, to where the river lay black and shining. Her coat was still undone but now she reached into her pocket and pulled out her own phone. Falk could feel her thoughts sliding to the evening that lay ahead, the same question rising in her. *Stay or go?*

'Do you have time for a drink?' Falk heard himself say the words with a faint sense of surprise. He'd been thinking it, but it seemed his head was a half-step behind his mouth, stumbling to catch up. 'Seeing as we're both here?'

Gemma turned to him, her own face still.

It felt like a long moment, as Falk watched her calculate whatever she was weighing up. She turned her beer mat over, then flipped it facedown again. 'Does the drink come with a life-affirming motto?'

'You have my word it will not.'

'Well. When you put it that way.' That smile again, and Falk felt a rush of something he could only describe as relief. She put her phone back in her coat pocket. They turned together towards the bar and the back of her hand touched his.

Stay.

Chapter 7

The surface of the reservoir lay still as glass as Falk and Raco approached. They had been walking for no more than about ten minutes, first in single file along the narrow track leading down from the festival site, then side by side when it widened. From the old parallel rut marks carved in the dirt, this stretch had clearly once been accessible to vehicles. Now, according to the signs Falk could see, it was walkers only.

They slowed as up ahead the track opened out even further, incorporating a small ledge of earth and rock bulging out from the main trail. A waist-height wooden fence guarded the edge. The body of water lay far below.

Raco stepped off the main track and Falk followed him to the guardrail, testing it with his palms before he put any real weight on it. It certainly felt sturdy enough.

The sun had set now and above them, a slim crescent moon hung silver and pale against the rapidly darkening sky. Below, the reservoir followed the natural pattern of the land. Even in the gloom Falk could see it stretching out, vast and open in its centre, then twisting and curving to fill the turns and gullies that formed the banks. It was big. Bigger than he remembered. The opposite bank was just visible across the swathe of water, but he couldn't see the westernmost edge, or the dam that lay somewhere to the east. The festival grounds felt far behind them, but Falk could hear a distant low thrum of music and crowd noise undercutting the stillness.

Testing the wooden safety barrier once more – still solid – Falk leaned over and looked down. To the left and right, the rocky embankment mostly formed a medium-to-steep slope from the hiking track down to the water's edge. Up here at the ledge, though, it fell away abruptly in a sharp drop.

'How far's the fall?' Falk asked.

'Depends on the water level.' Raco threw a small stone over the railing. They watched it tumble, hitting the surface and sinking without sound. The water gently rippled. 'But last year it was twenty-three metres.'

'Fair way,' Falk said as they both stared down. 'The water's so –'

A sudden blast of music sliced through the air behind them, and Falk and Raco turned in unison. The sound was far closer and louder than anything drifting from the festival, pumping out from somewhere in the dense bushland that rose up on the far side of the track. Through the music, Falk caught a burst of girls' laughter and the sharp clink of bottles in a bag. A young male voice followed, the words deep and indistinguishable. The voice was lost as the music was cranked up another notch.

'They've started early this year.' Raco checked his watch.

'That's the famous opening night party, is it?' Falk scanned the tree line again. The bushland was thick and dark. He could see nothing. He wouldn't know anyone was up there if not for the noise.

'Yeah. One of our town's oldest and proudest traditions,' Raco said. 'I'm only half joking – it's been going on since I was a kid. Before that, even. Probably about as long as the festival's been running, realistically.'

'This is where Zara was headed last year?' Falk knew they weren't far from the festival in terms of distance, but the dense bushland and the relative stillness of the water made it feel very isolated. 'Charlie was okay with that?'

'Yeah, well, he kind of had to be. He was up there himself every year back in the day, we all were. Me. Kim, as well. Everyone, really.' Raco listened to the throb of music and laughter for a minute. 'It's not as bad as it sounds from down here. It's mostly kids from the high school, some of their mates back from uni for the break. A few regular tourist kids used to come too. Let off some steam, catch up over a few more drinks than we should while the adults were busy with the festival.'

'So will Sergeant Dwyer be along at some point to break it up?'

'Yeah, earlier each year, from what I hear,' Raco said. 'He hates it, but the rest of us are all suckers for nostalgia. We all did it, and it never got broken up when I was that age, but –' He looked a little misty-eyed at the memory. 'My dad was the sergeant then, so maybe he went easy on us.'

Falk scoured the tree line once more. He could still find no break in the growth.

'Can they see us from up there?'

Raco rubbed his chin. 'Depends. Short answer: yes, if they want to. You maybe can't tell in this light but there's a small gap in the trees, somewhere around –' He pointed up, slowly moving his finger along – paused – backtracked, then dropped his hand. 'Yeah, well. Somewhere, anyway.'

'What's the longer answer?'

'They can see down, but it doesn't necessarily mean any of them are actually looking. There's a clearing up there, set back from the tree break. That's where all the action happens. Or used to, anyway. Unless getting drunk and trying to talk to girls has changed massively since my day – and I dunno, look, maybe it has – but that's where we used to hang out. No-one was too bothered about checking out a view they'd grown up with.'

Raco turned back to the water. It was a silky pool of ink now, under the night sky.

'That's one of Zara's issues, though. She reckons one of them up there last year – her, specifically – would have noticed Kim down here.'

'What do you think?'

'Silently stepping off this edge?' Raco's eyes were almost black in the evening light. 'I think you could be here and gone in ten seconds.'

They both stood with their palms on the barrier, considering that.

'I keep thinking about the day Charlie first met Kim,' Raco said suddenly. He straightened, removing his hands from the rail. 'She was on her bike. She was fifteen then, I think, because Charlie had turned seventeen. We were still living in our old house, over near the police station, and we had this big front yard. Me and Charlie and Ben were out there one afternoon, messing around, kicking a footy and stuff, and this girl rode by. Kim's hair was really long back then, and it was tied up in a ponytail, kind of swinging behind as she was cruising along, doing these big lazy loops on her bike along the road. She'd moved here that week with her family, so none of us had met her yet, and I remember as she rode by, Charlie was like, *whoosh* –'

Raco had a faint smile as he whipped his head from left to right, following the imaginary path of the long-ago girl and her bicycle across the silent water in front of them.

'And Charlie just dropped the footy, ran to the driveway, grabbed his bike and was –' Raco opened his hand like a puff of air. 'Gone. Straight after her. And that was it.' His smile faded. 'For as long as it lasted, anyway.'

Falk thought back to Charlie and Kim on the phone last year. As far as separated couples went, they seemed to have avoided the bitterness that usually followed. 'What happened with them?'

'They just burned out eventually,' Raco said. 'Maybe they liked the idea of each other more than they actually liked the reality, because they kept gravitating back. It was all intense for those first few years, and they managed to keep it going on and off through uni. I mean, Rita loves that story of how they met, but really it was a teenage thing that probably lasted way longer than it was meant to. Then when Charlie was – what, twenty-five? – Zara came along and he and Kim tried to do things seriously. But realistically, I'm not sure they would have stayed together without her.'

Falk nodded. 'Charlie wasn't upset when Kim ended up marrying another local bloke?'

Raco raised his eyebrows. 'Yeah, well. There wasn't much he could do about it. He and Kim weren't together anymore.' He paused, as though he was remembering something. 'The break-ups when they were younger used to hit him pretty hard. The arguments would get worse and it took them longer to get back together each time. But Charlie's mellowed with age, like we all have, I suppose. So that's helped. And Rohan hasn't lived here for a while, so he wasn't exactly local in that sense. I mean, he and Charlie and the others were all friends at school and Rohan's folks are still here, but after he left for uni, he never really came back. He and Kim were both working in Adelaide when they got together over there.'

'Still. Small world.'

'God, yeah, can feel that way. Especially around here. I don't think it was a huge surprise, though. They used to be friends, both had this place in common, so there was that shared family background, but Rohan's more –' Raco paused, considering. 'I dunno. He's an engineer, so he's different from Charlie. Charlie –' He stopped again, and Falk caught a flicker of guilt. 'Charlie had a bit of a habit of letting Kim down. Like with that stupid birthday visit last year. I mean, why couldn't he plan ahead for once and organise something, so everyone knew what we were doing and it wasn't a last-minute scramble?'

Falk thought back to the phone call last year. Disappointment, punctuated by awkward, tense silences.

'I know it's not really Charlie's fault, but it's shit that that was the last time we spoke to her.' Raco looked down at the water. 'Kim was always one of those people you were happy to run into, you know? After talking to her, you'd walk away feeling better than you did before. That's what I remember most about her, all the way back to that first day on her bike. Maybe that wasn't so true lately, though. I don't know. I hadn't seen her for a few years.'

'Was that confirmed, what Zara said about her having post-natal depression?'

Raco nodded.

'She had it after Zara was born as well, apparently, but it

sounds like this time was worse. We found out later she'd been on antidepressants for a while before she was even pregnant with Zoe. So it wasn't just postnatal.'

'She didn't tell anyone?'

'Rohan knew, but says he didn't realise the full extent of it.'

'What do you think?'

'Well, she didn't tell anyone else at all, as far as I know, so it's believable that she was hiding things.'

Falk nodded. It was a warm night and the moon was rising. The way the water pooled out in front of them, shining and placid, it looked almost inviting. 'Had anything like this thing with Kim happened before around here?'

'Anyone jumped?' Raco shook his head. 'There are old stories, but not in my time. Everyone knows this is a dangerous spot, though. We all warn the kids not to muck around.' Raco leaned against the barrier and sighed. Near his hand, Falk could see a small plaque screwed into the wood. He tilted his head but it was too dark to read the inscription at that angle. Raco saw him looking and glanced down.

'Accident. Few years ago now.' Raco guessed his question. 'Back when the track used to be open to cars as well as walkers, and –'

He broke off as behind them the music abruptly spiked, bass booming from the tree line in a new, faster tempo. It stayed ear-splittingly loud for half a minute before someone more responsible presumably stepped in, the volume dropping a few notches and the song changing from something Falk didn't recognise to something else he didn't recognise. He scanned the bushland again. He still couldn't see anyone, but even without the music this time he had a definite feeling of movement somewhere in there.

'Sounds like they're all arriving now,' Raco said.

'How do they get up there?' Falk asked.

'The clearing? There's a turn-off a minute or two back along there.' Raco pointed down the track towards the festival grounds. 'Nothing official, just a little trail through the bush.'

Falk peered into the dark. The track was empty, as far as he could make out. He hadn't heard or sensed anyone coming at all. He turned back to the reservoir. At odds with the hidden activity in the bushland, the water remained eerily still. He leaned over the railing again.

'It's so calm. You feel like she'd still be right there, below the surface.'

Raco nodded. 'Zara really can't get her head around the fact that she's not.'

'I can see why.'

'Me too. I'd look at this water and think the same. In the end, Charlie and I found a local waterways expert, got her to meet Zara out here and talk to her about the currents and things.'

'What did she say?'

'She explained things like how the dam was partially open this time last year. And we'd had good rainfall, so there were a couple of feeder streams that had water coming in. The filters create movement too.' He sighed. 'Would have been quite interesting, actually, in any other scenario. But basically, once Kim hit the water and plunged below a certain depth, the underwater currents could have pulled her literally anywhere.'

'Right.'

'Yeah, so we're talking like fifty stadiums' worth of liquid, plus there's a natural gully in the centre, so it's sixty metres deep in places. I don't care what Zara's seen in the movies or online, the divers can't search that deep. Just can't do it. You need sonar equipment on a boat.'

'Didn't you try something like that?'

'Yeah, of course, we've tried everything realistic. But to do it indefinitely you need unlimited cash or a lot of luck.'

Falk nodded. Neither spoke for a long moment.

'Is this –' How to phrase it? Falk could think of no subtle way. '– the town's drinking water supply?'

It actually didn't really bother him. He'd grown up in the country; he knew what ended up in dams and rivers. Every drop on Earth was recycled water, when it came down to it.

But Raco was shaking his head. 'No.' He flashed a wry smile. 'Probably get more people lining up to fund an underwater search if it was. We get ours from further upstream. This is privately owned, some agribusiness consortium. Livestock and vineyard use, maintaining river levels.'

'A few wineries in that consortium, I'm guessing?'

'Yeah, definitely. Want to keep the growers in business, protect their investments.'

Behind them, the music had ratcheted up another notch and Raco checked his phone.

'Time for the appeal?' Falk said.

'Soon. We'd better head back. Be interesting to see what comes of it.'

Falk looked over. It was hard to see Raco's face now in the dark.

'Zara's not here,' Falk prompted.

'No.'

'Just us talking.'

'Okay.'

'So what are you thinking about all this? Something still to find?'

Raco didn't answer immediately. He stood with his hands in his pockets, his back to the reservoir, listening to the noise from the party.

'Hard to say,' he said finally, and they started to walk. 'Maybe. Whether it makes a difference to what happened here or not, I dunno. But there's usually someone who's sitting on something useful, isn't there?'

Yes, Falk thought as they fell into step together back down the trail, leaving behind the vast spread of water and the laughter ringing from the trees. That was true. But Falk knew Raco well now, or well enough, at least, to be pretty sure that wasn't all that he'd been thinking.

Chapter 8

'Shit.' Raco's eyes were heavy with guilt as they dropped to the handful of missing person fliers still clutched in his fist.

Falk had managed to give out the last of his by the time they approached the vineyard stall, but Raco had mostly seemed to forget he even had them. He'd been unusually subdued as they'd made their way up from the reservoir, battling back through the festival crowd along paths that were lit up now night had fallen. As they saw Charlie's stall ahead, Raco frowned at the remaining fliers in his hand.

'Here.' Falk beckoned and Raco gratefully passed him half the sheets, and over the next few minutes they worked together to press them onto every person who passed. Most barely glanced down before shoving one in their pocket or bag.

'This feels –' Raco's voice was resigned. He didn't finish his thought.

Falk knew exactly what he meant, but they stayed anyway until their hands were empty.

The stall was still busy, Falk could see as they finished up. The large man who'd been stacking boxes in the back of the tent earlier was now positioned up front, alongside the two young women. He was pouring samples for a big group, and nodded a greeting as he saw Raco approach.

'They've gone on ahead, mate.' The bloke put down the wine bottle and wiped his hands on his jeans. He batted away a persistent moth hovering around a light near his head. 'Zara wanted to get there early. Charlie says to call him when you're near the stage.'

'No worries,' Raco said. 'You coming?'

There were potential customers circling, but the man's eyes fell instead on a stack of fliers lined up neatly at the edge of the table. Kim Gillespie gazed back at him from the printed paper.

'Yeah, look, I wouldn't mind.' He turned to the employee nearest him, who was already nodding. 'You'll be right, will you? Twenty minutes?'

'Absolutely. All good, Shane.' The woman stapled a flier to the receipt she was about to hand to a waiting couple. 'Take your time.'

'Great. Thanks.'

The man eased himself out from behind the table, having to duck his head to avoid brushing the tent canopy, and joined Falk and Raco on the path.

'Did you two meet last year?' Raco asked as they began to walk. 'Aaron –' He stopped as his phone lit up. 'Sorry, this is Charlie now.' He lifted it to his ear. 'Yes, mate, we're heading over –'

The guy extended a large calloused hand to Falk. 'I don't think we did meet, did we? Shane McAfee.'

'Yeah, I know, actually.' Falk introduced himself. 'I saw you a few times at the MCG. Great player.'

'Oh yeah? Thanks, mate.' Shane McAfee's tone was light but Falk could tell he was pleased. He had an interesting habit of pausing slightly, as though considering the words before he chose them, and was more softly spoken than Falk would have expected. 'That's going back a bit now.'

Twenty years at least, by Falk's reckoning. Shane was his age but with all the height and breadth of a professional AFL player. He was clearly still fit, but with the softened stocky look of a former elite athlete now left in charge of his own meal plans and exercise routine.

'You into the footy, then?' Shane asked as they walked.

'Yeah.' Falk nodded. 'Since I was a kid. I grew up in regional Victoria, so . . .'

'Pretty much inevitable?'

'Pretty much. Plus my dad absolutely loved it. Played a bit himself when he was young, country league stuff, you know. Liked to go to games, watch it on TV. We were at that grand final, actually,' Falk said. 'The year you –'

'Yeah.' Shane smiled at the memory. 'Yeah. Now that really is going back. You probably weren't barracking for us, hey? Being from Victoria?'

'Well, no. The other guys.'

'I owe you an apology, then.' Shane's face broadened into a grin. He didn't sound the least bit sorry but Falk could hardly blame him.

It had been the kind of game that Falk still felt lucky to have seen in person, despite the result. He'd been living near uni then, deep into his studies and barely making the fifty-minute trip back across Melbourne to his dad's place even for holidays, let alone weekends. If Falk had been forced to stop and consider his relationship with his father, he'd have said honestly that a bit of distance had been good for them. Their interactions had been laced with a polite formality and it was only years later, after his dad had died, that Falk reflected that *good* was probably not the right word for it at all.

Falk had been flipping unenthusiastically through a textbook in his student house when his dad had called. His voice had been filled with a pure energy that Falk hadn't heard in years. A raffle had been drawn at the agricultural supply business where Erik Falk worked, and guess who was now the proud and lucky owner of a couple of tickets to the grand final? The thrill was instantly infectious and Falk's desk chair had clattered to the floor as he rose and punched the air.

It was also only later that it occurred to Falk there were literally dozens of other people his dad probably could have invited to that game – workmates, neighbours, his dad might even have had friends, Falk didn't really know – and any one of them would no doubt have jumped at the chance. But footy, especially this kind of footy, transcended family drama – that went without saying – so Erik Falk had of course invited his son.

They'd met at Flinders Street Station wearing their identical team scarves. The careful, loaded courtesy that usually hovered between them evaporated over four quarters, somewhere between the celebrations and commiserations. Afterwards, they'd crammed into a pub for a few beers together and picked over the game, agreeing with mirrored passion that it should have gone their way. At the train station, they'd hugged goodbye in a movement both spontaneous and instinctive. Falk had inhaled. His dad's footy scarf had smelled exactly the way he remembered from when he was a kid. And all those years later – far too late by then – Falk thought it had been one of the best days they'd ever had.

'That was a great game,' was all he said now to Shane McAfee as they walked side by side. 'A good day.'

'Yeah.' Shane sounded a little wistful himself. 'Really was.'

Shane cleared his throat and Falk wished he knew him well enough to ask what he was thinking. What would all that have been like for him? The pressure and adrenalin on the field, and the emotion and energy coming from the stands. Shane would have been barely into his twenties, pretty much the same age as Falk had been, but instead of being one of a hundred thousand faces in the crowd, he'd experienced it all from the heart of the action. One of the sweaty, dirty, victorious chosen few who got the chance to run on that ground.

If Shane was reliving it at all now, he gave no sign, focusing instead on the busy path ahead as he walked. He didn't really need to, not with his bulk. The crowd tended to part for him.

What had happened to Shane McAfee? Falk tried to remember. He felt he should know, because the guy had been an exceptional player. Injured out, it had to be. Precisely *because* Shane had been such an exceptional player, and yet after that game Falk couldn't recall thinking about him ever again, right up until last year when Raco had pointed him out, working behind the table of Charlie's vineyard stand.

'You grew up here, then?' Falk said now, easing his way around a noisy family who had stopped dead in the centre of the track.

'Yeah, mates with Charlie. Greg, too.' Shane nodded at Raco, who was a pace ahead of them, still on the phone. 'I worked in Melbourne for a while after the footy, did a bit of radio commentary, things like that, but –' He shrugged. 'Ended up back here. It's good,' he added quickly.

'You still play at all?'

'Not really. I tried the social stuff for a while, but it's not the same.'

'No.' Falk pictured the crowd at the MCG. 'I bet.'

'Plus it wrecks my knees. Not worth it, end of the day, not for the social stuff. I coach the local men's team, though.' Shane ran his eye up and down Falk. 'You play? Like your dad?'

'No.'

'Used to, though?' Shane continued his appraisal. 'Look like you'd have the foot speed.'

'Just at school, a bit at uni,' Falk said. 'Nothing serious. And not for ages.'

'Everyone says that.' Shane looked faintly amused. 'Never too late.'

'I'm really not sure that's true,' Falk said, and they both smiled, slowing on the path as Raco paused in front of them.

'Yep, all right. See you there.' Raco hung up and turned to Shane and Falk. 'Charlie says they're over by the left side, near the speakers. This way, I think.'

They fell into loose single file as they picked their way through a sea of picnics towards a large central stage. The music was getting louder and up ahead a band bathed in spotlights was playing a fast number. Falk saw Shane bend to pick up something from the ground, then straighten again, barely breaking stride. He held a crumpled flier, a dusty boot print stamped over Kim's face. Shane ran his large thumb over the dirty mark, then folded the paper carefully into quarters and slipped it into his back pocket.

They found Charlie and Zara by the stage, along with a

group of the volunteers Falk recognised from the vineyard stall. Zara was clutching a page of handwritten notes, her eyes moving over the words. Joel stood at her side, his arms folded across his tall teenage frame, reading over her shoulder. Charlie was frowning at his phone, managing to seem oddly alone amid the crowd. Glancing up, he saw them approach and clicked off his screen.

'Hi, mate.' Shane had to raise his voice over the music. 'The girls are looking after the stand. I'll head back soon, I just wanted to –'

'It's fine.' Charlie waved a hand, then checked his watch. He looked like he'd rather be anywhere else. 'Time this got started anyway.'

As if on cue, the band struck their final chord, the note ringing out as the stage lights changed from bright blue to a soft yellow. A sound technician beckoned Zara over to a set of stairs leading up to the stage, where she was joined by Rohan Gillespie and Sergeant Dwyer. All three listened intently as the tech guy demonstrated where to find the on–off switch on the hand-held microphone.

You ready? Falk saw rather than heard the man say, and the three of them nodded. Sergeant Dwyer was the only one who looked like he meant it. The technician squinted across the stage, raised his hand and signalled to someone on the other side. *Good to go.*

Falk knew before he knew. He felt it even as he turned his head and looked up across the empty expanse of stage to the darkened wings. And he was right. Because there she was.

Gemma Tozer's hair was cut a little shorter sixteen months on, and the navy winter coat and patterned dress had been swapped for dark jeans and a linen shirt. As he saw her now,

Falk allowed himself to admit – completely silently and just to himself – that he'd been half looking for her all night. More than half looking, really. He exhaled.

'All right, mate?' Raco's voice caught him by surprise. Falk had briefly forgotten he was there.

'Yeah. Why?'

'Nothing. Thought you said something.'

'Oh. No,' Falk said, but Raco wasn't paying attention anyway, his focus fully on Zara, who was scanning her speech rapidly now, her brow furrowed.

Falk turned back to the stage. Gemma was currently bathed in an absurdly flattering golden light, giving her the effect of a warm glowing aura.

Oh, for God's sake. Falk watched with a touch of amusement. *That* hardly seemed fair.

She signalled something back to the technician then turned, her gaze running out over the crowd. Falk suddenly felt acutely conscious that he was staring and dropped his eyes to the ground.

Jesus Christ. He almost laughed, embarrassed on his own behalf. He wasn't sixteen.

Stay.

He levelled his gaze. Gemma's attention had returned to the stage.

And it was ridiculous, Falk told himself. Because it was dark, and there was a bit of distance between them, and his face was one in a hundred, and there was maybe – probably, to be honest – some serious wishful thinking at play on his part. But still. He looked at Gemma standing in the wings.

What was different? A tiny change in her expression, or a shift in her posture? Maybe? Basically nothing. But at the same time, Falk's skin was tingling like there was a faint new charge in the air. It felt, as the golden light on stage lifted to a crisp clean white, just close enough to something. And he wondered if, a moment earlier, she'd been looking at him too.

Chapter 9

The Southbank bar had transformed from standing-room-only to space-to-breathe in a matter of minutes as the footy crowd moved on to catch the start of the game. Gemma pounced with targeted precision on an empty table – a good one, looking out on the city lights reflected in the Yarra – and the bartender found it in his heart to forgive their earlier time-wasting and serve them. As they settled in their seats, Gemma made a passing reference to a TV series that Falk had also been watching, and the work of dissecting the book versus the adaptation propelled them well into a second drink. Falk went to the bar and when he came back, she'd taken her hair down. He'd proposed dinner before his glass was even empty.

She'd smiled. 'Sounds good.'

The rain obliged by holding off as they walked side by side across the bridge over the Yarra and into the heart of the city. Falk suggested a restaurant he'd heard good things about, and they left the main street cross-sections and wandered instead down the side lanes until they reached a small place with a sign outside. A serious young guy with an apron and complicated facial hair checked a handwritten ledger near the door, then without a word led them through the tight knot of chairs and place settings to a tiny table squeezed into a corner. The room was toasty after the damp night air and they shrugged off their coats, seated elbow to elbow with an infatuated couple at the table next to them. Falk and Gemma grinned at each other over their menus, and when he shifted in his chair, his knees brushed hers.

'What's it like running the festival?' Falk asked after they'd ordered.

'Interesting.' She sat back, apologising as she elbowed her neighbour who had reached out to clasp his lover's hand. He barely noticed. 'It's fun and the community's behind it, so that helps. A lot of us out there grew up with it, so there's this huge nostalgia factor. But then the festival's got bigger over the years which means different considerations have to come into play, and Marralee's still essentially a small town, so –' She shrugged.

'A lot of diplomacy required?'

'Yes. *So* much. Great, thank you –' she said, as he poured the wine they were sharing. She took a sip. 'Mmm, nice. Have you ever been?'

'To the Marralee Valley? No.' Falk tried the wine himself. She was right, it was nice. 'But I grew up in a small town. Where Greg Raco works now, actually.'

'Okay, yes, so you know what it's like.' Gemma smiled over her glass. 'Balancing all the politics. Although, really, it's only because people care. There's a definite sense of local ownership. And it's an exciting feeling, seeing it come together every year.'

Her enthusiasm was refreshing. Most people Falk knew vaguely loathed the way in which they made a living.

'Have you always –?' Falk stopped as their waiter edged his way over to them, balancing plates in both hands. Noticing that the small candle in the centre of their table was unlit, he tutted, put the plates down and whipped a box of matches from his pocket.

'No, it's fi–' started Falk, who was not keen on open flames in any context.

'No trouble.' The waiter misinterpreted his hesitation as politeness – or possibly, it occurred to Falk, romantic nerves – and with a reassuring smile and a flourish that seemed a little unnecessary, he struck a match and lit the wick.

'There.' He positioned the candle carefully between them. 'Much better.'

It wasn't. But it would be okay, Falk told himself. He closed his eyes briefly then opened them. He could cope with this.

Gemma was watching him across the tiny flame as the waiter squeezed away. Falk wasn't sure if she'd noticed the burn scars on his left hand or, knowing Raco, put two and two together, but as soon as the waiter was out of reach, she pointed to the offending candle, flickering innocently.

'Sorry, would you mind if I blew this out?' She circled her finger to indicate the room. 'It's just this place has a kind of snug, flammable vibe, and I'm flying back to Adelaide first thing so, you know . . .' She smiled. 'I'd really rather not get stuck because I've knocked it over and caused an incident.'

Falk looked at her. *Stay.* He just nodded.

'Great. Thanks.' She leaned in with pursed lips and, job done, picked up her silverware.

'You're heading off tomorrow?' he said as they began to eat. He tried to keep his tone casual. 'Just here for tonight?'

'Yeah. Got to get back. I've got a seventeen-year-old at home, even though I'm sure he's in no particular rush to see me.' Gemma focused on her food, but she was gauging his reaction to that information, Falk could tell.

'What's his name?'

'Joel. He's my stepson, technically, but –' She paused to save a twirl of pasta threatening to fall off her fork. 'He's a smart kid, and no trouble, really. Can be trusted on his own for a night, at any rate.'

'That's good.' Falk was curious what the current relationship status was between Gemma and her stepson's father, but she didn't offer an explanation and so he didn't ask. 'Have you always lived there?' he said, instead.

'In Marralee?' Gemma swallowed and shook her head. 'I grew up there, but I was at uni in Sydney and then after I graduated I worked in the States for a few years. In California.'

'Oh yeah? You don't have the accent at all.'

'No, I'm not sure I ever did. And it was a while ago now.'

'You were in the events industry there?'

'Not even close, actually.' Gemma laughed. 'I should make you guess, people are always surprised. I was in programming back then. The whole silicon start-up scene. I worked for one of the tech companies.'

'Really?' Falk was impressed. 'Which one?'

She nodded subtly towards a businessman a few tables away who had his laptop open to a website and was scrolling and typing one-handed as he ate. 'The big one.'

'Seriously? What was that like?'

'God, full on. It wasn't quite as big back then, the competitive landscape's changed, obviously. But yeah, I got an internship from uni, managed to turn that into a job. Working mainly on all the back-end functionality that goes into the consumer product.' She took a sip of wine, remembering. 'Looking back now, it was a crazy few years, but I learned a lot.'

'I can imagine.' Out of the corner of his eye, Falk saw the waiter lighting a candle at a neighbouring table with a familiar flourish, before zeroing in on their own unlit tealight with concern written all over his face. He took half a step towards them, but was fortuitously derailed by a request for more water. Falk turned his attention back to Gemma. 'Do you still do it at all?'

'The programming?' She shook her head, but not unhappily. 'I can still remember some of the stuff I used to work on – muscle memory, I guess? – but I think you become obsolete in about five minutes these days, let alone this many years.'

'So what brought you back here?'

'From the States to small-town SA? A few things, really.' Falk waited for her to elaborate but instead she looked at him over her glass. 'Would you ever go back to live in your home town?'

Falk blinked. 'God, no.'

'Okay.' She laughed. 'That was pretty definitive.'

He had to laugh too. 'I suppose it was.'

Falk's feelings about Kiewarra ran deep, but in fact had softened considerably in the last few years. Still, just because he could look back on his memories of the place with a new fondness didn't mean he was in a rush to make a whole lot of fresh ones. But that was a story for another day, so instead he said: 'I like it better here.'

'In the city?'

'Yeah. Well, Melbourne specifically. And the job and everything.'

'Enjoy working for the AFP?'

'I do, yeah. For the most part. I like the investigations, the financial stuff. Seeing where the money takes you can be pretty eye-opening. It's not for everyone, but it suits me. Some of the other stuff – the meetings and politics and paperwork – are a little less –'

As if on cue, his phone beeped in his pocket. They both heard it. He ignored it, but it beeped again, then twice more.

'Shit, sorry.' Falk took it out to turn it to silent. 'I thought I'd better leave it on in case Raco –'

'No, don't worry,' Gemma said. 'Go ahead. I've got to go to the bathroom anyway.'

She wiped her hands on her napkin and stood. She held the fabric of her dress clear of the table as she edged out and Falk felt the faint heat from her body as she passed. He watched her cross the room. His phone beeped again, insistent, and he dragged his eyes downwards.

When she came back, he was still deep in it. He looked up as she squeezed by.

'I'm so sorry. We're right in the middle of this –' He cut the excuse short, hit *send* and turned to her. 'Sorry.'

'It's okay.'

'No. It's not, it's rude. Work's just hectic, but still . . .' He put his phone down.

'Busy time?'

'Yeah, it always is, but I recently got placed – for God's sake, I'll –' A return reply bounced in. Marked *urgent*, of course, but they always were. He tapped back a single-word response, put his phone on silent and buried it in his coat pocket, where he felt it buzz almost immediately. He made himself ignore it.

'I got placed a few months ago onto this taskforce and it's –'
He felt his phone buzz again. *Ignore*.

Gemma was watching his face closely as she took a mouthful and chewed.

'Is it a move you wanted?' she asked.

'Yeah. I'd been trying to get on that team for a while.'

'Well, congratulations.' She tipped her glass to him. 'That's great.'

'Yes. Thank you.' He meant it, but she caught the undertone.

'Not what you expected?'

'Well . . .'

It was a good question. By and large, the job was what he'd thought it would be, he supposed. He'd known it would be a lot of work, and it was. But he'd wanted it. He'd pushed to be part of it. So yes, in that sense, it was both what he wanted and expected.

'It is. But it's also quite –' Falk felt his phone buzz again. He placed both hands on the table to stop himself reaching for it. '– demanding.'

'Yeah. I can understand that,' she said, in a way that made him think she actually could. 'Be careful what you wish for?'

He smiled back. 'Something like that.'

She topped up their glasses and seemed to decide something. 'It was like that in California.'

'Yeah?'

'A bit. I'd really wanted to be part of it and the work was challenging and it pushed me in a good way, but – I don't know – there were things I hadn't really expected as well. The culture, for example. It was all a bit cut-throat because the tech bubble had been –' She shrugged. 'Well, a bubble, with all the lay-offs and job insecurity and losses and everything else that brings, so the whole industry was raw for a long time. I stuck with it for most of my twenties, so I had the full experience, but eventually I wanted a change, I suppose.'

'So you came back?'

She took a bite and swallowed. 'Not at first. I did the travelling thing for a while, burned through some savings, let off some steam, trying to work out what to do next. I ended up in London, and was at one of those Aussie backpacker parties. You know, where you go along with some random person from your hostel and end up seeing both your cousin and your high school nemesis?'

Falk smiled. She was playing it lightly, but it had been a happy memory, he could tell.

'Anyway, I went along to this thing and – surprise, surprise – I ran into this man I'd grown up with back in Marralee but hadn't seen for a while. Dean Tozer. We reconnected, I guess.' She bought a moment by taking a sip of wine. Falk waited.

'Dean worked for an accountancy firm and had been seconded to London for six months, but he had a son – Joel – from a previous relationship. Joel was –' She counted back lightly on her fingertips with her thumb. 'He was seven then. Living with his mum back here in Australia. But she was a dancer professionally and had been offered a steady role with a cruise ship line, so when I met Dean he was about to head back to Marralee so she could take that up and Joel would live with him for a while. He left London, I hung back long enough to make it clear to myself and him that I wasn't following him back –' She laughed. '– and then obviously I followed him back. I wanted to though, I was ready to be somewhere that felt more like home.'

The waiter swept by and Gemma paused and fiddled with her glass on the table. Falk could feel a cloud gathering.

'So yeah, Dean and I were together, with Joel, of course, and then Dean died. And that was nearly five years ago now.'

Falk looked at her. 'I'm sorry.'

'Thank you. It's okay. I mean, it wasn't, obviously, but it was a little while ago now.'

'Unexpected?' Falk asked, although he could guess the answer. This had been no gentle hospice goodbye, there had clearly been a cleaving in two. Before and after.

'It was an accident. So, yes. He was hit by a car. It was –' Gemma searched for the word. 'Horrible, honestly. The police were involved. It was a really bad time.' She closed her eyes for half a beat longer than usual, almost like a tiny reset, then opened them and gave Falk a small smile. 'I'm sorry, I've never found a good way to tell that story.'

'No. Well, some stories aren't good ones.' They looked at each other over their unlit candle. Falk could see her sadness, tired and old, surfacing like it needed a glimpse of light and air before submerging again. 'I'm really sorry to hear that, Gemma.'

'Thank you.'

He could tell she wanted to change the subject, and felt around for a natural link.

'So that's when you started working with the festival? When you moved back?'

'Yes.' Gemma sounded relieved to be on firmer ground. 'It was different from the tech stuff but . . .' She shrugged.

'Kind of the point, I'm guessing?' Falk said.

'Exactly. I volunteered at first with the festival committee, and I was quite good at all the organisation and planning so I got a paid job pretty fast. Took on some more senior roles within the team, and when the director role opened up, I got it.'

'That's great. And you're happy there? Not tempted to head back overseas?'

'No.' Gemma shook her head. 'I suppose you can never rule anything out, but no. Joel and I did talk about leaving after, you know, Dean's accident. Fresh start or whatever. But in the end neither of us really wanted to. Joel's at school, he has friends, support. We both do. And Marralee's a beautiful town, great community. I mean, Greg would tell you.'

'Yeah,' Falk said. 'Maybe I should get him to invite me, check it out myself. I hear they've got a pretty amazing festival.'

'They do.' She smiled at him across the table. 'And maybe you should.'

They stayed late, and when their plates were clear and the wine was gone, they stood and edged their way out, stepping onto the cold street. Before he even really thought about it, Falk reached over and took her hand. It was raining again, with all the intensity of a brief passing shower, and they stopped under an awning to wait, watching the cascading water light up white and gold under the streetlights. The rain drummed against the awning, and the hum of the city at night rumbled all around them. It was cold, but Gemma was standing close and her hand was warm in his.

He turned to say something – what, exactly, he wasn't sure – but stopped as he saw her looking up at him in a way he felt pretty sure he recognised. They smiled at each other in the dark and Falk thought how some things just seemed right as he stepped in, bent his head, and kissed her. He felt her smile, her fingers tight in his own, as she kissed him back in the cool quiet night. The rain stopped first.

Chapter 10

The Marralee Valley Annual Food and Wine Festival offered many things to many people, but fortunately the picnic crowd seemed a happily settled bunch. Even so, some were clearly in two minds about whether to stay or go as they watched the band leave the stage and Sergeant Dwyer climb the steps instead, holding a microphone. A look of anguish crossed Zara's face as a handful of groups began packing up their blankets and paper plates, but most appeared to take the view that having arrived early enough to grab a prime spot, they'd prefer to keep it, thanks very much. As Sergeant Dwyer waited for his cue, Raco leaned over to Falk.

'Back in a minute, just going to say g'day to Naomi.' Raco paused, considering and rejecting a thought. 'It's probably better to introduce you tomorrow, if that's okay? When it's easier to talk.'

'No worries.' Falk hadn't met baby Henry's godmother-to-be last year – the scheduled coffee catch-up had been shelved along with so many other things after that opening night – but he watched now as Raco made his way over to a blonde woman with skinny jeans and shiny blonde hair. Falk recognised her from the vineyard stall earlier, where she'd been talking to Charlie and Shane. So that was Naomi Kerr, was it?

The woman pushed her hair over one shoulder as she reached up to hug Raco, her shirt lifting to reveal a slice of flat torso above her waistband. She said something Falk couldn't lip-read beyond the word *Henry*, and Raco promptly whipped out his phone, photo at the ready. At first glance, Naomi wasn't quite what Falk had expected, but then again, he'd never really considered himself typical godparent material either.

The stage backdrop suddenly changed and a hush of sorts fell over the crowd as Kim Gillespie's face appeared on a large screen.

It was the same photo as on the fliers, but this time with the words *Have you seen me?* written in bold across the top, with a hotline number below. Sergeant Dwyer waited for the swell of muted chatter to fade. When the crowd was as close to quiet as could reasonably be expected, he raised the microphone.

'Kim Gillespie. Please take a moment now to have a close look at the photo behind me. Kim's family has not seen or heard from her for twelve months. We are appealing for information from anyone who was at the opening night of this festival last year and may have had any contact with her, however brief.'

Dwyer was pretty good, Falk thought. Most eyes were on him now, half-eaten sausage rolls temporarily forgotten.

'If you were on site then, particularly between the hours of 7.15 pm and 10.30 pm, and believe you may have seen Kim, please contact me or my fellow officers at the station or via the details here on the screen. We're particularly keen to hear from anyone who may have noticed Kim around the east exit. That's the one all the way towards the back of the site.'

As Dwyer pointed east, Falk glanced over at Joel Tozer. The teenage boy had kept his reaction tightly controlled earlier at the stall, but this time he gave a funny reflexive shake of the head in – what? Embarrassment? Frustration? Falk couldn't tell. The expression on his face as he watched Sergeant Dwyer made Falk wonder if the cop had given him a hard time over his statement. Possibly.

Falk thought back to what Gemma had said about her stepson over dinner in that Melbourne restaurant sixteen months earlier. The boy could be trusted, she had thought. On some things at least, such as being left home alone. Still, Joel insisting Kim had not gone through the east exit complicated things, and complications – in Falk's experience – were rarely welcomed by even the best cops.

Falk allowed himself another fleeting glance at the stage wings. Gemma was still there, but now with a small frown on her face as she also watched her stepson. Her phone lit up in her hand and she checked the screen, frown deepening, then stepped back and melted into the dark. Falk waited, but she didn't reappear. Under the bright stage lights, Sergeant Dwyer was running through the facts.

'Kim Gillespie, aged thirty-nine, was last seen wearing –'

The officer wasn't using any notes, Falk noticed. The bloke had the details of times and descriptions seemingly at his fingertips. He seemed fully across the case, for someone who hadn't been there at the time.

'Where was he last year?' Falk murmured as Raco edged back through the crowd to join him.

'Who, Dwyer? Shit, sorry –' Raco shuffled his feet off an

irritated woman's picnic blanket. 'Er, camping, Dwyer was. Out in the Flinders Ranges. Personal leave.'

'Busy time of year to be taking leave, isn't it?'

'Definitely.' Raco nodded. 'I know Dad was never allowed, back when he was running things. But Rob Dwyer's daughter died last year, a couple of months before the festival, so I guess, under the circumstances . . .' Raco shrugged. 'I feel for the bloke, but it was bloody unlucky timing. It took a few days to actually get hold of him after Kim disappeared, do you remember?'

'Yeah, vaguely.'

'Okay, so that's why. Him and his wife had gone off on their own to the middle of nowhere. Turned their phones off, trying to get their heads straight.'

Falk watched the officer address the crowd. His head seemed screwed on pretty straight now. His appeal was calm and clear and he came across as wholly focused. Whatever he'd missed in those few days, he appeared determined to make up for now.

'What happened to his daughter?' Falk asked.

'Drank too much at a party and suffocated on her own vomit.'

'Bloody hell.'

'Yeah. A couple of her housemates over in Adelaide found her in the morning. She was only about twenty-two I think, so —'

Raco fell silent abruptly as up on stage, Sergeant Dwyer turned to introduce Zara. The officer drew the crowd's attention one last time to the photo and phone number on the screen, before passing the microphone to the girl.

'Has Zara told you what she's going to say?' Falk asked.

'No.' Raco glanced towards his brother. Charlie didn't react as his daughter crossed the stage. 'Reckon I can guess, though.'

Zara made eye contact with someone in the wings and the image behind her dissolved. A video clip began playing instead. There was no sound and it had clearly been shot on a phone. A younger, smiling Kim Gillespie silently sang – *happy birthday to you* – as she held out a homemade cake. Sun filtered through the windows and the candles on the cake flickered. Kim's gaze moved slightly off-centre as she locked eyes with the person filming, with the air of a private joke passing between her and whoever was behind the camera. Falk glanced over. From the expression on Charlie's face, there was no question at all it had been him.

'This is my mum, Kim.' Zara was nervous, but her unchecked emotion only drew more eyes to the stage. 'And I know some of you will have heard what happened here last year, but the facts –'

It was a more polished version of the speech she'd delivered at the vineyard stall and Falk heard Raco sigh. A slideshow continued behind her, with photos and videos spanning several years. Purely from an appeal perspective it was better to use only recent photos, the cop part of Falk couldn't help but think, but at the same time he could see why Zara had chosen them. They helped drive home that Kim Gillespie had been a real person, as urgent and vital as anyone watching and Falk felt something shift in the mood of the crowd. Kim had walked among them – recently, here – living and breathing and probably also smelling the popcorn in the air and trying to avoid trampling on picnic blankets.

'My mum would never do this to her family –'

On screen, Kim was laughing now, understated but bridal

in a simple cream gown. Zara, then fourteen years old and in flattering bridesmaid pink, was at her side, eating cake and trying to pretend she wasn't thoroughly enjoying herself. Rohan was wearing the traditional smart suit and had the happy, slightly stunned smile favoured by grooms everywhere as he held Kim's hand.

Another scene from the wedding followed, of Kim with her arms around an older couple who were clearly her parents. They lived in Canada, Falk remembered now, but had rushed over last year after it had happened. He ran his eyes quickly over the crowd of supporters. No return trip for the anniversary, he guessed. Some experiences were not ones anyone wanted to relive.

'Someone here tonight knows something –'

Zara was gathering momentum as the image behind her faded and resolved. Kim at the vineyard this time, laughing with Rita, their heads close. Falk felt Raco breathe out sharply.

'Where did she get that?' Raco muttered even as the picture changed again.

Kim at the finish line of a ten-kilometre charity fun run. Flushed but pleased, she raised a celebratory cup of water to her fellow runner, who herself appeared to have barely broken a sweat, her blonde hair pulled high in a ponytail.

Falk turned in time to see Naomi Kerr caught completely off guard to find herself up on the screen. Maybe Zara hadn't felt she needed permission to use photos of her own mother, but she clearly hadn't sought it from Naomi. The woman stared glassy-eyed at the picture until it disappeared.

'I want to finish with a message for my mum,' Zara said, as behind her now Kim was holding a baby. It was Zoe, judging by Kim's age. The baby in her arms looked brand new; Kim herself looked exhausted. An unconvincing smile was plastered across her face.

'If you hear this and if you can come home, Mum, please come home.' Zara paused. 'And if you can't, I want you to know we're all working to find you. Okay? That's it, I guess. Thank you.'

The awkward smattering of applause morphed into a rumbling murmur as she lowered the microphone and passed it to Rohan. Falk wasn't surprised. People were always interested in the husband.

If Rohan noticed, and Falk couldn't imagine he'd missed it, he didn't react.

'Thanks, Zara,' he said simply, and he took her place as the screen changed back to the standard missing person photo. No emotive montage for Rohan. It was the right decision, Falk thought. What had seemed moving and heartfelt from Zara could have easily come across as manipulative from Rohan. Instead, the man's wife simply gazed out. *Have you seen me?*

'I sometimes feel like I got to meet my wife for the first time twice.' Rohan launched straight into it. 'The second time was on a Sunday afternoon on Glenelg Beach. I was going for a run along the sand and Kim was there, in the sea with her daughter, Zara.' It felt like a moment where Rohan might have naturally paused to remember, had he been telling this story to friends. But he was not, and this crowd – while not hostile – was certainly keeping their acquaintanceship at arm's length, for now. He carried on.

'I'd known Kim for a lot of years. We were at school together – that's where I met her for the first time – and we were friends then, part of the same big group.'

Charlie didn't react to that, his arms folded and chin tucked down into his chest, but Falk saw Shane nodding.

'Kim and I went our separate ways after school, with uni and first jobs and things,' Rohan continued, 'until that afternoon on the beach when I saw her again. And I knew straight away it was Kim because she had this way about her that drew you in. It's hard to describe, but everyone who remembers her knows what I mean.'

Charlie reacted that time: a tight instinctive dip of his head in agreement.

'So Kim was standing knee-deep in the sea,' Rohan said. 'And I stopped running and probably said something smooth and witty like: "I didn't expect to see you here."'

A light but genuine laugh flitted through the crowd. It was smart of Rohan to humanise himself, Falk thought. Calculated or not, for an appeal to work, people needed to care.

'And Kim probably said something genuinely smooth and witty back. I wish I could remember what, because it worked and that was it for us. We were together for three years, we have a daughter who's just turned one –'

Raco leaned in, his eyes still on Rohan. 'I tested that gap in his night myself. In case you were wondering.'

Falk smiled. He had in fact been wondering exactly that. 'The eight minutes?'

'Yep,' Raco said. 'It was only six, actually. Sergeant Dwyer checked it out too, I know. But I walked it myself anyway. Once with Zara. A couple of times on my own.'

'To put her mind at rest or –?'

'Pretty much. And mine, I suppose. Just in case. I mean, I like Rohan. So I'm not saying anything by this, but –' He shrugged. 'Spouses, statistically, you know? Gotta check 'em. You can't not check them.'

'No. Obviously. How long did the walk take you?'

'Seven minutes thirty, at a steady pace. I did it in the high sixes a couple of times. So no detour. If anything, he hustled.'

'Couldn't have got back here?'

'To the grounds? No way. Not possible. So that was –' Raco sighed. '– a relief, I suppose.'

Falk watched Rohan on the stage. His wife's face still loomed large behind him. 'Does he know?'

'That I checked him out? I doubt it. Not specifically. But he was obviously questioned at the time, so he'd know Dwyer would've. I think he sort of welcomes it, though. You'd have to feel a bit guilty for leaving Kim alone, don't you reckon?' Raco paused. 'Plus, he's not an idiot. He knows he's bloody lucky it's only six minutes and not more.'

That was true, Falk agreed. He could still recall Rohan Gillespie's official movements from a year ago, partially because his own had helped corroborate them.

After Falk had seen him at the base of the ferris wheel waving goodbye to his wife and child on the ride, Rohan Gillespie had continued chatting to the Queensland tourist couple and their tired toddler for a few moments more and when they'd asked about the shortest route back to town, he'd offered to show them. They'd all walked together through the festival grounds and were captured on the CCTV camera at the main west exit. They had carried on through the car park and strolled towards the main street, a fifteen-minute walk.

At the edge of town, Rohan had taken the couple's phone to snap a photo of the family in front of a vertical floral wall. The image was time-stamped 8.17 pm. He had then pointed them towards their hotel the next block over, wished them a good stay and – here fell the gap – continued on alone. Six minutes later, he was again captured on CCTV, this time walking up the steps into his parents' favourite Italian restaurant. Surrounded by forty other diners, he and his parents had sat for more than two hours over three courses and picked through the implications of Rohan's father's recent cancer diagnosis.

Shortly before 10.30 pm, Rohan had put his parents in a taxi, stood on the street outside the restaurant and phoned his wife. When the call had gone through to voicemail, he'd sent a text instead. *Are you still up? On my way back now.* In fact, he'd gone back inside to pay and spent a further five minutes chatting with the owner and her husband. He was showing them pictures of newborn Zoe when his phone rang to let him know his daughter had been found at the festival grounds, alone.

'I'm an engineer, by profession,' Rohan was saying now, and Falk focused again. 'I've done that my whole career, so there are some things I feel I know how to do well. I know how to make sure buildings don't topple and bridges don't fall down. And part of the reason I know how to do that is because it's very logical. If you do one thing after another, you get the result you expect. But over this past year –'

Rohan faltered for the first time, his face flickering with something like disbelief. His *wife* was missing. He looked like he was learning it for the first time. His wife was *missing*. He exhaled. It echoed loudly in the microphone.

'Kim was really creative,' he said at last. 'She worked in marketing with design and branding, so she could always think outside the box. We saw the world in a different way, and I wish I could ask her what I should do now, because she'd have ideas that I can't seem to come up with.'

Rohan's expression was darkening with every word.

'But Kim's not here, and she hasn't been for a year. And all I can think to do for me and Zoe is fall back on logic. Because that logic tells me that someone here tonight has information that could tell us what happened to my wife last year.'

The crowd was still, and those watching had fallen quiet in a way they hadn't for Dwyer or even Zara.

'There'll be people listening to me now who saw Kim here. We're about to have a minute of silence to think about Kim, but while we do that, I'll ask you to keep something else in mind.' Rohan was slowly scanning the faces turned towards him. 'If you were one of the people who flagged a sighting with the police, thank you. But think again now; look around. Is there anything else you can remember about that moment?' There was no hiding the edge in his voice. 'And if you saw Kim last year and *didn't* tell anyone – for any reason at all – now's the time. Okay? Don't leave it another day. We're not interested in why, but we need to know what you know. So think back. Please. What did you see?'

In the wings, Falk saw the tech guy give a signal and Rohan nodded.

'So on behalf of Kim and her family, I'll ask you to please join us now for a minute's silence.'

Rohan lowered the microphone and walked across the stage to stand beside Zara. A soft chime of an electronic bell rang out and most of the crowd bowed their heads, at least a little, and many shut their eyes.

Falk had settled his weight when he felt Raco shift beside

him. He glanced over. Raco's head was up and at first Falk
thought he was looking at Zara, but no. Raco's focus was
instead off to the side, where Sergeant Dwyer stood at the
very top of the stairs leading down from the stage.

'All right, mate?' Falk said under his breath.

Raco didn't reply, just gave a tiny nod in the direction of
the other officer. Falk followed his gaze. Dwyer had a good
view from the top of those stairs. And his head was not bowed
either. Instead – Falk could suddenly see what Raco had
already spotted – Dwyer was making the most of his vantage
point. His face was lifted and his eyes were wide open, sliding
slowly and methodically, one by one, over the gathered friends,
supporters and members of Kim Gillespie's family.

Chapter 11

'Hey, you two,' Rita said softly as Falk and Raco came out onto the verandah.

The vineyard had been still and quiet and the cottage lights low when they'd pulled up. They'd found Rita sitting outside, Henry dozing against her chest. She had a book in one hand and was patting his back with the other. Just beyond the verandah, a small metal fire pit glowed against the dark of the night.

Rita put down her book and reached out to her husband. 'How was it?'

Raco took his wife's hand. 'Okay, I think.'

'That bad?'

He smiled at her. 'Just a hard couple of hours.'

'Where is everyone?'

'Zara's still there –'

After the appeal, Zara had simply taken another handful of fliers and shrugged off Charlie's suggestion that she call it a night and come home.

'I've got my key. I'll be back before eleven,' she'd said and disappeared into the crowd with Joel. Falk was glad no-one else seemed to have had an appetite to do the same. It hadn't even been 9 pm but he'd felt drained.

'And Charlie's inside.' Raco glanced towards the kitchen. 'He'll be out in a minute.'

'No worries.' Rita shifted Henry's weight. 'I might try putting this one down.'

'Here. Let me have him for a minute.' Raco took his son and nestled him against his shoulder.

Rita stretched, her back clicking. She noticed Falk's eye on the fire pit below and her expression softened. 'It's okay, they're just lights.'

Falk craned his head to see. She was right. Instead of glowing embers, there was a nest of solar-powered bulbs.

'Charlie gave in after I wouldn't let him light it for, like, three years. Used to piss him off in winter, but tough shit.' Raco smiled and pointed to his neck. The skin where his son rested, breathing heavily, had an odd, puckered quality to it. 'Couldn't really argue with this, made him look like an arsehole.'

Falk turned his own left hand over. The skin there had improved a lot, but he could still see the scars.

'The lights are nicer anyway,' said Rita, and Raco ran his free hand over hers.

Falk settled into his chair, listening to the nocturnal chirps floating from the vines in a gentle chaotic rhythm. 'How was the fire season this year?'

'Back in Kiewarra?' Raco said. 'Yeah, not too bad this time. Cooler summer, you know.'

'And, hey –' Rita put her glass down. 'You heard the river's running again?'

'Yeah,' Falk said. 'I did. That's great.'

It was. Raco had emailed through some pictures. The locals had lined the banks in the rain to watch as the water had finally forged its way through for the first time in years. Even in the still images, Falk could sense their joy and relief.

You should see it, Raco had written. *Beautiful sight.*

I should, Falk had replied, both of them knowing that he probably wouldn't. Not now, at least, but maybe – he thought – one day.

Things had changed a bit in Kiewarra in the last few years. His friends Barb and Gerry Hadler had sold up – their own house, their son's farm – and moved along the Great Ocean Road. Granddaughter Charlotte was learning to bodyboard. Falk had been to visit them four or five times, and Barb Hadler regularly texted him blurry photos of birds on their porch and the sun over the waves.

A nice bloke from Gippsland called Paul had bought the farm from them, plus the Deacon property next door, looking to roll up his sleeves and make a go of things. He had succeeded, apparently, in both a professional and personal sense. On his second night in town, he'd gone to The Fleece for a drink and spotted a tall blonde woman sipping a white wine and making friendly conversation with the wild redheaded barman. Paul had asked if he could buy her next glass and a few months ago they'd got married in the local church.

'Gretchen sends her best, by the way,' Rita said, reading Falk's mind.

'How was her wedding?'

'Yeah, good, you know. Small.' Raco glanced at his wife, who was watching Falk over the rim of her glass with a look he couldn't interpret. 'Very small, really, mainly immediate family, couple of locals. How many, Rita?'

'A few,' she said simply.

'Just a few,' echoed Raco, and Falk had to smile.

'It's really okay, mate, I didn't expect an invite.'

Gretchen had called to tell him, though. They'd chatted for a while, catching up. It had been nice. She had, in fact, implied that an extra spot could probably be found for an old friend, should he want it, but Falk could tell they were both relieved when he didn't take her up on the offer. He'd wished her the best and truly meant it. She'd done the same, and he knew her well enough to know she'd meant it too.

'Her bloke all right?' he said now.

'Paul? Yeah, seems it.'

'Really good with Lachie.' Rita looked over her shoulder as the back door opened and Charlie stepped out, a bottle under his arm and glasses in his hands. 'The kid can't get enough of him. Always tearing around together.'

'Good,' Falk said. And it was good. He accepted the glass Charlie was offering him. 'Thanks.'

'No worries.' Charlie opened the bottle of red and poured, then lowered himself into a chair with a heavy sigh. He had a large book wedged under his arm and pulled it out now and passed it to Raco. 'Zara got it from here, by the way. That photo with Rita you were asking about?'

'Oh yeah?' Raco reached out with his free hand and opened the book on the table.

Falk could see it was in fact a thick album with photos printed onto the pages.

'Zara had it made up last year,' Charlie said. 'Went through all the photos in the house, all the pics on the computers. Found everything she could of Kim and put it all together. I think she was planning to give it to Zoe, but ended up keeping it.' He swirled his drink, then took a long swallow. 'I guess she can always print another copy.'

'What's this about?' Rita asked, leaning over to see.

'Zara did a slideshow at the appeal,' Raco said, flipping through the pages. 'You were in it, a few others too. I hadn't seen that photo before. Was just curious where it'd come from.'

He found the page he'd been looking for and turned it so Rita could see.

'Yeah, I remember that visit. Kim and Rohan had got married not long before. That was a nice week.' Rita turned another couple of pages, Kim's face appearing again and again, before gently closing the cover.

'Can I –?' Falk asked, and Rita passed it to him.

The photos were in rough chronological order. Kim as a baby smiled out from the opening page, followed by missing teeth and Santa visits and a first day at school. Falk flipped forward, then stopped because suddenly there was Charlie. He was sitting on a wall with Kim. Their faces were unlined and their hands were flat on the brickwork, fingertips touching.

'Did tonight go like you wanted, Charlie?' Rita asked gently.

'Well, what I really wanted was to help Zara.' He took another deep swallow and considered. 'So, as far as that goes, I'm not sure.'

'Give it time to settle,' Raco said. 'See how she feels in a few days. I think it was still worth doing.'

'Hopefully.' Charlie rubbed his eyes. 'I suppose we were lucky Gemma said yes to it at all. Some of the committee didn't want to approve it, did I tell you?'

'The appeal?' Raco was whispering now as Henry stirred. He rose delicately and began to pace a slow circuit up and down the verandah.

'Felt it was too much of a downer for the opening night. I can see their point, to be honest.' Charlie stifled a yawn and glanced at Rita. 'Oh, I caught her on the way out to say thanks and she said hi, by the way.'

'Gemma?' Rita said.

'Yeah. And to you, mate.' He nodded at Falk, then leaned back and closed his eyes. 'Said you guys met once a while back? In Melbourne or something.'

'Oh. Yeah.' Falk tried to keep his voice casual. 'That's right.'

Raco, still pacing, didn't seem to notice, but Rita certainly did, her interest instantly piqued. Honestly, the woman had the instincts of a bloodhound when it came to any hint of activity in Falk's largely dormant love life. They eyeballed each other steadily across the table, and Falk suddenly had the strong sense that while Raco could barely remember him and Gemma crossing paths, this was not news to Rita. Finally, a tiny smile on her lips, she looked away, leaving Falk wondering what exactly she'd heard.

'Rohan and Shane didn't want to come back for a drink?' Rita returned her attention to Charlie, who opened his eyes.

'No. Shane said he'd stick around at the stall. And I guess Rohan needed to get back to Zoe.'

'What did he talk about at the appeal?'

'A few things,' Charlie said. 'How he and Kim met –'

As they chatted, Falk turned several more pages of the album. He was deep in high school territory now. Kim with her pony-tail. Charlie's hair was certainly a statement, although so was his younger brother's, and Falk couldn't stop himself flashing a grin at Raco. Raco was still rocking his son and laughed when he saw what Falk was looking at.

'Tread carefully, mate,' he whispered. 'You're one choice comment away from being invited to step into your car and drive yourself back to Melbourne.'

Falk smiled and turned another page. Footy games, parties, the usual rites of passage.

'God, look at that. I remember my own formal,' Rita said suddenly, leaning over for a closer look at the ill-fitting suits and shiny dresses. 'I went with Caleb Maloney. Wait. Maroney?' She shook her head and turned back to the book. 'And there's Shane. Wow, he was big, wasn't he? Even then.' She tapped a kid already head and shoulders above the others in the group shot. 'And Rohan, there. Charlie.'

Falk pointed to a blonde girl he also thought he now recognised. 'Is that Naomi?'

'Let's see.' Rita leaned in. 'Yep. I'm sorry you haven't met her yet. But she's coming to the house tomorrow, by the way. The priest wants to meet you both.' She winked at Falk. 'Brief you on your godparenting duties.'

'Okay. Sounds good,' Falk said, with as much enthusiasm as he could manage at that time of night, and Raco laughed.

'Power through it, mate. It's a fifteen-minute chat.'

Falk smiled and went to close the album, but Rita put a hand out.

'Oh God, look at Dean,' she said, turning the page to better see a young guy captured laughing at something just out of shot. 'That's a lovely one. Zara should make a copy of that for Joel.'

'Let's look.' Charlie leaned in and stared at the boy without saying anything more, then handed the album back.

'That's Dean Tozer,' Raco said quietly to Falk over the baby's head. 'The bloke in that accident I started telling you about

at the reservoir? With the memorial plaque. He died about –
what? Is it five years ago this year?'

'Six.' Charlie didn't have to think about it.

'Gemma's husband.' Rita glanced at Falk. 'Joel's dad.'

Falk nodded. He looked at the man, back when he was still
a boy. He had been stocky, with freckles running along his
arms and a friendly open face. Falk wondered what exactly
had happened. Car accident, obviously. Unexpected, Gemma
had said. The police were involved.

'Hit-and-run,' Charlie said, guessing his question. 'Start of
festival weekend that year. Early morning while he was out
walking his dog.'

'Shit, really?'

'Yeah. Back when you used to be able to drive along the
reservoir track. Some people used to try to go that way to
avoid breath tests on the highway.'

'And it was at the Drop? Same spot as Kim?' Falk felt
himself frown at that and Raco caught the look.

'I know, mate.' He shrugged as best he could with Henry
in his arms. 'We all hear how that sounds, but the fact is, the
rest of the reservoir's pretty flat and safe. If an accident's going
to happen, it's pretty much always going to be at the Drop.
It's a blind bend, then you've got walkers stopping there,
catching their breath, looking at the view or whatever, so it's
a bad mix. That's partly why they blocked the track off to cars
after what happened to Dean. Service vehicles only now. So,
I dunno. I guess that's better, at least.'

Falk looked over at Charlie, who was frowning into his empty
glass but had not reached for a refill. 'I'm sorry, mate. That's
rough.'

'Thanks. Yeah. Dean was a good bloke. Kim was mates with

him, too, so maybe – I dunno.' The frown deepened. 'Maybe she was –' Charlie stopped again. He pushed his empty glass away and sighed. 'Jesus. I really don't know. Anyway. On that cheery note, think I'll call it a night.' He pulled himself up with a low groan. 'Or at least lie awake listening until my bloody daughter comes home.'

''Night, Charlie.' Rita watched him disappear inside then shook her head. 'God, I'm such an idiot,' she said in an under-tone. 'I can't believe I brought up Dean.'

'No, it's fine. He'll be right. It's just with Kim and everything else.' Raco rubbed her shoulder with his free hand, and looked across at Falk. 'Charlie and Dean were good mates, at school and then again when Dean moved back here. So he took it pretty hard when he died. Obviously.'

'Shane too,' Rita said. 'I think maybe more so, even.'

'They were friends as well?' Falk asked.

'Yeah, all of them. Charlie, Shane, Rohan, Dean.' Raco looked at the album, still open on the table at Dean's picture. 'But Shane was first on the scene. He was out running and saw there'd been an accident. Had to make the call to the police.'

Falk nodded slowly. He thought about the memorial plaque, and pictured Gemma's face across the restaurant table. He could guess the answer before he even asked: 'So did they get the driver?'

'No.' Raco shook his head. A light went out somewhere inside the house and Dean Tozer's face darkened in shadow. 'Never did.'

Chapter 12

Falk and Raco sat together and listened to the hum of the night as they looked out over the long rows of vines. Rita had taken Henry inside and Falk could hear her now moving around the kitchen.

'You going to wait up for Zara?' Falk asked as Raco yawned.

'I don't think I'll make it. I hope she's feeling okay, though.'

'It's bloody hard when someone's not found,' Falk said. 'I can see why she's hung up on things.'

'I know. But a lot of these theories she grabs on to just go nowhere. I mean, Kim being out there still?' Raco rubbed the corners of his eyes. 'Think that through realistically for one second. Where's she supposed to have been living for an entire year? What's she doing for money? I mean, Kim was my family too. So I'll follow these things up, for her as much as Zara, but . . .' He waved a hand in futility. 'Things lead where they lead, you know? I can't change that because Zara wants it to be something different.'

'No.' Falk thought back over the evening, and the appeals for answers. Not just from Zara and Rohan, but from the sergeant, too, with his unexpected – to Falk, at least – scrutiny of the gathered supporters. 'What are your thoughts on Dwyer, out of interest? He seems the curious type.'

Raco looked faintly amused. 'He is, isn't he? Which is what you want, I suppose. But yeah, look, he's solid. Good with the locals, good at the job, I would say. My dad trained him up, actually, back when this was one of his early postings, so you'd hope so.'

'The way he was watching all of you tonight, at the end,' Falk said, and Raco nodded. 'You worried?'

'No.'

'Not at all?'

Raco seemed to weigh something up for a moment, then hauled himself out of his chair and disappeared inside the house. He returned a moment later with a large bound folder in his hands and passed it to Falk.

'Been keeping a few notes of my own about all this.'

'Yeah, mate. So I see.'

It was a thick file and Falk ran his thumb over the edge. He wasn't surprised Raco had his own resources, but this was even more comprehensive than he'd expected. He glanced over and Raco shrugged.

'Yeah, I know. Look, it's for peace of mind, mostly. So when Zara asks something I can give her a decent answer. Anyway, feel free to flick through. Maybe you'll see something I haven't.'

'I doubt that,' Falk said, meaning it.

'At this point, I'd be happy if you did, honestly.' Raco gathered up their empty glasses. 'And you never know, fresh pair of eyes.'

'Well.' Falk was less convinced. 'Maybe.'

After they'd said good night, Falk walked back to the

guesthouse on his own. It was very peaceful, he thought. Away from the lights of the cottage, the vineyard took shape under the silvery moon. The perfect rows gleamed in the pale light, and the distant hills rose up around the valley in their tones of black and grey. Above, the night sky was huge. The stars glowed. He stood for a minute, drinking it in.

Finally, the mosquitoes biting, he unlocked the guesthouse and let himself in. He flicked on a couple of lamps, bathing the room in a warm low light, and put Raco's file on the bedside table. Opening the fridge, he poured himself a glass of water, then went to the bathroom, turned on the taps and took a long, hot shower.

He emerged feeling better, more relaxed and his head clearer. He put on the t-shirt and shorts he usually slept in and stood at the window, rubbing a towel over his hair. Through the blinds, Falk could see the edge of the house. It was all in darkness except for a soft glow from one window. He mentally tracked the internal layout and decided it was Zara's room. There was some movement of shadow behind the curtains. So the girl was home, but she wasn't sleeping, he thought as he hung up his towel. Or at least not yet.

Falk brushed his teeth and sat on the bed. He settled back against the headboard, his hand reaching towards the light on the bedside table but his eyes on Raco's file. Five minutes, he decided. He was ready for sleep, but also curious what exactly his mate had found to fill a folder quite so thick.

The answer, Falk could see immediately when he opened the cover, was a robust and practical job typical of Raco's policing style these days. Maps – of the town, the festival site, the reservoir, the bushland – had been catalogued and annotated with notes and times and helpful lists of key points. Raco had summarised some witness statements, including Falk's own, and had managed to get his hands on photocopies of the originals of others. The bartender in the ale tent. The couple who had seen a woman arguing with a man in the car park.

– she had on dark jeans or pants. I could not see her top clearly because she was leaning into the car on the driver's side, but it was white or light coloured. The woman sounded annoyed and said to the driver something like: 'If you are lying to me, I will find out.' I did not hear his response because we were walking away and –

Falk turned the page. Another one, this time from a woman in the ladies' toilets.

– waiting in line and I could hear crying from inside a cubicle. It was the second or third cubicle on the left. It was a woman and she was upset and I considered asking if she was okay, but there were a lot of people in the line and I felt like it wasn't any of my business. I go to the festival every year and you do get people who have overdone it and are emotional. I heard a mobile phone ring from inside the cubicle and the woman stopped crying. She answered it and she said: 'Hello.' And then: 'I'm still here. Where are you?' I was at the front of the line by then so went to use the toilet myself and did not hear any more. I knew Kim Gillespie between the ages of approximately sixteen and twenty. I was friends with her mother, Deborah, before she and her husband moved to Canada and since then I have run into Kim from time to time when she came back to Marralee to visit. I believe it was Kim's voice I heard –

Falk moved on, marking spots to return to when he felt more alert. It was an interesting collection of material. Raco had said he'd compiled this to help Zara's understanding, but there was information in there that Falk highly doubted he'd ever show her. Studies of body decomposition rates in South Australian waters, for one. Several times, Falk found himself staring blankly at a page for several minutes, trying to work out its significance. An algae report, or the minutes of the previous year's festival committee AGM.

Falk yawned and half-heartedly opened a worn envelope to find a packet of grainy night-time photos. They had the familiar blurred quality that instantly dated them as having been taken before smartphones and instant edits. He recognised Kim in the first photo, no more than sixteen or seventeen at the time, but with a beer bottle in her hand. It was dark and her face was lit by something out of shot. A campfire, Falk guessed from the glow. She was sitting on a blanket with her legs tucked under her and was making a face at the camera.

Falk could feel exhaustion creeping over him, and he'd seen plenty of photos of Kim that evening. He started to replace them in the envelope, then stopped as something on the back of a picture caught his eye. He turned it over. It was a number in Raco's handwriting: *11*. Falk flicked through the rest of the shots. Each had been numbered, from one to thirty-six. Recently, too, he guessed. The ink looked far fresher than the photos.

Falk checked inside the envelope again and found what he'd been hoping for: a folded sheet of paper, also with the numbers one to thirty-six in Raco's writing. Falk scanned the list.

3. Kim.

4. Kim, Naomi, ??

Falk searched through the photos until he found the ones numbered three and four. Number three showed Kim sitting alone on the picnic blanket with her beer. In four, Kim was in the same spot but had been joined by Naomi, along with an unnamed teenage boy with cropped hair and a bottle in each hand. He was leaning over the girls, his arms heavy on their shoulders. Both girls' faces were fixed in tight, dutiful smiles, but neither looked particularly happy about it.

Falk shuffled through the rest of the pictures. From the clothes, he could tell they'd all been taken on the same evening. A party around a campfire, almost everyone holding drinks. He didn't recognise most of the faces, and flicked back and forth to the list.

15. Me and ?? Maybe Wade's cousin? Raco had written against a photo of himself, laughing like best friends with a tall bloke whose name he obviously could no longer recall.

16. Shane, Jen C, Charlie, ?? Shane, huge next to Jen C, was bending down to plant a drunken kiss on her cheek. Her eyes were bright and she was pink-cheeked with what looked like pure delight. Charlie was grinning at the camera, his arm snug around the waist of an unnamed girl who was decidedly not Kim.

Falk paused. Raco may not know the girl in the photo, but anyone could recognise the flirtatious energy in the shot. How had Kim felt about that, Falk wondered, if she'd even been aware? He worked through the images again, more slowly this time. He could find none of Charlie and Kim together.

He paused at shot number nineteen, though, labelled in Raco's neat handwriting: *Dean, Rohan, Gemma.*

The scene was badly lit and Falk had not recognised her immediately, but he could see it now. She looked softer and very young, but so did everyone. He looked from her to Dean. If there had been any hint of the romance that would blossom, it was derailed quite neatly by Rohan, bang in the middle of the pair and tipping a beer to the photographer, his face flushed. He wasn't alone in that. Every one of them looked worse for wear.

Falk continued, through faces and names that meant nothing to him. At the end of the list, Raco had added a few names that didn't seem to correspond with any of the images:

Dean's friend, short, dark hair, from Warrnambool.

Kyle.

Ryan S.

Tania's cousins x 3

Falk checked the back of the photos and the envelope for any further explanatory notes from Raco, but there were none. Another question to add to the algae reports and the AGM minutes. He leaned back against the bedhead and briefly considered texting Raco, but immediately decided against it. Whatever it was had waited this long, it could wait until the morning. Tired now, he sorted the pictures back in order, looking at Gemma's face for a moment longer than the others, then slid them back into the envelope and turned out the light.

Falk had kissed Gemma under the awning at the corner of the dark Melbourne laneway until the rain had passed. They'd taken each other's hand as they'd stepped back out onto the slick pavement and headed through the city towards Flinders Street Station, where the trams and trains went to a lot of different places. Falk's flat in St Kilda, for example. Gemma's hotel in Richmond as well. Falk wasn't quite sure what might happen next, so instead he concentrated on what was happening right then. Walking along together, the city lights shining, her hand in his.

At the station, they both hesitated on the footpath outside. *Stay or go?* Then Gemma glanced over his shoulder to the late-night newsagent near the ticket gates.

'I need to top up my travel card,' she said.

'Right.' Was that a signal for him to say goodbye and leave? Falk wondered. But then she'd smiled.

'I'll be back in a minute.'

'Okay. Great.'

Even as he spoke, Falk felt his phone buzz in his pocket and he pulled it out as she disappeared inside the shop. He stood near the door, his shoulders hunched against the wind, scanning a long string of work messages and tapping out a few fast replies.

'Hey.'

He glanced up at Gemma's voice as she came back out of the newsagency. She looked happy to see him. Falk put his phone away.

'So, this was a complete impulse buy, but I actually got you something.' She had her travel card in one hand and was holding something out to him with the other. 'Here.'

Falk looked down at the gift. It was a week-to-week office diary with a blue ballpoint pen.

'And it's really so nice of you to try to look grateful.' Gemma laughed as she caught his expression. 'But, seriously, the most organised person I've ever known gave me this tip.'

'A paper diary?'

'Yeah. It's good when you've got a lot on. Does the same as a phone calendar but without beeping at you all the time with meetings and things. The idea is that you feel a bit more in control of the day because you check it when you're ready, not the other way around.'

'Does it work?'

'For some people. It does for me. Your taskforce sounds pretty busy. I thought it might be worth a go.' She frowned. 'And then I also bought you the pen because I've drunk too much and forgot you probably already own one.'

'Well, you can really never have too many.' Falk flicked through the diary. Maybe he'd had a bit too much to drink himself, but he was genuinely touched. 'Thanks, Gemma. I'll give it a try.'

Falk lifted his eyes to hers and she smiled back at him, pleased. Her face was a little flushed under the station light, with her hair hanging damp around her shoulders. And all at once he had the sudden urgent sensation that something was about to pass him by. He turned to the back of the diary and held out the contacts page.

'Gemma, can I grab your number?'

She took the diary and the pen straight away. Once back in her hands, though, she seemed to pause. As Falk watched, her expression dimmed and she stood there, thinking, as the seconds ticked by. She pressed the pen against the paper for what felt like a long time. Falk just waited, but she still didn't write anything.

'I think –' She tapped the pen on the page, then wrote a *G*. She stopped again. The pen now hovered an inch above the diary. Gemma glanced up at him, then down again. She breathed out and closed the cover. 'I think it's actually better for both of us if I say no. I'm really sorry.'

'Oh.' Falk blinked. He couldn't think what to say. 'Okay.'

He wasn't often sure about these things, but he'd been sure this time. In his mind, her number was right there in the book she was now handing back to him. He had already jumped ahead, debating whether to text or call as a follow-up the next morning. Before or after her flight back home? Call, he'd decided. After the flight, when hopefully she'd have time to talk. Instead, he turned the empty diary over in his hands, then slipped it into his coat pocket. He took a breath and a longish moment to recalibrate expectation with reality.

Gemma was watching him. 'I'm sorry,' she said again.

'No, God, please don't, there's no need –' He was replaying the entire evening in his mind, though, skipping ahead and rewinding, trying to find the flaw. It really still felt like a yes. 'I think I just got the wrong –'

'No, you didn't –' She stopped.

Falk waited, genuinely curious, but when she didn't go on, he said: 'It's honestly fine, you don't have to explain.'

A pause. 'Thank you.'

He'd kind of hoped she would, though. Was it her late husband? he wondered. On some level that had to be part of the equation for anyone, but it didn't feel like the whole answer. Falk had been around grief – spouses, children, friends – enough times that he was pretty well attuned to the complexities involved. This felt like something else, though. He ran through the last few hours again: the bar, the drinks, the walk, the restaurant, the candle –

'It's nothing you did, Aaron. It's not you.'

He smiled at that, and despite herself she smiled back.

'Really,' she said.

'Okay.' He nodded. He'd take her word for it, but he'd love to know what it was, in that case. 'Well.' He breathed out. It was a no. All right, then. Move on. 'Thanks anyway, Gemma, for tonight. I really had a great time with you. It was a lot of fun.'

She was wavering, he could tell. But then she simply nodded. 'Yeah. It was.'

'And I'm glad I got to meet you.'

'Me too.'

Stay or go?

Go.

He couldn't help it, he paused for a moment, hoping for a last-minute change of heart. But all she said was: 'Good luck with the new job.'

'Thanks. Have a safe flight home.' He raised a hand. 'Well. Bye then.'

'Goodbye.'

Falk turned and headed off towards the tram stop. He thought he could feel her watching him for a way, but when he glanced back, she had gone. The spot where they'd been standing outside the station was now occupied by a pair of teenage girls embroiled in a teary argument.

No.

No number, no text or call debate, no follow-up. It was a no. And that was her choice to make and her decision was fair enough. But Falk still wished it had been a yes.

Chapter 13

Falk had spotted Gemma only twice during his brief visit to Marralee twelve months earlier. The first, perhaps not surprisingly, had been at the festival. It had been just after 8 pm on the night Kim Gillespie would later disappear and the sky was dark. Falk had been walking back from the HQ caravan, having tried and failed to deliver Charlie's safety reports into Gemma's hands personally, when suddenly there she was. Just beyond the ferris wheel, a little further along the path.

She'd been deep in conversation with a blonde woman Falk hadn't recognised at the time, but now knew to be Naomi Kerr. Falk had paused, considering what to do. Above him, the ferris wheel had circled slowly on its axis.

His impulse had been to walk straight up to Gemma and say hello, but instinctively he'd been able to tell this wasn't a great time. Both women were talking fast, standing close to hear each other over the noise. Naomi had seemed agitated, her hands moving in quick, tight gestures. She'd made a point emphatically and in response both women suddenly lifted their heads and looked in Falk's direction.

He had thought – hoped – for a second that Gemma would see him, but she and Naomi had been focused on something else, their gaze settling beyond him. Gemma had nodded, firm but calm – *Okay, I understand* – and Naomi had looked slightly mollified.

It had been that same moment that a feedback loop had screeched from the ride's speakers behind Falk and he'd automatically turned; the moment he'd caught Rohan Gillespie's eye, vaguely registered him talking to the Queensland tourist family, seen him waving up to the top carriage. And that – as Falk would have explained to the interviewing officer later if the guy had pressed him at all – was why two and a half hours before Kim was reported missing, his own focus had not been on her at all. It was instead on Gemma, who had been *right there* on the path before he'd glanced away, and was maddeningly, frustratingly gone by the time he'd looked back.

He did see her once more after that: the following day, in those strange black hours when the urgent question of Kim's whereabouts was taking on a surreal nightmarish quality. Falk had spotted Gemma leaving the police station as he'd been arriving to make his own statement. From the pavement on the other side of the road, the main street traffic moving between them, he'd watched her come quickly down the station steps. She'd got into her car, started the engine and driven away. If she'd seen him standing there, she hadn't acknowledged it.

Falk had kept the diary, though. The pages were crinkled with pen marks and crossings-out. The days had been crammed full of meetings and reminders and corrections and calls to return and questions to check and reports due. But it still didn't have her number.

*

Falk and Raco sat outside the guesthouse, drinking coffee in the morning sun while five-year-old Eva attempted to thread dandelions into a crown. Falk had woken up naturally before his alarm, which was somewhat unusual, and he'd lain in bed for several seconds bathed in the light from the window and trying to remember where he was. Now, he and Raco watched in silence as the back door to the house opened and Zara wandered out. She crossed the verandah and walked down to the grounds, absorbed in her phone. She was hunched too far over to properly see her face.

'She told me she thought yesterday went quite well,' Raco said.

'That's something, at least.'

Raco swallowed a mouthful of coffee. 'Hopefully she won't get her hopes up too high, but there's not a lot that can be done about that.'

Falk thought he was probably right. 'I got through some of your file last night.'

'Yeah?' Raco drained his mug. 'Anything –?' He stopped as the door opened again and this time Rita appeared on the back verandah, shielding her eyes. She spotted them outside the guesthouse and waved for them to join her.

'Naomi must be here.' Raco pulled himself out of the chair. 'Come on, Eva. So, yeah,' he said to Falk as they began to walk, 'any thoughts?'

'It's pretty thorough, mate,' Falk said. 'No stone unturned.'

'Or clutching at straws.'

'What was the significance of the AGM minutes?'

'Which ones?'

'The festival committee. Last year.'

'Oh, them. There was a plan to do a safety audit. I put the

minutes in so I remembered to follow up, but nothing new came out of it.'

'And the algae report? With the spring and summer bacteria levels?'

Raco frowned. 'Dunno, might have to remind myself. Think it was something to do with indicating water movement.'

'There were some old photos too,' Falk said. 'Numbered, names listed. Taken at a party.'

'Yep.' Falk caught the change in Raco's voice. 'I know the ones.'

Raco looked like he wanted to say more but instead lifted his hand to greet the second woman now waiting for them on the verandah. 'G'day, Naomi.'

Naomi Kerr stood next to Rita, holding baby Henry on her hip.

'Hi, Greg. And Aaron. Hello. At last.' Naomi smiled, bright and warm. Her sunglasses were not quite dark enough to hide her swift look of appraisal, up and down. 'Good to finally meet you.'

'You too,' he said.

Naomi was small, her head barely reaching Falk's shoulder. She was wearing leggings today and they were skin-tight and glossy black, ending mid-calf to show a smooth, tanned ankle. Beneath her lightweight fleece, a fitted t-shirt hugged her body.

'Thank you both again for doing this.' Rita took Henry back as he started to whine and motioned vaguely for them all to sit down. 'And Father Connor has another appointment after this, Naomi, so you should be back at the clinic for –'

'That's fine.' Naomi waved her hand. 'I've swapped to the afternoon roster anyway.'

'Naomi's a GP,' Raco called as he disappeared into the

kitchen and re-emerged with a jug of water and some glasses. 'At the medical centre in town.'

'Speaking of . . .' Naomi pulled out a chair but didn't sit, her gaze settling on Zara, who was now under the shade of a distant tree, staring at her phone. 'Make an appointment for her to come in and talk to someone, even if she doesn't want to. We've got a new woman recently started who's very good.'

'Thanks,' Rita said, and Raco nodded as he poured. 'We'll tell Charlie.'

'How's the general feeling this morning? Thank you.' Naomi accepted a glass of water and pushed her sunglasses onto her head. She had the reassuring presence of a medical professional, and Falk was starting to get a sense of why the Racos had chosen her to be his counterpart.

'We're all just keen to see what comes out of the appeal,' Raco said. 'Would help to have some answers, whatever they look like.'

'Absolutely.' Naomi's face softened, her eyes still on Zara. 'I think that would help a lot. It's hard not to try to imagine what was on Kim's mind.'

'Yeah.' Raco cracked his knuckles the way he sometimes did when he was silently debating something and Rita discreetly winced at the sound. He stopped and nodded towards Falk. 'We were actually just talking about that opening night party.'

Naomi's gaze slid back at that. She didn't ask what he meant. 'I've been thinking about that too.'

Falk frowned. 'What's this?' he asked, and Raco and Naomi simultaneously drew breath then locked eyes with an identical *sorry, you go* gesture.

'Go ahead,' Raco said. 'You found her.'

There was a pocket of silence when all they could hear was

the hum of insects. Rita was stroking her son's hair with an expression Falk couldn't read. Naomi stared down at her hands for a moment, gathering her thoughts, then looked up at Falk.

'You'd have heard about this bushland party that happens at the festival every year? All the local teenagers and any tourist kids they can drag in go up behind the reservoir on the first night and get absolutely shit-faced.' Naomi glanced at Henry in Rita's arms. 'Excuse my language.'

Rita smiled, pushing back her chair. 'I don't think he minds. I need to get him changed anyway.'

'And look,' Naomi went on as Rita disappeared indoors. 'Unpopular opinion here, because I'm aware I'm a hypocrite who used to do this myself, but that's one tradition that needs shutting down. Before some kid has a bad reaction to something, or falls down the embankment and breaks their bloody neck, or slips and drowns in that water, because I know no-one wants to hear it, but it will happen.'

'But teenagers'll always –' Raco started, but she shook her head.

'No, Greg. Come on. You know where the border of my property is. I hear those kids coming and going and I'm telling you it's not like you remember. Back then it was all people we knew and a handful of out-of-town cousins or whatever. This has grown with the festival, and as I keep saying, as a doctor and concerned resident – local busybody, whatever, I don't care – it's getting out of hand. Anyway,' Naomi swatted a fly away irritably, 'for all the good it does me to keep saying that.'

Her tone was level and brisk but underneath she sounded a little uneasy, Falk thought.

'So something happened involving Kim?' he asked.

Naomi and Raco exchanged another look and then she nodded.

'We're talking years ago,' she said quickly. 'But it was a big night, that one, because a lot of us had turned eighteen by then. Me, plus Charlie and Shane and Rohan, and another friend of ours, Dean.' His name sounded faintly different in her mouth than the others and she cleared her throat. 'Anyway. It was obvious Shane was going to be drafted by one of the footy teams, and the rest of us were off to uni after the summer, so it was the last time we were all going to be around for this thing. I mean, people did come back, there were always a few older faces home for a visit or whatever, and there were younger kids as well. You would have been – what?' she asked Raco.

'Fifteen.'

'Yeah, I went for the first time when I was fourteen.' Naomi's eyes turned back to Falk. 'But the point is, there were a lot of people there that year. A lot of drinking, possibly more than usual. And for whatever reason, maybe because of that, I wasn't really into it that night. The whole thing just felt off.' She glanced at Raco. 'You thought so too?'

'Yeah,' he said. 'Everyone got really drunk really fast and there was definitely a weird atmosphere. There were all these kids there we didn't know –' Naomi was nodding in agreement as he spoke. 'The dynamic was wrong. Little fights kept flaring up, over stupid stuff. And Charlie and Kim had fallen out before they even got there.'

Beyond the verandah, Falk could see Charlie out among the vines. Shane was there as well. Falk hadn't seen him arrive but the pair were talking, their stances almost identical from that distance. Shoulders hunched and arms folded across their chests.

'Do you know why Charlie and Kim weren't getting on?' Falk asked, and both Raco and Naomi shook their heads.

'It would have been nothing,' Naomi said. 'Charlie says he doesn't remember and I can believe it. They were always breaking up and making up, even then. So they'd had another argument, and of course Charlie did the mature thing and spent the whole night talking to girls and trying to make her jealous. And Kim, being sixteen, did what you'd expect – drank too much, pretended she didn't care what her boyfriend was up to and went off every five minutes to secretly cry behind a tree.'

'They got like that sometimes.' Raco sounded weary thinking about it. 'But basically at some point, Kim had had enough and she left. I didn't actually see her go, but when I realised, I wasn't surprised.'

'No, me neither,' Naomi said. 'I know it must have been still pretty early – only about 10 pm – because that was when I decided to leave myself. I was trying to find someone to come with me so I wouldn't have to walk back alone, but no-one wanted to. So in the end I just went.'

Naomi paused and Falk sensed that uneasiness again. He just waited.

'I found Kim near this spot where the track hits the reservoir trail.' Naomi motioned a meeting point with her hands. 'She wasn't even on the path. Probably five metres deep into the bushland, kind of half propped up against a tree. I had a torch with me because it got really dark out there – still does – but I only saw Kim because she had some sequin detailing on her top and it caught the light.'

Naomi took her sunglasses off her head, opening and closing them in her hands.

'So I stopped, and I called out to her. And she didn't answer. She had her eyes shut and there was no-one else around –' Open, close. '– and it was dark and for this horrible second, I thought she was dead.'

Naomi tossed her glasses on the table and reached for her water. The memory still troubled her, Falk could tell. But as she looked up again, he had a sudden faint but unshakeable sense of something being a fraction out of place.

'I mean, she wasn't dead, obviously.' Naomi's voice was brisk. 'Thankfully. But God, she was absolutely wasted. So drunk. More than I'd realised, for sure. I could see she'd thrown up, there was this puddle of vomit beside her. So I went over to check on her. She had vomit all up the back of her top and in her hair. She was still really out of it so I took her arms –' Naomi lifted a hand lightly as though reaching out. '– and pulled her up.'

Something about the gesture – the specific, precise way Naomi moved – set the oddly false note ringing again in Falk's head. The story felt edited, he realised suddenly. To what degree, he couldn't tell. Possibly not by much at all. Or no more than was to be expected after twenty-five years, with all the gaps in memory that might entail. Falk looked across the table at Naomi, straight-backed and clear-eyed. Trusted by the Racos. He could believe she was recounting this as closely as recall allowed. But even so, no story had just one side.

'So Kim was at least on her feet.' Naomi took a sip of water, her fingers trailing through the condensation as she put the glass back on the table. 'She was pretty unsteady, but back then me and my friends were helping each other get home drunk every weekend, so it wasn't much more than I was used to. I could tell she'd been sick so I was hoping she'd start to sober up. I got her onto the path, but something –' Her face hardened. 'God, I don't know. The whole thing felt wrong. I checked her clothes. Because with the vomit on her back it looked like she'd been lying down in it and her skirt was –' Naomi's hands fell to her own thighs. 'Kind of rucked up. But her undies were still on and I remember feeling –' She stopped again. Breathed out a sigh. '– relieved, I suppose, because at least they seemed fine. As far as you can really tell something like that, anyway. So I straightened her clothes, but to be honest I was freaking out myself by then because we were alone and I had a really strong –'

Naomi hesitated, touching a hand to her chest.

'You know that adrenalin sensation,' she said, finally. 'That you just dodged a bullet? Like when you hit the brakes in time and miss that other car? Or slip with a kitchen knife on the chopping board but get away with it? Well, that's what it felt like out there with Kim. Like I'd come along and interrupted –' Naomi could tell she didn't need to spell it out. 'Well, you can both guess as well as I can. Something bad.'

Chapter 14

'Did Kim say anything?' Falk watched Naomi across the table. 'Once you had her back on the path?'

A light breeze swept through, rustling the vines below the verandah. The sun came out from behind a cloud and Naomi slipped her sunglasses on again. It made it hard to read her expression but her mouth was a firm line as she shook her head.

'She was past the slurring stage even, so no. I walked her home. Helped her get into her bedroom without her parents realising the state she was in.' She drained her water glass. 'I went around to see her the next morning, though, to check if she was okay. Ask her what had gone on. God, she was so hungover. She did remember some parts, like arriving at the party, Charlie being a dickhead and her being upset about it, but after that –' Naomi's eyes flickered behind her dark glasses. 'Not much. Not deciding to leave, or who she left with – if anyone. Not me finding her, not getting home.'

'A lot of blank space there,' Raco said, frowning into the light.

139

'Yeah. I told her how I'd found her, what it looked like, but honestly, she seemed embarrassed as much as anything,' Naomi said. 'I know it sounds stupid, sitting here as adults, but back then . . .' She shrugged. 'Kim didn't want Charlie or anyone at school finding out. And what can I tell you? I was a teenager myself and I thought no real harm had been done.' Naomi gave a dry, humourless laugh. Underneath Falk sensed rather than heard that faint false note again. 'So I did what she asked. Never brought it up again, never told anyone.'

Falk nodded slowly. 'Until when? Last year?'

'Yep.' The word was clipped and Naomi's face was set. 'After Kim abandoned her newborn in a public place and walked off alone to take her own life a hundred metres from where it had happened. So at that point – yes, big pat on the back for me for finally stepping up. I told Sergeant Dwyer, because I thought – I still think – it was relevant to her state of mind.'

They were all quiet for a moment.

'It's not a cop-out to say things were different back then, Naomi,' Raco said. 'We were all young. And the three of us can sit here now thinking the word "assault" and considering consent issues under the influence because we're both police and you're a GP and it's twenty-five years on. But that's not always how it was. And definitely not when it came to teenage girls drinking at a party.'

'I know. I do. And I believed Kim at the time when she said she was okay. But, Jesus –' Naomi took off her glasses and ran a distracted hand through her hair. 'It's just so bloody sad. I wish I'd done things differently, that's all.'

'Did Kim ever tell anyone else?' Falk asked.

Raco and Naomi exchanged a glance and shook their heads.

'I don't think so,' Raco said. 'The first I heard of it was in the week after she disappeared, when Dwyer asked me if I could tell him anything. It was news to Charlie and Shane as well, I know. Even Rohan, I'm pretty sure?' he said, and Naomi nodded.

'Yeah, she hadn't told him either.'

'Are you surprised she didn't tell anyone?' Falk could tell Naomi had asked herself the same question, probably a few times. Still, she thought about it again now.

'Not really. I mean, she never mentioned it again to me, so I could imagine she didn't talk about it to anyone else. It was almost like it had never happened until –'

Naomi stopped as Rita put her head out of the door. 'Sorry to interrupt, Father Connor's car's pulled up.'

'Okay, thanks.' Raco finished his water and made to stand.

'So that's why you catalogued the party photos?' Falk asked him, pushing back his own chair. 'Working out who was there?'

Raco nodded. 'It's impossible, though. There were kids there who aren't in the pictures, people I never knew and don't remember. And where Naomi found Kim, it wasn't far from that main reservoir track –' Naomi was nodding in confirmation. '– so anyone could have come along there. Someone from the festival. Dog walker. Late-night jogger. You'd never know.'

From inside the house, they heard the front door close.

'That's him.' Raco immediately straightened and hurried inside. Falk watched him go and suppressed a smile. Father Connor was *in the building*. Naomi caught his eye. She also looked a little amused, and the tightness in her face relaxed.

'Come on.' She stepped around the table, slipping her honed body through the gap between the chairs. 'We'll get through this together.' She linked her arm through Falk's. 'Do you have kids, Aaron?'

141

'No,' he said. 'You?'

'Three.'

'Really?'

'They're with my ex-husband for the school holidays.' She peered up at him from beneath her eyelashes. 'You sound surprised.'

'Oh. No.' He was. Definitely.

'Sometimes people are,' she said with the kind of confidence unique to a woman who knew she looked spectacular in leggings, and Falk had to smile back.

A round white-haired man who exuded the welcoming warmth of a freshly boiled kettle was already settled and waiting for them in the kitchen. He was slipping biscuits from a plate on the table to Eva, who was cramming them into her mouth with gusto while Rita made coffee. Henry was dozing so Raco passed him to Falk and then hovered, getting in everyone's way.

Falk pulled up a chair next to Naomi, ready to engage in his first real conversation with a representative of the church since – when? He tried to think. Organising his father's funeral, possibly. Before that, he couldn't remember. Falk had never been religious, but after a while he had to admit there was something innately soothing about sitting here in his friend's sunny kitchen, drinking good coffee and holding his sleeping godson-to-be while listening to this affable man talk about how a child was a blessing and it took a village.

Afterwards, Naomi asked a couple of questions that Falk suspected were more out of courtesy than confusion, and which Father Connor was delighted to answer. He finished by pumping their hands and congratulating them on their roles so enthusiastically that it was almost as though Falk and

Naomi were the proud new parents themselves. As he rose to leave, Falk felt almost disappointed. He could have sat there longer.

'Well,' Naomi said, when she and Falk were alone again. She leaned back in her kitchen chair and smiled at him. Raco had taken Henry back, and the soft murmur of him and Rita saying goodbye to the priest floated along the hallway. 'I think between us we'll manage, what do you reckon?'

'I think so,' Falk said, although possibly believing it for the first time.

'So. No kids of your own.' Naomi was still looking at him. She raised an eyebrow. 'How about girlfriends? Got one of those?'

'Nope.'

'Oh my goodness. *More* than one, Aaron?'

He laughed. 'No. Fewer.'

'I see. Just curious.' Naomi flashed him a teasing smile. She wasn't interested herself, he felt sure, but was watching him with the private satisfaction of a woman who'd received the right answer.

'Does –' he started, then stopped as Rita reappeared. Her face was a little worried. 'Everything okay?'

'Oh. Yes, thanks.' Rita let Falk top up her coffee mug, but her face didn't change.

'You sure?' He glanced at Raco, who also seemed flat.

'It's just . . .' Rita swallowed a mouthful of hot coffee and grimaced. 'Is this whole thing ridiculously insensitive?'

'What thing?' Naomi blinked. 'The christening?'

'Father Connor mentioned Kim in passing as he left.' Raco's voice was a little subdued. 'Saying he was glad we'd rearranged after last year.'

'But so many people are going to make that connection,' Rita said. 'Remembering why we cancelled. The fact it's the anniversary. All of it.'

Naomi reached across the table. 'I realise people are always claiming to know what someone would have wanted after they're gone, but honestly, Rita? Kim would've supported you in this.'

'Yeah. I mostly feel that too.' Rita's mouth tightened. 'But then I can't stop thinking about last year. That I should have made more of an effort at the festival. I mean, Kim had a six-week-old baby, for God's sake, I know how hard –'

'Come on.' Raco put his palm on her back. 'Don't.'

'I know, but I keep coming back to that moment early on, at the toilet block. I had the chance to catch her then and I still didn't bother.' Rita looked to Falk for support. 'You remember?'

'Yeah, Rita, I do, but –' It was clear from her guilt that they recalled the incident differently.

They hadn't been at the festival long and the opening night crowd was continuing to grow as twilight drew in. Falk had been standing with Rita, watching Raco and Eva on the carousel, when Rita had leaned into the pram, sniffed and said: 'We need a toilet stop.'

To Falk, who was draining his beer, that hadn't sounded like a bad idea either. 'I'll come with you.'

Rita had waved to Raco, released the pram brake and she and Falk had wandered over together. The toilets were housed in an ugly grey cinderblock structure that at least looked clean and well maintained.

'Oh my God, look at that queue,' Rita had said as they approached, and Falk followed her gaze to the line snaking out of the women's side and around the corner. The entry to the men's side beckoned, wide open and empty, and Rita rolled her eyes.

'You go ahead,' she'd said to Falk. 'If I'm not out before the festival closes, tell my husband to send supplies and –'

'Rita, hey. How are you?'

Rita had turned at the voice. 'Rohan! Hi there, how nice to see you.'

The man waiting outside the toilet block was jiggling a pram with his foot, and in each hand held an ice-cream, one almost eaten, the other melting fast. He'd seemed a little stressed but had smiled as they'd gone over.

'Rohan, this is our friend Aaron,' Rita had said, distracted as she'd peered into the pram where a baby girl was asleep. 'Oh, is this Zoe? She is so beautiful. Look at that hair. Congratulations.'

'Thank you. You too.' Rohan had grinned approvingly at baby Henry. 'He's a fair size, isn't he?'

'Definitely feels it when I pick him up.' Rita's smile had fallen away as she glanced at the endless line for the women's toilets. 'Is Kim inside?'

'I'd really hope so, by now.'

'That slow, is it?' Rita had said, nodding at the melting ice-cream.

'Yeah.' Rohan's face had clouded as he scanned the queue. 'I mean, it looks to be moving but –' He'd shrugged. 'If you see Kim in there chatting, tell her Zoe and I are about thirty seconds away from eating this ourselves.'

Rita had laughed. 'I'll –' She'd stopped, inhaling sharply as the door to a nearby portable toilet creaked open. An elderly woman with a stick stepped out. On the door that slammed shut behind her was both a wheelchair and a parent-and-baby sticker. There was no-one else waiting.

'Oh my God, I'm sorry, this is a parental perk I can't say no to.' Rita had spun the pram around smartly. 'Really lovely to catch you, Rohan. Tell Kim I'll call her.'

'No worries.' Rohan had raised his wife's dripping ice-cream in farewell.

'I'll see you back out here,' Rita had shouted over her shoulder to Falk as she'd peeled off, making a beeline for the empty cubicle.

Falk had said goodbye to the man who was now trying to stop melted vanilla trickling onto the pram and had gone into the men's toilets.

He'd been at the sinks when he'd heard a familiar voice through the open window. Raco, he'd thought immediately, but no. The pitch was deeper. Charlie.

'Hey,' Charlie was saying. 'Before you head off, you said hi to your mum yet?'

'Dad. No –' Zara had sounded frustrated. 'I'm supposed to be meeting Sophie *right now*. They're all waiting for me.'

'Zara, mate, seriously. Come on, don't make me do this. Rohan and Zoe are right there. Your mum won't be far off. At least say hello to your sister.'

'She's a few weeks old, she really doesn't care.'

'Your mum will, though.'

'She won't.'

'Of course she will. They've come all this way to see you.'

'Dad,' Zara had snapped. 'Jesus, she won't. Stop trying to force it.'

'Force what?'

'The family thing.'

146

'We are all family.'

'No, we're not. Not like that. Whatever you do or don't do. Why can't you –?'

'Hey. Watch it, thanks. Don't speak to me like –'

'Okay, fine. Sorry. But you really need to stop.'

'Stop what?'

'You know what. This. About Mum. Look, I've got to go. Okay? My friends are waiting for me.'

'Zara –'

'Tell Mum I'll talk to her tomorrow.'

Falk had washed and dried his hands and walked outside. He'd half expected to see Charlie making conversation with Rohan, but neither man was there. The spot where the pram had been parked was empty, except for a splattering of ice-cream drips in the dust. Falk had leaned against the wall and waited and a minute later Rita came out of the parents' cubicle.

'All good?' she'd said, and Falk had nodded and together they'd headed back to find Raco and Eva.

In the Racos' kitchen a year on, Rita was fiddling with her coffee mug.

'And I knew she was upset about Charlie and Zara not being at home that night, and it still didn't cross my mind to go in and talk to her. Just make that effort. I was so focused on myself and what was easiest –'

'You had a baby to cope with,' Naomi said.

'Yeah, but so did Kim. That's even worse, because I knew how hard it was, and I still did nothing. And then afterwards, you remember how the next day or so someone reported that they'd heard a woman crying in the toilets –'

'That was a lot later in the evening,' Raco interjected. 'And it's a wine festival. There's always someone crying in the toilets.'

Naomi gave a small smile. 'He's right. And look, we all have our own guilt about this. I'm not even talking about –' Her eyes flicked up to Raco, then down again. '– the reservoir stuff. I'm talking recently. I mean, do you know how long it'd been since I'd spoken to Kim? It was more than a year, I worked out later. And I hadn't seen her properly since her wedding. I called a couple of times when the baby was born, didn't get through. I didn't keep trying, though, just sent her a gift and left it at that.' Naomi sighed. 'So yeah, Rita, we all have things we wish we'd done differently.'

'Like what?'

They all looked up at the voice from the doorway. Zara was watching them. Falk hadn't heard her approach and could see from the others' faces that they were also wondering how long she'd been listening.

'Hi, sweetheart,' Rita said, gathering herself. 'Lunch isn't far off, but do you want something now?'

'No, thanks.' Zara's gaze was still fixed on Naomi. 'What do you wish you'd done differently?'

Naomi met her eye. 'I was saying I wish I'd been a better friend to your mum.'

Zara watched her for a long moment, then: 'So are you here to see my dad again?'

'What? No. I'm here for –' A flicker of something crossed Naomi's face and she waved a hand towards Raco and Rita.

'For the christening meeting,' Rita said, frowning.

'Oh.' Zara suddenly looked drained. 'Is my dad around, though?'

'He's outside somewhere,' Raco said. 'What do you need?'

'Can someone please drive me to the festival site? I'm meeting Joel.'

'Sure, I'll do it after we've fed the kids.'

'I'm going to be late, he's already down there. And I want to drop off another box of fliers at the stall.'

'Well –'

'I'll drive you,' Falk said.

Zara looked over in surprise. 'Yeah? Thank you. I'll get my stuff.'

'You don't have to –' Raco started as she disappeared down the hall, but Falk shook his head.

'It's fine, happy to.'

'Yes,' Naomi said suddenly. She visibly brightened. 'He *should.*' She whipped her head around to Falk. 'It's a great festival. You should definitely go, Aaron. Check it out properly. It's actually run by a very good friend of mine.' She drained her coffee and stood, gathering her fleece as she shot another glance at him, coy now. 'You know her, I think? Gemma Tozer?'

'Yes,' Falk said, carefully. 'She was at the festival last night.'

'Of course. Of course.' Naomi pursed her lips thoughtfully and nodded. She leaned a toned hip casually against the table. 'But you've met, I mean. Before last night. In Melbourne, right?'

'Yeah.'

'Great. How nice. And tell me, what did you and Gemma get up to out on the town in the big city? Few drinks, dinner?' Naomi glanced at Rita, who was doing her best not to appear wholly invested. They were enjoying this.

'That sounds about right.' Falk couldn't help but smile himself.

'Fabulous,' Naomi enthused. 'And I don't know about you, but I always think Melbourne is so beautiful at night, all lit up.'

'It is.'

149

'Did you – I don't know – get the chance to take a walk at all? Soak up the atmosphere?'

'A little. It was raining.'

'Ah. Yes.' Naomi managed to look practically misty-eyed. 'Although, in the right circumstances, a little rain can be quite pleasant in itself.'

'It can.'

'Well, I have to say, it sounds like it was a really lovely evening.'

'Yes, thanks, Naomi.' Falk saw Zara reappear in the hall, ready to go. 'It was.'

'Mmm.' Naomi zipped up her fleece, flipped her blonde hair over one shoulder and fixed him with a conspiratorial smile. 'That's what I heard, too.'

Chapter 15

'They all pretend that they were still friends with her,' Zara said out of nowhere.

'Who does, sorry?' Falk looked over as he turned into the festival car park. They had driven in silence most of the way to the site. He had been lost in his own – not unpleasant – thoughts, largely involving a replay of Naomi's words on a loop. *That's what I heard, too.*

Zara shrugged in the passenger seat. 'All of them. Naomi. Rita, even. Like they're so sorry they didn't go and speak to my mum on that last night. But it wasn't unusual or anything. Naomi said it herself, she hadn't really talked to Mum in a year. Probably hadn't seen her for two. Rita would be the same, if you asked.'

'Well, adult friendships can be like that, sometimes.' Falk touched the brake as a parking attendant indicated for him to wait, then directed him to an empty spot. 'You can go for long stretches without –'

'Yeah, I get that. And I know Mum wasn't the easiest person to get hold of. Over in Adelaide. New husband. New baby.

But everyone acting like it was so out of character that they hadn't made the effort to catch up with her –' Zara fiddled with her seatbelt. 'It just annoys me, that's all.'

Falk looked at Zara and remembered that call in the Racos' kitchen last year. Kim on the phone screen, Zara leaning forward to tap her finger against the glass, cutting off her mum as she spoke. Falk doubted, as he drew the car to a stop, that Kim's dwindling friendship circle was the whole issue here.

'So.' Zara was staring out of her window as Falk killed the engine. 'Do you want me to show you why none of this stuff about Mum makes any sense?'

When he didn't answer, she twisted in her seat towards him.

'My uncle's probably shown you his notes, hasn't he? The ones he thinks I haven't seen.' She frowned when he didn't respond. 'I mean, you're a cop too, right? So? What did you think?'

Falk shook his head. 'Zara, I honestly don't know enough to even –'

'My uncle says you're good at working stuff out, though.'

'He's good at that himself. Excellent, actually. So I'd be inclined to trust his judgement –'

'But he thinks there's something wrong, too.'

There was a silence, broken only by the distant lilt of music and the chatter of families passing by the car.

'You've seen his notes,' Zara said. '*All those notes.* You know it's true. How many hours have gone into that huge file?'

Falk pictured Raco's folder. Heavy. Exhaustive. 'He says he did that for you.'

'No.' She gave Falk a look. 'It's not for me.'

He didn't reply and they stared at each other for a minute.

'So.' Zara unclicked her seatbelt. 'You want me to show you or not?'

Falk paused, then reached for the doorhandle. 'Yeah. I do.'

They walked across the festival site together, stopping only to drop off the box of fliers at Charlie's stall. The same two young women from the night before were back again, still pouring samples and cheerfully answering all the same questions. Falk followed Zara through the crowd, past the rides and admin tents to the east exit, where they paused only to duck under the rope. It was as quiet as ever. A different first-aid volunteer was sitting on the chair nearby. He lifted his eyes briefly before dropping them back to his phone.

Falk and Zara walked in single file along the bushland trail, the sounds of the festival fading behind them as the path flattened out and broadened.

'There was this theory going around for a while,' Zara said as they hit the broad dirt track that circled the reservoir. 'People didn't tell me directly, but I knew anyway. That my mum came looking for me because she was upset, about me cancelling my birthday thing to go drinking, or whatever. And then –' Zara focused on her feet. 'I don't know, they said she was so depressed that she changed her mind and went to the Drop instead.'

'I see,' Falk said.

'I don't think that makes sense, though.' Zara's voice was firm. She had thought it through, Falk could tell. 'I mean, if Mum was seriously so pissed off that she'd leave her *six-week-old* child to find her teenage one – which she literally never would, by the way – then why didn't she actually come and get me? She knew I was right up here.'

Zara slowed and indicated for them to step off the main track and onto a thin side trail. Not even a trail, more of a subtle fracture through the bushland. Falk wouldn't even have noticed it, but now something deep inside him instantly recognised it, plain as day, as the route to a teenage drinking spot. He followed Zara through the trees and could briefly see the official reservoir track continue the other way, the water wide and silent beside it, before the branches closed in again and it was lost from sight.

'If Mum wanted to find me, she would have found me,' Zara said as she picked her way up the small trail. The bushland was thick on both sides and Falk could no longer hear the faint hum from the festival. 'Why would she just walk past?'

'I don't know,' Falk said.

'No.' Zara shrugged. 'Well, it's a hypothetical question anyway, because she didn't come down this way.'

Falk said nothing to that, and Zara glanced back, disappointed. *You too?* She turned away and he felt a bit bad. They continued on. The uphill path was uneven and wildly overgrown and suddenly took a steep turn. Falk could see where the slope fell away. He wouldn't want to navigate his way down here after a few too many. What had Naomi said? It was only a matter of time before some kid fell and broke their neck. Beloved teenage tradition or not, Falk was tempted to agree.

Ahead, Zara pushed a large overhanging branch aside and all at once the path gave way to a clearing. It was unofficial, but Falk could see that years of use had left it as established as any campsite. A charred metal fire pit in the middle was surrounded by a circle of fallen trees, the trunks worn almost smooth from being sat on over the years. A few bottles and empty wrappers lay scattered about and a handful of dirty crushed cans had been shoved under one log. This space had clearly held dozens of people – recently – but it was deserted now. Zara looked around, a little perplexed to find it empty.

'I thought Joel –' she started, and pulled out her phone.

Falk walked a slow lap, overcome with the distinct sensation of having been there before. He wondered for a moment if it was a throwback memory to when he and his three closest friends used to go to a clearing a bit like this, at the top of a lookout in a different town and another time. But no, he realised as quickly as the thought arrived, he simply recognised the surroundings from the photos he'd seen in Raco's file. The space looked different in daylight and the colours were much brighter than they'd been on the faded prints, but this was the place. Things obviously hadn't changed much over a couple of decades, but Falk wasn't really surprised. A good drinking spot was a good drinking spot.

Zara frowned and slipped her phone into her jeans pocket. 'He'll be down at the water.'

She walked to the edge of the clearing and eased an armful of overgrown shrubbery aside, revealing an unexpected natural gap in the bushland. Falk looked beyond her. A tree had fallen at some point in the distant past, creating a window effect through the trunks and scrub. Zara motioned for Falk to follow and they took a handful of steps before she stopped, the view spread wide in front of them. Below, Falk could see down to the reservoir. The broad dirt track was some distance below them but clearly visible. As was the Drop. A tall lean figure was standing there, right by the safety railing, his hands on the barrier and his head down. A dog lay docile at his feet. The water pooled out in front of him, vast and still.

'Joel! Hey!' Zara's voice echoed out, and a flock of startled lorikeets took off from a nearby tree.

The young guy turned. Unlike Raco yesterday, he seemed to know exactly where to look to spot the source of the voice. He raised a hand. Zara pulled out her phone and texted something, and a moment later the boy looked at his own screen then nodded. He raised an arm and pointed. *I'm coming up.*

Satisfied, Zara put her phone away and watched as he called his dog and stepped away from the railing. Only part of the track was visible, Falk realised now as the boy vanished from sight. It curved close to the bushland, hiding sections to the right and left. Falk took half a step forward.

'Careful.' Zara put out a hand. 'It's a bit loose around here.'

'Right. Thanks.' Falk stepped back and they stood side by side, looking out.

'You can actually see really clearly at night. The bushland's so dark that the moon kind of bounces off the water and lights everything up down there.'

Zara glanced at Falk with her mouth set and her eyebrows raised, as though her point was self-evident. 'So someone would have seen Mum,' she explained, when he didn't immediately respond, a note of exasperation creeping in. 'There was a whole group of us up here. Some people were here all night. Every year it happens. It's like, a tradition. This spot right here –' She tapped her heel into the ground to indicate where they were standing. A small circle of ground was worn bald. 'People are always standing around here. Because it's nice to look down on the water while you chat.'

Falk looked pointedly behind them to the crushed beer cans dumped in the clearing.

'Yeah, okay,' she conceded. 'And obviously have a few drinks. But what I'm saying is, you can *see*.' Her voice caught. 'If my mum had gone down there and climbed over that railing, someone would have –'

Zara stopped and they both turned at the sound of footsteps crunching through the bushland. Two sets, light and heavy. The overgrown branch lifted and Joel appeared in the clearing, his dog following.

'Hey,' Zara called. 'We're over here.'

Joel walked across the clearing to join them as Falk watched, a little surprised. The young bloke had got up there faster than he'd expected; it couldn't have taken him much more than a minute. A combination of youth and familiarity, he guessed. It was the first time Falk had seen him up close, and he found himself looking at Joel with curiosity. Gemma Tozer's stepson. He had that odd teenage ability to look both older and younger than his eighteen years, depending on the way his face fell. Joel's angular frame and dark hair didn't bear much resemblance to the few photos Falk had seen of his father at the same age. Dean Tozer had been sturdy and grinning, his sandy complexion a little pink from the beer in his hand.

'This is my uncle's friend, Aaron,' Zara was saying. 'He's a cop too.'

Joel simply nodded. 'Hi.'

He showed some interest but no recognition. So Gemma had not mentioned Falk, not that he would have expected her to. The dog, a bundle of energy and mystery pedigree, lavished Falk with friendly attention.

'I was showing Aaron how much you can see from up here,' Zara said, and Falk glanced at Joel to gauge his reaction. The boy's eyes had settled on Zara but moved away quickly as she turned. Other than that, he gave nothing away, just squinted a little into the glare, his arms folded.

Falk looked down again. The view to the reservoir was clear, that was true, but it was not broad. He could see the track at the point where it swelled out to form the Drop, where Joel had been a moment earlier, but on either side it was hidden by bushland. He couldn't make out the path beyond that for more than a dozen metres in either direction. Falk took a couple of careful steps to the side. Even at the best vantage point, he could see only a little more towards the festival side. The other way was now completely obscured.

'What was it like up here?' He turned to Zara. 'On opening night?'

She shrugged. 'Just the usual thing, I guess. A bunch of us get together to catch up.'

'I mean, last year specifically. How many people were up here?'

'Maybe forty. Fifty? I'm not sure.'

Falk looked around the clearing. It wasn't huge. 'So it gets pretty packed?'

'Yeah.'

'Noisy?'

'I suppose.'

'Music playing?'

'Yeah, of course.'

'Got the fire going?'

'Yeah. If there's not a fire ban.'

'Was there last year?'

'No. So, yeah. There was a fire.'

Falk didn't even bother asking how much they'd all been

drinking. He looked down to the reservoir again. It didn't really matter how many people had been up here that night. He knew how sessions like this got and, view or no view, there was no way this gap was being watched at all times, let alone by someone still sober enough to see and remember.

His eyes moved along the part of the track that was hidden, one side and then the other. He thought for a long moment. He couldn't imagine this vantage point had been well monitored, but was it naturally good enough to rule out a struggle taking place down below? Falk weighed up the scenario silently, imagining it playing out. The sudden flash of a forced movement, the oddity of a cry for help in the night. That probably would have been enough to draw the eye, maybe. Or maybe not. It depended on how noisy the party was and how violent the struggle.

A lone woman in the dark, though. That, Falk could picture. Even standing in the broad light of day, he could imagine the music, the flickering lights of the fire, the booze, the hormones. Raco was right. Kim Gillespie could have slipped herself over the edge and plunged into the silent water below without anyone even glancing up from their beer.

'I saw Naomi,' Zara said suddenly, as though reading his mind. That desperate note was back again. 'Her property borders the reserve, a bit further up –' She pointed away from the festival. 'She walked home this way. I was standing here, and I noticed her myself.'

Falk didn't reply. He heard Joel shift his weight.

'So if you're thinking someone down there wouldn't necessarily be seen,' Zara said, 'I'm telling you they would have.'

'Zara's mum didn't come this way anyway.' It was the most Joel had said since arriving and he shrugged when they both looked over at him. 'I was working near the east exit. I would've seen Kim. I didn't.'

'So I hear.' Falk watched him. 'Tell me about that.'

'There's nothing to tell.' Joel's voice was quiet but his eye contact was solid. 'I was stationed at the first-aid tent. I was there for two and a half hours, no break. Kim didn't come past. That's it.'

Falk waited, but he said no more. As if that really was it. 'You would have seen a few people come through, though?' he asked, finally. 'On their way out.'

'Not many. That exit's hardly used. Naomi came through, like Zara said. That was around 9.30 pm. She said bye to me as she passed. That she was heading home. Viv and Graham Marsh, they live on the property next to Naomi's. They left pretty early, after the kids' fireworks. They had their grandsons with them. The little one was having a meltdown.'

'Who else?' Falk said.

'Like I said. No-one. No adults, anyway.' Joel glanced at Zara. 'Just kids heading here.'

Falk nodded. 'You didn't want to join them?'

'No.' The answer came fast. Joel looked faintly troubled by the suggestion. Falk just waited and eventually the boy took a breath.

'The festival week's a bit –' Joel stopped. No eye contact now; instead he frowned out towards the water. 'It doesn't matter. I just don't get involved in it. But Gemma – she's my stepmum – she's the director and a couple of first aiders had called in sick and legally they need a certain ratio. I've done the training, and she was stuck so I said I'd help her out. She got them to put me in an easy spot, just to make up the numbers.'

Falk still said nothing and Joel shrugged, his shoulders tight and hunched.

'Look, my dad was killed by a car.' Joel didn't bother trying to hide the edge in his voice. 'Six years ago, during festival week. So I don't know what to tell you. When I say Kim didn't come past me, it's not some stupid bloody joke to make things harder for everyone.' He jerked his head in the direction of the Drop, a tiny controlled movement. 'I mean, my dad died right there. I know what that feels like.'

Joel's face was dark and Falk followed his gaze out through the bushland to the water glinting below.

'I'm sorry, mate.' Falk looked down at the Drop. The danger spot, Raco had said. Everyone knew it. 'Do you mind if I ask what happened?'

Joel shrugged. 'Dad used to come down here most days to walk Luna –' The dog perked up at her name and he reached down to rub her head. 'Early, like six-thirty in the morning. But on that day, Gemma and I were having breakfast and it was nearly 8 am and he wasn't back, which was –' He swallowed, frowned. '– weird. So Gemma was texting him, to see if he'd gone into town or something, and then Shane called – Shane McAfee, he works with Zara's dad,' Joel clarified, and Falk nodded. 'Anyway, Shane had been jogging around the reservoir and said he'd found Luna on her own, barking and stuff. The safety railings around the Drop were smashed and so he'd tried to call my dad and couldn't get through.'

Joel's hand rested on Luna's ears.

'The festival had opened the night before, and the cops always did breath tests on the highway in the mornings. They've closed off the track to cars now, but you used to be able to drive along there, skip a section of the road. They reckoned someone over the limit used it as a short cut to miss the testing.'

'Right.' Where Gemma's grief had seemed worn-in, Joel's still felt raw and jagged. 'I'm really sorry to hear that, it's –'

'Yeah. I know. Thanks.' Joel waved the condolences away, embarrassed. 'The point is, my dad was knocked into the water and they didn't find his –' A tiny hesitation. '– his body for five months and nine days, and that was –' Joel cleared his throat. 'I dunno. A really shitty five months and nine days. And Sergeant Dwyer's never managed to find out who did it, so it's still pretty shitty, to be honest. So yeah, I know what everyone thinks. That I'm full of it, or wasn't watching the exit, or I'm saying this for attention or whatever, but I'm not.'

'Okay, mate.' Falk nodded as Joel crouched to stroke his dog, conveniently hiding his face. 'Understood.'

Zara's eyes slid from Joel to Falk and back again, her expression morphing from sympathy to frustration.

'But don't you think that's all a bit of a coincidence?' she said, her gaze zeroing in on Falk. 'I mean, his dad not being found for months? My mum is still missing. This is not a big town, how often does something like this happen? Don't you think it's at least possible there's a connection?'

There was a silence, and Joel stood again. They were both watching Falk carefully, waiting for his response. They looked abjectly miserable and Falk felt a wave of compassion, deep and complex. Zara was only seventeen now, and Joel couldn't have been more than twelve or thirteen when he'd lost his dad. Formative ages to go through something like that. Standing there in the bushland, Falk had a sudden sharp flash of cancer clinics and the disinfectant smell of the respite care home and the sun shining hot and harsh overhead at his father's funeral.

Losing a parent was pretty formative in its own way at any age, really.

He looked from one to the other. 'Okay,' he said. 'Tell me.'

'Well, I mean, there are lots of similar things,' Zara said. 'My mum and his dad knew each other. Our parents have all been friends since school. What happened to them both happened around the opening of the festival, at the reservoir –'

'But you reckon Kim didn't even come down here,' Falk said to Joel, and caught the look that passed between the teenagers. Interesting. They at least acknowledged the cracks in their theory.

'Well, what I'm saying is that Kim didn't come through the east exit.' Joel's voice was firm.

'Yeah.' Zara nodded quickly. 'Something's happened to her, that's obvious. But the point is, it's not what everyone thinks. Not Mum leaving her own baby and coming down here to –' She stopped, and pressed her mouth into a line.

'Look, Kim's shoe was found in the water, so the reservoir's involved somehow,' Joel said. 'But there are other ways you can get down here. There's a car park a few kilometres up, near the far end. Or you can come in through one of the hiking tracks. People with properties nearby cut through the bushland all the time to walk dogs and go running and things. You can't drive in off the highway anymore, but the physical road still exists.'

They fell silent, waiting, and Falk tried to work out the best way to respond. He didn't know what the answer was, but he knew enough to tell that there was at least one real connection there, and that was grief and uncertainty. He didn't blame them. It was a lot for anyone to take on.

Zara sighed with the disappointment of someone realising

they may be wasting their time. 'We're just saying it's not as straightforward as –'

She stopped. They had all sensed movement on the track below. Falk shifted and together they peered down through the gap. He could see a shadow cast against the trail. Someone was down there, hidden on the far side by the bushland. All three of them had felt the additional presence immediately, Falk noted with interest. Okay, it was daylight and there was no rowdy party going on behind him, but still. Maybe Zara had a point. He stood next to the two teenagers in silence, watching, and after a minute the figure came into view. Sergeant Dwyer.

'Oh.' Zara breathed out, her interest immediately evaporating. 'It's him again.'

The officer stood for a moment, his back to the bushland and his palms flat against the safety railing, staring out at the water. Whether he sensed the scrutiny or not, Falk wasn't sure, but suddenly he straightened and turned, his focus directed up towards them. Like Joel, Dwyer seemed to know exactly where to find the break in the trees. He could see them, Falk could tell. No-one moved for a second, then Dwyer raised his arm, pointed and beckoned. A request, but a clear one.

Come down here, please.

Zara frowned and next to her, Joel lifted a hand and pointed at his own chest. Dwyer shook his head slowly. Adjusted his arm a fraction.

You.

Falk blinked, then lifted his own hand and pointed to himself. Dwyer nodded this time. He paused, long enough to check he'd been understood, then turned back to the water to wait.

'You've been summoned.' Zara's voice had an odd note.

'Looks like it,' Falk said. 'See you later, I guess.'

Zara nodded but didn't move as he made to leave, her eyes still on the officer. Falk stepped back into the clearing, then stopped at the sound of footsteps following.

'Hey.' Joel paused to clip Luna back on her lead. When he stood again, he and Falk were almost eye to eye. 'So, listen. Dwyer won't help you with anything,' he said, matter-of-factly. 'Just so you know.'

'No?' Falk kept his tone neutral.

'No. He only comes across as okay at his job because there's no real crime around here. But when something big happens – my dad, Kim –' Joel shrugged, like it was obvious. 'Then he has no answers.'

Falk said nothing. Investigations, he knew from bitter experience, were often less straightforward than they appeared from the outside. Joel picked up on his hesitation.

'I mean, you ask me and Zara what we think happened to her mum, and yeah, of course we don't know.' The boy nodded down to the reservoir where Sergeant Dwyer was waiting. 'But he should know. He should definitely know. That's his whole job, right? That's a fact.' Joel's voice was low and steady. 'And here's another fact for you. It took nearly six months to find my dad in that water, but in the end they still found him. Take a guess how many people in the past fifty years have drowned in the reservoir and never been seen again?'

'Go on.'

'Kim would be the first.'

Chapter 16

Falk knew Zara and Joel couldn't see him as he left the clearing and navigated his way down through the bushland, but he sensed their eyes following again as he approached the Drop.

'G'day.' Sergeant Dwyer was waiting by the safety railing. He introduced himself as Falk joined him. 'Lucky to spot you up there. Can cross you off my catch-up list.'

'Right.' Falk squinted back up towards the trees. He couldn't see any sign of the teenagers, but felt sure they were still there.

'A little higher.' Dwyer squinted himself, then pointed. He looked older in broad daylight than he had last night, his hair silver in the sun. 'Find the fallen tree – you see it? There, looks darker from here – and straight up from there. Got them?'

Falk suddenly did. The blue of Joel's jacket, the shadow of Zara's hair by his shoulder. It wasn't easy, though. The benefits of local knowledge, he supposed.

'Anyway, thanks for coming down,' Dwyer said. 'I would've come up but I try and show a bit of respect for the kids' territory, when I can, at least. Not sure they'd agree, but there you go.'

166

Falk was tempted to believe him. Fit and wiry, Dwyer wouldn't have had any trouble making his own way up that narrow path to the clearing in a matter of minutes if he'd wanted to.

'Like I said, just wanted a quick chat,' Dwyer said, in a tone very similar to one Falk often used himself when saying that exact phrase. 'We didn't get the chance to meet last night. Or last year, obviously.'

'No,' Falk said, curious rather than concerned. 'That's right.' He leaned against the safety barrier. Screwed into the wood between him and Dwyer was the small brass memorial plaque he'd noticed the previous evening.

In memory of Dean Tozer, Falk was able to read now in the sunlight. *Loved and missed.*

The paintwork along the railings on either side had been freshly graffitied. It was the mindless scrawl of kids with a black pen and too much booze and time on their hands, rather than anything targeted, Falk could see, but still unpleasant. Sticky food remnants were smeared on the wood, and there was a series of dirty boot marks next to the plaque where someone had tried to balance on the railing. Falk suddenly pictured Joel standing there earlier, his shoulders stooped as he presumably took in the sight of his father's memorial plaque surrounded by all this mess.

'This all would've happened last night.' Dwyer followed Falk's gaze down to the vandalism, his face set. 'Kids come here every year, get carried away. Not my favourite annual event, by a long way. But –' He gave a deep shrug. 'Being a cop here, it's a balancing act. You're AFP, I hear?'

Dwyer seemed neither threatened nor particularly impressed as Falk nodded.

'In town for the christening, that right? Godfather to Greg and Rita's youngest.' Dwyer looked over. 'So you must know the family well? Part of that circle?'

'Not really. Greg and Rita, yes. I've known them for a few years.'

'How about the others? Charlie, Shane McAfee? All their mates? Naomi Kerr, she's godmother, isn't she?'

'Yeah. I just met them, though. Don't know them well.' Falk could tell his answers were being appraised, he just wasn't sure why yet. He pictured Dwyer at the appeal the night before, and the way he had run his eyes over Kim's family and friends. Falk shut his mouth and waited.

But Dwyer simply nodded, considering, then glanced back up to the bushland, his eyes following the downed tree up to the break where Zara and Joel had been. There was no sign of them now.

'Those two aren't happy with me.' Dwyer reached out and rubbed a thin strip of dirt off the memorial plaque, then used his thumbnail to pick out a dead leaf caught between the metal and the wood. 'They tell you their connection theory? Looking to link Dean Tozer and Kim?'

'They mentioned it, yeah.'

'They tell you I don't take them seriously?'

'That seemed to be the feeling.'

Dwyer didn't seem put out, simply resigned. 'It's not that I don't take them seriously, it's more that I think they're wrong on that specific point.' He found a cleanish spot on the barrier to lean against. 'You ever had any call to police a small town?'

'No, but I grew up in one.'

'Like Marralee?'

'More run-down. Doing it a lot harder. But the same where it matters.'

'So you'd probably get it. Place this size – you can get lucky for years and years, dodging those big incidents. But not forever, and when they happen they hurt us all. Not least because most people know each other, so when two separate things happen to two separate people, they can feel closer than they are.'

Falk thought he probably agreed with that. He looked out at the water. There was – the recurring realisation always presented itself as new – so much of it.

'Joel said Kim would be the first person in a while not to have been recovered from the reservoir,' Falk said and next to him, Dwyer nodded.

'Yeah, and look, he's not wrong, technically. But what's the catch with stats? They can show anything.' The light bounced off the water, reflecting ripples across the sergeant's face. 'We haven't lost anyone in the last fifty years because in the last fifty years we started putting up railings and warning signs. And there's better education about wild swimming, and kids all learn water survival at school. And if a drowning does happen, we've got better boats and techniques for recovering the body. Go back another hundred years, when this was just a lake and a glorified watering hole, and it's a different story.' Dwyer ran a thumb over the edge of the plaque. 'More than five months it took us to find Dean Tozer's body. A bloody eternity for Joel and Gemma, believe me, I know. But we found him in the end.'

'No luck getting the driver?' Falk said. 'No judgement, just interested.'

Dwyer sighed through his nose. 'You know how it is,' he said, eventually. 'Sometimes you just don't.'

Falk nodded. He did know.

'But we found Dean,' Dwyer said. 'And I haven't given up hope on Kim, either. She was a really nice woman. She deserves better and I don't like not having answers.'

Falk sensed that was true. Dwyer seemed both personally and professionally dissatisfied that this whole distressing episode was not neatly, if sadly, squared away.

'Anything come from last night's appeal so far?' Falk asked, and Dwyer gave a noncommittal shrug.

'One or two things. Had a few people come forward, couple of potentially interesting sightings. One near the pram bay looks promising, a mum who was getting her kids' bikes out. Timing would work, so we're checking that out. We'll see.' He frowned. 'Info's never really been the problem, though; the issue's always been more sorting through what's useful. Woman in her late thirties or early forties, average height, medium build, brown hair, wearing dark pants and a light top? I've got a dozen people who saw someone matching that description at a dozen different places over the same hour. They can't all be Kim.' He sighed. 'But you never know. New things do come to light. They have before.'

Falk heard the change in his voice. The bushland towered behind them. 'You're talking about the attempted assault?' he asked. 'When Kim was a teenager?'

Dwyer's grey eyes flicked over. 'You heard about that?'

'Naomi told me. This morning.'

'Well, yeah, that's one example. That took absolutely everyone by surprise, so it seems.' The odd note was unmistakable this time.

'Naomi said she never told anyone about that until Kim went missing last year. But, what?' Falk watched him. 'You think that's not true?'

'No, I think that probably is true. And I can believe Kim never told anyone herself.' Dwyer frowned. 'Just interesting to see reactions when it came out. Everyone so shocked. These men who were hot and heavy eighteen-year-old boys them-selves not so long ago, now all clutching their pearls at the suggestion one of their drinking mates might see a young girl worse for wear and try to take advantage?' He made a noise of disbelief. 'I'm not saying they knew, but no-one's that naïve. Or in that much denial.'

Neither spoke for a minute, watching as a small brown bird hovered and came to rest on the water, sending ripples across the surface.

'When I said new things came up, I was actually thinking of Kim's mental health,' Dwyer said eventually, and Falk looked over. 'The postnatal depression, or pre-pregnancy as well, as it turned out. She'd been on medication for more than a year, apparently, kept it to herself. But yeah, that assault allegation wasn't something I saw coming.' He rubbed a hand over his chin. 'Still not sure what to make of that. Like I was saying, two separate events can sometimes feel connected.'

He turned away from the water, staring up at the deep silence of the bushland for a long time.

'Jesus, I bloody hate that opening night party,' he said quietly. His eyes were still on the trees. 'And whatever Zara and Joel think, I know what they've gone through. My wife and I lost our daughter last year, unexpectedly. It's bloody hard. That's why I wasn't around when Kim disappeared to take care of the initial investigation myself. I wish –' Dwyer stopped, frowned. 'Well. We can only play the hand we're dealt. But Zara's kidding herself if she thinks that any of those kids up there would have noticed one woman walking alone down this

171

track. Every year I break up that party, and every year I climb that trail with a couple of officers and not one of them looks up from their drink long enough to notice until we're chucking water on their campfire and checking IDs. So, yeah, I also think Zara's wrong about that.'

Dwyer's gaze dropped back to the railing and a dirty boot print near his hand.

'Thing is –' He was silent for a long minute. 'I don't think she and Joel are wrong about everything.'

Falk hadn't expected that. 'In what way?' he asked.

Dwyer's grey eyes narrowed. He seemed to be considering his answer, then he nodded back in the direction of the festival. 'You headed up?'

'Yeah, I suppose.'

They pushed away from the safety rail and started along the track. Dwyer waited until they were past the hidden turn-off to the drinking site, the small trail naturally concealed once more by the overgrown shrubbery, before he spoke again.

'Tell me this.' He glanced at Falk as they walked. 'When it comes to Kim, I reckon something is bothering your mate Greg. What do you think?'

Falk thought about the thick file back at the Racos' guesthouse. He had agreed when Zara had suggested the same, and he privately agreed now. But Raco's reasons were usually sound, so Falk just shrugged. 'What makes you say that?'

'Yeah, fair question,' Dwyer said as Falk fell into step behind him. They'd left the wide reservoir track and begun making their way up the thinner trail leading to the grounds. Falk had been right, the sergeant was fit and the pace was fast.

'Greg and Charlie's dad trained me, did they tell you that?'

Dwyer continued. 'Good bloke, Les Raco. Great bloke. Excellent officer. My first real posting was here in Marralee, working under him back in my early twenties. I went elsewhere for a while, then came back ten years ago or so when Les retired. So I've known Greg since before he was Zara's age. Kept half an eye on his career out of interest. What happened with the two of you over in Victoria a few years ago –' Dwyer gave Falk a tight nod of understanding. 'Tough business, that. So knowing Greg as I reckon I do, he's not the type to waste a lot of time raking over old ground and gathering documents and such without good reason.'

Dwyer looked back to get Falk's reaction. Falk shrugged, then nodded. That was demonstrably true. Raco was practical and reliable. He didn't create problems where there were none. Satisfied, Dwyer turned and kept walking. Up ahead lay the fence and the festival's deserted east exit. The sound of the crowds and the music beyond was growing louder.

'So, you may not know Greg's wider family and mates well,' Dwyer said. 'But I do. And the thing about them – the thing about a lot of people around here – is that those circles are close-knit. Once you're in, you're in. They care about each other, they look out for each other. And I'll tell you, what's bugging me is the same question that's keeping your good friend and mine awake at night, I reckon.'

'And what's that?'

'Kim had come back home for the first time in more than two years. She's here, surrounded by heaps of people she knew – this tight extended family, friendships that go back decades. And yet not one of them admits to having a conversation with her all evening.' Dwyer stopped as they reached the top of the track. He lifted the rope so Falk could duck under, watching his face as he did so. 'What are the odds of that, do you think?'

Falk considered this as he stepped back onto the festival grounds. A different first aider was in the chair now. She was engrossed in a novel and did not look their way.

'It's not impossible,' he said.

'No, not impossible. But it doesn't smell right, either,' Dwyer said. 'So when I look at our Sergeant Raco having a dig around, I can't help wondering if he's maybe heard something in that inner circle of his. Knows something more than he's shared.'

Falk stared at the officer. 'I really couldn't say.'

'Would he tell you?'

Would he? Falk thought of Raco. The way their friendship had evolved over the past few years, growing from the vulnerability of initial trauma into something steadfast and solid. 'Yeah. He would.'

Dwyer gave a knowing smile. 'And what are the chances you'd tell me?'

'Well, exactly.' Falk flashed a knowing smile of his own. 'I trust the bloke. Completely. So I'd obviously be having a good long one-on-one chat with him before I did anything like that. But honestly, if it were something relevant, I think he'd already have told you himself.'

'Even about –? Sorry.' Dwyer broke off as his phone buzzed from his pocket. He checked the screen, lifted it to his ear and listened for a moment. 'Yep, be right there.' He hung up and turned back to Falk. 'Sorry about that. So you reckon Greg would speak up, do you? Even about his own family and friends?'

Falk didn't really need to think about it. 'Even then. If he really felt it was the right thing to do, yeah.' He was preaching to the converted, he suspected. 'As I think you already know, mate. Greg Raco's moral compass points true north. He's not the kind who keeps secrets easily. Not about something as serious as this. It's not in his nature.'

'Perhaps not, but –' Dwyer's phone buzzed again. He glanced down and exhaled something close to a sigh. 'All right, look, I'd better keep moving. We'll talk again.' He didn't move immediately, though, instead squinting across the grounds at something Falk couldn't identify. 'For the record, I happen to agree with you about Greg Raco. Whether I can necessarily say the same for the rest of them, though . . .'

Dwyer lifted his shoulders in a light shrug. He raised a hand in farewell and, without waiting for a response, turned and headed off. Falk watched the officer walk away, growing smaller across the field. Then he stood there alone in the mild spring warmth for a long while, mulling over that very same question himself.

Chapter 17

The vineyard was quiet as Falk pulled up and parked next to Raco's car.

He walked through Charlie's house, finding the kitchen empty now, and then stepped out onto the verandah. He could see no movement among the vines, but across the dirt driveway, the door to the vineyard's office stood open. The slam of a desk drawer and a muffled swear word floated out into the still afternoon air. Falk looked around once more, then wandered down the steps and towards the noise.

'G'day.' Falk leaned against the open office door and looked inside.

'Oh. G'day.' Shane McAfee glanced up, then down again. He was behind a desktop computer, his bulky frame crammed into an office chair and his face flushed despite the air conditioner rattling full pelt in the corner. He was looking at the screen like he was staring into an abyss. 'Thought you might be Charlie.'

'No.'

'Is he out there?'

'Haven't seen him.'

'Right.' Shane tapped a couple of strokes on the keyboard and swore again, under his breath this time. He ran a hand over his chin and wiped the sweat on his shorts, then sat back heavily. 'Don't suppose you know anything about spreadsheets?'

'A bit,' said Falk, who knew an exhaustive amount. 'You need some help?'

'Charlie needs these latest invoices added to the winter quarter figures but the accountant's started us on this new system and –' Shane pointed to the screen as Falk edged past the filing cabinet to see. 'Here. The column spacing's blown out but when I tried to fix it I lost a whole bloody section.'

'It won't be lost.' Falk leaned in and immediately recognised the accountancy program. He'd recently spent a whole week using it to trace several million dollars in disguised income. He reached over and moved the mouse a few times. 'It's usually still in there somewhere. You just do this, and then this. And – yeah – there. That what you needed?'

'That's the one. Yes.' Shane breathed out. 'Thank God for that. Cheers, mate. I owe you one.'

'And look, you're importing the hard way. It's a lot easier if you go here and then drag that over –'

'To where?'

'There. Yep, that's it.' Falk spent a couple of minutes showing him, then stood back and watched as Shane completed several rounds himself. The guy frowned as his weathered fingers coaxed the mouse across the desktop. The other hand was idly massaging his left knee joint.

'That's so much bloody easier,' Shane said. 'You do this for work or something? I thought Greg said you were police too.'

'Financial division with the AFP,' Falk said. 'So, yeah. I do this quite a lot.'

'You like it?'

'Working with spreadsheets?'

Shane smiled. 'The job.'

'Yeah, I do,' Falk said truthfully. 'It's interesting.'

He could tell Shane was expecting him to say more, but both the conversation and the spreadsheet had triggered a well-worn sequence in Falk's head. He could immediately feel the virtual heft of unanswered emails weighing down the phone in his pocket. He hadn't thought about or communicated with work for at least twenty-four hours, which was something of a record lately. He was on leave, he reminded himself, but it was already too late. He was thinking about it now.

'It's good that you like it,' Shane said, bringing Falk back into the room. 'Lucky to find something you enjoy.'

He seemed to mean it, which was somewhat rare. Most people went out of their way to slide in a back-handed comment about the perceived dullness of Falk's chosen field. Falk watched him for a minute, working away at the computer. 'When did you retire from footy?'

'Earlier than I wanted to.' Shane gave a rueful smile. 'Not long after I turned twenty-four. Only got to play one more full season after that grand final you were at.'

Falk nodded, because all of a sudden he was back there again. Sitting with his dad and watching this guy play what probably ended up being the peak game of his career. 'Injured out?'

'Yeah, third quarter of the second game the year after. Against Collingwood, that one was. Tore my ACL.' Shane's hand dropped to his knee again. 'The physio and recovery techniques are better now, but back then –' He shook his head. 'Game over. Never got back.'

'That's a real shame.'

'Yeah. I thought so too.' Shane shrugged. 'Happens, though.'

'What did you do afterwards?'

'God. *Everything*, at first. Went a bit nuts for a while. I was at a loose end, but I had a fair bit of money – or it felt like it at that age, anyway – and the bouncers at the VIP nightclubs all recognised me, so –' Shane stopped, pointing at the computer. 'Sorry, do I copy these figures to here? Or here?'

'The first one. Yep, exactly.'

'Great, thanks.' He nodded. 'Yeah, so it was all a bit of a blur for a while, but at least it was fun, and then . . .' Shane paused. He shot a glance up at Falk, the faintest trace of humour in his face. 'Then, I don't know if you remember, but this one photo kind of surfaced of me in a pretty compromising –'

And just like that, all at once, Falk did remember. That's right, *that* had been Shane McAfee. The image had been everywhere for five minutes and all these years later Falk could instantly conjure it in his mind. Not the frequent photos of Shane stumbling red-faced and sweating out of a nightclub and into the early hours with a string of different women on his arm, or the few of him in front of an unidentified white powder smeared across a grubby glass coffee table, but that single very unfortunate one, involving a bottle of his own urine and a dare at a dinner table at a Sydney black-tie function.

It took a significant mental leap to reconcile this large, softly spoken man with *that* guy – *disgraced former footy star Shane McAfee* – captured in notoriety in newsprint and online, and

Falk scrambled for an appropriate response. Shane just shrugged, and gave a small self-deprecating smile.

'Don't worry, mate. What can you really say?'

'For what it's worth,' Falk said, 'I had completely forgotten about that.'

'Lucky you.' Shane grinned. 'Although, to be honest, I couldn't remember a thing about it myself either by the next morning. Other people definitely could, though, and the photo was right there, so my commercial endorsements and media work and everything were gone. Club distanced itself, which wasn't surprising, really.' For the first time, he sounded a little sad. 'I apologised, obviously. Went for a stint in rehab.'

'Then you came back here?'

'Yeah.' Shane moved the mouse and clicked. He was getting the hang of it now. 'It was a bit shit at first, but I couldn't think what else to do. And everyone knew I'd left with this golden chance and then here I was, back again with a dodgy knee. But Charlie was still around. Kim too. So that was good,' Shane added, but his face clouded at her name. 'They were together again, and Charlie had just bought this place. Kim got pregnant with Zara not long after, so Charlie couldn't really afford to take me on, but he did anyway. And yeah, been here ever since.'

On the computer in front of Falk, Shane dragged the final file into place, then reached across the desk for a pen and a piece of paper.

'Anyway. This –' Shane nodded at the clear screen. '– was really useful. I'd better write it down so I remember next quarter.'

'I can send you a link that'll help. Especially if your accountant updates again, which is possible. This system isn't a great one, to be honest.'

'Yeah, wouldn't put it past him. He's always changing things around. Reckons it's more efficient, but –' Shane grunted in dismissal. 'Maybe for him, I guess.'

'You can't get Charlie to use someone else?' Falk said. 'This doesn't need to be hard.'

'Maybe. It's tricky, though, because this guy's the local operator, and we all try and support each other around here.'

Shane hauled himself up and the desk chair squeaked with relief. He went over to the small fridge in the corner and took out a bottle of water and a couple of glasses. He held one up to Falk, who nodded.

'Back in the day, the local accountant used to be this mate of ours, so he used to do everything for us with the books. He was really good. Like you just then, he knew all the tricks.' Shane passed Falk a glass, then took a long swallow from his own. 'Made it all make sense.'

'You can't use him anymore?' Falk said.

Shane examined his water for a moment. 'No. He died. It was shit. Hit-and-run.'

'Dean Tozer?' Falk said, and Shane looked up in surprise.

'Yeah. Did you know him?'

'No. But I was just out at the reservoir with Zara and I met his son. Charlie mentioned him last night, too. I didn't realise he worked with you, though.'

Shane nodded. 'Not just with us, he did the books for most people in town. He was a smart bloke, worked for some big accountancy firm in London for a while so knew what he was doing. Then when he moved back here to look after Joel he started up on his own. It was good, you know. He understood the businesses around here, and everyone liked him so we all used him.' Shane concentrated harder than he needed to on refilling their glasses. He took another deep drink before he spoke again. 'So Joel was out at the reservoir, was he? How did he seem?'

Falk pictured the tall, subdued boy. 'A bit sad, I would say.'

'Right. I might go around and see him later. Dunno if he mentioned it, but Dean died during festival week. Six years now, but it's still hard. Especially this time of year.' Shane paused, swirling the water around in his glass. The man seemed to want to talk, but stayed silent.

'I saw Dean's memorial plaque,' Falk said eventually. 'On the barrier near the Drop.'

'Yeah.' Shane looked up. 'You ever attend accident scenes? As a cop?'

'Not for a long time, but when I was younger, yeah. A couple.' Falk still remembered them, though. One in particular, where neither the driver nor passenger had been wearing a seatbelt. The inside of the car had looked like a pizza. 'Not something I'd be keen to repeat.'

'No. Me neither.' Shane's soft voice dropped even further. 'It was me who found Dean. I mean, the scene, really. Dean wasn't there.'

'Rita said something about that,' Falk said as Shane studied his own hands, frowning.

'Yeah. I'd sometimes jog around the reservoir track, try to keep the fitness up, you know. Not that often – or not as often as I should – but every few days or so. Dean used to walk his dog down there most mornings, but earlier, so I'd usually miss him.' The creases in Shane's face deepened. 'Then on that day I saw Luna – Dean's dog – and I remember thinking he must have been running pretty late. But I knew straight away something was wrong because Luna was in the middle of the bloody track, making this –' He cringed at the memory. '– howling noise. I've never heard her do that. I thought she was hurt but she wasn't, just shaking. Circling and yapping.' Shane shook his head. 'The safety railings were a mess. Posts all broken and the middle section gone. Like it had been completely torn out. When I looked over the side there was a big chunk of wood hanging down, all splintered. And Luna was there on her own and Dean was nowhere. No sign of any car.'

'You could tell that's what had happened?' Falk said.

'I guessed. From the damage to the barrier.' Shane was quiet for a long moment. 'I had a smash myself once. Years ago, not long after I retired, back when I was still drinking. Hit a fence. No-one else was involved, but . . .' He shook away the thought, didn't look at Falk. 'And down at the reservoir it had that same feel about it. Hard to describe.'

Falk knew the one. He'd felt it at accident scenes himself, years ago. As though the air itself absorbed the moment of impact, pulsing with it like an echo.

'I actually tried to call Dean. While I was standing there.' Shane seemed faintly mystified by that. 'God knows why. Maybe in case he'd been thrown clear or something and was injured. He didn't answer. Of course. I couldn't even hear his phone ring, but Luna was bloody howling and barking, so who knows? I remember looking down into the water again. Couldn't see anything. Didn't know how long it had been since the crash. So then –'

Shane drained his water glass, put it on the desk with a sharp tap.

'I called Gemma. I called her instead of Sergeant Dwyer because –' Shane's usual soft-spoken rhythm was undercut by a streak of anger. 'Jesus, I really don't know. Because I was hoping she'd say Dean was at home, or at the hospital, but that doesn't make any bloody sense because Gemma and Joel never would've left Luna like that. So I can't even remember exactly what I said, but that was how they found out that Dean was gone. Which wasn't great.' Shane exhaled and rubbed a hand over his face. His voice steadied, returning to something closer to normal. 'I mean, I used to think I did some bloody stupid things back when I was playing, but sometimes I wonder. I wish Gemma and Joel had found out in a better way.'

'Sometimes there is no good way to hear something.'

'Maybe. There're bad ways and worse ways, though, aren't there?' Shane managed a small smile, then nodded at the computer. 'Anyway, so that's the story of why I'm sitting here now stuffing up spreadsheets requested by some accountant who thinks I'm an idiot.' He paused, his mood lifting a notch as something occurred to him. 'He'll be absolutely shocked I'm not calling asking for help this time. I reckon he enjoys it, actually, the way he talks to me. People like to pigeonhole, you know?'

'That's very true.' Falk nodded.

'Do it to ourselves even, hey?' Shane picked up his empty glass and tilted it at the computer. 'Like how you're good at this stuff, but reckon you can't play footy.'

Falk smiled. 'Well, that's a fact, mate, not an opinion.'

'You *don't* play, that's not the same thing as *can't* play.' Shane cast an appraising eye over him. 'What are you, around my age? You look fit enough. And height like that? I spent years looking at blokes on the field and working out how good they were, and I reckon you could be okay.' He considered. 'Or okay for around here, anyway.'

Falk had to laugh. 'Which is saying what exactly?'

'Not a huge amount, true.' Shane grinned as a shadow passed outside and Charlie appeared in the doorway. 'But not nothing.'

'They'll be in the drawer, here. I'll just –' Charlie was saying to Raco as they came in, five-year-old Eva clattering behind them. They stopped when they saw Falk and Shane.

'Hey, you're back.' Raco smiled as Charlie squeezed past to rummage through the desk. 'How was the festival?'

'Yeah, okay,' Falk said. 'I –'

'Guess what we're doing?' Eva interrupted. She held up Duffy, the doll Falk had sent her when she was born. Its features had partly worn away through love and handling, giving the doll a slightly grotesque appearance, but Eva didn't seem to mind. 'We're taking the tractor for a ride.'

'Oh, great. Sounds like fun.'

'You can come too,' she said, with beaming benevolence.

'I don't know, mate, I should probably –' Falk's phone was feeling very heavy again in his pocket. What he should do was go to the guesthouse, dig out his laptop and blast through the most pressing of the messages. But Eva had already taken both him and Raco by the hand and was leading them outside.

Charlie slammed the desk drawer shut, keys jangling in his palm, and followed them out into the sun. Falk looked back, raising his free hand in farewell to Shane, then gave in for the moment and let Eva lead him down towards the vines. He breathed in the deep, fresh air, soaking in the sense of spring leaves and fledgling fruit all around.

'Was the festival site busy?' Charlie asked as they walked. 'I called the station earlier to see how the appeal went and they said Rob Dwyer was already down there.'

'Yeah.' Falk hesitated. 'I ran into him. He said a few new reports came in. Reckons a couple are worth chasing up.'

'Right.' Charlie frowned slightly. 'That's good. Something, at least?' He glanced at his brother for confirmation and Raco nodded.

'After a whole year, any new information's good,' Raco said, then turned to Falk. 'He mention anything else?'

'About the appeal? No.' Falk met Raco's eye. Kept his voice neutral. 'Sounded like he might have one or two thoughts simmering away, though.'

'Rob? Yeah.' Raco flashed Falk a knowing smile over his daughter's head. 'I'll bet he does.' They exchanged a silent look of understanding. They'd talk later.

Eva dropped their hands suddenly and ran ahead to the tractor that was parked in the large shed at the far end of the vines. She placed Duffy carefully up on the seat then climbed in herself, positioning the doll on her lap.

'You know what would be *so* fun?' she said, as though the idea had only just struck her, even as she fixed Falk firmly in her crosshairs. 'If *you* drive us.'

'Me?' Falk laughed. 'No, Eva.'

'Oh.' Her face fell. 'Why not?'

'For starters, I've got some work I need to do.'

'Mum says you're on holiday.'

'That's true.'

'So why do you have to do work? That doesn't make any sense.'

'Also true, Eva.' Falk smiled. The kid made a good point. 'Still, I think this is something I'd better leave to your dad or uncle.'

'Oh.' She looked immediately devastated. 'Okay,' she managed, bravely.

'Don't be dramatic, kiddo.' Charlie grinned and hefted a bag of what smelled like fertiliser clear of the wheels. 'It's different from a car. Not everyone can drive one of these.'

'Although . . .' Raco said. He was leaning against the tractor, watching the conversation unfold with amusement. 'I'll bet you a thousand dollars, Eva, that your uncle Aaron can.'

'*Really?*' Eva and Charlie turned in unison to look at Falk, one in delight and the other in surprise.

Raco laughed. 'I've seen the exact property where this guy grew up. There's no way he doesn't know his way around one of these things. You, hand him the keys.' He pointed at Charlie and then Falk. 'And you, leave the work for once. Give the kid a ride.'

Falk looked up at the machine. Raco wasn't wrong. Falk had learned to drive a tractor before he'd learned to drive a car, and his dad had taught him both. It had been a long time, though, since he'd done this. He stood there in the cool of the shed, with the shafts of sunlight warm across the dusty floor, and all of a sudden, it was twenty-five years ago and he couldn't wait another minute. Falk stepped forward and climbed up, feeling the long-forgotten but instantly familiar sensation of being in front of the controls. He took the key from Charlie and turned it. The sensation was immediate. He knew how to do this.

'Okay.' Of course. He'd always known how to do this. 'Let's go.'

'Try to avoid the crop, preferably,' Charlie called after them, but he was smiling.

Falk pulled away, out into the bright light, the little girl beside him and the land and the sky huge ahead. Raco and Charlie strolled along behind and, after a while, Rita and Henry came out and joined them, chatting as they wandered slowly through the vines. Falk and Eva sat side by side and she sang songs and recounted meandering stories as they trundled along, drawing long lazy laps in the afternoon sun until dinnertime.

Chapter 18

When Falk ran these days, it was alone on a treadmill, with earphones blocking out his surrounds. The windows of the twenty-four-hour gym nearest his work looked out onto a tall glassy office block tenanted by an investment banking firm and Falk used to clock up the kilometres watching a shadowy figure stare at a screen in the building opposite.

The guy seemed to work long hours, even longer than Falk. Or perhaps not, perhaps just a different shift pattern that also kept him at his desk well into the night. Either way, that was where they both found themselves, three to five evenings a week and some weekends. Once, about a month ago, the guy had stood up and stretched, as he tended to do every now and again. This time, though, he'd walked to the window and raised the sun blind that had stopped being useful hours earlier and stood there, a middle-aged man with a late-night cup of coffee in his hand. He and Falk had stared at each other through two panes of glass, ten floors up, the dark sky a sliver above them and the lights of the city streets far below, and then Falk had dialled up the volume on his headphones and the guy had turned away and gone back to his desk. For reasons he couldn't articulate, Falk didn't use that treadmill anymore.

This evening, though, Falk tied his laces and pulled the door of the guesthouse closed behind him. The sky was pink and orange and the air still thick and warm. The kitchen lights glowed from the cottage. Dinner had been cleared away and Raco and Rita were putting Eva and Henry through their regular bedtime routine.

Falk jogged to the end of the driveway, then turned right. He hadn't been this way before, and went where his legs took him along the empty country road, paying enough attention to be sure he could find his way back. He ran for a while before the road turned a gentle corner, and up ahead Falk saw the lush green of the vineyards give way to an open park. Falk slowed as he heard the familiar sound of a distant football bouncing against the ground. He stopped, leaning against a playground fence to catch his breath. Beyond the slide and swing set, a figure was running an unhurried length of a community footy oval.

The player was too far away for Falk to make out his face, but he recognised him simply by the way he moved. Shane. It could be no-one else. Even with the extra years and a few extra kilos, Shane McAfee still had it. He bounced the ball as he ran, control and grace in every step. At the fifty-metre line he drew his leg back and kicked in a smooth sweeping motion. The ball sailed through the centre posts, clean and clear. It was beautiful to watch.

Shane stood for a long moment on the silent oval in the growing twilight, hands on hips. At last, he ran a palm over his face and slowly walked across the empty field to retrieve the football. Falk suddenly felt like he was intruding on an intensely private moment and he turned away, picking up speed again and continuing down the track before Shane saw him there.

Falk clocked up another couple of kilometres and was just wondering whether it was time to turn around when he spotted the old reservoir track. He hadn't known there was access along here, but suddenly there it was, a subtle break in the bushland. He'd run past it even as his eye snagged on the faded sign.

East Reservoir. No public vehicle access. Hiking permitted.

Falk dropped his pace to a walk, his breathing heavier now, and went back to look. The geography in his head shifted and slotted into a new position as he tried to get his bearings in relation to the body of water that he realised must be hidden behind the trees. Somewhere in the distance, he could hear the soft hum of the country highway.

The reservoir entrance was wide enough for a single truck or car to pass through, but was barred by a waist-high metal gate. The gate was padlocked to a post that didn't quite meet the bushland at the side, so walkers over the years had simply stepped around, wearing the packed earth smooth.

Falk checked his watch, then the sky. There was still plenty of soft light left in the evening, but that could disappear fast and he didn't know his way well. Still, the path was clearly marked and if he kept the water on his – he consulted the sparse map in his head – on his left, he should eventually end up at the festival grounds. He could find his way back from there if it came to it.

He stepped around the gate and ran a few paces along the dirt path, emerging sooner than he'd expected from the trees. Right in front of him lay the reservoir. It stretched out ahead, almost black now the sun had gone. How many stadiums' worth of water had Raco said? Whatever the number, Falk could believe it. From this angle, it looked vast and deep in a whole new way.

Falk dragged his eyes back to the trail and started running again. The bushland on his right hummed and sang with late bird call, and the track ahead was wide and smooth with a gentle gradient and he soon fell into a rhythm. He was focusing on his breathing and trying, somewhat unsuccessfully, not to think about work when he spotted the figure up ahead.

It was hard to make out any detail amid the deepening gloom, and whoever it was had their back turned. They were standing at a safety barrier which – Falk realised with a jolt of surprise – was guarding the Drop. How far had he come? He looked at his watch. Judging by his pace, he could only be a kilometre or so from the gate. The distance was less than he'd expected.

Up ahead, the figure was hunched over, doing something to the railing. Falk pictured Dean Tozer's memorial plaque and, more specifically, the mess and graffiti left after the previous night.

'Hey!' His voice was sharp and the person startled and dropped what they were holding.

Shit. It was Joel, Falk realised straight away. Tall and lean, the boy frowned into the poor light, relaxing only a fraction when he saw who had spoken. He bent to retrieve the item now rolling around by his feet. Luna was at his heels, tail twitching, watching them both.

'Sorry, mate.' Falk raised his arm and slowed to a walk for the final stretch, catching his breath. 'I didn't mean to scare you. I saw someone had made a bit of a mess last night –'

Falk stopped as he reached the Drop. In Joel's hands, he could see now, were a damp cloth and a bottle of cleaning fluid. Falk looked up and their eyes met, almost level. The young bloke shrugged and looked away, embarrassed.

'It's not like anyone else is going to do it,' Joel muttered, turning back to the railings. He sprayed the solution on the woodwork around his dad's plaque and scrubbed hard at a black mark near one corner.

Falk nodded slowly. He ran a hand over the barrier nearest him. It was clean and damp under his palm, the crusty residue from earlier wiped away. Joel looked to have cleaned about half the length of the railings.

'How often do you come out here and do this?' Falk asked.

Another shrug. 'Dunno. Whenever it needs doing.' Joel took a water bottle from his backpack on the ground and poured a little on the cloth. 'Otherwise it stays like this for ages. It's owned by some business group, so they don't give a shit, they'd leave it like this all year.'

In memory of Dean Tozer. Loved and missed.

The plaque near Falk's hand was now gleaming. The dirt and boot prints were mostly gone, but the graffitied pen markings remained stubbornly scrawled across the woodwork.

'You'll need turps or something for these,' Falk said.

'I know. We've run out at home.' Joel sprayed some more cleaning fluid on the wood. 'This was better than nothing for now.'

Falk nodded. It was growing dark. The kid still had a bit to do.

'You got a spare cloth?'

Joel looked up in surprise. 'You don't have to help. I can do it myself.'

'Yeah, I can see that.' Falk leaned against the clean barrier and watched Joel for a minute. 'My own dad died, a few years ago now. Cancer. Drawn out. Expected. So, no memorial like this. But he's got a grave back in Victoria and I'll tell you, if some drunk dickheads left it in this state, I would be un-believably pissed off.' Falk nodded at the bag on the ground. 'Seriously. Let me give you a hand, mate.'

Joel didn't respond immediately, but Falk saw him run an eye over what was left to do. A beat passed, then he reached down and pulled another cloth from his bag.

'Thanks.' The word was almost lost in the soft rustle of the bushland.

'No worries.'

They worked silently side by side for a while, as the sky over the water turned a deeper purple. They were on the final stretch when Joel rolled his shoulders, loosening his neck.

'So what did Sergeant Dwyer have to say earlier?'

Falk frowned as he rubbed the corner of his cloth over a particularly tough grey mark that seemed baked on. 'He thinks you and Zara are on the wrong track.'

A short laugh. 'No surprise there. What does he reckon the right track is, then?'

'Well, yeah,' Falk said. 'Be interesting to know.'

'He didn't say?'

'Not to me.'

'Because he doesn't know himself. Not what happened to Kim. Not who killed my dad. I mean, Jesus, how hard is it to find a car with that much damage?'

Falk said nothing, but stopped scrubbing for a minute and looked around, more closely this time, at the surroundings. The track, the bushland, the Drop, the barrier. Falk didn't know anything especially useful about resolving traffic accidents. It was a world away from his day-to-day operations, but even applying basic investigation techniques he could appreciate that this scenario could be a tricky one. No witnesses, early morning, quiet roads in and out, hundreds if not thousands of agricultural sheds big enough to hide a damaged vehicle. Assuming it was a local vehicle at all, which felt like a pretty big assumption to make. Falk could hear the faint pulse of the festival music through the trees and he pictured the size of the crowd. A lot of people, with a lot of vehicles. Jump on the highway, head home. A car could be across the border and into Victoria or New South Wales in a matter of hours. Falk looked at Joel, whose face was hard as he wrung out his cloth.

'Does Dwyer know what kind of car it was?'

'Blue Toyota. Or possibly Holden. And yes,' he said, as Falk took a breath, 'before you ask, I do know how common that type of vehicle is. Sergeant Dwyer's made that point a few hundred times.'

'Right.' Falk nodded. To be fair, Dwyer wasn't wrong about that. 'But I was actually going to ask how he knows. CCTV somewhere or –?'

'Oh. No, there was nothing like that.' Joel examined the barrier in front of him. 'From paint scratches left on the wood.'

'And they checked all the locally registered vehicles, I'm guessing?'

'Apparently.'

Falk was still thinking about that when Joel spoke again.

'Hey.' The boy's tone was overly casual. 'Was Zara okay when she got home? She was a bit down when she left this afternoon.'

Falk blinked, catching up with the change in subject. He pictured Zara at dinner. She had said very little, concentrating on her plate, seemingly miles away.

'She seemed no worse,' he said truthfully.

'That's good.'

Falk looked over at Joel in the growing darkness. He took personal and professional pride in not jumping to conclusions, but at the same time some things were clear without having to ask. For example, it was as obvious as if it were written in the night sky above them that this kid had a serious thing for Zara and she did not feel the same way. Falk watched Joel for a moment, tipping clean water onto his cloth. He could remember that feeling, at that age. Pining after a girl. The acute sharp pang of longing that was both pleasant and painful.

Gemma, can I grab your number?

I think . . . no.

The memory flared without warning and, almost amused, Falk pushed it straight back down.

'So what's the situation with you and Zara? Are you two together, or –?' Falk knew the answer but was interested in Joel's take. The kid was already shaking his head.

'No. We're just friends.' He was quiet for a minute. 'But we're pretty good friends, I guess. Now, obviously, but even before this. Our parents were close, so we've known each other a long time. Zara was really good when my dad died. And then all this with her mum . . .' Joel shrugged, and an edge crept into his voice. 'So we kind of look out for each other, I suppose. Which is why I wouldn't make things harder for her by lying about not seeing Kim that night. For the record. Again.'

'I don't get the impression people think you're lying, mate.'

Falk had nearly reached the end of the barrier he was working on. 'I reckon honestly it's because they remember themselves at your age. How reliable they were. Or weren't, more likely. Most people probably look back and think they wouldn't have trusted themselves to be sure, at your age and in that position.'

'What about you?' Joel looked over. 'Would you have trusted yourself?'

'No.' Falk's answer came so quickly even Joel smiled. 'I did a couple of pretty stupid things as a kid, like everyone. I wouldn't have taken my word for it.'

The boy nodded. He doused a scrawl of graffiti with cleaning fluid and lifted his cloth but didn't move, paused mid-thought. He seemed to be debating something. Finally, he started to clean, but more slowly now. He glanced sideways at Falk.

'So, that night last year –' Joel was hard to hear. His head was down and he was focused on the railing. 'I was already stationed at that first-aid post when I saw Zara go out of the east exit. She was with a couple of other girls from our school, but she saw me and came over and said hi. Asked if I was sure I didn't want to come, because a lot of our friends were going. But I really didn't want to because –' Joel tossed his cloth on the barrier and reached down to stroke Luna's head instead. 'Because I couldn't face it, or whatever. Being here, at this time of year, drinking and having to pretend like it's all fine.' He frowned in a way that made him look suddenly younger. 'And anyway, I was already working by then. I'd told Gemma I'd do the whole shift so I couldn't just leave.'

Joel scratched his dog's ears as he stared at the scribbled graffiti, still stark and legible despite all their work. 'Anyway. We all knew Dwyer wasn't going to be around to shut things down that year, so there was already this feeling that things could get a bit crazy out here. And Zara said she might not stay too long because her dad was giving her grief about needing to spend some time with her mum.' Joel paused. 'I thought there was maybe a chance she'd end up coming back before my shift was over. So –' He stopped again, for longer this time, then shrugged. 'So, I was kind of half looking out for her. At the exit. In case she did come back early or something, you know?'

Yes. Falk looked over in the dim light. Yes, he did know what Joel was trying to tell him but didn't want to spell out loud. There was no need to, anyway, because Falk could picture it now, with vivid, hormonal clarity. To be that age, watching a girl he liked leave with her friends, trailing the faint tantalising promise of return. Falk knew that feeling well and he also knew, without a shadow of a doubt, that he himself would have had one eye glued to that exit for the entire night, too.

'Okay,' he said, and gave a small nod. Even in the growing dark, he could see a flush creep up Joel's face and neck as the boy picked his cloth up again and busied himself scrubbing the last few marks. Falk gave his own barrier a final wipe, and they both stood back to inspect their handiwork. The painted wood shone white in the early moonlight.

'What do you reckon?' Falk said.

'Yeah. Good. Heaps better.' Joel seemed as close to happy as Falk had seen him, and reached out to take his dirty cloth. 'Thanks for –'

He stopped as they both heard the movement along the track at the same time. Falk listened. Footsteps against the packed dirt, coming from the direction of the festival. They turned together, but it was Joel who recognised her first.

'Oh. It's just my stepmum.' He raised his hand. 'Gemma?'

'Joel? Oh, good. You're here.'

Falk remembered her voice even as the figure was still taking shape and then, all at once, he could see her for himself. He straightened, suddenly a little self-conscious in his sweat-damp running gear, and watched Gemma Tozer come along the track. She was wearing jeans again, and her shirt was creased at the elbows. Her hair was up, Falk noticed, like the first time he'd seen her, sixteen months ago in the packed Southbank bar.

Gemma's relief at seeing Joel morphed into baffled surprise as she drew closer, absorbing more of the scene in front of her with each step. She blinked, her eyes moving from her stepson to the barrier to the memorial to the cleaning cloths in their hands and then, finally, coming to rest on Falk.

'Hi,' he said.

'Hello, again.'

He smiled at her, automatic and impulsive. He couldn't help it.

And there in the dark, with the evening sky huge overhead and the water still and calm below, she smiled back. He breathed out. They stood looking at each other for a drawn-out beat, then Gemma glanced past him to Joel, who was busy zipping his cleaning stuff into his backpack.

'This looks really nice,' she said, running her hand over the shining wooden barrier, pausing only briefly at the scrawled graffiti. 'Great job.'

Joel shrugged and waved his free hand towards Falk. 'Aaron helped. He's Zara's uncle's friend –' He stopped as Gemma nodded.

'Yeah. We've met once, actually.'

'Oh, right.' Joel shrugged, his stepmother's social life clearly

199

of limited interest, and swung his bag onto his back. He was taller than Gemma and had to look down to make eye contact with her when they spoke. 'Are you coming home too?'

'Not yet. I'm on site until close tonight. I just came to check if you were down here, because –' Gemma's voice was light, but Falk caught the undertone. 'You know, sometimes you're down here.'

They all glanced at the plaque, then Joel crouched and clipped the lead onto Luna's collar.

'Yeah, well. All done now,' he said, in a tone that was probably meant to be reassuring but just made Gemma press her lips together in a line. He noticed and gave her a small smile as he turned to leave, raising a hand to Falk. 'Thanks again.'

'No worries.'

'Text me when you're home,' Gemma called after him, and the boy nodded without looking back. Falk stood beside her and they watched him disappear in the other direction down the track. The night suddenly seemed very big and quiet and Falk took a breath.

'Listen, I hope I wasn't overstep–'

'Thank you, that was –'

They caught each other's eye.

'Sorry,' he said. 'You go.'

Gemma hesitated. She glanced again at the memorial plaque and the clean barriers, then looked at Falk and nodded back towards the festival.

'Let's get a drink. Please. If you have time?'

'Yeah. Great. That sounds –' Falk stopped. His hands fell to his pocketless shorts. 'I actually don't have any money.'

They both looked down, taking in his running gear, then

back up, where their eyes met again. Gemma looked faintly amused.

'You're okay. I've got one or two connections up there. And I'm pretty sure I owe you, anyway.' She turned, but not before Falk caught her smiling, just a little to herself. 'You know, from last time.'

Chapter 19

The caravan that served as the on-site headquarters was empty, Falk could see as he followed Gemma across the grounds. The lanterns in the large tree overhead bathed the area in a soft glow and she nodded to the folding chairs underneath.

'Grab a seat.'

Falk settled into a striped fabric director's chair that was surprisingly comfortable as Gemma unlocked the caravan and went inside. She reappeared in the doorway a moment later, holding up a range of drink options in turn. Falk's earlier run was starting to catch up with him and he could feel the pleasant warm burn building in his legs as he pointed gratefully at the cold water.

'Me too,' Gemma said, coming out with two glasses and a filled glass bottle. She pulled up the chair opposite and then reached into her jeans pocket and put her phone on the table. 'Sorry, I'm still on duty so I have to keep an eye on it.'

'No worries, I know that feeling. Thanks,' he said, as she poured the water for them both.

'Well.' She lifted her glass. 'Welcome, Aaron Falk.'

'Thank you.' They looked at each other as they drank. He took a long deep swallow. Where to start? 'Hey, I used the diary, by the way.' That seemed as good a place as any. He'd been kind of wanting to tell her that for a year. 'The one you bought at the station.'

'You mean, the one I randomly forced on you.' Gemma laughed, a little embarrassed. 'God, I couldn't believe I'd done that later. The wine went to my head a bit. So how did you find it?'

'Useful,' Falk said, truthfully. 'For all those reasons you said. Made the work chaos feel a bit calmer. I bought a new one this year, actually.'

'Oh yeah?' she said lightly, but looked quite pleased. 'And how is the taskforce going? Is the chaos manageable?'

'Just about.' Although Falk suddenly, maddeningly, pictured his phone. Lying on his bed back in the Racos' guesthouse, heavy still with calls to return and emails to be answered. He gave himself an invisible mental shake to clear the image. 'Speaking of work, though. Gemma, this festival is –'

He waved a hand effusively to indicate the entire complex operation. The night air was soaked with music and the steady hum of laughter and chatter from people enjoying themselves. Benefits for local producers too, Falk guessed. Not to mention jobs created and money generated for the town. He could only imagine the amount of work it took to make the Marralee Valley Annual Food and Wine Festival a success.

'It's a serious achievement,' he said. 'Amazing. You don't need me to tell you that, but congratulations. Really.'

'Thank you. Yeah, we're all pretty proud of it.' She smiled. 'I'm happy you got to see it.'

'Yeah, I am too.'

Falk watched Gemma across the table. Her hair looked darker under the low light from the caravan and the trees. She hadn't taken it down this time, he noticed. He'd vaguely wondered at times what it would be like if he ever found himself in this situation with her again. They'd spent one evening together sixteen months ago and Falk was acutely aware that he'd probably airbrushed and edited at least some of it without meaning to. But here in the warm spring air, sitting in front of each other in the flawed flesh, he felt the same as he had on that cold wet Melbourne night. *Stay.* She was watching him too. He sat there in his running clothes and drank his water and tried to read her face. They both blinked as her phone suddenly buzzed loudly against the table. Gemma leaned forward.

'Joel's home. Good.' She sat back, but her face showed a trace of tension now. 'Listen, thank you. For helping him clean up the plaque. It means a lot to him. And me, as well.' She paused. 'I guess Joel told you what happened to Dean?'

Falk nodded. 'Shane McAfee brought it up as well.'

'Right.' Gemma sounded sad for a moment. 'Yeah, they both find the festival difficult, with the anniversary of Dean's accident.'

'Do you?' Falk asked, curious. 'Being so involved here?'

'Well –' She hesitated. 'The anniversary itself's never my favourite day, obviously. But the festival, no. I don't feel the same way they do. I don't have that association, I guess, maybe because this is a year-round job for me. And . . .' She glanced out across the site. 'I mean, we already lost Dean. Who was a huge important part of life for me and Joel. I really didn't want to lose this as well.'

'Yeah,' he said. 'I can understand that.' Grief hit people in different ways, though, and Falk found himself picturing Joel once more. Down there at the reservoir on a Friday night, a lonely figure with his cleaning cloths. From Gemma's frown, he suspected she was thinking the same.

'Joel had actually been doing pretty well for a while,' she said. 'I mean, it's six years now since Dean died and he seemed to be going okay. But then last year – God, that whole nightmare with Kim.' Her voice was tight and she picked at her thumbnail.

'Were you and Kim close?' Falk asked.

Gemma's nod was automatic, but then slowed. 'We definitely used to be. When we were at school, and then again when I moved back. Dean and Charlie were friends and Zara and Joel were around the same age. Did you know her?'

'No,' Falk said. 'We never met.'

'Kim was the first one who said I should go for this job, as festival director.' Gemma smiled a little at the memory.

'Really?'

'Yeah. I didn't think I had any real chance when it came up, but one night Dean and I were at the pub with her and Charlie and Naomi, and we were talking about who might go for it and then Kim went and got a piece of paper from the bar. She made us all sit there and list everyone and then compare my strengths and experience against theirs. And we were laughing and everything, but by the end it made me feel like, yeah, I could actually do this. And she was right. But if it wasn't for Kim, I probably wouldn't have applied.'

'Good on her.' Falk smiled. 'And you.'

'Thanks. She was always doing things like that. Or she used to, anyway.' Gemma's smile faded. 'We'd grown apart in the last few years, so I hadn't seen her for a while.' She examined the glass in her hand, and Falk could hear the guilt.

'Rita said something similar,' he offered, not sure if it would help or not.

She gave him a small smile and nodded. 'It all got a bit tricky for a while after Kim and Charlie split up and she moved away. It's no excuse, but time passed and we lost touch a little. But she was still my friend, and what happened last year was –' She struggled to find the right word. 'God. So disturbing. And then Joel got dragged right in. He was only seventeen then, so it was a lot at that age. Any age, really. Losing Dean was bad enough, but this left him feeling very –' Gemma shrugged sadly. '– alone, I think.'

Falk nodded. 'Is his mum in the picture?'

'Not so much.' Gemma refilled their glasses and sat back in her chair. 'It's not bad blood or anything, but she got married a few years ago and lives out near Port Pirie. Has two little kids now, so it's hard for Joel. She definitely does her best, but she and Dean got together pretty young and Joel probably came along before either of them was ready. And now he's this awkward teenager and his mum has a whole new family that she *was* ready for, and I'm not saying she doesn't love him – not at all.' She shook her head. 'But it's different. And whatever you say to Joel, he's smart enough to –'

Gemma stopped as they both suddenly sensed movement from the dimly lit patch of ground behind the tree. She leaned forward and craned her neck to see.

'Just me,' a voice called, and an older man wearing a festival t-shirt appeared out of the gloom. He had a backpack slung over his shoulder and was frowning at a dull metal bolt in his oil-stained fingers. He raised his free hand and Gemma settled back in her chair.

'Bloody canopy pin's coming loose on the Chardonnay

Revival tent again,' the man said. 'I'll replace it for now, take a proper look in daylight.'

'Great, thanks, Kev,' Gemma said as he paused in front of the caravan and held the bolt up to the light to examine it. 'Do you need anyone to help?'

'No, you're all right. Matty's already over there.' The man went inside and they heard the sound of rummaging. He emerged a moment later with a toolbox and smiled at Gemma. His gaze moved to Falk, where it lingered for a moment and cooled.

'I delivered Charlie Raco's signed waivers to you last year,' Falk said, answering the man's unasked question.

The guy snapped his fingers. 'That's right, you did.' The curiosity on his face flickered again, now laced with mild suspicion. 'All right, well.' He kept his eyes firmly on Falk. 'I'm on the mobile if you need me, Gemma.'

'No worries, thanks, Kev.'

The bloke nodded smartly, then lifted a hand in farewell and headed off across the grass.

'So, wait a second.' Gemma laughed and leaned her elbows on the table as he left. 'Does that mean *you* were the "intense bloke" that he warned me was acting a bit strange?'

'Yeah, apparently so,' Falk said, but he was smiling too. He watched the man disappear into the night.

'Kev's words, not mine. He can be a little dramatic. The festival brings out some odd types occasionally, though, so he's just watching out for me.'

'Fair enough. And look, maybe I was a bit intense.' Falk shrugged. 'I was just conscious it was a pretty transparent attempt to see you.'

Gemma tilted her head. In the tree above, the lanterns swayed as the night air breathed through the branches. 'Is that right?'

'Yeah.'

'Well.' They looked at each other for a moment. She seemed about to say something more, then changed her mind, reaching for the water to top up their still full glasses. 'You know, I thought I did see you last year, actually.' She put the bottle back on the table and checked her phone again.

'Near the ferris wheel?' Falk said.

'No, it was by Charlie's stall. But I was quite far away and by the time I got nearer you were gone.' She frowned a little. 'I don't think I saw you by the ferris wheel –'

'It was around the children's fireworks. You were talking to Naomi. She looked kind of serious, so I didn't want to interrupt.'

'Oh.' Gemma smoothed a strand of hair off her face as she thought back. 'Yeah. I remember that, actually. She'd walked in along the reservoir track and was worried the kids' party in the bushland was already getting out of hand. She wanted me to get the officers on duty to go and check.'

'Did they?'

'I asked them to, but no, I found out later they didn't go. Sergeant Dwyer normally stamps it out before too long, but he wasn't around, and no-one else did.'

'Sounds like Naomi's pretty keen to see the party stopped altogether.'

'She is. She'll get her way, too, just watch,' Gemma predicted. 'You've met her, have you?'

'This morning. She's Henry's godmother.'

'That's right, of course. She's a great choice. A lot of fun, very smart too.' Gemma sipped her water. 'And you've met Shane as well?'

'Yeah. I knew who he was already, though. My dad and I followed the footy. We saw him play in a grand final years ago. Great day. Amazing game. He was incredible.'

Gemma nodded. 'So I've heard. I was always at uni or in the States, but the others used to go and watch him when they could. Charlie and Kim, Naomi. My parents as well, they were big fans. They were at that grand final too.'

'Oh yeah?' Falk said. 'Are they still around?'

'They live in Stirling now, near my older sister and her three girls. So not too far. What about your dad?'

'No, he died a while ago. He would've loved to have met Shane, though.'

Gemma smiled. 'Dads do love meeting Shane.'

'You know, he would've really liked all this as well.' Falk shifted in his chair to look back at the grounds. The sounds and the lights and the aroma of food and wine had sparked a memory Falk hadn't known he'd had.

'The festival?' she asked.

'Yeah. We had sheep at our place back home but once, when I was about fourteen, we had to transport some to Clyde, which was a couple of hours away.' He paused to let the memory rise to the surface and take shape. 'They had this local produce festival on – nothing as good as this, much smaller – but we spent the rest of the day there and it was pretty fun. Then the whole drive home I remember Dad going on about how someone should set up something like that in Kiewarra. Diversify, attract visitors to the region. He reckoned people would love it. That it would breathe life back into the town.'

Falk couldn't believe he'd forgotten this.

'It was funny,' he said. 'He was so keen that for a minute I thought he was about to park in front of the council offices and roll up his sleeves and demand the permit forms or whatever. He didn't, obviously. I mean, he had to work so hard at our place he didn't have time for anything else, but he never stopped bringing it up, either. We only lived in Kiewarra for a couple more years, and every autumn we'd make that trip out to Clyde and check out the festival and bring home some organic cheese or whatever. So, yeah.' Falk smiled to himself as he remembered. 'He would have really enjoyed this. Maybe even more than meeting Shane.'

'Well, that is high praise.' Gemma grinned. 'It's nice that you and your dad were close.'

'Oh.' Falk blinked, the memory suddenly blurring a little. 'No. We weren't, really. Unfortunately.'

'No? Oh.' Gemma seemed genuinely surprised. 'Sorry. It just sounded like you were. Going together to the festivals and the footy or whatever. And you obviously got how Joel was feeling down there tonight with his dad's plaque.'

'Anyone would understand that, though,' Falk said.

'They really don't.' Gemma shook her head. 'That stupid vandalism shows they don't.'

Falk didn't reply, but found himself thinking about what she'd said. He'd never considered himself and his dad in that light, but the way Gemma had said it made it feel . . . what? Sort of true. Maybe.

The phone buzzed again on the table between them and Gemma leaned forward and tapped the screen.

'Oh, well. All good things . . .' she said with a rueful smile. 'That's me summoned, I'm afraid. Issues at the Chardonnay Revival tent.'

'Right. No worries.' Falk tried not to sound disappointed as he drained his glass and pulled himself out of his chair. 'Far be it from me to hold up chardonnay's comeback. Is that really a thing, by the way?'

'Oh my God, yes. Absolutely it is. What is it they say? Wait long enough, and everything comes around again.' Gemma paused. She was looking at Falk in a way that reminded him a little bit of Melbourne. 'Speaking of which, it's been nice to see you.'

'Yeah. You too, Gemma.'

She was poised to go but still didn't move. Above, the lanterns shone in the dark and the soft beat of music floated over from a distant stage. The sounds of crowds were all around them, but outside the caravan, they were alone.

'Listen –'

'I –'

They both stopped. Gemma smiled and her eyes fell to her phone, silent in her hand. Falk could tell from her face that she was considering something. What, exactly, he wasn't sure, but when she looked up again, she seemed a little awkward.

'Aaron, I wanted to explain, about last year.'

'You really don't have to.'

'I know, but I want to. Because I had a really nice time with you – back then, and again just now –' She shifted her weight but didn't come any closer. 'And when you asked for my number in Melbourne, it wasn't that I didn't want to see where things could go.' She gave a small shrug. 'I just think it's pretty obvious where that would be.'

'Is it?' Falk was genuinely surprised.

'Yeah. It really is.' Gemma looked at him in the low light. 'I mean, tell me, what does that diary of yours look like?'

He pictured it. The pages were creased and thick with meetings, appointments, reminders, deadlines.

'Busy, right?' She read his face. 'It has to be, with the kind of job you do. Seven days a week, probably?'

She waited as though hoping Falk might contradict her, but he had to nod.

'So, what happens?' Gemma said. 'We exchange numbers, and then what? Even with the best will in the world, we're not going to be chalking up regular visits and three-day long weekends. Realistically.'

'We could try.' He wanted to, he realised. He *would* actually try. 'Give it a go.'

'Yeah, true. We could,' she said. 'But say it actually works. Then what? The long-term situation's even worse. You've worked hard to get where you are, I have too. I don't want to leave here. And last I heard, Marralee's a long way from an AFP hub.'

'Well, yeah. Okay. But –'

Gemma waited. Falk tried to think of an answer to that. He couldn't.

'Ten years or so ago –' she said, when it was clear he wasn't going to go on. Her voice softened. 'Look, Aaron, I wouldn't have been saying any of this when I was younger. You wanted my number back then, you would have got it, no question. But that's not where I am now. And I've got Joel to think about too. So I don't know exactly what the right relationship looks like, but I know it's not an interstate romance. It's just not, I'm sorry.'

She did sound it, he thought. But the regret seemed matched by resolve.

'I've done the whole *will-he, won't-he, wait-by-the-phone* thing in the past,' Gemma said. 'And it's not for me anymore. I don't need snatched weekends and champagne and sunsets. I want help bringing in the supermarket shopping and someone to talk to and watch TV with. The day-to-day stuff, you know?'

They looked at each other and finally Falk nodded.

'Yeah, look, I do know. And that makes sense,' he said at last. 'I just wish –'

She waited, but eventually he had to shrug. He managed to find a smile, despite himself. 'I wish I had an answer, though.'

'I know. Me too.' Gemma's phone buzzed again in her hand.

'You'd better go,' Falk said, and she nodded. 'But –' He stopped. He wanted to say something more, but couldn't think what. 'Thanks for telling me.'

'No, that's okay,' she said. 'Thanks for understanding. Because it's really not you, or anything you did. The opposite, if anything. I just know myself too well and when I look down that road –' Gemma shook her head, a small smile on her face as she turned to leave. 'Honestly, in the best possible way, I could see myself wasting so much time on you.'

Chapter 20

Rita and Raco were sitting outside the guesthouse when Falk trudged up the vineyard driveway. They had a bottle of wine open on the small table between them; Rita was reading a novel while Raco had his head tilted back with his forearm across his eyes, possibly asleep. Falk smiled, glad to see them. It had felt like a long walk home, not least because whichever way he turned it, and he'd tried a few different ways, he thought that ultimately Gemma had probably got it right.

'That was a long run,' Rita called softly as she saw him. She pulled the third chair closer, and Falk sat down gratefully. 'Drink?'

'Why not? Thanks,' he said as Raco stirred and rubbed his eyes, blinking hard. 'I haven't been running the whole time. I bumped into Gemma.'

'Oh, yes?' Rita threw her husband a smug look. 'And?'

'And we had a drink. Talked a bit.'

'And?'

'And unfortunately, Rita, that's all there is to report.'

'For now?'

'For good, I think.' Falk kept his voice light. 'But for a few very valid reasons. So yeah. It's fine.'

He braced himself for a string of questions or reassurances or romantic plotting, but instead Rita simply reached out and rested her hand gently on his. Her palm was warm and comforting against the back of his hand, and Falk suddenly felt his throat constrict. Out of absolutely nowhere, for one very long, very real moment, he actually thought that he might start to cry. He focused hard on the glass in front of him and swallowed twice, three times, until the sensation passed. Neither Rita nor Raco said anything, just sat with him, surrounded by the hushed sounds of night.

'Mate, I have to tell you,' Falk cleared his throat noisily, 'Sergeant Dwyer thinks someone in your friends and family circle is lying about not seeing Kim that night.' Abrupt, he was aware, but at least it moved the conversation on. 'He thinks it's unlikely no-one spoke to her, given how close you all are.'

'That's what he was saying to you this afternoon?' Raco reached up, cracking his shoulder joints. He exchanged a glance with Rita, but neither seemed shocked or even surprised. 'I thought something new might have come out of the appeal.'

'No. He was asking about you. All of you, I mean.'

'Yeah, fair enough. I would too, in his shoes, wouldn't you?' Raco reached over and splashed the remains of the bottle between their three glasses. 'I like Rob Dwyer, but I don't think he's right about this. That was a busy night at the festival. Crowds like that? You could be next to someone and still miss them. And we all thought Kim was here for a few days, so the urgency to catch her right then wasn't really there.' He glanced at Rita, who nodded. 'Not for us, anyway. And that's before you even wonder if Kim was actively avoiding people she knew, for whatever reason. Mental health, who knows?'

Falk could see that Rita agreed and, thinking about it, he was inclined to as well. Not least because he suddenly – again – pictured Gemma. They had both apparently spotted each other last year without the other noticing. It wasn't impossible at all. 'So you're not worried?'

'About that?' Raco shook his head. 'I know there's a personal connection with Dwyer having worked with my dad, but if he really thought there was something solid to pursue, he'd do it. And –' He glanced past Falk, to his brother's house. The kitchen lights were on, but Falk could see no movement inside. Still, Raco's voice dropped a notch. 'The fact is – and Dwyer knows this – all the alibis are pretty good. For everyone in Kim's circle.'

'You've checked them out?' Falk said and glanced at Rita, who raised her eyebrows a fraction over the rim of her glass. This was not news to her.

'Yeah, look, don't shout it around the dinner table or anything,' Raco said. 'But yes, of course. And not because I don't trust my own friends and family. Because I do. But Kim was family as well. And there are always going to be questions around something like this, so I'd rather know what we were all dealing with than get a surprise.'

Falk nodded. He could see a shadow in the windows now. Zara maybe. 'So the movements on the night are good?'

'Yeah,' Raco said. 'Not perfect, but when are they ever? Most people were on the festival site all night, seen multiple times by one or more people. When it comes down to it, I've heard a lot worse. You would've too.'

'Who are we talking about?' Falk said. 'Charlie? Shane?'

'Yep.' Raco's voice was very quiet now. 'Rohan, obviously, although we know where he went. Naomi. Gemma. Zara, I guess, if we're being really thorough. Us –' He waved a glass towards himself and Rita. 'You, technically.'

'Good enough to rule them out?'

'In the real world, yes.' Raco nodded. 'And I say that as someone who cared about Kim. But yes. There are gaps of a few minutes here and there, but we're talking short. Not hours, not even half-hours. No-one left the site alone, except Naomi, and Zara and Joel both saw her heading home. Shane drove back here to the vineyard a bit before 9 pm to grab another couple of crates. But he's on CCTV leaving via the main exit, and he passed one of Charlie's seasonal workers on the way back. Stopped to give her a lift the rest of the way to the festival and was back at the stall quick enough. Time frame's reasonable.'

Falk nodded. That was useful to know, at least. If Raco was satisfied he'd checked things out, then he'd checked them out.

'But –' Falk glanced at the guesthouse door and pictured the folder of Raco's notes sitting on the bedside table, thick and meticulous. 'You do think something's wrong.' It was a statement rather than a question.

'Well. Not exactly.' Raco hesitated. 'Look, it's nothing solid. But it's the baby for me. Kim leaving Zoe alone like that. I think about our two –' He and Rita both instinctively turned towards the house where Eva and Henry were sleeping. 'And I cannot imagine Kim doing that. I just can't. There were so many people around who she knew and trusted, why not leave Zoe with someone? She could have made any excuse – anything at all – and handed over the baby and walked away, but at least then she would have known Zoe was safe. And, okay –'

He glanced at Rita, and Falk could tell they'd had this conversation before. 'I know people do things that are out of character when they're struggling. I get that. But that was seriously out of character for her. So much so.'

'Right.' Falk looked over to Rita. 'What do you think?'

Rita reached across and took her husband's hand. A silent, private warmth passed between them. 'Honestly, I think mental health can be complicated. I'm not sure it helps to judge what Kim did that night against the woman we knew.'

Raco squeezed her hand. 'Look, you're probably right.' He sighed. 'It's just when I think about Kim, I can't believe this was – I dunno – her *ending*. Something this bloody sad and lonely. She deserved a happy life. Better than this, anyway.'

They fell silent and Falk could hear the breeze whisper through the vines.

'Maybe there is something else, though,' he said finally. 'Joel's sticking to his guns about Kim not leaving the festival by that exit.'

'She did, mate.'

'But there are other ways to get to the reservoir, he's right about that –'

'It doesn't work –'

'But if she went another way then it opens up –'

'No. Mate –' Raco stopped him. Not annoyed, simply exhausted. 'I get what you're saying. But Kim left that way. She had to.'

He stifled an enormous yawn and Rita stood, resting her fingers lightly on Falk's shoulder and then her husband's as she reached to gather the glasses. *Enough for now.*

'Let's call it a night,' Raco said. 'But I'll show you tomorrow.'

'Yeah.' Falk nodded. 'Okay, mate.'

They said good night, Rita stretching up to give him a soft kiss on the cheek, and Falk let himself into the guesthouse. He turned on the lights and sat on the bed, alone, then got up again, rummaging through his bag until he found his work diary. He sat down once more and opened it. He ignored the meetings and reminders clamouring for his attention and instead turned the pages slowly, one by one, looking through the entire year for a three-day weekend when he was completely free. He checked all fifty-two weeks and couldn't find a single one.

Chapter 21

The good folks of the Marralee Valley were not the types to waste a sunny Saturday morning, and the festival grounds were as busy as Falk had ever seen them. He'd left Raco and Rita in the vineyard driveway, packing the kids into their car, and walked to the site rather than squeeze between the child seats. He'd followed the main route, approaching the festival via the car park rather than the reservoir, and had still beaten them there. From a shady spot near the entrance he watched the Racos approach, Henry complaining bitterly from the pram as Eva swung from her dad's hand.

'Listen, I can wrangle them both if you want.' Rita nodded to the kids as they all met outside the gate. 'Just not for too long.'

'I wouldn't do that to you, my love.' Raco smiled and gave Rita a kiss. 'All right, Eva. Say bye to Mum. She and Henry are going to check out the baby rides while you and me and Aaron do some investigating.'

'*Really?*' Eva's face was instantly alert and serious. 'What are we looking for?'

Raco put his hands on his knees so their eyes were level. 'Ways to get in and out of here.'

Eva frowned, then pointed to the main entrance beside them, a bottleneck already forming. 'That's easy. There are lots of ways.'

'Well,' Raco said mildly. 'We'll see.'

He straightened and together they walked over to join the crowd waiting to get inside. Henry's pram saw him and Rita waved breezily through the side gate, while Falk, Raco and Eva stood in the line for the turnstiles.

'So, the entrance is always staffed,' Raco said to Falk as they shuffled forward, and they both looked over to the workers in festival t-shirts on either side of the queues. 'They keep an eye on the numbers coming in, open the side gate. Watch for potential troublemakers as well, so they can get security involved if they need to.'

Raco took Eva's hand as they passed through the turnstiles and rummaged in his pocket for some cash for the charity collectors inside the gates. Falk did the same, pulling out a handful of coins and dropping them in the nearest collection tin.

'Thanks, mate.'

Falk stopped and looked up at the familiar voice. Even then, it took him a moment to recognise the speaker. Sergeant Dwyer seemed a different man out of uniform. He was dressed in jeans and a checked shirt, collecting alongside a kind-faced woman who Falk guessed from their body language must be Dwyer's wife.

'G'day, Eva. Gentlemen.' Dwyer nodded at the three of them, smiling as he held out the tin for another passer-by to drop in a donation. 'Appreciated, thank you.'

Falk looked past him to the sign propped up nearby. Each

day had seen a different charity on the gate and this wasn't one he was hugely familiar with. He recognised the logo and branding, though. A support network for families of those with alcohol abuse issues.

'This is my wife, Cathy, by the way.' Dwyer nodded to the woman waiting patiently for Eva to painstakingly deposit Raco's coins into her tin one at a time.

'Hello.' Cathy looked over and smiled. She had a badge pinned to her shirt showing a photo of a young woman captured in a spontaneous glance. A surprised, amused look lit up her eyes, but for just a moment, her frozen long-gone gaze reminded Falk a little of Kim Gillespie. The similarity ended there, though; this woman was years younger, with fair hair framing her face. *Caitlin Dwyer*, he read, above the charity's logo and dates of both her birth and her death. What had Raco said about her? Falk thought back. Choked on her own vomit after a party the previous year. According to her mother's badge, Caitlin had been just twenty-two.

'I'm very sorry about your daughter.' Falk turned back to the sergeant.

'Thank you.' Dwyer's reply was steady but there was something deep and sad behind his eyes. 'Doesn't get much easier, but we try and make a point of talking about it. Not a popular topic this time of year –' His eyes followed a couple clinking past with a large case of wine bottles, their young children trailing in their wake. 'But a community like this, there's a drinking culture built in and youth alcohol issues don't get much attention. People think it's just kids being kids but some of them –' His eyes slid to his wife's badge then quickly away. 'They can't handle it. Oh, great, thank you.' He held out his tin as another passer-by reached over.

'All right,' Raco said as Eva finally dropped in her last fifty-cent piece. 'Well, good to see you, Rob, Cathy. We'll let you get on.'

'Thank you for the money, sweetheart,' Cathy said to Eva. 'Here, let me give you a sticker. Enjoy the rides.'

'We're not going on rides,' Eva announced. 'We're investigating the exits.'

Dwyer's mouth twitched into a half-smile. 'That right, Eva?' He spoke to the girl, but his eyes flicked to Raco's for a measured beat. 'Well, that sounds very interesting. Make sure you let me know what you find out, won't you?'

Falk watched as Dwyer and Raco held each other's gaze a moment longer, then Raco inclined his head. Understood. One cop to another.

'Well, that sounds like our cue,' Raco said as a large group clicked through the turnstiles and Cathy held out her tin hopefully. 'Let's keep moving.'

Raco rolled his eyes good-naturedly as they walked away, but didn't seem too put out.

'Bloody Dwyer. It's quite hard to stay annoyed with him, though.'

'Sad about his daughter.' Falk glanced back. Cathy was shaking her tin again. 'Not surprising he's not a fan of the opening night party, I suppose.'

'No. He'll have that shut right down within a few years, I reckon. Cathy told Rita once they think it's where Caitlin learned to drink, and they're probably right. Although, from what I hear, she picked it up pretty fast anyway.'

'Gave them a bit of trouble, did she?'

'Yeah, a lot of heartache.' Raco's eyes dropped to the charity sticker on his own daughter's t-shirt. 'Still does, I guess. But that's the thing about Dwyer, he knows how it feels for families to lose someone. The pain's real for him. And I get that Zara's frustrated, but you can't accuse him of not taking Kim's disappearance seriously. Okay –' He slowed. 'Let's stop here for a second.'

Raco indicated a small gap between stalls. It was off the track, but they could still see the entrance clearly. Falk thought he could sense Dwyer watching them, but when he looked over, the officer was focused on a new group coming through the turnstiles.

'So, for the sake of argument,' Raco said, tucking Eva in beside him, 'if Kim didn't go through that back east exit, she had to leave some other way.' He pointed to the crowds streaming in. 'But I've never thought going out the entrance was a realistic option.'

Falk observed for a minute, watching the strong one-way flow of traffic, the staff monitoring the situation on either side of the gate. Anyone trying to push the wrong way through the tide of prams, scooters, wheelchairs, families linking arms and strolling couples would surely be noticed.

'I reckon you're right,' he said finally. 'Someone would remember.' He looked up at the CCTV camera installed on a temporary pole. 'That's one of the new ones?'

'This year. Yeah. No camera then.'

Falk nodded and turned back to the entrance. Both sides were flanked by stalls packed tight together, selling impulse items to get people in the spending mood, small handmade soaps, ice-cream. Behind the stalls, a two-metre-high chain-link fence formed a snug barrier.

'What do you think, Eva?' Raco said lightly to his daughter. 'Would you try and get out this way?'

'No.' The girl frowned, like it was obvious. 'I'd go out the exit.'

Raco's smile moved from her to Falk. 'Me too. So let's check that out.'

Falk and Eva followed him through the crowds along a short loop of track, past more rows of stalls. A painted sign saying *RIDES* directed people deeper into the festival grounds, and below it another marked *EXIT* pointed the other way.

Falk glanced to the right and caught a glimpse of the Penvale Vineyard stand. Shane was there, he could see, the man's height putting him half a head above the crowd. He was with a casual worker Falk didn't recognise and they looked to be doing a brisk trade. A stack of Kim's fliers was in a prominent position on the table and as Falk watched, a woman took a flier, glanced over it, then went to put it back. Shane motioned for her to keep it, but she smiled and shook her head, reaching instead for a bottle of red and turning it over to read the price. They disappeared from sight as the crowd shifted around them and Falk walked on.

It only took a minute to reach the large west exit, quiet at that time of day, and they again tucked into a spot just off the path. Falk had been through the exit several times now, but tried to look at it again with fresh eyes. While the entrance had been closely controlled, the west exit was wide open. No turnstiles here, simply a tall wooden archway over the broad track, leading out to a sea of cars glinting in the morning sun.

'They've got to make it easy for large numbers to get out quickly if needed. Same reason they've got the east exit at the back, for overflow.' Raco nodded towards a security guard sitting on a stool at the side. 'There are two guards in the evenings, same as last year. Alert the cops to any obvious drink drivers, anyone who's overdone it and looks like they might cause trouble on the way home.'

Falk glanced upwards. There had been one CCTV camera on the exit last year, he knew, but he could see at least two more now.

'Kim didn't come out this way,' Raco said. 'That's a one hundred per cent guarantee.'

'You watched the footage?' Falk asked.

'Yep. Six hours' worth.'

'The recording was complete? No edits?'

Raco shook his head. 'Time stamped. All looks right. It's legit.'

Falk frowned. 'And no sign of her at all?'

'None. I mean, there's a bit to get through and there are a lot of people, but the footage is clear. Good quality. If you take your time, you can see the faces. Dwyer's watched it too, obviously. Charlie as well. And Zara. A few times, I think. If Kim had come this way, one of us would have spotted her.'

'Okay,' Falk said. 'So she didn't come out this way.'

'No,' said Raco. 'Unless you're seeing something I'm not.' He looked down at Eva, who was busy gathering long stalks of grass into a makeshift bouquet. 'Or you, mate.'

Eva just smiled benignly, but Falk shook his head. He stepped up to the exit and ran a hand over the chain-link fence bordering it.

'Can we follow this the whole way around?'

Raco nodded. 'We can try.'

It wasn't easy, though, Falk realised quickly. The fence ran close to the back of the stalls, which were in turn packed deliberately close to discourage casual visitors from wandering behind and messing with supplies or the electrical wires that snaked across the ground.

They picked their way along in single file, Eva between them, and Falk stopping every now and again to examine the mechanism joining the fence links. The boundary may have only been temporary but it was sturdy, slotting together smoothly. As they made their way through, stallholders popping back to grab fresh stock or snatch a breath of air threw them curious looks.

Eventually, they emerged from the back of the tents and Falk felt the relief of stepping out into the open again. He blinked, the sudden daylight harsh after the shade from the canopies. Up ahead, he could see the east exit, the rope slung across it as always. The first-aid stand nearby was currently staffed by a woman in a wide-brimmed hat.

Falk looked back up along the fence they'd just followed. At two metres, it was reasonably high all the way around.

'I guess theoretically it's possible Kim felt up to scaling a fence six weeks after giving birth.' Raco read his thoughts. 'But I know Rita couldn't have.'

'No, I think you're right,' Falk said. 'Not even the physical factor, but with all those stallholders coming and going. They'd have noticed her doing something like that. Plus some of them must have known her.'

Raco nodded. 'It's exactly the same down the other side.' He squinted, pointing a finger to where the fence picked up again on the other side of the exit and continued around the grounds.

'Maybe there was a gap?' Falk said. 'She could have slipped through?'

Raco shook his head. 'I checked.'

'Last year?' Falk was surprised.

'Yeah, walked the whole route the next day. Like we did just then.'

'I don't remember that.'

'You were at the station giving your statement,' Raco said. 'I probably didn't mention it because, I dunno, it seemed a bit paranoid. Especially because there was nothing to see. The fence was complete, same as now.'

'Right.' Falk's eyes ran along the boundary, settling inevitably on the only gap. The first-aid volunteer near the east exit had her head buried in a novel.

'Joel's a good kid,' Raco said. 'Serious, conscientious, for sure. But he is still a kid.'

'Yeah.' Was the word of a teenager stronger than a solid chain-link fence? Falk wondered. Probably not, no matter who it was.

Eva sighed dramatically, hot and losing patience. 'Can we stop investigating and go on a ride now?'

'What do you reckon?' Raco said to Falk, who nodded.

'Yeah, Eva. Let's go,' he said. 'I think I've seen what I needed to see. Thanks for your help, mate.'

'No worries,' she said, skipping ahead a little as they turned away from the exit. They headed back into the heart of the site, the music and laughter growing louder as they neared the rides. Falk glanced over at Raco, keeping his voice too low for Eva to hear.

'What about cars? Ones with on-site access. Could someone have driven her out, maybe hidden in the back seat or boot? A few hours later, when it was quiet?'

'There's access through the main exit, but it's only for emergencies during festival hours,' Raco said. 'I checked with

Gemma last year and she says no vehicles entered the grounds at all during the actual festival that night, and there would've been almost none moving about. Too many pedestrians and kids to do it safely. Vehicles could technically have driven in later, but it would've probably been after Kim was discovered missing. In which case, where was she during the initial search of the site?' He gave a shrug. 'I'm not saying it couldn't have happened, but it wouldn't have been easy.'

Falk walked on for a minute, running scenarios in his mind. 'Doesn't really feel right, either,' he said at last. 'How would it work? Drag her into a vehicle, even with people around?'

'It's easiest if she'd got in willingly.' Raco's voice had dropped so low it was hard to hear. 'But that raises a whole lot of other questions. I mean, whose vehicle? And does that mean it was a mentally sound decision? Because if so, why not also decide to leave Zoe with someone she trusted?'

Falk thought about that. He pictured Kim, with her new baby tucked up in her pram, and tried to play it out in his head. His eyes fell on Eva, running in front of them, and something dark slowly crept into his thoughts.

'There'd be one easy way to make Kim get into a car. Or to hide somewhere. Do anything really,' Falk murmured. He nodded at Raco's daughter. 'Threaten her child.'

Raco blinked. Long and slow, his face instantly tight. He didn't respond, but his eyes locked on Eva as she picked up pace and ran a few steps ahead.

'Eva!' Raco's voice was unusually sharp and she turned, hurt.

'What? I can see Mummy.'

'Oh.' Sure enough, a little further up the path stood Rita. She was holding Henry against her chest, her hair falling down

229

her back as they both craned their necks up. The little boy lifted a chubby hand to the sky, marvelling at the ferris wheel creaking and clanging above them.

'Wow, can we go on *that*?' Eva called, running towards her mother, who broke into a smile as she saw Raco and Falk following.

'How did you go?' she asked.

'As expected,' Raco said, and Falk nodded. They came to a stop on the path by Rita, and Falk looked up himself.

'Whereabouts was her carriage?' he heard Raco ask quietly, and Falk pointed.

'Right near the top. Around where that one is, or the one next to it.'

Raco tilted his head back and shielded his eyes. Falk watched the top carriages move and thought, yet again, about those few seconds a whole year earlier. He tried to slow the scene down, freeze it in his mind to examine it more closely.

What had he seen? There had been the pram bay, near the base of the ride, where Zoe Gillespie would be found alone two and a half hours later. The path ahead. Gemma had been there, of course, talking to Naomi – the whole reason Falk had stopped walking at all. He'd seen Rohan too, underneath the ride, talking to those Queensland tourists before looking up. Falk gazed up at those carriages now and wished – not for the first time – that he had focused a little longer when it had mattered. If he'd been less distracted, would he have seen something that would have made a difference? Any clue as to what had been going through Kim Gillespie's mind, in those final few hours?

'*Dad.*' Eva was pulling at Raco's hand. 'Can we please go on this one?'

Raco was still squinting up, his face hard to read. He nodded slowly. 'Yeah, Eva. Let's go on this one.'

They bought three tickets and joined the queue, waiting among couples and families until the attendant directed them into a carriage of their own. Falk sat on one side and Eva and Raco on the other as the attendant locked the door behind them, enclosing them safely in the capsule. The wheel started to turn and Eva shifted in her seat, making the carriage sway gently as she pressed her face to the vertical safety bars.

'Here we go,' she called as they lifted into the air.

Falk leaned against the bars himself, watching the view change as they glided upwards. They were nearly at the top when the ride slowed and shuddered to a halt to let people on and off below. Not far from where Kim's and Zoe's carriage had been, Falk guessed, when he'd seen Rohan wave from the ground.

Had Kim hesitated at all before waving back? Falk really couldn't be sure. But gazing down, he could understand why she might have. It felt even higher up here than it appeared from below. The people seemed small and much further away than he'd expected. Falk could believe it might take a moment to notice what was going on.

And there was a lot going on, he realised. Turning in his seat, Falk could see right across the festival grounds. All the way, from the main entrance to – he twisted in the other direction – the distant white flash of the first-aid station tent visible near the back exit. Beyond that lay bushland and the reservoir.

'I can see *Mummy* and I can see *Henry*.' Eva pointed them out in turn, then thrust her arm through the bars and waved. On the ground, a handful of people waved back. 'Daddy, look.'

She tugged at Raco's sleeve with her free hand. 'You're not even looking.'

'Sorry,' Raco said, with a cursory glance down.

Eva had been right, Falk saw, Raco hadn't been looking at his family. Instead, he'd been doing exactly the same as Falk. Running his own gaze right across the wide, expansive view beneath them.

Falk didn't need to ask why. A year earlier and a couple of dozen metres lower at ground level, Falk might not have been able to make out much at all. But from this height . . . his eyes met Raco's over the top of Eva's head. They were thinking the same thing, he could tell immediately.

Up here, from the vantage point of this bird's-eye view, Kim would have been able to see everything that was going on below.

Chapter 22

Falk left Raco and Rita once again battling with the kids' car seats and walked back to the vineyard alone, thinking hard. He beat them this time, too, and was about to let himself into the guesthouse when he heard his name being called.

'Aaron. G'day. Do me a favour and come and try this, mate.' Charlie appeared in the doorway of the large barn. He had a bottle of red in his hand and was holding it up to the light, frowning slightly.

Falk walked over. The barn had been closed since he arrived, but he followed Charlie inside now to find a large cool space with high ceilings and exposed beams. Wide shutters lay open to let in both the breeze and the glorious view of the vineyard stretching out beyond. The concrete floor looked recently swept and the place smelled clean and fresh. Someone – Charlie, presumably – had started to set out trestle tables and chairs.

Falk could see another man rummaging in a storage cupboard across the room. Rohan, he realised as the bloke straightened and stepped out, brushing dust from a barbecue gas canister. At the far end of the barn, Zara was sitting cross-legged in a patch of sunlight, blowing bubbles for Zoe. Naomi was there too, a forgotten stack of silverware half organised on a table in front of her as she sat absorbed by the sight of the one-year-old stretching up her soft little arms to the bubbles floating in the air.

'Great space,' Falk said as Charlie handed him a glass with a splash of wine in it.

'Thanks. We hire it out for weddings sometimes. Getting it ready for tomorrow.'

'This is for the christening?'

'Yeah, well, afterwards at least.' Charlie grinned and nodded at the wine in Falk's hand. 'Anyway, have a taste of that. Rohan?' He beckoned, holding up the bottle. 'It's last year's grenache. Thinking about opening some for tomorrow.'

'Oh yeah? G'day.' Rohan nodded to Falk as he came over. He accepted a glass, examining the liquid before taking a sip. 'I won't have any more, I'm driving. But yeah, good. Tannins are nice and smooth.'

'I thought so too.'

'Definitely. Come up well, mate.'

'What do you reckon?' Charlie turned to Falk, who took a swallow. He had never been a big drinker and, although he didn't tend to admit it out loud, usually chose wine based on price and what fell at eye level on the shelf. He focused now on the inside of his mouth. The wine was . . . *nice*. Think of another word. *Red* came to mind. Charlie was watching for his reaction, genuinely interested, and Falk felt under pressure.

'It's –' He took another sip. '– fruity?' he tried.

'Really?' Charlie frowned at the bottle. 'It's supposed to be at the slightly lighter end.'

Falk smiled. 'That's probably what I meant then.'

Charlie grinned at that. 'All right. Just tell me this, do you like it?'

'Yeah,' Falk said honestly. 'I do.'

'Great. That's all I really need to know,' Charlie said, reaching for a fresh glass as Naomi wandered over. He poured a taste for her without needing to ask and their hands brushed as she took it. Across the room, Falk saw Zara watching.

Naomi took a sip as she turned to Falk. 'Hello, good to see you again.' Her voice was warm and she stretched up and kissed him lightly on the cheek, then looked past him to the door. 'Is Henry back too?'

'On their way. Shouldn't be long.'

'I hope so.' She glanced at her watch. 'I'll have to head off soon. Just wanted to see the little man himself ahead of tomorrow.'

Zara's eyes slid from Naomi to her father and back again, then down to the tube of bubble mixture in her hand. Naomi drained her glass and placed it on a nearby trestle table.

'That's a nice one, Charlie.'

'Thanks, I'm pretty happy with it. Good to get another opinion, though. Shane's no help, now he's completely off the booze.'

'Still?' Rohan seemed both surprised and impressed. 'That's great. Not at all?'

'No. Been a few years now,' Charlie said, and Naomi nodded.

'Well,' Rohan said. 'Good on him. Goes to show.' He put down his own glass, then stepped over to a nearby stack of chairs and lifted off the top two. 'We're placing these along here, mate?'

'Yeah, great.' Charlie moved their empty glasses out of the way, and turned to Falk. 'And listen, I've been meaning to say, thanks for helping Shane out the other day. He said you showed him a short cut with the invoices or something.'

'No worries, it was no trouble.' As Falk went to grab a couple of chairs himself, he noticed a small bottle of paint thinner among a box of supplies. He thought for a moment, then picked it up. 'Hey, can I use some of this?'

'Sure.' Charlie waved a hand. 'Help yourself to anything.'

'Thanks,' Falk said. 'And it was easy. Showing Shane. He got it straight away.'

'Of course he did.' Naomi looked up from her phone at that, fixing her gaze pointedly on Charlie. 'He's a smart guy. He just hates that accountant you're using.'

'He doesn't *hate* him.'

'He does, Charlie. Open your eyes. That's why he's so stressed lately. He's constantly worrying about stuffing things up.'

'Shane's fine.'

'No, Charlie. I'm not sure he is.' Naomi's brow creased. 'Not about this.'

'Okay, but that's dealing with accountants for you. It's no-one's favourite part of the job, is it? Shane used to tie himself in knots getting the paperwork ready for Dean as well.'

'Not in the same way.'

'Yeah, Naomi, pretty much in the same way. Dean was always having to chase him for stuff. It caused issues then, it's causing issues now.' Charlie was sounding a little stressed himself. 'Look, Shane's got a lot of strengths, and okay, this isn't one of them, but it still needs to get done, doesn't it?'

'Well, whatever, Charlie. It's your business. I'm just saying, he's not happy.' Naomi checked the time again. 'Anyway, I'd love to hang around all day and help you boys set up, but I've got to get back to the clinic.'

'Have there been any updates on Dean, by the way?' Rohan asked quietly as he lifted a chair down from the stack, and Naomi paused. 'Every time I talk to Rob Dwyer these days it's about Kim and I forget to ask.'

'Not as far as I've heard,' Naomi said, and beside her Charlie was also shaking his head.

'I think technically they're still looking for the blue car,' he said. 'But it's been – how long now? Six years. Doesn't feel like anyone's holding their breath.'

'Bullshit, isn't it?' Rohan put down the chair with a clatter and rubbed his eyes with his finger and thumb. His voice had changed, and taken on a hard edge. 'Dwyer's a joke.'

Naomi hesitated. 'I suppose –' she started, but Rohan shook his head.

'He is.'

The barn swallowed up noise, but Falk saw Charlie glance towards Zara and Zoe. They were still chasing the bubbles, and didn't seem to have heard.

Rohan exhaled, deep and heavy. 'Sorry.' He took a breath in, then cleared his throat. His voice sounded closer to normal. 'Sorry.'

'No, Rohan, we get it.' Naomi put a hand on his back. 'We –'

They looked up at the sound of a car crunching to a stop on the drive. A moment later a door slammed and Henry's babble floated in through the open barn door.

'That sounds like your godson.' Rohan smiled at Naomi. 'Thanks. I'm fine. Go and say hello.'

Naomi just looked at him, then put her arms up and drew him into a long hug. Charlie turned back to the chairs, his face hard to read.

237

'I know it's difficult,' Naomi said as she pulled away. 'We all feel the same.'

Rohan nodded and she gave his hand a final squeeze, before walking over to greet Rita at the door and scoop Henry up into her arms. Eva weaved past her mother's legs, making a beeline for the bubbles. Outside, a car lock beeped and a moment later Raco appeared.

He headed over, waving an arm at the work they'd done around the barn. 'Wow, this is looking very –'

'What's wrong?' Charlie cut him off immediately. He put the chair he was holding down with a sharp tap against the floor, and frowned at his brother.

If Raco had a professional fault, Falk thought, it was his lack of a poker face. The guy wore his emotions all over him. Despite his smile, it was as clear as day that he was still thinking about their discussions at the festival.

'Nothing's wrong.' Raco glanced at Falk, who'd had a few more years to perfect the art of inscrutable neutrality, then at the other two men. 'Why –?'

'Has something happened? You've been at the site, right?' Rohan was already reaching for his phone. 'Has something come from the appeal?'

'No.' Raco shook his head firmly. 'Look, no, mate. I'm sorry. If there was anything, we'd hear from Dwyer.'

Rohan's face tightened at the mention of the sergeant. 'Yeah, I suppose,' he said, as he breathed out slowly and put his phone away. His eyes found his daughter and rested there for a long minute. Eva was encouraging Zoe to chase the bubbles now, holding out her hands to help the little girl balance. Finally, Rohan frowned and turned back.

'Hey, has Dwyer asked any of you to go over your statements

from the night?' He blinked as Charlie shook his head, then looked to Raco and Falk. 'No? What about Shane? Naomi?' Rohan glanced to the barn door where Naomi was still talking to Rita.

'I don't think so,' Charlie said. 'Not that I've heard.'

Rohan gave an odd reflexive laugh. 'Just me, then.'

There was a silence.

'He can ask the rest of us anytime, though,' Charlie said. 'We're always around.'

Rohan didn't look convinced. 'I suppose so.'

'Can I ask what he wanted to check?' Raco said.

'Mainly things I thought we'd already gone over,' Rohan said. 'A few times. Like, why didn't Kim and Zoe come to dinner with me and my parents?'

'And what did you say?'

'The same.' Rohan watched the girls playing and lowered his voice. 'That Kim and my mum didn't always see eye to eye. I mean, nothing serious, they got along okay. But Kim wasn't keen on dinner with them, not on the first night. Which was fine, because it wasn't really a social thing anyway. I wanted to talk to my dad about the tests he'd been having. Recovery, care implications, stuff that's a lot easier in person and without a baby dominating things.' He shook his head. 'But Kim could have come. Of course she could have, she was my wife. She was the one who said she didn't want to.'

Raco nodded. 'Maybe –'

'I should have questioned it,' Rohan cut across him suddenly, as though Raco hadn't spoken. 'I didn't, though, did I? Because it was easier for me if she and Zoe weren't there. But I should have.' He pulled a hand down his face. 'Jesus. Kim always held her cards so bloody close to her chest.'

Charlie made a soft noise in his throat and Rohan looked up sharply.

'You don't agree, mate?' His voice had barely changed, but somewhere in there, Falk heard a blade-fine edge.

'No, I do, actually.' Charlie's voice too had the faintest undercurrent. He pushed a chair in and it scraped against the concrete floor. 'Of course I do. We've all learned stuff about Kim over the past year.'

'Like what?' Rohan was watching him closely now.

'Mate. You know what.' Charlie didn't meet his eye. 'Like why she completely avoided the reservoir for the best part of twenty years.'

Rohan's face went still for a moment, as though processing. Confusion crumpled into a frown. 'What are you talking about?'

'Jesus, Rohan. Come on.'

'You mean –?' The man looked genuinely lost. 'What Naomi said? About what happened at the opening night party back at school?'

'Yeah, of course.' Charlie glanced towards their daughters, and dropped his voice. 'And don't pretend Kim had told you about it either, because I bet she hadn't.'

'No, but –' Rohan was still staring at Charlie. 'But – sorry. What do you mean she *avoided* the reservoir?'

It was Charlie's turn to stare. 'I mean exactly that. Kim never went down there. Ever, really. She didn't make a big deal of it, just always had some excuse. The weather, or other plans, or she wanted to go the long way. Stuff like that.'

'But she lived here for years.' Rohan sounded incredulous. 'Everyone goes down there.'

'Before the night of that party?' Charlie said. 'Yeah, then.

But not after. I can't think of a single time. I mean, did she go down there with you?'

There was a silence, and Falk could almost see the memories flickering behind Rohan's eyes.

'No. But we didn't live around here when we were together,' Rohan said at last. He looked disturbed. 'Have you told the police?'

'Yeah, of course. I told Dwyer at the time that Kim must have been in a seriously bad state to –' Charlie concentrated for a long moment on straightening a chair. Cleared his throat. '– do what she did, because normally she never went near the reservoir.'

Rohan stood very still, his eyes fixed on Charlie. 'I really wasn't aware that she didn't like to go there.' They all heard the soft note of disbelief.

'Well.' Charlie shrugged. He pulled another chair down and the stack rattled. 'Maybe I'm wrong. You were married to her. You would know.'

There was a silence. The two men looked at each other, then Rohan shook his head just once, a tight, frustrated movement.

'Zoe?' He raised his chin and called across the barn. 'Time to go, sweetheart. Oh, great, thanks,' he said as Zara carried the toddler over and passed her into his arms. Both girls seemed to pick up on the atmosphere instantly.

Zara glanced at her dad. 'What's going on?'

'Nothing,' Charlie and Rohan said at the same time, and Rohan hoisted his daughter higher on his hip. 'Listen, thanks for playing with her, Zara. It's nice for her to get to see you.' He raised a hand, managing to take in everyone but Charlie. 'Right, we'll catch you all tomorrow.'

Charlie didn't say anything. He leaned against a table and watched as they walked away. At the barn door, though, Rohan suddenly seemed to hesitate. He squinted towards the sunlight, then back again, as if silently arguing with himself.

'Forget something, mate?' Charlie's voice was light and strange, and he gently shook Raco's hand off his elbow.

Rohan stood for a moment longer, then shifted Zoe to his other arm, and walked back towards them. He stopped a few paces short of where he'd been standing.

'Didn't go down there for nearly *twenty years*.' Rohan let the words hang in the air. 'I mean, did you ever ask her *why*?'

There was a long silence. Charlie didn't move, but something complicated shifted behind his eyes even as his face went slack, and his gaze fell to the ground.

Rohan seemed strongly tempted to say more, but kept his mouth pressed shut in a hard, thin line. He looked sad rather than surprised, Falk thought as the man turn to leave, while Charlie just sighed and pushed a chair under the table like nothing had happened. More than sad, in fact. To Falk, Rohan looked very much like a man who'd had something he'd long suspected finally confirmed.

Chapter 23

'Aaron? Wait!'

Falk was almost at the end of the vineyard drive when he heard the voice behind him. He turned. Zara was jogging towards him and he stopped until she caught up. The cottage beyond looked still and peaceful in the afternoon sun, but Falk was glad to be getting out for a bit. Once Rohan and Zoe had left, Charlie had muttered something about work and had been holed up in his office ever since. Raco had gone in at one point to talk to him but re-emerged quickly. He'd shrugged at Falk and shaken his head.

'He does this. Works through things on his own. He'll be right in a few hours.'

'Is that true, do you reckon?' Falk had wondered. 'That Kim avoided the reservoir?'

'I don't know. It's possible. Thinking back, I actually can't remember her down there myself, but that's not saying much.' Raco's eyes were on the closed office door. 'Charlie would know, to be fair.'

'If he is right,' Falk followed the train of thought, 'does that make it more or less likely Kim would go down there to end her life?'

He and Raco had stood side by side, watching the light filtering across the vines as they silently played out scenarios.

'I wish we had a sense of what she was thinking then,' Raco had said finally. 'Like with the view from the top of the ferris wheel. Say she did spot something she wasn't supposed to, or something that upset her –' Raco stared out unseeing at the rolling valley and the huge sky. He shook his head. 'I don't know. I can't get past this feeling that we're missing something.'

Falk felt it too. A translucent shimmer of a thought hovering in the distance, dissolving and reappearing without warning. He'd tried to grasp it. There was nothing to hold on to. 'I'm not sure what.'

'Me neither.' Raco had glanced back at the house as a child's irritated squawk pierced the air, and breathed out a heavy sigh. 'For God's sake. I'd better give Rita a hand.'

Falk had watched him head off, then let himself into his guesthouse. At something of a loose end, he'd sat and stared at his closed work laptop for several minutes, then instead picked up the bottle of paint thinner he'd found in Charlie's barn. He'd dug around in the cupboard under the sink, emerging with a handful of cleaning cloths, and headed out into the afternoon.

'Thanks,' Zara said now, as she caught up to him, a little breathless. She pointed to the bottle of paint thinner under his arm. 'Are you going to the Drop? To wipe off the graffiti?'

'Yeah, thought I'd see if this stuff worked.'

'It does,' she said. 'We've used it before. I'll call Joel, tell him to meet us.'

'He doesn't have to,' Falk said. 'I just wanted to stretch my legs. He's probably got better ways to spend his Saturday.'

'He probably doesn't. Anyway, he'll want to.' Zara finished texting and put her phone away. They walked together in companionable silence, taking the back route past the park and the oval. No Shane today; instead a group of young girls were chasing around after each other, scrambling for the footy.

'Hey, what were my dad and Rohan arguing about before?' Zara said as they reached the reservoir turn-off, the gate still closed and locked. She seemed subdued as she stepped off the main track and around the barrier.

Falk considered what to say. Honesty usually worked. 'It was about your mum.'

'Obviously. But what specifically?'

'I think in essence it came down to who was closer to her.'

'Oh.' Zara sounded fed up. 'I wish Dad wouldn't do stupid stuff like that, trying to get one over Rohan. He can't seem to stop, though. I think because he still loved her.'

'Yeah?' Falk looked over.

'Yeah. She'd moved on, but he hadn't really. Not in the same way. He acted like he was fine with her and Rohan and they were all friends or whatever but –' She shook her head. 'After she got married, Mum had to tell him to back off in the end, because he was calling her too much, like they were still together.'

That was interesting, Falk thought. He wondered if Raco was aware. Probably.

'It's so awkward,' Zara said. 'Watching someone chase someone who's not interested in them.'

Was she also talking about Joel? Falk wondered. Along the track, he could make out a distant figure that he guessed was the boy on his way to meet them.

'Like Naomi,' Zara said, and Falk looked over, a little thrown by the change in direction.

'What about her?'

Zara frowned, incredulous. 'How she obviously likes my dad?'

'Do you think so?' Falk said, considering it. He had to admit, he did find Naomi's relationship with Charlie a little hard to define, but he hadn't quite got the sense of an unrequited romance there, either.

'Oh God, *yes*. I definitely think so. She's always coming around to the vineyard. Like, all the time. Making some excuse to stop by, dropping something off, arranging group drinks like they're all still eighteen or something.' Zara wrinkled her nose. 'It's weird. Especially as Naomi looks so good.' The teenager considered. 'For her age, at least.'

'And your dad's not interested?'

'I guess not.' Zara shrugged. They were nearly at the Drop now, and sure enough Falk could see Joel waiting, Luna at his feet. He raised a hand, his expression lifting as he saw them. After a second, Zara smiled and waved back. 'Otherwise something would happen between them, right?'

'Probably,' Falk said. 'That's usually how it goes. If both people feel the same way.'

Zara gave a small smile. 'Yeah. That's kind of the key, isn't it?' She raised her voice and called out to Joel. 'Your cleaning service has arrived.'

'Thanks,' Joel said as they got nearer, looking happy when he saw the paint thinner. 'Great, this is the brand we used last time. And listen, I can get this back to you later,' he said to Falk. 'You don't have to stay and do this.'

Falk wondered if that was a hint to leave him and Zara to it, but Joel seemed to mean what he said. And the late-afternoon sun was warm and the water was shining, and Falk was in no real rush to get back to the vineyard. He picked up one of the cloths. 'It's okay. Let's see this in action.'

Zara had been right, it was good stuff. She got out her phone and streamed some upbeat music Falk hadn't heard before while the three of them worked, the bushland rustling gently around them and the barrier growing clearer as they moved along. Not entirely clean, though, Falk noticed with irritation. The paint was simply too old, and the graffiti and dirt had soaked in over the years, leaving ugly grey marks and patches. Still, it was better. He could tell by the chatter and occasional ripple of laughter that Joel was pleased.

The sun was a little lower in the sky when Zara stretched, lifting her arms over her head. She relaxed back against the barrier and watched Falk for a minute. He could tell from the way she was tossing her cloth from one hand to the other that she was working up to saying something. He just waited.

'So, Aaron,' she said eventually. 'My uncle says you work in financial policing.'

'Yep.' Falk nodded.

'People get killed over that kind of stuff, right?'

He looked up at that. 'Money? Yeah. All the time. Why?'

Zara wasn't focused on him now, though. She was instead fixed on Joel, and the pair were conducting an intense silent conversation with their eyes. Something they'd discussed before, Falk could tell, from the way she was gesturing with tiny tilts of her head.

247

'Why?' Falk asked again.

Zara gave a single sharp nod this time. Joel looked vaguely mutinous, but sighed deep and long, then took a breath.

'So –' He seemed unsure where to start. 'Did you know my dad was an accountant?'

'Yeah.'

'Well.' He glanced at Zara, who communicated something forcefully with her eyebrows. 'Do you reckon it's possible his accident was deliberate rather than just an accident?'

It was always *possible*, Falk thought. Whether it was likely or not, he really didn't have enough information to guess. Joel's face was serious, though.

'What makes you say that, mate?'

The guy shrugged. 'Just been thinking.'

They looked at each other for a minute.

'Okay.' Falk rested against the barrier. He chose his words carefully. 'Well, let's walk through that. Your dad mainly did the accounts for a lot of people in town, right?' Joel nodded. 'So that would suggest he wasn't involved in anything illegal. Because if he was, it would've come out by now. Probably as soon as the next person took over the books.'

Joel looked a little relieved, which he hid by being instantly defensive. 'He absolutely wasn't like that –'

'No, mate, I'm not saying –'

'What if he *uncovered* something illegal, though?' Zara piped up. 'Through his work?'

That, thought Falk, was actually not impossible. But, still.

'Look, it does happen. But then whatever it was would have to be major enough to justify really extreme action.' Falk rested a hand near the memorial plaque. 'But also small enough that it hasn't come out another way in the past six years. So that narrows the options a bit.'

'Dad wouldn't have got himself involved in anything bad. He wasn't into anything like that. But he could be –' Joel hesitated. '– outspoken, I guess. He said what he thought. Not everyone likes that.'

'Okay.'

'Or maybe someone wanted to take over his business or –?'

'Did someone? Take it over?'

'No. After he died, it just closed.'

'Right.'

'But he used to walk Luna at pretty much the same time every day.' The dog raised her head at the sound of her name. 'So people knew he'd be here in the mornings.'

'Okay.'

Falk looked at Joel. He thought he understood what the boy was reaching for. A reason. There was something almost unbearably tragic in randomness. The thought of millions of minor inconsequential events cascading into a single moment.

'The thing is, Joel,' Falk said. 'If someone wanted to target your dad, this would be a pretty complicated way to do it. For starters, the outcome isn't –' What word to use? '– guaranteed, I guess. And I don't even do traffic, mate, but I can tell you it's hard to fake something to look like a genuine hit-and-run. It's not only the collision itself, there are angles of impact, tyre marks –'

As he was talking, Joel suddenly pulled out his phone. He started scrolling through, fast, then tapped the screen. He held it out silently. Falk looked down, taking a long moment to process what he was seeing. A video. Of the reservoir, the track, the barrier lying broken and splintered –

'Shit. This is the accident?' Falk blinked, blindsided. But yes, he could see that it was. The aftermath, more accurately. 'Where did you get this?'

'I took it myself. From up there.' Joel glanced at the bushland. The clearing was once again invisible to Falk.

'Does Sergeant Dwyer know you have this?' Falk looked up from the phone. 'Does Gemma?'

Joel nodded. 'Now they do, yeah. Not at the time, though. I was supposed to wait at home but –' He stopped and shrugged. 'I came here anyway. No-one would tell me what was going on.'

Falk took the boy's phone and after a moment, tapped his finger against the screen.

The video started playing but at first the image barely moved. The only change was in the way the light caught the gentle ripples on the water. The barrier had been violently wrenched from its holdings and what remained hung at a jarring angle. Part of the track was roughly marked off with police tape but there was no sign of life. Falk watched on, almost startled when a figure suddenly appeared at the edge of the screen.

Gemma.

Very slowly, she walked to the Drop. Her back was turned to the camera and her face hidden. She stopped where the barrier should have been, almost exactly where Falk himself stood now. Her hands hung loose by her sides as she stared down into the water. It was a very intimate moment, and Falk felt uncomfortable seeing it without her permission. He touched the screen and moved the video on. A full minute later, Gemma still hadn't moved.

Sergeant Dwyer had, though. He appeared initially in the corner of the screen, then worked his way steadily across the visible area. Falk watched as he carried out his silent work. Examining the posts, moving slowly from one side of the track to the other. He made a short phone call then, finally, he also stopped. Dwyer stood a few paces behind Gemma, his arms folded across his chest.

Falk paused the image. He couldn't see the sergeant's face at that angle, but his body language was clear. He was watching Gemma's reaction, Falk was certain. It wasn't an unreasonable response from the police officer, he knew. Necessary, even. But it still bothered him a little to see. He started the video again.

Dwyer must have asked Gemma to move back from the open gap because at last she turned. Her posture was rigid, a sense of shock radiating from her. Dwyer said something and, finally, she nodded and took a few hesitant steps and then a few more. The edge of the screen sliced through the path and she was gone.

Alone now, Dwyer walked over to the Drop himself and stood on the brink. His hand brushed against the smashed barrier and he withdrew it quickly, examining his palm for a moment. Then he leaned over and stared down into the water for a long beat. At last, he straightened, lifted his phone to his ear and stepped back onto the track. He walked a few paces and the camera lost him, too. The Drop was deserted. No-one appeared again, and the video ended.

Falk exhaled. He went to hand the phone back to Joel, then stopped. The final scene was still on the screen and he scrolled back to those last empty frames, pausing and pinching the images to enlarge them. He frowned. He felt like there was –

'What is it?' Zara said. She was watching him closely, Falk realised, and he shook his head.

'I don't know,' he said, truthfully.

But something did feel a bit – what? *Off.* Falk frowned. Did it? Or was it just a reaction to seeing footage so confronting? He scrolled back again, uncomfortably aware of the kids' scrutiny as the seconds ticked on. He could sense their hope building and shook his head. He wasn't going to do this to them.

'No. I'm sorry. It's nothing.' Even as he said it, he could almost believe it. On the screen he could clearly see the trademark signs of an accident. The skid in the dirt where the tyres had failed to grip. The vicious edge of the broken barrier.

He clicked the screen off and handed the phone back to Joel. The boy looked disappointed and Falk hesitated again. Because somewhere, buried deep beneath a dusty pile of long-unused basic police training skills, a faint alarm had been activated. Falk waited. The alarm continued, soft but insistent.

'Listen.' He spoke before he could stop himself again. 'It's hard to see detail in daylight.' He tapped his own phone and held it out. 'That's my number. Send me the video and I'll take a proper look later.'

'Yeah? Great.' Joel swiped at his own screen, and Zara gave Falk a small smile.

Thank you, she mouthed over the boy's bent head.

Falk nodded, still uneasy, and picked up his cloth. Zara joined him and together they gave the barrier in front of them a last going-over. They were nearly done, and Falk heard Joel's phone buzz in his hand.

'Oh. Sorry, it's just Gemma. I'll show her what we've –' Joel held out his phone and snapped a photo of a stretch of sparkling barrier. He tapped a few words, then lowered the phone, message sent. A minute passed, then two. Then the buzz of a reply. Joel ran his cloth over the last of the markings with one hand and checked the message with the other.

'So, Gemma's not working tonight and asks if you two want to come to the house for dinner?'

'Sure,' Zara said easily. 'What are we having?'

'Lasagne, I think.' Joel looked at Falk. 'You?'

He hesitated. 'She definitely means both of us?'

'Yeah.' Joel sounded surprised at the question. He held out the message. 'She said.'

Ask Zara and Aaron if they want to come back here for dinner. So she had.

'Great, I'm pretty hungry.' Zara was already tidying up the cleaning supplies. 'Come along,' she said as she reached out for Falk's cloth. 'Why not?'

Well. There were probably a couple of reasons, he thought. Maybe even good ones. But standing there in the early-evening sun with the invitation right there on screen, he was struggling to think of them.

'I'm letting my dad know.' Zara got her own phone out and glanced up, fingers poised. 'So, you're in?'

As if there had ever been any real doubt.

'Yeah.' Falk nodded. 'I'm in.'

Chapter 24

Falk couldn't be certain, but Gemma answered the door fast enough that it was distinctly possible she'd been waiting in the hallway.

'Oh.' Joel blinked as it swung open before he'd had the chance to turn his key in the lock. 'Hey. We're back.' He dumped his backpack beneath a gleaming side table. 'This looks nice and tidy.'

'No it doesn't,' Gemma said quickly.

The house was a low-slung white weatherboard cottage on a leafy block of land. Falk had followed Joel and Zara from the reservoir up through the bushland on an unmarked but well-worn trail. They'd emerged at the top onto a quiet paved road, much like the one outside the vineyard and followed it for a few minutes past driveways that each wound their way to a house set back among the trees. Falk had looked at them with curiosity, the windows glowing as the sun dipped lower, turning the sky a deep pink. As the road rounded a bend, Luna barked and ran ahead, up a neat gravel drive lined on either side by tall eucalypts that rustled in the breeze. Home.

'Hello. Come through,' Gemma said now as she stepped back to let them into the hall. She was wearing a casual linen dress with a pattern that reminded Falk a little of the first time they'd met, in the Southbank bar. The high-ceilinged hallway had been painted cream and a colourful rug covered dark wooden floorboards. A lamp on the side table – which did indeed have a faint telltale aroma of fresh furniture polish – threw out a warm light. Gemma's eyes met Falk's in a mirror on the wall.

'I'm glad you could come. I hope you all like lasagne.'

Falk loved lasagne.

The kitchen was bright and airy, with soft music playing from a speaker on a shelf lined with cookbooks. Gemma set them to work putting out plates and glasses and jugs of iced water and a bowl of salad, and then the four of them sat around a large table made from reclaimed wood and served themselves second helpings from the deep dish on a heat mat in the centre.

Zara quizzed Falk about the best case he'd ever solved, so he told them his most fun story, about the actor and the casino car park and the flat tyre and the bricks of money where the spare was supposed to be, and they'd all laughed. They talked about the festival and Gemma said it was going well, on track so far to meet their projections for this year. The kids were thinking ahead to uni. Zara was pretty set on Adelaide the following year, Joel was hoping to be studying in Sydney after the summer. Both he and Gemma seemed confident he'd get into the course he wanted.

Afterwards, they loaded the dishwasher and Joel and Zara slunk away to watch something on his laptop in the living room. Falk helped Gemma wipe down the table, then she opened the fridge and put two cold beers on the counter. She peered around the door to where the teenagers were still occupied and nodded to the verandah.

'Do you want to sit outside for a while?'

'Sounds good.'

The night was still warm and Falk could hear the cicadas chirping in the dark and the music playing softly from the kitchen. The verandah looked over a garden lush with native plants. Beyond lay the bushland, a little darker and deeper, and above, the sky was heavy with stars.

'Well. Cheers.' Gemma pulled up a couple of well-loved outdoor chairs and Falk sat down next to her. They looked out at the evening, Luna flopped at their feet. 'And thank you for helping Joel today. Once again.'

'It's no trouble. But, look –' Falk hesitated. He didn't want to ruin the atmosphere, but his conscience had been nudging him all night. 'I have to tell you, Joel showed me a video earlier. Of the scene after your husband's accident. And he sent it to me because it sounds like he – and Zara, to be fair – have been working themselves up that there's something suspicious about what happened.'

Gemma's eyes slid towards the house, where Joel was visible through the kitchen door, still slumped on the couch with Zara. 'I see.'

'Yeah. I didn't ask him to show me – I didn't even know it existed. But something like that's obviously really personal and –' Falk wished he knew her well enough to guess what she was thinking. 'I didn't want to have watched it without you knowing.'

'Okay.' Gemma twisted her beer bottle around in her hand, then took a long sip. 'I know Joel did take a video. And thank you for telling me.' She met his eyes, then frowned. 'So, what, he just had it to hand? There on his phone?'

'Pretty much.'

'God. Well, that certainly doesn't seem . . .' Gemma shook her head. 'Ideal.'

'No. But –' Falk thought about his few conversations with Joel. The way the topic often turned the same way. 'Look, I don't know him at all, obviously. But I get the impression he just really misses his dad. It could be as simple and as complex as that.'

'Yeah. He does.' Gemma moved in her chair to see her stepson better through the doors, her face carrying the same quiet dismay as when she'd found him spending his Friday night cleaning the memorial plaque. 'It's just sometimes I really worry that Joel'll leave next year to go to uni and he'll find it too hard to come back here again. Step-parent won't be enough anymore and he's going to slip away and be out there in the world all on his own. Like our family never happened.'

She blinked hard, then twisted back and lifted her bottle to her lips.

'I'm so sorry,' she said to Falk, taking a swallow. 'This is not at all your problem.'

'No, it's okay. I get it.'

She managed a small smile. It faded fast. 'I don't really want to know, but just tell me: is the video bad?'

'I would say yes. Not graphic. But sad.'

'I can't watch it.'

Falk shook his head. 'I really don't think it's necessary. Not if you don't want to.'

'But why is Joel bringing this up now?' she asked, as a murmur of conversation floated out from the house. Zara was saying something Falk didn't catch and Gemma tilted her head as the talk died away again. 'Has something new happened?'

'I don't know. But it didn't sound like a new idea.'

'After the accident,' Gemma lowered her voice a little, 'there were a few horrible whispers. Not most people – most people were great – but a small handful. Because the police hadn't found the car involved and for ages – more than five months, in the end – we couldn't find Dean either. And no-one ever said anything to my face, but of course I still heard things.' She glanced inside, the words even softer now. 'So did Joel. Stupid stuff. Like that Dean had run off with a client's money. He was out there somewhere living the high life with – what? – whatever few thousand dollars he might have been able to skim from the fertiliser supplier or something.'

'I'm sorry, that's hard.'

'It really was. And *ridiculous*.' Gemma waved a hand in disbelief and frustration. 'Even practicalities aside, Dean would *never* have done that. And everyone here knew it, but some idiots always like to talk. Then months went by and the water levels dropped and finally a routine trawl found Dean. His remains, anyway. They did the tests, even though it was obviously going to be him, and it was only after that that it started to feel different.' She shrugged. 'For Joel as well, I thought. A little bit better, if that's possible. To at least have had it confirmed.'

Inside the house, Falk could see Joel and Zara still absorbed in the screen.

'But Joel took some of the whispers to heart?' he said, and Gemma nodded.

'And look, it would have been impossible not to. Those months we were stuck waiting were honestly indescribable. I found it hard enough as an adult, and he was only twelve then.' She looked down at her feet for a long minute and then, completely unexpectedly, a tiny smile crept across her face. She reached over and stroked Luna's head. 'It's almost kind of funny where your mind goes under stress, though. In my absolute worst moments, the thing I kept coming back to again and again was that I knew Dean hadn't left us because, honestly, he would have taken the dog.'

Falk laughed in surprise, and she did too, shaking her head at the memory.

'I mean, Dean loved us. Of course he did.' Her face was lighter now. 'But he had a real soft spot for Luna.'

The kitchen floor creaked behind them, and they both turned as Joel put his head out.

'Gemma, are you saving the rest of that lasagne or can I have more?'

'Go ahead, you can have it,' she said, her eyes widening in amusement as he disappeared back inside. 'God, I know teenage boys are always hungry but he is *always* hungry.'

'I can't blame him, it was really good.' Falk held her gaze. 'And hey, thank you for inviting me, by the way.'

'Thank you for coming.' She sipped her beer and glanced back at him. 'It's a very mixed message, isn't it? I know that. I'm sorry. I just thought . . .' She considered for a moment. 'Actually, I'm not sure what I thought. When are you leaving again?'

'Friday.'

She nodded and gave him a small sideways smile. 'Maybe that was it.'

They sat together, drinking beer and watching the night for a while.

'I couldn't find any clear weekends.' Falk finally broke the silence. 'You were right.'

Gemma looked over at him. 'No, well, a lot of people can't. It's modern life, isn't it?'

Falk nodded. It did seem to be, at least in his experience.

'Raco and Rita think I work too much.' He frowned. He hadn't really known he was going to say that. It was true, though. 'They don't give me a hard time about it, because they're not like that, but I know they think I miss out on stuff.'

'And what do you think?'

'Well. I guess from their position, with their rock-solid marriage and great kids, I'd probably feel the same.' He would definitely feel the same, he suspected. 'But at the same time, it kind of suits me now. Genuinely. I mean, yeah, the job has long hours and stress, but if I wasn't getting anything out of it, why would I keep doing it? There's a lot I really like about it.'

'Yeah?' Gemma had turned to look at him, interested. 'Like what?'

'Working things out,' Falk said. He hesitated, but the night was warm and the beer was cold. 'I really like that moment when you've been untangling something for ages – years sometimes – and it can feel like it's all going nowhere, but then suddenly one thing changes and it's like –' The memory of the sensation was enough to make him smile. 'The world makes sense. Everything fits together and it's so clear. I love that bit.'

'That must feel really good. Although,' she tipped her beer bottle knowingly, 'I believe the official term you're looking for is "cracking the case".'

'Apologies, yes, I didn't realise you were across the jargon.' He grinned and she laughed. 'But yeah. That's the one. It does feel good. Like it's restored the balance a bit. Set something right.'

She said nothing, just watched him for a minute.

'The problem is all the late nights and weekends to reach that,' he said eventually and shrugged. 'The resolution's great, but it takes a lot to get there.'

Gemma swung her beer bottle thoughtfully between her fingers.

'I suppose there's annoying stuff with every job,' she said. 'I guess the key is knowing when you're just tired of the paperwork and politics, and when the whole job isn't right anymore. It's hard to spot that line.' She screwed up her eyes a little, the way Falk noticed she did when she was thinking back. 'It took me a really long time to decide to leave California.'

'Did it?'

'God, yes. So long.' She lifted her bottle and took a sip. 'Mainly because it wasn't terrible. Not at all. And in some ways, it was exactly right. It was challenging. I was good at it. But day to day, there were lots of things that started adding up. I had friends, but I never had time for them. I was always tired, I had this whole country on my doorstep that I never saw because I was working. But I'd put in so much effort to get that job, I thought it was what I wanted. And it actually was, some of the time.'

'How did you decide in the end?'

'I made a list.'

'Really? What, pros and cons?'

'Yeah.' She looked a little embarrassed but there was no need. Falk was himself quite fond of a good long list. 'But the thing was, it was actually pretty even. And I think that's why I'd been finding it so hard to decide, because there wasn't a clear winner. So at first, that felt worse because I obviously wanted to make the best choice, right? But one day I was at my desk, and I remember thinking if there was no clear winner, maybe that meant there was no loser either. The decision was hard because both options were decent ones, with good and bad points. So if there was no wrong answer, maybe I could –' She shrugged. '– choose, I suppose. What kind of life I really wanted to go after.'

Falk took a swallow of beer and thought about that. The house creaked and settled behind them. Out ahead, he could see the distinctive silhouette of the land and trees against the inky night. The sky was clear and he could smell the eucalyptus in the air. 'Are you happy with what you chose?'

'Yeah, I am. It's not for everyone, I get that.' Gemma smiled. 'God, my teenage self would be *furious* with me. But that's part of living, isn't it?' She looked over and met Falk's gaze. 'What we want changes.'

He watched her for a moment longer and then, almost involuntarily, moved his hand. A distance both tiny and huge, across the arm of his chair, until his fingertips touched hers. A beat passed, then he felt a warm spark rush through him as she pressed back. They sat like that, side by side, looking out at the sky and the bushland, until the verandah door slid open with a clatter.

'Dad says I have to come home. Oh –' Zara's head appeared. Her gaze flicked down to their hands then up again, her eyes dancing with surprise and faint amusement. 'Sorry. My grandma's arriving tomorrow for the christening and he doesn't want me out late. So . . .' Her voice was coy. 'When are you going home, Aaron?'

'Well, I guess that would be right now, Zara,' Falk said. He felt rather than saw Gemma smile, and she gave his fingers a final small squeeze as they stood. Falk helped her carry the bottles in, and they looked at each other across her kitchen as Zara rattled around gathering up her bits and pieces to leave. Gemma's arm brushed Falk's as they moved through to the hallway.

'Bye, Joel,' Falk called from the front door, and the boy gave a wave.

'Thanks, Aaron. See you.'

'And hey, good luck at the christening tomorrow.' Gemma leaned against the porch post as they stepped into the night, the light spilling out behind her. 'Your big moment. We'll look for you there.'

'Yes. That's right.' Falk smiled. 'And thanks again for tonight. This was –' What? A lot of things. 'So nice.'

'Yeah.' She smiled back. 'It was.'

The street was quiet as Falk and Zara walked along, past the homes and down through the bushland again towards the now-familiar reservoir track.

'Gemma's awesome,' Zara said out of nowhere, into the dark. 'She's a good person, you know? I like going to their place.'

'Yeah,' Falk said. 'That was fun.'

He could feel her curiosity buzzing, but he said no more.

'I always think she's pretty as well.' Zara cracked first. 'Not like Naomi is, obviously, but different. She has a nice face.' She looked over so expectantly that Falk had to laugh.

'She does.' He pictured it. She really did.

As they neared the water, Zara's expression dimmed a little.

'And, hey, thanks again for helping Joel,' she said. 'With the clean-up, and the video.'

'I'm not expecting to be much help with that.' Falk looked over until she met his eye. 'I need you to be realistic.'

'No, I know. But just taking him seriously is good.' She picked up a stone and threw it into the dark water as they walked. She had a good arm. 'He deserves to be listened to. And I know Dad thinks I'm clutching at straws, believing what he says about Mum not coming through the exit near him, but I do believe him. I know Joel would tell me the truth because that's how he is. He's not doing it for any other reason.'

'Like what?'

'Well, the fact that he likes me.'

Falk, who privately agreed with that assessment, kept his face neutral. He remembered what it was like to be that age, and felt a certain solidarity with the young awkward guy with his cleaning cloths and quiet way. 'You think so?'

'Yeah.' Zara smiled and shrugged. 'I do think so. But he knows we're just friends so he doesn't push for anything more. He's good with it, acts normal. That's why I like him. But still —' She flashed Falk a little witchy glance, her voice suddenly lighter. 'Sometimes things are obvious, right?'

'I suppose.'

'*Definitely*, I think.' She glanced back in the direction of Gemma's house so meaningfully that she nearly cricked her neck. 'Because you can just tell, can't you?'

Her smile was infectious and Falk couldn't stop his own. 'Tell what?'

'When there's love in the air.'

Chapter 25

Young Henry had brought out the sun for his christening day, and Falk woke early to the light filtering through the blinds. Outside, the vineyard was still quiet and he lay for a while in the cool linen sheets, staring at the guesthouse ceiling and thinking about the night before.

He had liked Gemma's place, a lot. Liked just being there, sitting around the wide kitchen table, eating lasagne from mismatched plates. But it had been the small things as well. The basil had apparently come from the row of herbs she was growing with mixed success in pots along the windowsill; and as he'd been leaving Falk had realised the large framed painting in the entrance hall that he'd assumed to be modern art, with its bold blue strokes creating no discernible image, was in fact a piece of childhood artwork by Joel.

The house had felt . . . *familiar*. The word came to Falk instantly and he rejected it just as quickly. He had never lived somewhere like that, with herbs in window pots and a child's painting hung like it was art. *Welcoming* was perhaps what he was reaching for, he decided, while at the same time picturing his own flat, lying empty back in St Kilda.

His place was absolutely fine, no argument to be had there. Good location. A decent long-term investment. Falk kept it clean and it was fully functional in the sense that it met all his needs. He frowned now up at the guesthouse ceiling. He could obviously grow herbs in his kitchen if he wanted to. Pick his own basil leaves and make lasagne. There was nothing stopping him. Although lasagne was a bit of a hassle for one. Lots of leftovers.

Falk's thoughts skipped to Joel, hanging out of the verandah door, asking to finish off the food. He'd been much more relaxed at home. Different from earlier, down by the reservoir with his phone and that deeply unsettling video of broken barriers and angry tyre marks and early grief.

Falk closed his eyes and listened. His subconscious had been picking away at something overnight, he suspected, because his internal alarm had started up again. The soft insistent warning was a little faster, if anything. He pushed back the bedsheets and got up.

He showered and dressed, then switched on his laptop, transferring Joel's video to the larger screen. Falk watched it play out – taking in the silent aftermath, Gemma rigid with shock, Dwyer scrutinising the scene – then went back to the start and ran it again. He was still at it an hour later when there was a knock on the door.

'G'day.' Raco put his head in. 'Thought I'd check if you needed anything before we head over to the church later.'

'If you want somewhere to hide from your extended family, mate,' Falk said, his eyes still on the screen, 'you don't have to lie about it to me.'

'Thank God.' Raco flopped into the armchair with a sigh. 'I can't stay long or Rita'll divorce me. I just need a breather before the rest descend.'

Ben Raco, the eldest of the three brothers, was escorting their mother down from Brisbane, Falk knew, along with Ben's pregnant wife and their three children. They'd flown into Adelaide last night and were driving over this morning.

'When are they arriving?'

Raco rubbed his eyes. 'Any minute. I mean, I love them, but all together they can be a bit much sometimes.' He sat back, then almost immediately leaned forward again. 'What on earth are you watching?'

'Dean Tozer's hit-and-run scene.'

'Seriously? Where did you get this?' Raco hauled himself up and came over, moving in for a closer look as Falk told him. They watched the video run through one loop in its entirety, then Raco frowned. 'And you think something's off?'

'Yeah, but I can't work out what. It's really annoying. Might be nothing; it's been bloody years since I looked at one of these.'

Raco's eyes darted over the screen as Falk set it playing again, then he reached out and paused the image. 'Where's the glass?'

Falk stopped. 'What glass?' He looked at what he was seeing. Made himself think. 'From the headlights?'

'Yeah.' Raco moved the scene back a few seconds, then let it run again. He pointed to the splintered wood of the barrier. 'You can see from the force – this break here – this has to be a front corner collision. No sideswipe. They changed the cross-roads out near the Maxwell place earlier this year and we've had a heap of single-vehicle smashes lately. Pain in the arse.

But yeah, no way you're getting out of that with your headlight intact. Should be a whole load of shattered glass all over the ground here.'

'Shit. Yes.' Falk could see it now.

They were both still for a moment, examining the screen. Falk went back to the start and moved through the video again, freezing it every few seconds. The ground was blurry in every scene.

'It's hard to tell,' Falk said finally. 'How small are these fragments likely to be?'

'It depends,' Raco said. 'But there'd be a lot of them. It was a sunny morning, we should be seeing some reflection at least.'

'So, it's been cleared up?' Falk said.

'Looks that way to me. You can tell a lot from the type of glass. Make, model, approximate year sometimes.' Raco's face was hard. 'Bloody cold, though. I don't know what the reservoir level was that year, but depending on the drop, Dean could've still been alive in that water. And instead of calling for help the driver sets about clearing the area?' He shook his head. 'It never stops amazing me, you know? What people'll do.'

'Desperation makes people do all sorts, I suppose,' Falk said.

'So true. This feels a bit weird, though.' Raco frowned at the screen. 'If it was someone trying to avoid a breath test on the highway. To have enough in your system to cause this accident, but then the presence of mind to clean up afterwards?'

'Might not have been a great clean-up job,' Falk said. 'There could be glass we can't see, and I'm guessing these are the paint marks.' He zoomed in on a shadowy patch against the broken white wood. The detail was lost over the distance.

'Probably not much they could do about the paint,' Raco said.

'No.' Falk thought of the graffiti marks around the memorial plaque. They were much fainter thanks to his cleaning efforts with Zara and Joel, but hadn't been erased entirely. He ran his eyes over the reservoir track, deserted in the paused image. 'Time would have to be a factor as well. I wouldn't want to be hanging around there too long afterwards.'

'No way.' Raco shook his head. 'You never know who's going to come –'

He stopped short at the sound of a car pulling up on the driveway. They both listened to the creak and slam of four doors followed by a babble of excited voices rising steadily to fever pitch. Raco sighed, then smiled despite himself. 'Sounds like my cue.'

'Good luck.'

'Thanks.' Raco paused at the door. 'And listen, I know it's all a bit crazy today, but thanks for being part of it. Seriously. Me and Rita are really glad you're here.'

Falk smiled. 'Me too.'

Clothes ironed, suits on and shoes shining, Falk and the Raco family walked to the church together. It was a white wooden structure on the leafy edge of town, surrounded by towering gum trees. The branches swayed as they threw dappled light down on the crowd that was already gathering outside in a mist of perfume and hugs and good wishes.

Falk immediately looked around for Gemma. He couldn't see her yet, but he did spot Rohan. He was with Zoe, who was dressed in a floral playsuit and giggling as her dad chased her around the far end of the car park. Raco looked pointedly over at Charlie, the wordless message crystal clear. Charlie sighed and nodded.

'Yep. I'll sort it,' he said.

Falk watched as he trudged off across the gravel. As Rohan saw Charlie approach, he stopped running after his daughter and straightened his back, his shoulders suddenly tense. The two stopped a short distance away from each other. Falk couldn't hear the muttered exchange but after a loaded pause, they both took half a step forward and awkwardly shook hands. Shane, whose formalwear made him look very much like a man awaiting a court appearance, stood nearby, taking it in. Falk saw his large chest rise and fall in a sigh, before he made his way across the car park to join them. He was welcomed with open relief by both men.

'Come on, Father Connor's calling us in,' Falk heard Rita say, and looked down as she took his arm and gave his elbow a squeeze. 'And, hey, welcome officially to the extended family. I honestly can't think of anyone we'd rather have than you.'

Falk stopped mid-stride at the steps of the church and put his arms around this gorgeous generous woman and bundled her into a firm hug. Releasing her, they laughed and followed the priest inside. Naomi was already waiting at the top of the aisle in a clingy cream dress, her crown of blonde hair shining as she radiated an energy that threatened to overshadow even Henry himself. She gave Falk a wink as he came to stand next to her.

'God, some men just scrub up beautifully,' she said, running an approving eye over his suit.

'Thanks.' He smiled. 'Although I think you've outdone us all.'

Naomi smoothed a hand down the pale fabric and raised an eyebrow. 'Not too bridal?'

'Only in a good way,' he said truthfully.

'I knew I liked you, Aaron.' She laughed, but as the priest approached, Falk saw her eyes flick towards the church door. He wondered who exactly she was looking for, as she turned away again, disappointed. Perhaps Zara's suspicions had some basis after all.

Falk put the thought aside as they stood together in a patch of sunlight, listening to Father Connor's last-minute instructions and watching the Racos' friends and family wander in to take their seats. Falk tried to focus on what the priest was saying but instead found his own gaze drifting away, moving over the familiar and unfamiliar faces filing into the church until – *at last*, there she was. Gemma's hair was down around her shoulders and she was wearing a yellow dress that suited her in a way Falk couldn't quite articulate. He watched her, hoping she'd look up and see him.

'– if that sounds all right to you, Aaron?'

'Yes. Absolutely.' Falk heard his name and abruptly tuned back in to the conversation. 'No worries.' He nodded firmly to hide the fact he wasn't sure what he was agreeing to and, next to him, he sensed Naomi stifle a laugh.

Gemma was moving up the aisle towards a spare seat, and when Falk glanced over this time, he felt a little leap as he realised she was looking back at him. She held his eye and smiled encouragingly, opening her palm in a little personal wave. And right then, as the tiny subtle connection zipped between them, Falk could almost imagine a different day. A day a bit like this, with the suit and the sunlight and a dress at the other end of that aisle. The air thick with love and celebration. He could see it – feel it, maybe? – and for a second it all seemed so vivid and real that he was a little startled when Rita suddenly handed him a struggling Henry. Falk mentally lurched back into the room, the reality faintly coloured now by a strange, disoriented longing. He blinked, and breathed slowly in and out.

'All right.' Father Connor checked his watch, then gave Falk and Naomi each a final reassuring smile. 'Show time.'

There was a short service before the christening itself, and Falk sat between Raco and Naomi in the warm space, letting the words wash over him.

When his moment arrived, Falk looked down at Henry and thought about the trust the Racos were placing in him. He'd always suspected on some level he was doing this purely for them – a gesture of their mutual friendship, offered and returned. But as he spoke his words, here and now, he discovered to his mild surprise that it felt like something more. A tangible bond being woven between Falk and his godson.

Okay, Henry, he thought. *Starting now. But for real, this time.*

Naomi played her own part with her usual competence and grace and then, faster than Falk had expected, it was all over. He craned his neck, trying to spot Gemma as the guests trooped back out into the sunshine, but had to give up as he was swiftly led aside for family photos. Lots of them, it seemed, in all possible combinations until various members were released one by one. Finally, it was just Henry, his parents and his brand new godparents left alone to stroll home to the vineyard in peace.

'Well. That was absolutely lovely,' Naomi said. She had insisted on pushing Henry's pram while Rita and Raco walked along arm in arm. 'Keep me in mind for the next one, won't you?'

'We're done,' Raco said with a grin, at the same time as Rita said firmly: 'God, no. No more.'

'Fair enough.' Naomi smiled and accepted a cracker from the box Rita had conjured from Henry's baby bag. Hungry after all the excitement, the four of them crunched on handfuls as they ambled along.

'And how about you, Aaron?' Naomi said lightly, offering the box to Falk. 'Any thoughts on –?'

'Naomi,' Rita warned, but she was laughing. 'Don't.'

'Don't what?' Naomi's blue eyes were wide.

'You know what. Leave the poor man alone.'

'I was just going to make a *very* general observation that some kids – male teenage stepchildren, for example – might sound like hard work on the surface but –'

'Yep, we can all guess what you were going to say.' Rita smiled. 'Aaron included. So how about you don't and just hand me the crackers instead, would you?'

'Fine.' Naomi nudged Falk gently as they walked. She nodded back towards Rita and Raco. 'You do know they're as nosey and invested as me, don't you? They're just playing it cool.'

Falk smiled at her. 'I do know, yeah.'

'Good.'

They came around a bend in the road and up ahead, Falk could make out Joel and Zara walking together, their heads close. They must have fallen well behind the rest of the group.

'Is that something of Kim's that Zara's got on?' Naomi squinted into the light.

Over her dress, Zara was wearing a flowing blue fine-knit cardigan, despite the warmth of the day. She had it wrapped tightly around her, the hem flaring a little as she walked.

'Yeah.' Rita nodded. 'Rohan brought up some of Kim's clothes and books and things for her.'

'I thought I recognised it.' Naomi's smile faded. 'Is Zara

273

finding today hard with Kim not here? I couldn't see her face in the church.'

'A bit, I think.' Raco nodded. 'Kind of a reminder, isn't it? Knowing Kim would've been here along with everyone else.'

'I suppose so, but do you think –?' Rita started, then stopped.

Raco looked over at his wife. 'Think what?'

'Do you think Kim would've actually come, though?'

'Yeah, of course.' Raco frowned. They had reached the start of the vineyard driveway and Falk could see guests' cars parked at the other end. 'Why wouldn't she?'

Rita shrugged. 'I mean, I know Rohan's here, but he's only in town because of the appeal. And I hadn't seen Kim socially for a long time. A couple of years, at least. I just feel like she'd moved on from all this. Which is understandable, she'd have had new friends in Adelaide and work was probably keeping her busy.'

'No, she'd stopped working,' Naomi said suddenly.

Rita looked over in surprise. 'When she had Zoe?'

'Earlier. A few months before she was even pregnant, I think.'

'She never told me. Did you know?' Rita asked Raco, who shook his head.

'She didn't tell me either,' Naomi said. 'I only found out by accident when I was in the city one day, and realised I had a meeting in the same building as that design firm she'd gone to. I stopped by during lunch but they said she hadn't worked there for a while.'

Raco frowned. 'Seriously? Why wouldn't she mention it? Had she been fired or something?'

'No, I don't think so. The others in the office seemed friendly, but it was obviously a bit awkward because I'd shown up and didn't even know Kim wasn't there anymore. They said they hadn't seen her since she left. Asked me to pass on their best when I spoke to her.'

'And did you speak to her?' Raco said. They were weaving their way through the cars parked outside the cottage and Falk could hear music and laughter floating through the air.

'I tried,' Naomi said. 'I know I called her, probably would've sent a follow-up text too. Saying hello, asking if she'd moved on.'

'And what was the response?' Raco was still frowning, and Rita gently touched his arm as they headed around the side of the cottage to the barn where their guests were waiting.

'The usual for Kim,' Naomi said, as three different people spotted Rita and Raco and simultaneously set off towards them at a trot. 'She didn't reply.'

Chapter 26

'Strictly between you and me, it's any height restrictions for the AFP that worry me, you see. My grandson's always been a little – well, look, my daughter says I'm not supposed to use the word *short* in front of him, but I told her, Cheryl, I really don't know what else you'd call it –'

'Right. I understand.' Falk nodded politely, trying without success to catch Gemma's eye across the barn. He'd spotted her immediately, looking a little like a conversational hostage herself as she was cornered between tables by an older couple Falk didn't recognise. He'd started towards her only to be rather impressively hijacked by this woman who'd introduced herself as Raco's former clarinet teacher and was very keen to discuss the entry requirements her grandson might have to meet to apply for the federal police.

The barn itself had been transformed by the arrival of guests. Music was playing and bright tablecloths added to the festive feel. The whole back wall had been slid open to let in the view and Charlie and Shane had fired up the huge barbecue outside, where they were being heavily supervised by a group of men eyeballing the steaks. Most of the guests appeared to have brought something, which was a benefit of living in a food and wine region, Falk supposed, and the long table against the wall heaved with platters and bottles of wine.

'– so I told Cheryl I'd ask you, and she got quite annoyed with me – what a surprise! – and told me I wasn't to bother you but I –'

'Excuse us. He's needed, Rachel, I'm so sorry.' A firm voice cut through the verbal stream and Falk felt a hand grip his elbow. He looked down to see Naomi smiling up apologetically. 'Godparent duties beckon.'

Naomi led Falk away until they were out of the line of sight, then waved a hand before he could say anything. 'It's fine, you're welcome. She's lovely really, but there's a trick to getting a word in edgeways. I'll teach you if you end up being around here long enough to need it.' Naomi nodded across the room. 'So Gemma's over there – see her? Stuck with Neil and Carol Milton? Thought you might like to rescue her yourself.'

Falk smiled. 'Thanks, Naomi.'

'I like to look after my investments.' She grinned. 'Have fun.'

Naomi turned and Falk watched her weave away through the tables. She edged by Zara, who was chatting with a group of teenagers, and Falk saw the girl glance up, tracking Naomi as she passed. Zara lightly rolled her eyes and, catching Falk's gaze, mouthed *I told you so* as Naomi headed outside and made a beeline for Charlie.

Naomi joined him at the barbecue, leaning up and kissing him lightly on the cheek. Charlie smiled as she murmured something and gestured towards the party in a way that could only be complimentary.

See? Zara mouthed again, and Falk was about to nod in

agreement – he did see, yes – when he stopped himself. Naomi was still chatting, effusive and engaged, but even as Falk watched, her eyes were darting elsewhere. Somewhere beyond Charlie. Falk followed the trajectory and all of a sudden, he could see exactly where Naomi's gaze was landing. Ah. Falk smiled to himself. That possibly explained one or two things.

He caught Zara's attention once more, and motioned for her to look again. Not at her father this time – Falk tilted his head – but a little to the left. He saw Zara's eyes move and then settle in much the same way as Naomi's had. Arriving squarely on a man who, at an arguably unsafe distance from the sizzling hot grill, was keeping a crowd of blokes utterly spellbound as he re-enacted that time he'd won Mark of the Year.

Shane? Zara spun her head back to Falk, the dawning realisation morphing into baffled amusement. *Seriously?*

Falk smiled and shrugged. He didn't know for sure, but Zara could see the dynamic playing out across the sausages and steaks as well as he could. Smart, self-assured Dr Naomi Kerr may be engineering excuses to stop by the vineyard, but Falk would bet good money it wasn't Charlie she was hoping to see. Falk wouldn't have naturally put Naomi and Shane together, but he could picture it now he thought about it. The heart wanted what it wanted, he supposed. Falk wondered why Naomi hadn't acted on it, though. She didn't seem the type to hold back. He watched for another minute. Perhaps, he decided, because the whole time Naomi stood there, in that dress that clung like it was made for her and with a mildly perplexed look on her beautiful face, Shane barely glanced her way.

'Well, I'll say this for you. You certainly know how to wear a nice suit.'

Falk laughed and turned at the voice.

'Very kind, Gemma.' He held out his hands in a mock pose and she smiled. 'And you. You look beautiful.' She really did, he thought. Like she was lit from within. He glanced around. She was alone. 'I was supposed to save you from someone.'

'Neil and Carol.' She laughed. 'Well, you're too late, I saved myself. Actually, Rita did, to be fair. She says we should come and eat lunch at their table.'

The Racos' table was two pushed together, to accommodate highchairs and multiple children. Food was piled high and Charlie had surrendered the barbecue to other keen hands and was now pouring wine. He pointed Falk and Gemma to a couple of empty chairs.

'Squeeze in. You know our brother, Ben?' Charlie nodded at a friendly man who looked a lot like Charlie and Raco, just a few miles further down the track. 'He's a cop too, and bloody loves talking shop, whether you're interested or not. His wife, Dee. Their kids are – I dunno, somewhere around, anyway. And my mum, Diane.'

'Yeah, we spoke a little back at the church,' Falk said, shaking hands. 'Good to see you all.'

'I don't only talk shop, for the record, but as it happens we've got a mutual friend.' Ben Raco leaned over to Falk. 'You were both seconded on the same case a couple of years ago –'

Falk remembered the guy well. He was very smart but with a shameless talent for getting himself both in and out of trouble, and they spent most of lunch entertaining Gemma with stories of his exploits. Ben started recounting one that Falk already knew – had indeed heard told a few times, always in the same semi-horrified whisper – and as he nodded along, he found himself vaguely tuning in to a different conversation across the table.

'– was finding it harder to get in on time in the mornings. On Sunday nights, she'd always be really flat,' Rohan was saying to Raco. 'I know a lot of people feel like that, ahead of Mondays, but this was every single week.'

Kim, Falk could tell immediately. They were talking quietly, Raco leaning over his plate to listen, and Falk had to strain to hear.

'Was the problem that job specifically?' Raco said. 'The people she was working with, maybe? Or was it work in general?'

'In general, as far as I could tell. She complained about her boss sometimes, and I wondered for a while if she was being bullied even, but then I met her colleagues at a work drinks thing and that didn't seem to be the case either. They were nice enough, all looked to get along.' Rohan paused to pass another strawberry to Zoe, who was smearing them over her highchair tray. 'The best I could get out of Kim was that the work was too stressful.'

'But she used to run her own business here,' Raco said. 'That was the same work, wasn't it? Graphic design and logos and things?'

'Yeah, exactly the same.' Rohan nodded. 'But this carried on for a while and finally she said she wasn't happy and wanted to leave. We ran the numbers, decided it would be okay. So she did.'

'It's just that she kept it quiet that she'd left work. Naomi said she found out by accident.'

'She didn't tell Naomi?' Rohan glanced across the room in surprise. Naomi was by the buffet, examining the open bottles of wine. A small frown reached his eyes. 'I thought she had.'

A burst of laughter erupted from the end of the table, and Falk looked over to where Zara was sitting between Charlie and her grandmother. They were crowded around a computer tablet, looking at photos.

'I feel like I'm going to regret asking, but what's so funny over there?' Ben called.

'Just some of these pictures Zara's found.' Charlie was wiping his eyes in mirth. 'There are a couple of classic ones of you at Halloween, hang on –' He moved his finger over the screen, then turned the tablet so they could all see Ben dressed up in the same matching waistcoat and hat as his own toy rabbit.

'I'm going to get a photo book printed up,' Zara said. 'As a christening thing, but for us all, really.'

'Well, a little discretion would be rewarded, if you know what I mean,' Ben said, ostentatiously rolling a single dollar coin across the table to Zara.

'Ben, I'm seventeen.' She laughed and rolled it back. 'You'd have needed more than that ten years ago.'

'Oh, this is a very cute one of you, Zara.' Diane was still scrolling through, and Zara looked over as her grandmother stopped and turned the screen.

'No, that's not me, Nan.'

Diane peered through her glasses. 'That? That's you. Look at your lovely hair. With your mum.'

A momentary hush fell over the table at the passing mention of Kim, and Diane hesitated. The screen was still facing outwards, and Falk could see the picture was indeed of Kim, with a newborn baby in her arms. She was smiling at the camera but her skin looked greasy and she had dark circles under her eyes.

'No, Nan. That baby Mum's holding is Zoe.' Zara pointed across the table to the toddler now banging a spoon against her plate.

281

'Really?' Diane laughed. 'That's Zoe as a baby? My goodness, it goes to show. She could be any one of you grandkids
in that photo. Or the boys. She's got that same suspicious look
you all had. I used to call it the Raco gaze.'

There was a sharp pocket of silence.

'But Zoe's not a Raco, Nan. She's Mum's and Rohan's –'

'Yep, thanks, Zara. I am aware,' Diane said, the implications
of what she'd said clearly not lost on her. 'I mean, that's obvious.
Look at those gorgeous blonde curls she has now.' She waved
a hand towards Zoe in a half-hearted attempt at doddery
foolishness, then sighed. 'Oh, for God's sake. Look, ignore me.
At my age every new baby looks like a goblin in a onesie.
Anyway, she's clearly Rohan's.'

Diane was right about that, Falk thought. Now, at least.
The fine dark baby hair on Zoe's head in the photo had been
shed at some point over the past twelve months and regrown
into the beginnings of sandy waves. Her eyes were still brown
but not as dark as they appeared on screen. The child's face
had taken shape as she'd grown and, faux Raco gaze or not,
Zoe was now very much the image of Rohan, who at that
moment had his arms crossed and was staring hard at the
table.

'Diane,' Rita said, getting up. 'Speaking of grandchildren,
why don't you come outside and we'll get a few nice photos
with baby Henry.'

'Yes,' Diane said, rising. 'I think I better had.'

There was a beat of silence as she left, then Charlie laughed.

'Christ, do I even need to say this?' He stood. 'No, I'm not
even going to –'

He stretched over the remains of lunch, plates clattering,
and offered his hand to Rohan. There was a loaded moment,

then Rohan took it, his jaw relaxing a little. He looked embarrassed more than anything.

'You knew Kim,' Charlie said, still gripping the man's hand. 'You know she wouldn't. I might.' A flicker of a smile. 'But Kim would never.'

'Still. Nice try, mate.' Across the table, Ben flashed Rohan a grin that instantly lightened the mood. 'I keep trying to fob mine off as well, but those paternity tests are always coming back with the wrong answer.' He winked at his visibly pregnant wife, who rolled her eyes good-naturedly. 'Congratulations, here's another bloody one. And another.' Ben swept up a shrieking child as she ran past, and then a second one, turning them upside down as they squealed with delight. 'Wish I could work out how we keep getting them.'

Between them all, Raco blinked slowly and shook his head. *Family*, he mouthed at Falk. *Jesus Christ*. He reached for the bottle nearest him.

'Right,' he said to no-one in particular. 'Who else needs a drink?'

Falk smiled and sat back in his chair. He leaned over to Gemma, their elbows colliding as she turned towards him at the same moment.

'Do you want to get some air?' he said.

'Absolutely.'

The light in the vineyard was dazzling after the relative dark of the barn and they blinked as they emerged into the brilliant afternoon sun. Falk reached for Gemma's hand and it slid straight into his. They didn't talk as they walked together down through the vines, the fresh spring leaves shimmering full and green all around. They were alone out there, the distant music and chatter growing louder and then fading as they wandered together up and down the tracks. Falk found himself watching their shadows. Side by side, hand in hand.

At the far end of a row that looked pretty much the same as all the others, he finally slowed then came to a stop. Gemma, still holding his hand, glanced back the way they'd come. The sounds from the party filtered through the air, but the barn was hidden from view.

She nodded. 'This is a good spot.'

'Is it?'

'Yeah,' she said. 'Because if we walk up any further they'll all be able to see us kissing.'

Falk smiled at her. 'That's what's going to happen now?'

She smiled back. 'You know it is.'

And she was right. He put his hands to her face and his mouth on hers, long and deep. The sensation flooded through him like cool water and he could feel her body pressed soft and warm against his.

After what felt like both a long time and not long enough, they pulled apart and Gemma took a breath. Her eyes were bright, her fingertips laced through his own.

'Joel's going from here to a friend's house to play video games for the afternoon.'

'Okay.' Falk ran his thumb over her palm.

She closed her hand around his. 'So you should drive me home.'

Her house was silent and sun-drenched. They went straight to her bedroom, closing the door on a disgruntled Luna.

'Listen, Gemma, I do actually still need to leave on Friday. I'm giving evidence in court on Monday so I have to get up to speed –'

'It's okay. This unzips on the side here, not the back.'

'Oh, great, got it, thanks. And I can definitely have another look for clear weekends, but it gets tricky because I'm on a seven-day rotating roster so –'

'I know. I understand that.'

'I just –' He stopped.

'Aaron.' Gemma stopped too. Her lips were close to his, her fingers on his shirt buttons. 'Maybe I've been overthinking all this. I mean, people will always come and go. And sometimes you know when, and sometimes you don't.'

Falk nodded, his hands still.

'And we're both here right now.' Her eyes had flecks of gold near the centre. 'So I think we should make the most of it.'

'Yeah?'

'Yeah. There's something to be said for enjoying moments while you can.' She smiled and touched her lips to his. 'Those stupid Melbourne beer coasters might have had a point.'

He laughed and she hung his jacket on a chair. Then they lay down on her sun-lined sheets under the open window, and he kissed her back in that quiet house as the breeze and the soft lazy sounds of a Sunday afternoon floated by.

Chapter 27

The barn was empty and the vineyard drive had cleared by the time Falk pulled up in the dark. Light spilled from the cottage and he could hear the hum of relaxed talking and laughter through the open windows. His guesthouse stood dark but someone was sitting alone out the front in the night-time air. She had her head tilted back and her eyes closed.

'Hi, Rita.' Falk pulled up the other chair. 'Your turn to hide from the family?'

She smiled with her eyes still shut. 'I'm folding laundry, can't you tell?'

'Let me give you a hand with that.' Falk went into the guesthouse and came out with a jug of iced water and a couple of glasses. 'Have most people gone?'

'Everyone but the family.' She opened one eye. 'You're going to be invited to brunch tomorrow, by the way. I don't know if you've ever been to brunch with five children but I'd highly recommend a prior commitment if I were you. We're taking them to the festival tomorrow night for a last run before people start heading off. Say you'll catch us then instead.'

'Noted. Thanks.'

Rita smiled and straightened in her chair, reaching for her water. 'And how about you?' She looked at Falk now, her voice softer. He was still wearing his suit, his tie in his pocket. 'Have you had a nice day, Aaron?'

'Yeah. I have.'

He'd lain there with Gemma in the quiet and the warmth until the light changed. As the shadows grew across the room, she'd finally taken her hand off his chest and propped herself up on one elbow.

'I absolutely hate to say this, but –'

'It's okay. I'll head off now, before Joel gets back.'

'Is that all right? It's just this is his home too and –'

'Yeah, definitely. It's better. Can I see you tomorrow?'

'I'm on call for the festival all day tomorrow. I'll try to arrange a couple of hours' cover.'

'Great.' He smiled at her. 'Although, I actually still don't have your number.'

'I know.' She smiled back, then rolled over on the bed to reach her phone on the bedside table. 'Let's fix that.'

He had kissed her again at the front door, the sky already deepening above them.

Falk sat with Rita now, Gemma's number saved on his phone, listening to the gentle nocturnal buzz of evening settling in.

'I say this with complete neutrality.' Rita was watching his face. 'But if you were interested, Charlie would probably bring you in on this business –'

'Rita.'

'Aaron, I'm simply passing on the information.'

'Come on. Seriously. I can't. You know I –'

'I do know, and that's fine. It is. I have no stake in this, other than I care about you.' She fixed her large dark eyes on him so he couldn't look away. 'But supposing you could. Charlie would have work for you here.'

'Doing *what*? What on earth would I do here?'

'Everything. There's a lot you could bring to this. The business has been too big for him for a while now. He's looking for someone else. It doesn't have to be you. But it could be.'

'Rita. Jesus.' Frustration with the situation was making him irritable. He could not open that door. 'Please can we not –'

'What?'

'Pretend that's something I'm ever going to do. Please?'

'All right.'

She dropped it, as Falk had known she would. Instead, she simply reached out and rested her hand gently on his arm. He looked out at the night.

'I barely know her, Rita.'

'I know.'

They sat there a little longer, listening to the voices drifting from the house. Falk looked at the darkened barn, so still and silent compared with earlier. He thought back to lunch. It seemed a long time ago now.

'Charlie and Rohan are still on speaking terms, are they?' Falk said.

'After a fun little public dalliance questioning Zoe's paternity? I think so. They're as okay as they ever really are.'

'There's nothing in it, I'm guessing?' Falk would be surprised. Zoe looked very much like Rohan.

Rita was already shaking her head. 'I highly doubt it. Not just Zoe's features now but because Charlie's right, Kim would never have done that to Rohan. It wasn't in her nature.' She paused. 'Not in Charlie's either, no matter what he says. It was all stupid anyway. When Zoe was born she looked like Kim more than anyone. It's just that Kim had similar colouring to Charlie and the rest of them.'

A babble of chatter rose from the house and they both looked over. Falk could hear a voice that sounded like Raco's, although it could have been one of his brothers'. He couldn't make out the words.

'Greg's worried, though,' Rita said. 'About the whole thing with Kim.'

Falk frowned. 'Yeah. It feels like it's never sat right with him.'

'There's something more, though. He's mulling over things, I can tell. It's been hard to find time to talk properly these last few days, but he's got that look.' Rita swirled her water in her glass as she stared at the house. 'He's never liked the fact Kim left Zoe alone. He's always thought that was out of character.'

Falk thought back to the festival grounds the day before. How do you get a parent to do anything? Threaten their child. Maybe character didn't come into it. He looked over at Rita now.

'Were you surprised Kim would leave Zoe like that?' he said.

'The Kim I knew? Yes. Definitely. But I hadn't seen her in person for a couple of years.' Rita frowned. 'I'll tell you this, though. Being a new mother can be very, very hard. We know Kim was already on medication for depression, and some babies are a nightmare. You're not supposed to say it out loud, but they are. They wreck you. I mean, Henry's quite mellow, but Eva?' She pressed her lips together. 'And Kim had dragged her six-week-old all the way out here to see her teenage daughter, who had cancelled on her anyway. So she was probably feeling pressure to come to the festival, bring this baby along, and it's noisy and crowded, and her husband's heading off early to meet his parents. And suddenly she's all alone in the dark, and maybe her medication is unbalanced after the birth, maybe she's still in pain at times. And now she's stuck with this baby who's playing up yet again, and it's all simply too much. So she goes for a walk on her own.'

Rita looked across at Falk. They were both silent for a moment.

'That's what I think. Because I can see it happening.'

Falk nodded slowly. He said nothing.

'And the thing is,' Rita said, 'Zoe *was* relatively safe. I mean, it's not ideal, obviously. But she was tucked up in the pram. She was warm, clean, away from the elements. That pram bay is surrounded by festival staff, it's full of parents coming and going. It was always highly likely someone responsible would find her.' She shook her head. 'If I imagine what might have been going through Kim's head that night, I can think of much worse outcomes. Much worse.'

Falk looked out at the blackness. He could think of some too.

'Sergeant Dwyer doesn't believe Kim didn't talk to anyone she knew that night,' he said. 'But I guess if she was already feeling isolated –'

Rita nodded, as she reached over and refilled their glasses. 'And look, don't say this to anyone but Greg – and even he doesn't fully agree with me – but I didn't grow up here so I have a slightly different view on things.'

'And what's that?'

Rita put the jug down, her eyes on the house. The windows were glowing and someone had put on some music. Through the verandah doors, Falk could now see Raco moving about as he made coffee, a long string of mugs lined up.

'I love these people here,' Rita said. 'All of them, I mean, not just my family. And not because I have to get along with them, but because they are warm and genuine and kind. But whether they'd admit it or not, honestly whether they'd even recognise it, there was a rift when Kim and Rohan got together. There'd always been this . . .' She reached for the right words. 'Unspoken expectation, I guess, that Kim and Charlie would eventually end up back together. And when Kim and Rohan got married, they broke that. I mean, they didn't really break anything, obviously. Kim and Charlie had split up, there was nothing there to break. But logic doesn't stop feelings. And we can all get along and co-parent and raise a glass to the bride and groom, and Charlie can pay for as much wedding wine as he likes, but the fact is that sides were taken. For all sorts of reasons, because we have connections through this place, through our lives and work and family. And Kim knew that. She'd made a choice. A perfectly legitimate one. But when the dust settled, even *Zara* ended up here with Charlie.'

Falk watched Rita. For possibly the first time ever, she didn't seem able to meet his eye.

'I don't need to tell you, Aaron, what it's like to suddenly feel exiled from your own community by people you trusted,' she said softly. 'But I can imagine it's hard.'

Yes, Falk thought, as he stared out into the dark. It was very hard.

They sat together for a long stretch of silence until finally he looked over. Rita was still staring into her lap, guilt on her face. This time it was Falk who put his hand on hers.

'Did anyone talk to Kim about any of this?' he said, eventually.

'I don't think so. Not directly, anyway,' Rita said. 'The closest was not long after Kim's engagement. Zara heard her and Charlie having this stupid fight. Probably nothing that blew up into something, but he told Kim she was making a mistake, that Rohan wasn't right for her. Don't come crying to him when she realised that. That sort of thing.'

'And what happened?'

Rita gave a sad shrug. 'They were angry for a few days but had to keep it civil for Zara. Neither of them usually had the energy to sustain a grudge, so they made up. But the damage was done, you know? By everyone, really. Kim had been told. She'd made her bed. So a couple of years later, when Kim's struggling, and maybe her head's not quite right, and it's all feeling too much – does it surprise me she didn't come to any of us?' Rita gazed out over the silent vineyard. 'I'd love to say it does. But no. It doesn't at all.'

Chapter 28

Falk was unfortunately unable to join the Raco family brunch owing to an urgent work conference call. He had to raise his voice over the cacophony in the kitchen simply to deliver the excuse and Rita caught his eye over the top of two bawling red-faced girls. She inclined her head in surreptitious approval.

Save yourself, she mouthed without dropping her rigor-mortis smile.

Raco, wrestling one kid after another outside and into various car seats, raised a hand without even looking over. 'Yep, no worries.'

Falk watched Raco for a minute, his expression unusually flat and distant. It was hard to tell amid the chaos, but Rita was right, he thought. Raco was preoccupied by something, and it wasn't just the kids. Falk scooped up a dropped sunhat from the ground and followed him out to the car.

'Great. Thanks.' Raco plonked the hat on the nearest bare head as he tried to force the seat buckle to click into place. 'This bloody thing never – *there*. Got it.'

'Now's clearly not the time,' Falk said, as Raco emerged, sweating lightly. They both glanced at the kids, securely strapped in. 'But should we talk later? You thinking something?'

Raco hesitated, then sighed through his nose. He turned so he was facing away from the children. 'Not really. Just the usual Kim stuff. I keep coming back to a few bits and pieces, none of it new though.'

'No?'

'No. I wish there was. Anything to help shake things loose, you know?' Raco glanced back into the car as a high-pitched shriek was followed by a chorus of giggles.

'Yeah.' Falk felt the same low frustration, like there was an odd and unexpected blind spot in his peripheral vision. They both turned at the sound of another shriek, this time followed by crying rather than laughter.

'Anyway. Better keep moving.' Raco's mouth lifted up at the corners. 'And, hey, don't let them work you too hard on that sudden conference call of yours, mate, will you?'

Falk grinned. 'I'll try my best. Enjoy brunch.'

'Yep. I will also try. Catch you later.'

Falk waited until they were gone and the vineyard was quiet again before he put on his running gear. He set off down the driveway, taking the same route as before, moving along the back roads in the morning sun. He heard the faint familiar sound of the footy bouncing against the ground as the park came into view and he slowed to a walk, then stopped. He debated silently for a minute, then this time headed across the grass and playground to the oval itself, leaning against the metal boundary fence to catch his breath.

The sun was in Shane's eyes, Falk could tell, as the guy lined up while still in motion, pulling back his leg in a sweeping kick. The ball soared through the air, looking good before clipping the post at the last moment and ricocheting away. It bounced a couple of times, landing not far from Falk. Shane shielded his eyes, breathing heavily, his face shining with sweat. He grinned as he saw Falk there.

'Kick it back, mate,' he shouted.

Falk hesitated. Shane waited, then pointed at the ground.

'It's right there. In front of you.'

'Yeah. I can see it, thanks.' Falk laughed as he climbed the fence to retrieve the ball. He hadn't held a football in – how long? – years. He turned it over in his hands, feeling the familiar weight and shape. He shot a glance across the oval to Shane, who hadn't moved but suddenly seemed a long way away.

'Go on.' Shane was shouting again. 'I think everyone's crap, don't worry about it.'

'Yeah, okay, I'm going,' Falk called back. 'If you'd shut up and let me concentrate.'

Shane grinned, but closed his mouth. Falk tried to remember how he used to do this, then gave up. He ran a few steps and just kicked, letting instinct take over. They both followed the trajectory through the air.

'Nice one. Not bad.' Shane had to run to get himself under the ball, but at least it made the distance. 'Turn your wrists down further, you'll get a better angle.' He jogged a couple of paces and demonstrated as he smoothly punted it back.

Falk moved for the ball, watching and reaching up and catching it and then, keeping his wrists well down, curving around to kick it back as Shane ran past. He caught it and they ran together, back and forth up the oval in the morning light, until Shane pointed at the goalposts.

'Go for it.' He was panting.

Falk kicked. The goal was close and completely open, but they both cheered as the ball sailed through.

'You could be decent, you know? You're just rusty,' Shane said as he fetched the footy, his forehead damp. They walked together to the water fountain, breathing hard. 'How long's it been since you had a kick?'

'God, I don't know.' Falk tried to remember. 'Years, must be. And never on a Monday morning.'

'Yeah, it's good, hey?' Shane grinned. 'For now, anyway. It does get busier around here. You should see it in autumn. The whole town, all the vineyards, it's crazy. Charlie's good like that, though. Work hard when we need to, take it a bit easier when we don't.' He stretched his shoulders and squinted over at the track that led back in the direction of the vineyard. 'Was a good day yesterday, I thought. They all surface okay this morning?'

'I think so. They're at brunch. You stay late?'

'Not really. Walked Naomi part of the way home because it was getting dark. Sounds like she had a good time. Happy to be picked as godmother.'

'She seems like a good choice.' Falk pressed the button on the fountain. 'She's good fun.'

'Naomi? Yeah. She's great.'

There was definitely something wistful in Shane's tone. Falk swallowed and wiped his mouth. He pictured Naomi, dressed up and forlorn by the barbecue, and found himself wondering, somewhat unexpectedly, what Rita would do in this situation.

'Divorced, is she?' he settled on.

Shane was examining the footy, turning it over in his hands. 'Yeah. About eighteen months now.'

'She's not seeing anyone?'

'No.' The ball stopped moving momentarily. The word was almost territorial. 'Why?'

'Dunno. Small town. She wouldn't have stayed single too long where I used to live.'

'No. Probably not here either, most likely.' Shane frowned. 'We used to go out, actually. Me and Naomi. For a little while. Years ago. She could do better now obviously, but yeah. We were together then. Back in my footy days.'

'Oh yeah?' Falk hadn't known that, but found he wasn't surprised either. 'Didn't work out?'

'No. I stuffed it up. Usual story. Went to play a game over in Perth. Had sex with someone else in a nightclub toilet.'

'Well,' Falk said. 'That'd do it.'

'Yeah.' They'd wandered back to the oval. Shane lined up and kicked the ball. They watched it glide clean through the goalposts and bounce across the grass. He glanced over, his voice light. 'Why? She said something?'

'Naomi? Not to me.'

'No.' Shane shook his head quickly. 'Didn't think so.' He looked faintly but distinctly disappointed.

'Still.' Falk thought about Naomi, the visits to the vineyard, the way her eyes had sought out Shane at the church. She'd looked like a woman who could be convinced to forgive. 'Twenty years is a long time to stay upset about something.'

'I dunno. Depends.' A ghost of a smile flitted across Shane's face. 'Found myself in Perth a few times. Back in those days.'

He ran over to get the ball and they kicked it back and forth for a while longer until eventually a group of small boys making the most of the school holidays gathered around the goals at the other end. It was clear from the baffled look on their judgemental little faces that it was high time for these old blokes to make way. Shane checked his watch.

'Probably better head back anyway. Do some work.'

'Where do you live?' Falk asked as they started walking.

'Over by the reservoir, not far from Naomi. I keep some clothes and stuff at the vineyard, though. I'll shower and change there.'

Falk glanced over his shoulder. The turn-off to the reservoir lay somewhere behind them along the empty road, well out of sight. Next to him, Shane was twirling the ball in his hands as they walked, whistling softly through his teeth.

'I saw Joel again the other day,' Falk said. 'He was talking about his dad's accident.'

'Oh yeah?' Shane stopped messing with the ball. 'Has there been some news?'

'Not as far as I know. But can I ask you something about that? About finding the scene?'

There was a pause. 'Sure.'

'I know it was a few years ago now, but can you remember approaching it?'

'Yeah, mate.' A tiny, hard smile. 'I remember that day pretty well.'

'What did you see?' Falk hoped Shane would go down the path he wanted without having to be led.

'I dunno. I mean, it was bad. Luna was howling. Is that what you mean?'

'Yeah, that kind of thing. I mean, going on your own gut feeling, did you have a sense someone had left in a hurry? Or had it been quiet for a while?'

Shane's face creased. 'I think –' His eyes were on the road but his gaze was far away. 'I remember I was surprised when

I realised I was the only one there. Took me a while to get my head around that, you know?' He looked over and Falk nodded. 'Maybe because Luna was making such a bloody racket, it felt like Dean should be around. Or because you'd never really expect to be the first one to find something like that. But it couldn't have been too long after it happened, I reckon. Dean walked Luna around six-thirty most mornings, and I probably got there before eight.' He said nothing for a few paces. 'Long enough, I suppose. For something like that.'

'So, the first thing you noticed was Luna,' Falk said, and Shane nodded. They had reached the vineyard and turned up the driveway together. 'What next?'

'Probably that the barrier was broken. That was hard to miss. And there were tracks on the road, where the car had skidded.'

'Staying with the ground for a moment, what did that look like?'

'There were the marks, from the tyres. They'd gouged the dirt where the car braked.' Shane looked over. 'Is that what you're asking?'

'Anything else?'

'Like what?'

They were nearly back at Charlie's house, where Falk could sense the conversation would end. Shane hadn't remembered what Falk had hoped he would, which was perhaps useful in one way, but less useful in another. He'd have to ask.

'Was there broken glass on the ground?'

'Broken glass?' Shane's face was still. 'I'm not sure.'

'No rush, mate. Just think for a minute.' Falk waited, but no answer came. 'Can't say either way?'

'No.' Shane frowned. 'Why? Is it important?'

Falk shook his head. 'I don't know.'

Chapter 29

Marralee Valley's police station was nestled in the heart of the town. Falk had been there only once before, a year earlier, when he'd been invited in to give his statement the day after Kim's disappearance.

He parked now in the afternoon sun and went inside. The reception area was dim, painted the same dull industrial blue that he remembered finding a little oppressive last time. Falk had been kept waiting for a while that day, and could remember sitting there, silently running through what he'd seen at the festival, while wondering vaguely if the colour was a deliberate choice to make visitors feel immediately institutionalised.

Possibly, he'd decided, last year. Probably, he felt certain now, having since met and spent a little time with Sergeant Dwyer. Institutionalised people tended to be more cooperative, and these walls looked like they'd been recoated in the past few years. Dwyer was the type to insist that even the decor pull its weight, Falk thought as he went up to the reception desk and asked for the sergeant.

Out, came the reply. Due back shortly.

Falk left his name and a brief message, then pushed through the doors and back outside into the daylight. At the bottom of the steps he paused and pulled out his phone to call Gemma. He took a moment to enjoy the novelty of having her number right there, and felt a warm rush of exhilaration as she answered.

'Hey,' he said. 'Are we still on for later?'

'Yes.' He could hear that she was smiling. 'I've got cover for around two hours. What do you want to do?'

'I'll have a think,' he said, and so he did, standing outside the police station in the sun, watching the locals pass by on their daily business. After a few minutes, he straightened and joined the flow of foot traffic on the pavement, heading deeper into town in search of a few things.

Dwyer was back by the time he returned. Falk was loading his shopping bags into his car when he spotted the officer climbing the steps to the station. He slammed the boot and followed him in.

'Here to see me?' Dwyer said when he noticed Falk behind him. He didn't look too surprised. He unlocked a security door and motioned for Falk to follow. 'Come through.'

Dwyer's office was painted the same industrial blue as the reception area but in here it felt calm and, if not quite tranquil, then orderly. The space was tidy and highly functional, with neatly labelled filing cabinets squared away against the far wall and a window overlooking the main street. Falk took the visitor's seat across from Dwyer. Like the rest of the room, his desk was clean and as sparse as it was possible for a sergeant's desk to be. It held the only personal items Falk could see – a washed coffee mug and a framed photo of Dwyer, his wife and his daughter. They had their arms around each other and were smiling, but Falk could tell from the girl's age that the photo must have been taken years before she died. Caitlin Dwyer was still a child in the happy moment her father had chosen to remember.

'The Racos' christening went well, I hear,' Dwyer said, his eyes following Falk's to the photo.

'It did, thanks.'

'Good. I was hoping to stop in but I was on duty. Got tied up with something.'

His voice was neutral but something in it made Falk look up. 'Anything new from Kim's appeal?'

Dwyer didn't say yes, but he didn't say no, either. Finally, he leaned back in his chair. 'So, what can I do for you?'

'Right, yeah. I actually wanted to ask you about this.' Falk took out his phone and flicked through to find the video of the accident Joel had shared with him two days earlier. He held it out and Dwyer put on his glasses and leaned forward to see better. 'Joel sent it to me –'

'Joel did?' Dwyer stared at the screen for a long moment, then frowned. He sat back in his chair. 'Sorry, I assumed this was something about Kim.'

'No,' Falk said. 'Dean Tozer.'

Dwyer blinked, catching up, then leaned in again. 'Go on.'

'Joel said you knew he had this video?'

'Yeah. I did. I just haven't seen it in a while.'

Falk waited while he watched in silence. Dwyer's face was set, flickering just once as he reached the footage of himself observing Gemma, deep in grief. When the video finished, Falk rewound a little and paused on the clearest scene. Neither Gemma nor Dwyer were in shot and the ground around the smashed barrier was clear and unobstructed.

'I wanted to ask –' Falk pointed. 'Here. There doesn't look to be any broken glass from the headlights.'

Dwyer peered in for a moment longer. 'No.' He frowned. 'That's right. From memory, there wasn't much at all.'

'No? What did you make of that?'

'Same as you, I'm guessing,' Dwyer said. 'Driver attempted to clean it up.'

'Is that usual? In a situation like this?'

'Well, we don't get many like this, luckily. But attempting to conceal evidence after a traffic accident?' The officer pushed his glasses up his nose and thought for a minute. 'Yeah. It happens. Certain mindset. It's usually harder, though, because most smashes are on roads. Nothing much to be done about glass on tarmac. Here, though –' He pointed to the spot on the screen where the edge of the ground dropped away. 'Got somewhere to hide it.'

'So, what? They swept it into the water?'

'Yeah, wouldn't take much. Push it with the side of your boot or something. We recovered some fragments, but there's all sorts in that reservoir. Broken bottles, dumped rubbish. Got a few different results in, some not definitive at all. Hard to know what was useful and what was junk.' Dwyer glanced up. 'And Joel's been worrying about this, has he? Now?'

'The accident, yes. Not the glass.' Falk took his phone back and put it in his pocket. 'Sounds like he didn't know about that.'

'Maybe not. He was only, what? Twelve, then? And Gemma was pretty torn up, as you can imagine. I can't remember if we talked about it specifically or not. I would've tended to focus on any positive info. Which wasn't much, unfortunately.' Dwyer rubbed a hand over his clean-shaven chin. 'Joel all right, is he? Or struggling?'

'Bit of both, I think,' Falk said. 'Depends how you catch him.'

Dwyer didn't reply straight away. Outside in the hall, Falk could hear the sounds of a photocopier firing up. 'You ever meet Dean?' the officer said, finally.

Falk shook his head.

'Good guy. Well liked around here. Just a normal bloke, accountant, worked locally so most people knew him. It was a real shock. Walking his dog, wrong place, wrong time. And I'm well aware that boy of his thinks I haven't done enough.' Dwyer's eyes fell to the photo of his late daughter. He sounded suddenly deeply exhausted, for the first time since Falk had met him. 'But I understand how he feels. I really do.'

Dwyer sat for a moment longer, staring at the desk, then cleared his throat and checked his watch. He fixed Falk with a steady look, back to his more familiar self.

'Tell me something about Kim. Something I don't know.'

Falk gave a short laugh. 'Pretty sure you know everything I know.'

'Bullshit.' Dwyer was good-natured but firm. 'You were at that christening yesterday. Everyone relaxed, chatting. *Reflecting*. You can't tell me there was nothing.'

Falk started to shake his head, then stopped. There was possibly something, he remembered now.

'Well, you might already know this, but she'd left her job about a year before she disappeared. Resigned, but hadn't told anyone. Not here, anyway. Rohan said she was stressed about work in general, rather than anything specific.'

'Told you there was something.' Dwyer allowed himself to look smug for half a second before growing serious again. 'What was Kim doing for money, in that case?'

'Maybe nothing. She would have been pregnant not long after.'

'You'd expect Rohan would be earning a decent enough wage as an engineer.' Dwyer looked at Falk. 'Or are you thinking financial problems?'

'I really wouldn't know. Not about them. I always tend to lean into the finances, though. Part of the job. Rule it in until I can rule it out. Might be worth considering.'

'Yeah. I will.' Dwyer frowned. 'It's a shame Kim gave up her work, though. For any reason. She was good. We have community fundraising days every year, I do a bit for that addiction charity I'm involved with. Kim ran her own business so she used to design the posters and banners for us at cost.' He swivelled his chair a few degrees so he could see out of the window, onto the main street. 'Her office was just over there before she moved to Adelaide, so I'd see her most days, coming and going.'

Falk looked over Dwyer's shoulder. Across the road, he could make out what looked to be a shared office space. Two businesses – 31A and 31B, Falk could read if he squinted – with a shared frontage and entrance.

'That's where she worked, is it?' Falk said. 'What's in there now?'

'Print shop.' Dwyer pointed to the left-hand office, then the right. 'Lawyer.'

'Were either of those operating when Kim still worked there?'

'No.' At the question, Dwyer swung back a little in his chair to look at Falk. His expression was unreadable. 'They weren't.'

'What?' said Falk.

Dwyer paused, debating silently. 'You're going to read something into this.'

'I'll do my best not to.'

'You will, though.' Dwyer didn't sound judgemental, simply resigned to the inevitable. On the desk, his phone started ringing. He reached for it, but didn't answer immediately. 'You're going to see something that's not there. You will. But you'll be wrong.'

'Okay.'

'One cop to another, this is a small town. It's just one of those things.'

'Try me.'

'For a couple of years, Kim had the office on the right.' Dwyer picked up the phone. 'And until he died, Dean Tozer had the place on the left.'

Chapter 30

Dwyer was right, Falk hated to admit as he stood on the street in front of the office block that Kim and Dean had once shared. Falk's immediate instinct was to read a whole book into that.

He'd left Dwyer to his phone call and walked out of the station and straight across the road. Falk looked at the businesses now – 31A and 31B – and was fairly sure he could feel the officer's eyes on him through the station window. Falk didn't mind. If the situation was reversed, he'd be watching too.

Dwyer had been adamant, though, and Falk knew from personal experience that coincidences were almost daily occurrences in small towns. Still. He breathed out and consciously pushed his instinctive reaction down. Then looked again.

The offices were both nondescript glass-fronted spaces, with a view out onto the main street. There were two people working in the print shop, and a lone woman in the lawyer's office, who regarded Falk warily from her desk when she spotted him peering in. He moved on quickly. From what he could tell from the external layout, the businesses shared nothing but a front door and entrance hall. The occupants would see each other arriving and leaving, but not necessarily during the day. Not unless they wanted to, which Falk supposed they might. Kim and Dean had got along, from everything he'd heard, and they'd both been close to Charlie.

Falk stepped away and walked slowly the whole stretch up and down the main street, past some of the shops he'd been in earlier. He ignored them now, looking beyond the retail fronts and instead counting office spaces. He spotted eight that he thought looked suitable for small to medium businesses. About what he'd expected, give or take. If Kim and Dean had both wanted to work in the centre of town, the choice was not exhaustive. And that choice would have been dictated further by other factors, Falk guessed, such as lease availability. But the fact was, Kim and Dean had found themselves working side by side, for a while at least.

Small-town coincidence, Falk thought as he looked again at 31A and 31B. Sometimes it was just one of those things. Sometimes it wasn't.

'Aaron, mate. G'day.'

Falk heard the familiar voice, and in the reflection of the print shop glass saw someone crossing the street towards him. Charlie.

He turned. 'G'day.'

'Thought that was you.' Charlie was lugging two heavy-looking bags of some agricultural product Falk couldn't identify. He lowered them to the ground with relief and glanced at the office space behind Falk, his eyes lingering on 31B in particular. Kim's former workplace. A cloud crossed his face but he didn't say anything. When he looked back to Falk, his usual smile had returned.

'You heading to the vineyard?' he said. 'Want a lift?'

'No, thanks, I've got the car here,' Falk said. 'I'm catching up with Gemma soon, anyway.'

'Yeah?' Charlie didn't sound surprised by this, but there was a pause as he seemed to consider something. Then he nodded at the bags on the pavement. 'I'm parked around the corner. Got time to give me a hand with these?'

'Sure.'

Falk picked up the nearest one and followed Charlie along the footpath to a shady side street. When they reached his truck, Falk helped him heave one bag into the back, then the other.

'Thanks.' Charlie unlocked the driver's door but didn't open it. Instead he leaned against the side. 'Listen, it's so bloody hard to talk at home right now, people everywhere.' He flashed Falk a grin. 'There's not usually this much mayhem, by the way. It's mostly just me and Shane a lot of the time, getting on with things. You can hear yourself think, at least.'

'Right.'

'Yeah. So anyway, I think Rita might have mentioned, but if you were maybe looking to hang around Marralee –'

No. Falk's internal response was immediate, but he stopped himself before he spoke. Charlie caught it in his face anyway.

'That brother of mine giving me dud info, is he? Wouldn't be the first time.'

'Sorry.' Falk shook his head. 'Go on.'

'Well, the thing is, the business is bigger than it used to be. It's outgrowing the set-up I've got, so I'm having to start to think ahead. I've got Shane, obviously, and the casuals and seasonal teams, but I need someone else year-round. Steady pair of hands to help me and Shane –'

'With what, though?'

'God, all of it.' Charlie laughed. 'If you can find your way around a spreadsheet and a tractor, we'd keep you busy, don't worry about that. It doesn't have to be a boss–employee thing either, if that's what you're worried about. We could do a contractor arrangement if you want. That's what Shane has. I could pull together some numbers, see if it's even in the ball-park for you.'

'Charlie, mate, I know nothing about wine.'

'I can tell that.' But he was smiling. 'It's agricultural at this end, anyway, but to be honest, it's better to have people who aren't too fond of the finished product.' Charlie looked at Falk and shrugged. 'I dunno, mate, I realise it's a bit out of the blue. But from what Greg's told me over the years, you'd be good. There's nothing in this business you couldn't learn if you wanted to.'

'What about Shane? What would he think?' Falk wondered why he was even asking.

'Shane's the one who suggested it. I know how he seems, but he's a lot more switched on than he comes across some-times. Can spot an opportunity when he sees it.'

Falk considered that.

'I'm not an accountant, you know,' Falk said. 'Seriously. It's one thing helping Shane out with a couple of invoices, but I'm not trained or qualified. That's not what I do.'

'Understood,' Charlie said. 'I bet you're good at dealing with them, though.'

Falk had to smile at that. He said nothing for a minute, instead looking down the shady street at the town beyond. At the junction, a woman greeted a couple with delight as they spotted each other crossing the road. Beyond, three old men sitting outside the pub were arguing good-naturedly, cold beers in front of them. The afternoon sky was a dazzling blue above and on the far-off horizon, the rolling hills sat lazy and lush.

'No offence if you're not keen,' Charlie said, and Falk could tell he meant it.

'It's not that. It's –' Falk stopped. What was it? So many things. He shrugged. 'I mean, when did you last consider uprooting your life?'

'Well, never.' Charlie grinned and waved towards the town, the clear sky, the green hills, the flourishing vineyards invisible beyond. 'But I already get to live here.'

Falk smiled. 'I suppose that's true.'

'Anyway –' Charlie pulled the truck door open now. 'No pressure. Just wanted to flag it. Just in case.'

'Okay. Thank you,' Falk said. 'Really. The vineyard's great. And I appreciate the offer.'

'You don't need to thank me, you'd be helping me out, too.' Charlie started the engine and raised a hand out of the window. 'Take some time. Mull it over.'

Falk watched him pull away, and then stood for a while on the peaceful shady street. He didn't need any time, because he didn't need to consider it. But as he walked to his own car and drove to Gemma's house, Falk wasn't entirely surprised to find he could think about nothing else.

Chapter 31

Joel answered the door. Falk had pulled up outside Gemma's cottage, parking in the shade of the eucalyptus trees, and sat there for a while, listening to the soft sounds of the leaves rustling around him. Eventually, he'd got out and rung the bell.

'Hey. Gemma's on her way.' Joel stepped back to let Falk into the hall. He had his thumb wedged between the pages of a novel. 'She texted to say you might get here first. You want a drink or something?'

'No, you're all right, thanks, mate.'

Falk followed him through to the kitchen, where Joel filled a glass of water from the tap. He drank deeply, downing half of it in one go, then swallowed. 'You and Gemma heading out somewhere?'

'Yeah.' Falk hesitated. 'What are you up to?'

'I'm covering a first-aid shift at the festival, so don't worry.' Joel gulped the rest of his water and flashed a grin. 'You don't have to invite me along.'

Falk smiled back. 'Our loss.' He was glad, though. It wouldn't have been the end of the world, but he hadn't really planned for a three-person event.

'Even if I wasn't working, I should probably be studying anyway.' Joel sighed and tossed the book he'd been reading face-up on the counter. On the cover was a pale watercolour picture of a girl in a long dress and a bonnet.

'When do exams start?'

'First one's in a few weeks.'

'Then off to uni?' Falk said as Joel nodded. 'And then what, eventually?'

'Law, I think.' The boy didn't sound entirely enthused. 'Something that gets me a job somewhere else, anyway.'

'You don't like it here?'

'It's not that, it's just boring.'

'Find it a bit quiet?'

'Yeah.' Joel looked at Falk like nothing could be more obvious. 'Because it is.'

'That's not always a bad thing, though.' Falk looked out through the kitchen doors to the verandah where he'd sat with Gemma the first night he'd been there. The bushland was deep and still and he could hear the lorikeets calling to each other. 'Sometimes that can actually be a good thing.'

Joel was staring at him with a slight frown, unsure whether or not he was meant to respond. Falk didn't blame him. He cleared his throat.

'Listen, I had a closer look at your video. Of the accident.'

'Yeah?' Joel straightened immediately against the kitchen counter.

'Don't get excited, though. It was small stuff in the end.' Falk pulled out his phone. 'It's a bit hard to see on this screen but –'

'I've got it on the computer.' Joel put down his empty glass with a clatter and motioned for Falk to follow. Joel's bedroom was marginally neater than Falk might have expected, but that wasn't saying a lot. The boy swept an armload of assorted junk aside so Falk could lean in to see the screen on the desk.

'Yeah, there.' Falk pointed as Joel pulled up the video and paused it. He explained about the glass, and told him what both Shane and Sergeant Dwyer had said. 'So it doesn't really take things forward. I'm sorry.'

The boy was silent for a long time, trawling back and forth through the footage.

'Someone was trying to hide what they'd done,' he said finally. 'While Dad was still down there in the water?'

'It's possible, yeah.'

'Who would do that?'

'People do all kinds of things when they're scared or desperate,' Falk said. 'I'm not excusing it. It doesn't make it right, but it happens.'

'Unbelievable.'

Joel shook his head, his eyes still on the screen. He had one hand on the mouse, and with the other he absently reached across his desk and picked up a slender plastic jar. The container had been kept separate from the rest of the clutter, tucked in carefully at the end of a stack of books. It was a cheap screw-top thing, small enough to fit in Joel's palm, and the boy rolled it between his fingers as he scrolled with his other hand. Something was rattling around inside that Falk couldn't make out. Then Joel sighed and put it down, and the contents suddenly became clear. Falk blinked.

'What've you got in there, mate?' he asked, but he had

guessed now. Inside were a few small shards of wood, raw brown on one side, blue on the other.

'Paint samples from the broken barrier,' Joel said, without looking up from the screen.

'Seriously? Can I see?'

'Sure.' Joel pushed the jar towards him. It was an ordinary container, nothing official about it. Falk held it up and peered at the contents. The wooden shards inside were rough and uneven. He looked at the boy, who was still staring at the screen.

'Did you get these yourself? From the accident scene?'

'Yeah. A couple of days later. Scraped off a few bits with a penknife.' Joel sensed Falk's surprise and looked up. 'What can I say? I watch a lot of movies. And he was my dad, and he was gone, and no-one seemed to be able to tell me what was going on.' He shrugged, his voice quieter. 'I dunno. Just felt weird to leave it all to be cleared away, like it had never happened.'

Falk could understand that. But still. He imagined Joel, twelve years old, down there alone, penknife chipping against the wood. 'Does Gemma know?'

'Yeah. She didn't like having it in the house at first, but –' Joel's expression softened a little. 'I really wanted to keep it, so she let me.'

Falk turned the jar over in his hand, then stepped closer to the window to get a better look. He moved aside a dusty collection of *Star Wars* figurines and held the container up to the light.

'Can I open this?'

'Yeah,' Joel said. 'I do all the time. It's not a scientific sample or anything.'

In Falk's palm, the wood fragments were long and thin. He turned each one carefully to see the painted side. When he'd heard the car involved in the accident was blue, Falk had been picturing something different, he realised now. Something brighter, sportier. This was a dull flat tone. Falk turned the splinters back and forth, watching the colour change a little as it caught the light. He closed his eyes briefly and visualised a whole car painted this shade. The side panels, the doors. Around the headlights. He ran through makes and models in his head, picturing something large and then compact, old and then new, in motion and still and – Falk opened his eyes and stared at the wood chips. Deep in his consciousness, something twitched in recognition.

What was it? Had he seen this car before?

Falk closed his eyes again and tried to tease it out. He thought about the car park at the festival, and the rows and rows of vehicles with their paintwork glinting under the sun or reflecting the lights at night. There? He could easily imagine a car that would fit the bill, but could he remember one?

From down the hall came the sound of the front door squeaking open and then clicking shut. Both Falk and Joel turned at the noise.

'Hello?' Gemma called. 'I'm back.'

Joel quickly touched the mouse to close the video on the computer screen and glanced at the jar in Falk's hand.

'She's not sad the way she used to be.' Joel's voice was low. 'But she doesn't like to be reminded of it.'

'Right.' Falk slipped the wood chips back into the container, screwed the lid on and placed it carefully on the desk. He turned away, then immediately back again. He picked up the jar and held it to the light, then pulled out his phone and snapped a photo. He made sure to capture the paint colour on the wood. Just in case he ever saw it again.

Chapter 32

The winding road leading out of town was just as empty as it had been a few days earlier when Falk had driven in alone from Melbourne. He found it a little hard to believe it hadn't been longer than that and counted back through the week to make sure he was right. Either way, he was enjoying the drive more this time. A lot of things were better with Gemma around.

She was sitting in the passenger seat, and music played softly from the radio as they wound their way up through the hills. Gemma tapped the window as they passed the spot where she'd come off her mountain bike as a ten-year-old and broken her right wrist in *three* places. Falk told her about the time his mate Luke had persuaded him at age eleven to join him on their school roof and he'd slipped and fractured his left elbow. Just in the one place, but they'd both been lucky not to break their necks in hindsight.

The bushland grew heavier on both sides, filtering the light of the low sun and eventually Falk stopped talking and started watching the side of the road. When he saw what he thought

317

he was looking for, he touched the brakes. The gap immediately seemed to disappear. He glanced at the deserted road behind in the rear-view mirror, then slowed some more.

'No, you're right. It's there.' Gemma pointed to an almost invisible opening in the foliage. 'By that big tree. See it?'

'I do now, thanks.' Falk grinned as he turned the steering wheel. 'You've guessed our surprise destination, then?'

'I have.' Gemma laughed but she kept her eyes on him a moment longer, as though learning something new. 'I'm still surprised, though.'

'That's good.'

Falk followed the hidden track, bumping along the rough ground until the bushland thinned and then opened entirely. The spectacular lookout was yet again better than he remembered. The Marralee Valley stretched out below, its vibrant patchwork of greens now bathed in a deep orange glow from the sun hanging heavy in the enormous sky. There was no-one else there, Falk was happy to see as he pulled the car to a stop in the clearing.

'Oh my God,' Gemma said, as they got out. 'You know, it's been absolutely years since I've been up here. You forget how good it is.' She nodded back towards the hard-to-spot track. 'This used to be a bit of a local secret, or does every city blow-in know it now?'

'I don't think all of us yet.' Falk smiled. 'Raco showed me last year.'

'Well, I think we can forgive him.' Gemma wandered to the edge and Falk joined her at the barrier. 'As long as you're careful. Last time I was here, I brought a friend visiting from the States and she dropped her phone over the side.'

'Seriously? That was gone, I'm guessing.' Falk looked down

at the impenetrable tangle of bushland far below. The dense canopy covered the ground.

'Yeah, no chance. And it was a beta prototype she was testing, so –'

'She took the loss with humour and good grace?'

'You can imagine. I felt really bad, but what could we do? You can't get down there, but she didn't really understand the bushland around here. In the end I had to drive all the way around the perimeter to convince her she couldn't hike in.' She smiled over at him. 'So that soured the afternoon a little.'

'Good to know.' Falk turned away from the edge and headed back across the clearing. 'I'll keep hold of my belongings.'

'That's a strong start.' Gemma watched with curiosity as he unlocked the car boot. 'What have you got there, anyway?'

'Well.' Falk pulled out his bags of shopping from earlier and carried them over to the small picnic table. 'I know you said the other night at the festival that you didn't need champagne and sunsets.' He unfolded a tablecloth over the battered surface, then laid out two glasses and unzipped a chiller bag. 'But then I was thinking, no-one *needs* champagne and sunsets. They're just nice to have, like house plants or free wi-fi.'

'Seriously?' Gemma came over to the table. She was laughing, but the delight was real, he could tell. 'That's what we're doing tonight, champagne and sunsets?'

'Yeah, I thought we could give it a go. Although, it's technically a multi-award-winning sparkling wine from the Marralee region,' Falk said, pulling the bottle from the chiller bag and reading the label. 'It's one of the world class ones so I thought it made more sense with your connections to the local producers. And –' He rummaged through another bag. 'I've got a bottle stopper and some sparkling water as well, because as much fun as this is, I'm driving and you're back on duty later.'

'That's very responsible.'

'Also,' Falk looked at his watch, 'I've checked today's sunset time and we actually have to head off pretty much as soon as it's done to get you back on site by the end of your break.'

He glanced up. Gemma was leaning against the table, her head tilted as she watched him, and he stopped.

'Is this all okay?'

'Aaron.' She stepped around the picnic bench so they were face to face. She put her hands around his waist and he could feel the warmth of her skin through his shirt. 'Practical romance is my absolute favourite kind.'

'Yeah? Because some people don't like it.'

'Some people don't know how to live.'

He opened the bottle and she poured and they sat on the bench together, backs resting against the table as they watched the sun sink towards the hill. Overhead, the sky slowly changed, the colours growing rich and deep.

After a while, Gemma sighed contentedly and stretched out her legs in front of her. 'God, this is nice. Pretty great for a Monday night.'

It was, Falk thought. Right up there. 'I can see why you like living here.'

'Yeah?' She looked over. 'Fair warning, it's not always like this. Only when someone pulls out an unexpectedly lovely sweeping romantic gesture.'

'You might find it hard to believe, but this is my very first sweeping romantic gesture.'

'Really? Amazing debut.'

'Thanks. I'm happy you like it. Although I have to say, this bloody sunset –' Falk tipped his empty glass towards the glorious dying blaze, beautiful but brief. '– is starting to feel a bit like a metaphor. So Gemma, look, can we try and work something out for after I leave? Please.'

He really wanted the answer to be yes this time. He hadn't realised quite how much until he'd asked the question.

'Well,' Gemma started, but she was already nodding and he felt a wave of relief. 'I mean, of course. Obviously. I'd love to work something out too.' A tiny frown crossed her face. 'That's never really been the issue. It's more what that would look like.'

'Yeah. I know.'

'But –' What was left of the light was dazzling and Gemma leaned her head back and shut her eyes as she thought for a minute. 'I mean, Joel leaves for uni next year.' She turned her head and squinted at him. 'Maybe that changes the equation a bit.'

'Yeah?' An instant spark of hope flared, but Falk kept it contained. 'The festival still needs to be run, though.'

'It does. But I suppose I'm hardly the only person in the world who could do that.'

'You're too good at it to just stop, though. Would there be something similar you'd be interested in doing?'

'Something where?' He could tell she was considering it, at least. 'In Melbourne?'

'For example. That would obviously be highly convenient for me.' Falk smiled. He put his empty glass down and reached for her hand, their fingers intertwining. 'But it is also the nation's cultural capital. Thriving arts and events scene.'

'I know that,' Gemma nudged him affectionately, 'because Melburnians are always telling me so.'

'What can I say? We're very proud of it. And it's true.'

'Fair enough.' She laughed, and they looked at each other for a long moment. Finally, she shrugged. 'And, yes, probably. I'm sure if I asked around I could find something else.'

Gemma's eyes left his face and she turned back to the view over the valley. Falk watched her as she gazed out. The town below looked far away and peaceful in the dusk.

'I understand it's not only about the festival, though,' he said.

'No.' She smiled. 'But it's hard to explain without sounding really insular.'

'Have a go.'

'I suppose . . .' Gemma thought for a minute. 'There's a lot of good everyday stuff that comes with living here. Little things add up. Having close friends, recognising faces in the street. No commute. I like having time to read the books for book club, being able to stop for a spontaneous coffee with someone. I love the seasons here, the way the vines change. I always have. I missed that when I was away. And it's our friends and neighbours, obviously. The way they stepped up and were there for me and Joel when we needed it.'

'You don't get that everywhere.'

'No.' Gemma's eyes were still on the valley. 'You don't. And I've met people over the years – like when I was in the US – people who you just know will spend their whole lives chasing after something they hope will make them happy. And, okay, that looks different for everyone, and I'm not saying I couldn't be happy somewhere else. Because of course I could.'

'But you're happy now? Here?'

'I am.' She turned to him now. The sun was almost gone,

the sky growing deeper above them. The first star was out. 'I think our grass here is really green.'

Falk looked at her. *Stay or go?* The question felt bigger out here. He took a breath. 'Charlie asked if I wanted to work at the vineyard.'

Gemma said nothing at first, and he could almost hear her thinking.

'Well, now. That would be highly convenient for *me*.' She smiled. 'A big change, though.'

'Yeah.'

'Too big?'

Falk paused, then nodded. 'I think it might be. I'm sorry.'

'No.' Gemma squeezed his hand. 'Seriously. You don't have to be sorry for not wanting to chuck in your whole career. Especially for someone you barely know. I mean, neither of us should be.' She rested back against the table. 'It's good that work's important to you. And the AFP still needs someone to crack all those cases.'

Falk smiled. She was close enough that he could detect the faint scent of her shampoo and fabric softener. When he breathed in, it reminded him of being in her bedroom, with the sun on the sheets. He could feel himself slipping into somewhat uncharted territory.

'I suppose work is pretty important to me. Definitely on some level.' When he spoke again, he took his time. A quiet truth that he'd rarely, if ever, acknowledged was slowly shaping itself into words and he wanted to explain it right. 'That's not really why I can't see myself leaving, though.'

'No?'

'No. I mean, that's part of it.' Falk hesitated. 'But it's more that walking away from the job doesn't feel like a real option, because –' He stopped again. He knew what he wanted to say, but he'd never voiced it out loud before. 'Because I feel like I've sacrificed too much for it. I don't just mean the long hours and evenings and weekends, I'm talking about things going back years. Okay, for instance –' Having started, Falk found he couldn't stop. '– why did I stay at uni to study all the time instead of going home to visit Dad?' The example presented itself to him fully formed. 'There were so many weekends when I could have gone to watch the footy with him, or catch up for a drink or something. So many. I knew he wanted me to. But I never did, because I was working hard to get the grades I needed to move ahead. And I did get them. But Dad and I didn't get to the footy.'

The words carried the acid prickle of a shameful admission but when Falk looked over, Gemma didn't seem disapproving or even surprised. She was simply listening, and he could feel the soft steady movement of her breathing next to him as he spoke.

'And there are other times. I let people I really cared about slip away,' he went on. 'And I could give you lots of reasons why, but the fact I couldn't find much time for them has always played a part. Always. I've skipped birthdays, things that matter. Stuff that doesn't, but kind of does as well. Friday night drinks, swims at the beach. Relationships have just . . . faded. I barely see the Racos, who are honestly the best friends I've ever had.'

The hills were dark outlines against the night now. Falk could hear the soft hum and rustle of the bushland around them, the familiar sounds like fragments of conversations and faces he hadn't realised he even remembered.

'The job is demanding. It is. But I knew it would be. And

I knew I'd have to give up all kinds of things over the years that I can't get back now. And maybe that's okay. But to drop it mid-career, it would feel like –' He found it physically hard to say the words. 'Like that was for nothing.'

Gemma nodded, her face hard to read in the dark. The sun was completely gone.

'Anyway, so, yeah. That's why.' Falk cleared his throat and dredged up a small smile as he checked his watch. 'But, look, it's probably time we –'

Gemma didn't move other than to touch his hand. Her palm was warm and solid. 'We can be a little late.'

Falk hesitated, but then settled back on the bench. They sat together in silence for another minute, the night drawing in around them.

'Sunk costs are gone,' he said. 'I can accept that. You can't get them back, but –' He stopped again.

'They still cost you something.' Gemma was watching him with that expression again. Like she was seeing something new. 'I know. It's hard to walk away from that.'

'Yeah. It really is.'

She said nothing at first, thinking. Eventually, she took a breath. 'I can't speak for other people in your life, Aaron, because I don't know them.' Her eyes met his. 'But you knew them. And if you cared about them, I'm assuming they were fairly decent, reasonable people?'

Falk had to smile at that. 'Mostly, as far as I know.'

'So would they understand?' she said. 'If they'd heard what you just said?'

He thought about it. The answer was clearer than he'd expected. 'Probably.'

'They'd forgive you?'

He looked over. 'I can see where you're going with this.'

'So that's a yes?'

'Yeah. I think so.'

'And now that a bit of time's passed, would any of these normal, decent people have a huge problem with you forgiving yourself?'

He made himself consider, but he found he already knew the answer. 'No.' The word itself felt like a release. 'I mean, of course they wouldn't.' He looked across at Gemma. She still didn't seem surprised.

'What kind of farming was your dad in?' she said after a moment. 'Back in your old town. Sheep, was it?'

'Yeah.'

'What was his general position on chasing losses?'

Falk smiled. 'He thought it was bullshit.'

'I'll bet he did.' Gemma smiled back. 'And look, only you know what's going to be best for you. So I'm really not pushing one way or the other – as much as I'd love to, I'm not. But I do think it's worth stopping and looking around once in a while. Take stock. See if anything's changed over time.'

Falk didn't reply. He gazed out across the darkened valley once more, then he got up from the bench and reached for her hand. Gemma stood too and stepped in close as he wrapped his arms tight around her. He buried his face in her hair, and the smell of the shampoo and fabric softener blurred with the relief of the conversation and the memory of her sheets in the afternoon sun.

'Thank you,' he said, and he felt her shrug lightly against him and hug him tighter.

'Thank you, too. This was perfect, by the way. Sweeping, romantic. So practical.'

Falk smiled, his lips against her head. Night had fallen fully, he realised, when they eventually pulled apart.

'Well, I could seriously stay here for hours.' He glanced at the sky and reluctantly checked his watch again. 'But we had better head off if we're going to get you back.'

Gemma touched Falk's chest gently with her fingertips and looked up into his face. 'Do you know what my second favourite romantic trait is?'

'I'm hoping it's punctuality.'

'You read my mind.'

Chapter 33

They drove back to the festival in a silence that was warm and relaxed, if not fully contented. Unresolved decisions, Falk supposed. He watched the winding road ahead as Gemma stared out of the window, both wrapped deep in their own thoughts. The streets grew busier as they neared the grounds and when Falk turned into the car park, Gemma sighed and pulled out her phone. She scrolled through her messages and Falk glanced across at the passenger seat.

'Didn't miss too much?'

'No. It all seems –' She paused, though, her finger hovering above the screen.

He manoeuvred into a parking space as she tapped a button and lifted the phone to her ear. Falk could hear the tinny whisper of a voicemail, and looked over in time to catch her frown.

'Everything okay?' he asked as she lowered the phone.

There was another pause, a little longer this time. Gemma was staring at her screen, her face lit by the artificial glow. 'Has Greg called you as well?' she asked.

Falk turned off the engine and reached for his own phone. A few work messages, but nothing from Raco. 'What did he want?'

Gemma was listening to the voicemail again. She hung up and clicked the screen to black. The lights from the festival entrance shone bright through the car windscreen and the sounds of music and crowds floated through the air.

'He wants to know exactly when I last saw Kim.'

'Does he say why?'

'No.'

Falk kissed Gemma goodbye inside the main gates and watched her disappear down the path in the direction of the festival headquarters. When she was gone, he took out his phone and tried Raco, listening to the ringtone on the other end. No answer. Falk thought for a minute, then set off in the direction of the vineyard stall.

The Monday night festival crowd was lighter and easier to navigate, and Falk could see further ahead than he was used to. He spotted Raco's family and friends gathered around the stall before any of them saw him. The casual workers were once again behind the table, smiling and pouring for customers, and Falk saw Charlie unloading a crate of bottles. Shane was there as well, leaning against a post, chatting to someone. As he laughed and shifted his weight, Falk saw a blonde head appear. Naomi. She was laughing too.

'Hey, you made it.'

Falk felt a hand on his arm and turned at the voice. Rita.

'How was your evening?' she asked, interested but not intrusive.

'It was really nice, thanks.'

'Well, it's about to get even better because we're heading over to tackle the kids' rides in a minute.' She grinned. 'If you want to join me for the walk? Please say yes.'

'I would, but –' Falk scanned the group. Across the track, Raco's older brother Ben was shepherding his various children out of the way of passers-by while managing to simultaneously hold a conversation with Rohan. Zoe was watching them from her pram, looking bored. 'Where's Greg?'

'He's with Eva and Zara. They've gone to see Joel at the first-aid station.'

'By the east exit? Did he say why?'

'No. Just to say hello, I think.' Rita had caught the note in his voice, though, and frowned. 'They should be back soon.'

'Right.' Falk's eyes met hers. She'd lived with a police officer long enough that some things could go unsaid. 'Listen, has he mentioned anything to you?'

'About what? Kim?'

'Yeah.'

'Not to me. Not today, anyway.' Rita shifted her weight to glance beyond Falk, over to where the rest of the family was starting to move, gathering up children and belongings. She turned back. 'Go and talk to him. You know where we'll be.'

The east of the site was as empty as always and Falk passed only a handful of people after he cleared the rides and stalls and drew closer to the exit.

He spotted Raco straight away, alone, a few steps beyond the rope that hung across the break in the fence. He had his back turned and his arms folded across his chest as he stared out at the bushland. Joel and Zara were watching him in silence from the first-aid station, while Eva played with Joel's blood

330

pressure cuff. They all looked up as Falk came nearer and he caught a flash of relief cross the teenagers' faces. How long had Raco been standing there like that? Falk raised a hand to them, then ducked under the rope himself.

Raco turned at the sound. 'Oh. G'day.' His voice was flat and his eyes slid straight back to the reservoir track. He wasn't smiling.

'Hi, mate,' Falk said, stepping onto the path beside him. They stood shoulder to shoulder, looking down to where the body of water lay hidden beyond the trees. Falk hesitated, but only for a moment. If he couldn't trust Raco, he couldn't trust anyone. 'Gemma says the answer is around fifteen months before Kim disappeared.'

'Right.' Raco didn't sound surprised. He looked over, caught Falk's expression, and his voice changed. 'Don't worry. I've asked everyone.'

'Yeah? When they last saw Kim?' Falk felt a tiny thread of relief run through him. He hadn't really been worried, but still. Ahead, the silvery shadows on the trail shifted as the breeze rustled the trees. 'Why?'

'Just trying to get it clear in my head,' Raco said. 'So around fifteen months, Gemma reckons, since she had significant contact with Kim?' He nodded. 'Sounds about right.'

'Does it?' Falk frowned, trying to follow.

'Naomi says the same. Shane reckons a bit longer for him. Zara was in touch more often, as you'd expect, but even she found Kim hard to get hold of. Charlie says he hadn't seen her in person for a full year. Rita and I hadn't seen her in two.'

'Okay.' A fair while then, Falk thought. For all of them. But he wasn't sure what –

'Daddy?' They both turned to see Eva on the other side of the exit. 'Can we go?'

Zara was following a few paces behind and shrugged an apology. 'She says she's had enough.'

'No worries, don't blame you, mate,' Raco said, ducking under the rope and taking his daughter's hand. 'Yeah, let's go.' He turned to Zara. 'You coming too?'

Zara hesitated, then glanced towards Joel, who was patiently tidying up the equipment Eva had been fiddling with. 'I think I'll stay here for a while.'

'All right. Come on, Eva. We'll find Mum at the rides.'

Eva extended her other hand to Falk, swinging herself between him and Raco as they headed back into the site. The sounds and music grew louder as they drew closer to the attractions, the crowd filling in around them.

'So what's going on, mate?' Falk said as they walked.

'I really don't know. Been thinking, I suppose,' Raco said over his daughter's head. 'I mean, I get it that Rob Dwyer has a hard time believing Kim didn't talk to any of us on the night. For what it's worth, I can take his point on that.' He shrugged. 'But it was a really busy night. And then when Zoe was found alone, it didn't feel like a stretch to chalk up the whole night to Kim behaving out of character.'

Raco's mouth was a hard line as he swung his daughter. Screams from the rides echoed in the night air.

'But the thing is, avoiding us wasn't out of character for Kim lately,' he said. 'It hadn't been for a while. Rita was right the other day, saying that Kim wouldn't have come to the christening. She probably wouldn't have. She'd been pulling away.'

'You don't think it was just a distance thing?' Falk felt the weight of Eva's small hand gripping his. 'Her moving to Adelaide, maybe some mental health issues in there as well?'

'Well, yeah. I did think that. But if I take a step back, it feels like there's more to it. On the one hand, okay, it's a few unreturned phone calls or Kim not mentioning that she'd left her job, or never getting around to visiting. But for her to drift away from everyone she used to be close to feels . . .' Raco shrugged. 'Deliberate, I suppose. That night at the festival wasn't unusual. It was how things were between us and Kim. It's like she was gone before she was even gone.'

They slowed on the path to let a children's mini-train on wheels trundle across in front of them, groups of energetic kids and their tired-looking parents waving from the carriages. Eva dropped Falk's and Raco's hands to wave back and they both dutifully did the same.

'They friends of yours, Eva?' Falk asked as she enthusiastically waved them off into the distance, and she looked at him like it was a silly question.

'No. It's what you're supposed to do here.' Her tone had enough of Rita in it that Falk had to smile. 'It's fun.'

'You know what? You're right, Eva. It is.'

With the track ahead clear once more, they walked on, the lights from the rides throwing bright colours onto their faces. Falk turned back to Raco and had opened his mouth when the words simply disappeared. It happened without warning as, in a dormant part of his mind, something stirred. Whatever it was shifted, heavy and stubborn, only to resettle awkwardly. It left behind a mild but distinctly uncomfortable sensation, as though Falk had forgotten something he really needed to remember. He blinked in confusion. What had triggered that?

He walked on, doing his best to fade out the noise and bustle around him as he tried to capture the thought. A few paces ahead, Eva pointed at some people on a ride. And *there*. There it was again, another unwieldy shudder, before the sensation sank back into the depths. The uneasy feeling lingered, though, pulsing and persistent. There was too much going on around for Falk to get a clear read. Still, he waited. Nothing more. Finally, he gave up and looked over at Raco.

'So what are you thinking?' Falk said. 'With Kim?'

'I don't know. I mean, it probably doesn't add much in real terms. Doesn't change the fact that Zoe was found alone. Or that Kim must have taken herself out of that east exit, or that her shoe turned up in the water. But I can think of a few reasons someone might cut themselves off, and none of them are good. It's a red flag any way you look at it.' Raco glanced down at his daughter. 'You know, if a report like that came across my desk at work, especially with a baby involved, I'd have been asking questions straight away. Getting some of the health teams involved, I'd be thinking maternal welfare checks, that kind of thing.' New lines formed on his face. 'You can be too close sometimes. See what you expect to see, not what's really in front of you.'

The alert pulsing in Falk's head ratcheted up a whole notch.

'There's Mummy.'

Eva pointed and up ahead, Falk could see Rita standing by one of the baby rides. The concern hadn't quite left her eyes. Charlie was there too, talking to his older brother and Rohan, all three leaning in to hear each other over the music. Shane was checking his phone, frowning at the screen, but Naomi was nowhere to be seen. On the far side of the track, the ferris wheel rose up into the sky. It creaked and groaned through its lazy rotation.

'You coming over?' Raco said to Falk as Eva pulled on his hand.

'Yeah. I will. Be there in a sec.'

Falk slowed and stepped clear of the path. He watched Eva run ahead of her dad, arms outstretched and suddenly found himself picturing her just a few minutes earlier. Waving at the train ride, sounding a lot like her mother. The alert was coming faster and louder now because in Falk's head that thing that felt so heavy and stale and worn was moving again. Not just moving, but taking on a different shape. He closed his eyes and forced himself to focus. The shape was something he recognised, but as he turned it over and then over again, it shifted and re-formed in an unexpected way, catching a new light. And different shadows, too. Ones that made it look both familiar and like something else entirely.

Falk's eyes flicked open. He stepped onto the path and walked a few fast paces, stopping when he reached the base of the ferris wheel.

We see what we expect to see.

Falk ignored what was right in front of him and instead cast his mind back, re-creating the scene in front of him as clearly as he possibly could. This same spot, twelve months earlier. What had happened?

Gemma and Naomi had been there. A short distance along that same path, their heads close as they spoke. Rohan too, underneath the wheel itself, chatting to the Queensland tourists. Elsewhere on the grounds, out of sight, Raco and Rita had been with their children. Shane and Charlie at the vineyard stall. Zara making her way to the bushland party. Joel, lovesick and alone at the first-aid station. And Falk himself, here in this spot.

We see what we expect to see.

Falk looked up. Because now, he was thinking about more than just that moment last year. He was thinking about other things too. About Kim on the phone to Charlie and Zara. What was said, and what wasn't said. And Joel at the east exit sticking to his story. And Raco checking the fence perimeter. And the most efficient and terrifying way to make a parent do anything you might want them to do. And how Eva Raco, like her mother, was sometimes so very right.

We see what we expect to see.

Falk gazed at the ferris wheel, up to the top carriages rising high in the air. He lifted his arm and waved. He waited.

We see what we expect to see.

A dozen hands waved back.

Gone before she was gone.

Chapter 34

Kim

Charlie was calling her again.

Kim saw his name on her screen. She was sitting in the passenger seat of her husband's car, her six-week-old daughter asleep in the back. It had been a while, but she still recognised the bushland surrounding them. They were about half an hour from Marralee.

Kim glanced sideways at Rohan. His eyes were fixed on the road, carefully navigating the turns, travelling just below the speed limit. Had he seen Charlie's name on the screen? She couldn't be sure.

'Are you going to get that?'

Her husband didn't look at her when he spoke.

★   ★   ★

Kim's problems with Charlie hadn't begun with Dean Tozer's death, but it was then that they'd started to get worse.

Charlie had taken to disappearing for long stretches on

his own, coming back with grief clinging to him like vapour. Whenever Kim tried to talk to him, her attempts were brushed away, gently at first and then later with a dash of impatience. Silence and sadness crept through their house, seeping into the fabric of their days. Kim found herself alone a lot of the time. Standing in the kitchen, staring out at long rows of vines as she made a cup of tea or washed out Zara's lunchbox, listening for the sound of Charlie's key in the door. She knew those lost hours were being spent down at the reservoir, but the very first time she'd asked him about it, he'd lied – automatically and badly. That was unusual enough to be unsettling for them both and Kim hadn't asked again. She hadn't really needed to, she knew Charlie well enough to guess why he was going. He needed space to grieve for his friend in a way he felt he couldn't around anyone else. Including Kim herself. And she understood that. But still, this didn't feel right.

It was the hint of shame around the whole thing that bothered her most, especially after she started to suspect Shane was doing the same. Kim just hung around her empty kitchen, slamming drawers in frustration. They all missed Dean, and his death felt like a body blow. Of course it did. None of them needed to hide that from each other. She was desperate to throw some sunlight and air on their mutual pain, sit down together and open a bottle of something good and fill their glasses. Say out loud the words she was sure they were thinking so they could all agree it was a horrible, shit thing to have happened and, yes, it still really hurt.

Charlie wouldn't give her the chance. He seemed able to sense the conversation coming, even while Kim was still drawing breath, and immediately was *so busy* or *dead tired* or just *grabbing his keys on his way out*. He still went absent for hours at a time – Kim banged the cutlery drawer closed so hard the knives rattled – apparently safe and secure in the knowledge that she wouldn't come to the reservoir to find him.

She was considering it, though. Kim would go to the reservoir, if she had to. She simply preferred not to. But she would. And then, almost as if Charlie had been able to tell what she was thinking, he'd stopped going overnight.

It didn't help. The little arguments that had been brewing even before Dean died began flaring again like spot fires. Kim could sense both herself and Charlie keeping constant watch, racing to put them out before they ran too far. It was exhausting for him, too, she could tell. They both wanted to stop. They tried. They just didn't seem to be able to.

They only fought about small things, Kim would think as she lay awake at night, exhausted and fractious, listening to Charlie's slow breathing. But for how long did small stuff stay small? she wondered. How many years until it all added up into something too big to ignore? Kim stared at the ceiling, counting how many years she'd been with Charlie, and thought she knew the answer to that. She had known for a while, she suspected.

Sometimes Kim would catch an unexpected glimpse of Charlie, trudging through the vineyard or avoiding her gaze at the dinner table, and he'd seem older and bigger and worn in a way that she could barely reconcile with the clear-eyed boy from that first autumn day. She could still remember the sound of his voice, though. Calling out to her all those years ago as he chased her bike through the leaves, his face flushed when he'd caught up.

'Hey,' he'd said, breathless.

'Hi.'

And it was, as fifteen-year-old Kim had written in her diary, love.

Sometimes now, when Charlie occasionally laughed or they talked about their daughter, she could still take herself back to that moment. But a lot of the time, it felt like a story she'd heard about two other people.

Dean's funeral had been a lurid nightmare. It hadn't even been a funeral, technically. It had been worse, a memorial service, because they still hadn't recovered his body. Everyone had been there. Rohan had driven back to Marralee to attend.

Kim had been at the sink in the church kitchen fetching Gemma a glass of water and had watched Rohan draw up and park his clean black car considerately in a difficult spot. He was on time and dressed in an understated charcoal suit and she was struck by how he'd grown into the features that as a teenager had made him seem so awkward and self-conscious. Rohan had spotted her through the window. He'd smiled and raised a hand, his delight at seeing her transforming his face in a way that had caught Kim off guard. And she found herself, entirely inappropriately in that moment at the church sink, remembering how Charlie hadn't been the only boy who'd used to look at her like that.

The next few hours had been focused on helping Gemma simply get through the ordeal, and Kim hadn't come face to face with Rohan again until people were leaving. She'd been collecting empty glasses on a tray and she'd looked up to see him and his charcoal suit making their way across the room. Rohan had stopped every few paces, gathering up any used glasses in his path until both hands were full by the time he reached her. He'd held them out like an offering.

'Thank you.' She'd smiled, for what felt like the first time all afternoon.

'How are you?' he'd asked.

Kim was, she realised, happy to see him.

They'd chatted as Rohan had helped her clear the rest of the tables. He'd been working for an engineering firm in Sydney for a few years, but was now heading up their operations in Adelaide. Next time she was in the city, she should let him know. They should catch up. It would be great to see her. And Charlie.

Of course, they both readily agreed. And Charlie.

Kim had been in Adelaide a few times after that. She had never called Rohan. She had never mentioned the conversation to Charlie either.

Kim and Charlie had tried to work it out. Or maybe they hadn't, she sometimes thought later. They knew each other well enough to realise they'd reached the end, whatever was said or done. The separation had been sad and subdued. Charlie had dutifully asked her not to go, to give them another chance, but Kim had been able to detect the faint echo of relief beneath his words. She had been right at fifteen. It had been love. But they weren't teenagers anymore, and he was worn out too.

He didn't argue too hard against Kim's suggestion that she and Zara make a fresh start in Adelaide. It wasn't far away, and they both knew they would slip back to each other if they stayed too close. Habit and loneliness weren't good enough reasons to be together. It was one thing when it was just the two of them, but they wouldn't do it to Zara, this uncertain back and forth.

And things were good in Adelaide. Kim found a job she enjoyed, at a firm run by a woman she'd collaborated with on a design brief a few years earlier. She took up Pilates, discovered a great farmers' market. She was definitely happier, all things considered. If this break-up with Charlie felt worse than the ones that had come before, Kim thought, it was only because this time they both knew it was for good.

Zara, for her part, seemed to be simply waiting for her mother to change her mind and take them home. She completed one full week at her new school in near silence before looking at Kim over her untouched Friday night takeaway and asking if she could please go back to Marralee.

'Give it a chance,' Kim had said.

'How long?'

'At least a year.'

'And then I can go back?'

Kim wasn't about to make the rookie error of committing to that, but in a response that even she could tell reeked of desperation, she threw herself into showing Zara the best side of their new life. Months of movies and outings and restaurants and activities followed, until they were both exhausted and Zara still no happier. It had been with a growing sense of despair that they'd found themselves yet again at Glenelg Beach one Sunday afternoon, Kim half-heartedly splashing around in the water and encouraging her sad-eyed daughter to swim. She had been right on the cusp of flinging their damp, sandy towels in a bag and calling it a day when a jogger had unexpectedly slowed, then stopped. He'd shielded his eyes, squinting against the glare of the water.

'Kim? That you?'

And she discovered she was, once again, happy to see Rohan.

At first, it had been friendly coffees and platonic day trips. He'd actually managed to suggest a few things that even Zara had begrudgingly enjoyed. They'd taken it slow and steady, but Kim and Rohan had been something more than friends for six months before she finally told Charlie.

'Great. Good to hear you're happy,' Charlie had said. He was really trying to sound like he meant it, she could tell, which made her feel worse than anything else he could have done. But then he'd taken another breath.

'So. Rohan, eh?' There had been an odd note in his voice followed by a very long pause. 'You sure about that, Kim?'

She had hung up.

She was annoyed with herself later for not pushing back, because yes, thank you very much, Charlie, she *was* sure. Rohan had a reliable steadiness about him that Charlie had never had. Their relationship didn't have the same highs and lows that Kim was used to, but there was something about that that she found intensely comforting. Rohan was thoughtful in a holistic way. He was considerate, and not only to her. He conducted daily life in a considered way. Before Rohan did anything, he thought it through.

Kim and Charlie had had the argument anyway – of course they had – but later, after she was engaged. When it had all suddenly seemed real. Charlie had driven down to pick up Zara for handover and a passing comment about the house Kim now shared with Rohan had been clumsily delivered and badly received, and the two of them had found themselves throwing furious whispered words at each other in the walk-in pantry while Zara packed in her bedroom.

'– made yourself very clear, Kim, don't you worry about that. But Rohan, for God's sake. He's not the right –'

'What, and you are?'

'No. God, no. Not me. I am *done*. Okay? I'm so tired of this. Be with Rohan, if that's what you want. But don't you come crying to me about him, Kim. Understand? Please. I can't do it.' Charlie had had tears in his eyes. 'I don't want to hear it. Ever.'

'Fine. Got it. Keep your voice down.'

Charlie was angry and lashing out because he was hurt, Kim knew, but so was she. Later, still more shaken than she'd expected to be, she had told Rohan about the fight. He'd reached for his bookmark and got up from the couch and wrapped his arms around her.

'That's Charlie for you. I'm sorry.' He held her, tight and firm. 'For what it's worth, I think he's a bit jealous.'

That was true, Kim thought. But by then she knew Rohan better. And she suspected that Charlie was not the only one.

They'd all been on their best behaviour after that. Charlie had apologised. Zara told Kim that he'd sat her down at their kitchen table at home in Marralee and calmly explained his part in the break-up, and how the split wasn't Kim's fault. Or not only her fault. It didn't seem to make a difference, Zara was still desperate to go home to the vineyard, but Kim was grateful that Charlie had at least tried.

Their phone calls were now wholly and exclusively about Zara. They were short and rigid with courtesy. That was a reasonable outcome, Kim supposed, even if it felt like she was talking to someone she didn't know. She and Rohan invited Charlie to their wedding because Zara had expected it and Kim couldn't see how they could avoid it. He had attended,

Kim suspected, for the same reason. When the two men's paths crossed, both Rohan and Charlie were so jovial and good-natured that Kim wondered if she was the only one who could see they were both faking it.

Zara didn't even try to fake it anymore. She never settled into their new life in the way Kim had hoped she would. Her pleading was incessant.

'You said I only had to give it a year.'

'No, I said *at least* a year, Zara.'

'But it's been nearly two. Please.'

Kim braced herself for the arguments to escalate, but instead Zara seemed to sink lower, drawing further into herself in a way that was so much worse. Kim strung it out for another couple of months, hoping for a change of heart she knew wouldn't come. Eventually, after trying absolutely everything she could think of, she couldn't bear to see Zara so unhappy anymore. She called Charlie and they agreed their daughter would return to Marralee, for now at least. Zara had cried when Kim had told her, deep shuddering tears of relief.

'Thank you.' She had hugged her mother.

'I just want you to be happy.'

It was, Kim told Rohan later, the worst day of her life.

'Give her some time,' he'd said gently. 'She's confused and upset. It's not like she's chosen Charlie over you.'

It was, though, Kim thought as soon as he said it. That was *exactly* what it was like.

Zara had stepped seamlessly back into Marralee life, the transition easy and effortless, and it turned out she wasn't confused and upset there. She was happy and she had friends and as teenagers they all wanted nothing more than to go to the festival opening night party by the reservoir. The longest conversation Kim and Charlie had in more than a year was whether to allow Zara to go.

'What do you think?' Charlie said.

It was a good question. What did Kim think?

I actually do remember what it's like being your age, Kim had sometimes told Zara when they were still living under the same roof. *Believe it or not.*

But Kim didn't remember what it was like to be sixteen at that bushland party.

She remembered *wanting* to go. She remembered the crushing disappointment of missing it the year before because she'd been on holiday with her parents, returning to the gossip and buzz and the distinct feeling that she'd been left out of something special. She remembered fizzing with the anticipation of being part of it this time.

But when the day came around, Kim and Charlie had been arguing. She remembered that too. He'd kept her waiting for ten minutes at their meeting spot in the park and when he'd finally arrived she was brooding and angry, and he couldn't seem to understand why because it was only ten bloody minutes, after all. And okay, it *was* only ten minutes, but the week before that Charlie had completely forgotten they were supposed to meet at all. Kim had hung around for a whole hour then, before giving up and walking home alone, brushing away hot, furious tears. She hadn't told him, mainly because she was embarrassed at having waited for so long.

They were still arguing over those ten late minutes when they'd reached the campfire at the clearing. The party had already started and they'd looked at each other and it had occurred to Kim that if they were going to call a truce, this was the moment. If Charlie had moved first, with a gentle touch or a whispered apology, she would have responded. She was certain he would do the same. But the seconds passed and neither of them budged. Instead – Kim remembered this bit very well – she had turned her back on her boyfriend and opened her first beer of the night.

There were bits and pieces after that. Snatches of chatter around the fire, laughter at a joke she couldn't follow. Charlie didn't come over to her. Someone took a photo and the flash was blinding. Charlie was standing next to some girl she didn't know. A drink slipped from Kim's hand and splashed all over her shoes. She was holding a new drink and her shoes were still wet. Charlie was talking to a different girl. Then: blackness.

The campfire had gone out. No, not out. Kim just wasn't near it anymore. The bushland felt very still. She was lying down. Why was she lying down? Twigs and leaves were scratching her skin. She wanted to sit up. Her head spun and her ears rang in the silence all around.

'*Relax.*'

The word came from somewhere in the dark. Kim's heart lurched, snatching her breath away. She wasn't alone. Who was there? She tried to ask but couldn't find the words. She could taste vomit. The trees formed inky patterns that spun against the night sky. A hand on her leg. Her skin crawling under its clammy weight. Blackness, again. She could hear someone talking now. Or whispering? Fast words that she couldn't catch. They sounded angry, Kim thought. They sounded angry with her.

And then it was morning. The light was so sudden and bright it was painful. The sharp sticks and leaves had been replaced by cool, soft sheets. Kim was at home. Lying in her own bed. She pushed back the blanket. She was wearing last night's clothes. They reeked of vomit and alcohol.

When Naomi had arrived mid-morning, Kim had wanted her to laugh and say it was all no big deal. That Kim was being silly and that it was all nothing to worry about. But as they'd sat together on the fuzzy pink bedroom rug, Kim's whole body pulsing with a hangover and her mouth sticky and dry, they had looked at each other and Kim could see Naomi was in fact worried. Whatever had happened, it wasn't just nothing.

Naomi filled in the blanks – some of them – but not one that Kim had been waiting for and eventually she'd had to ask.

'Who else was there? There was someone else, right?'

A pause. 'There was someone else?'

'Yeah. Were they with you when you saw me?' Kim could hear the bright, false optimism even as she spoke. 'Helping, maybe?'

'No. Kim, no.' Naomi's voice was odd. She sounded scared, Kim realised. 'No-one was with me. Was someone there with you?'

'I thought so.'

'You saw them?'

'Heard them.'

Relax.

Kim could almost feel the breath of the word against her skin. She sucked in the stale air of her bedroom.

'Maybe not, then.' The backs of her arms and legs were patterned with faint red criss-cross scratches from the ground. 'If you didn't see anyone. I could be remembering wrong.'

Naomi didn't say anything to that. She just looked at Kim,

who was wrapped in her dressing gown, her hair dripping from the shower. 'Your clothes from last night were a bit –'

'Disgusting? I know. I'm sorry. They're in the washing machine.' They weren't. Kim had dropped them into the laundry basket, then fished them straight out, scrunched them in a ball and stuffed them into the bin instead. There was no point keeping them. She already knew she wouldn't wear them again.

'Oh.' Naomi fell quiet again. 'How are you feeling now? Are you okay?'

'Yeah.' *Was* she okay? Kim didn't allow the question to settle. 'Yes. I'm fine. Embarrassed, you know?'

'It's just –' Naomi had paused. 'I was thinking you could tell someone. If you wanted to. The police or someone. If –'

'No.' Kim's reply was quick. 'Naomi. *No.* What would I even say?'

No answer.

'I don't want anyone to find out. How messy I got, you know?' At the words, the icy trickle of a completely different type of fear began creeping through Kim. Their school was small. The post-party gossip was notoriously brutal. The gleeful buzz of rehashing what went right and what went wrong was only fun when it was about someone else. 'Naomi? Okay?'

'I know. But, what? Not even Charlie?'

He'd be upset, Kim knew immediately. Not with her – even during their stupidest fights he never got angry with her – but he'd blame himself. For being late to meet her at the park, for carrying on their ridiculous argument past the point that either of them wanted to, for not looking out for her. Charlie wasn't perfect, Kim knew, but neither was she and whatever this was, it wasn't his fault. It wasn't hers, either, a tiny voice whispered, but she pushed it aside. What she needed and wanted right then, more than anything else, was for everything to be back to normal.

'I just want to forget it.' Kim was suddenly strangely grateful for the blackness in her head. She couldn't bring herself to hold last night too close to the light. 'Seriously. Please don't tell anyone else. Not even Charlie.'

Naomi had looked like she might try to argue, but at last she nodded. 'Okay.' Kim felt weak with relief. 'Yeah. If that's what you want.'

It was. Kim had never again brought it up, so Naomi hadn't either. For a while afterwards, though, Kim had half feared new memories would resurface without warning. The sensation was strongest when she was down at the reservoir. The sight of the dense bushland with its hidden pockets would immediately trip something deep inside. It would creep over her, setting her heart pounding and sharp snaps of adrenalin zipping from her chest and through her limbs. Full fight or flight. It became almost unbearable and yet it didn't help her remember anything. Whatever was hidden in the blackness stayed there. But Kim hated her reaction to the reservoir. She felt out of control and very alone down there. And so, without mentioning it to anyone, Kim simply stopped going altogether.

Charlie noticed. Kim just didn't realise it until years later, one sunny afternoon not long after Zara was born. Charlie had been driving them home from a doctor's appointment, Zara tiny and soft, tucked up in her car seat in the back. They'd had a busy day already and the quickest way home, Kim knew, would be to turn off the highway and carry on down the track past the reservoir. She never drove that way herself, but she

wasn't the one behind the wheel now and as they approached
the turn, she felt the familiar unwelcome response kick in. She
was pressing her fingers lightly against the armrest, the intense
prickling feeling already building in her chest, when she realised Charlie had stayed on the highway. He was taking the
long way around.

'Are we going somewhere else?' Kim had asked, surprise
and relief washing through her.

'No. Just home.' Without looking, he'd reached over and
taken her hand. His voice was soft. 'You really don't like it
down there, hey?'

Kim had stared at his familiar palm, so warm and solid, and
she'd felt like she could breathe again. This wasn't the first
time Charlie had done this, she'd realised, as she suddenly
remembered all the times he'd quietly made it easy for
her – taking the slower route without comment, or suggesting
before Kim had to that they meet friends elsewhere for a walk.
How long had he been doing that for her? She wasn't sure.
Years, maybe.

'I've never liked it down there.' That wasn't the case, but
Charlie didn't call her out on it. 'I think the water or something
creeps me out.'

He'd looked over then. 'Yeah?'

'I mean . . . you don't know what's out there.'

'No. I suppose not.' He'd waited patiently, until it was clear
she wasn't going to say any more. 'Well. Whatever it is, we can
just leave it alone out there. If that's what you want.' He smiled
at her in her favourite way, the way that always reminded her
of the very first time she'd seen him. 'It doesn't have to come
home with us.'

And that was so true, Kim thought as Charlie had held her

hand and driven her and their daughter back to their cosy, baby-proofed house surrounded by vines. She'd known in that moment that she could have told him. Everything. What she remembered, what she didn't. How that all made her feel. And she'd known it would be all right. Kim could tell Charlie, but she still didn't want to. Not because she was worried anymore, but because in that moment she felt other things, too. Loved and safe and suddenly determined that whatever had happened all those years ago, it didn't deserve to take up space that could be filled by happiness instead.

So Charlie didn't know. But on the phone so many years later, discussing their teenage daughter and the annual party at the reservoir, Kim found herself wishing for the first time that he did. But it was too late now. They didn't have those kinds of conversations anymore.

'Let Zara go,' Kim said in the end. 'Tell her to be careful.'

Kim had less time than she might have had to dwell on things back in Marralee because here in Adelaide, for the first time in her life, work was not going well.

Rohan had come along for Friday night drinks to celebrate the end of a successful campaign and had been oddly subdued when they'd finally got home.

'Hey, I thought the Williams project was yours?' he'd said as they'd brushed their teeth in their master bathroom. The underfloor heating Rohan had recently had installed warmed Kim's bare feet.

'It is.'

'So why is Sarah talking about bringing someone else in on it?'

Sarah was her boss and a woman Kim had always enjoyed working with. She'd stared at Rohan in the mirror. 'Who?'

'That curly-haired man, I think.'

'*Jeff?* Bring him in how?'

'As a project supervisor.'

'But I'm the supervisor.'

Rohan had frowned and run his toothbrush under the tap. 'Maybe I got it wrong. It was noisy in the bar, maybe she meant for support.'

'But did Sarah say I needed support?'

Rohan had hesitated. 'It was really loud, Kim. I probably misheard.'

In bed, Kim had stared at the ceiling, analysing her recent conversations with Sarah. Rohan had rolled over.

'Sarah hasn't spoken to you about needing help to meet the brief?'

'No.'

'Well, look, that's on her. She should have done that first, before sounding out Jeff at a bar. It's unprofessional. God, I'm not surprised you're stressed there.'

'I'm not,' Kim said. 'Or, I wasn't, at least.' She was a little now, though, and it had taken a while to fall asleep. On Monday, she had booked some time with Sarah to discuss the Williams brief. Kim had turned up to the meeting to find that the working outlines of the central design concept were missing from her files. She spent the next three days trying to recover them. On Friday afternoon, Sarah suggested bringing someone else on board to help Kim re-do the work in time for the deadline. Kim, embarrassed and frazzled, agreed, and Jeff was duly summoned.

Rohan took her out to dinner to cheer her up and bought

her a book on toxic management techniques. He asked her which ones applied to Sarah, and when Kim said none of them seemed to, he'd laughed gently and told her she was always too nice.

Rohan left his phone lying about. On the kitchen counter, on the coffee table. Kim knew the passcode. She had known Charlie's as well, but Rohan seemed to offer his up as a sign of trust. He was always handing his phone to her, asking her to dig out an email, read from a recipe, get an address from his texts. She did the same, because it felt like something that was important to him and anyway, she had nothing to hide.

'What did Naomi want?' Rohan said one day as they were cooking dinner.

Kim had glanced up in surprise from the pan she was stirring. 'Not much. Just called for a chat.' She hadn't told him that Naomi had phoned, but it was recorded right there in her call history.

Rohan didn't say anything, focusing on the carrots he was chopping into neat batons on the wooden board.

'What?' she said.

'Nothing.' He gathered the vegetables together and scraped them into a baking tray. 'Really. I'm sorry. I'm just always vaguely aware that everything we say to Naomi or whoever eventually makes its way back to Charlie.'

Kim had laughed. 'I don't think that's the case.'

'No?' His question seemed genuine as he checked the temperature on the oven. 'They don't all talk to each other like they used to?'

Kim had stopped stirring the pan. 'Well, yeah, they do, but –'

'I suppose it doesn't matter anyway.' He shut the oven door and flashed her a smile. 'Let them talk.'

Kim looked at her husband. 'Does it bother you?'

'No. Not at all. It's fine.'

But Kim could tell it wasn't. And Rohan maybe had a point, when she stopped to think about it. She became more mindful of what she said on the phone, which was a little tiring but perhaps not a bad idea. She'd recount the conversations later to him and he'd put forward the odd suggestion or mild objection. And it worked for a while, but Rohan knew every time that someone from home called, and after a while tiring became tiresome. With everything going on at work, it was one more thing Kim could do without.

So the next time Naomi texted, Kim had simply ignored it. She'd flipped her phone over on the couch and turned back to her husband and the movie they were watching, and he'd slipped his arm around her and life was suddenly easier. She did the same the next few times, and again, and then again, and quite a few months passed before she realised she hadn't had any calls to ignore in a while.

Kim lost her car keys and was late for an important client meeting. Sarah was understanding. But it happened again, and then once more when her alarm didn't go off. Sarah had no choice but to give her a verbal warning, an exchange which was so horribly excruciating for both women that Kim couldn't hold back the tears over dinner that night.

Rohan asked if she wanted to hand in her notice. When Kim said that sounded a little extreme, he'd put his fork down, reached into his jeans pocket and dug out a clean folded tissue for her.

'You're crying, Kim. No job's worth making you feel like this.'

Rohan was busy with his own work, too, in a way that made him seem preoccupied at times. During a distracted conversation one night, he let slip the fact that Shane had cheated on Naomi, years ago when they were together and Shane was still playing. Kim already knew about that, because everyone knew about that.

'I guess that was just Shane back then,' she'd said. 'Some men are like that. Can't say no.'

And in that moment there had been a beat of pure silence in which she'd heard, unspoken but unmissable, the word *Charlie* pulse between them. She had stared at Rohan, who had busied himself shutting down his laptop. He wouldn't meet her eye.

'What?' Kim felt sideswiped. She tried to keep her voice light. 'Did Charlie?'

'No.'

'Did he? Rohan?'

'Kim, no.' He gave a short laugh. 'No.'

'You can tell me. I don't care.' Although she did, because of all Kim and Charlie's problems – and, okay, there had been a few – that had never been one of them. Or so she'd thought. Charlie had his faults, but Kim had always trusted him.

The idea that she had been wrong about that, that he might have been unfaithful and, worse, successfully hidden it from her, slipped into her side like a blade. She told herself she didn't believe it, while at the same time picking over old conversations and scrutinising mental lists of his casual acquaintances.

Rohan had changed the subject swiftly and not brought it up again, until eventually Kim had had to.

'Just tell me,' she'd said a few tormented days later. 'I'd rather know.'

'Kim, seriously.'

'Well, did the others all know? Gemma and Dean and everyone?' The idea that her friends had kept something like that from her made her want to cry.

'Jesus, Kim. Please, let's not.'

'What would Gemma say if I asked her, though?'

Rohan had looked at her strangely. 'Why are you even thinking about this now?'

'I don't know. You brought it up.'

'No. You did.' He was still watching her, concern all over his face. Finally, he'd shrugged. 'Look, ask Gemma then, if you really need to. Or Naomi. They'll tell you the same as I am.'

Kim felt ashamed by the way he was staring at her, and was simply too angry and embarrassed to have that same conversation with someone else. Next time the phone rang, Kim sent it straight through to voicemail.

She realised she felt stressed and sad, all the time. She went to the doctor about oversleeping and losing her keys. She came away with a prescription for antidepressants. Things got worse at work. She lost another file. She handed in her notice before Sarah had to ask her to. She went back to the doctor to see if her memory was okay. Another prescription was written and dispensed, along with a sleep aid to help her rest properly.

After that, Kim stayed home for a while, carrying out half-hearted job searches at the granite table in the kitchen that had been paid for with Rohan's engineer's salary. She started to feel sick in the mornings and then she stopped looking for work.

She had to go back to the doctor again, because now she was pregnant.

The baby looked just like Kim.

She and Zoe had been home from hospital for a week when she first caught Rohan staring at their daughter with an odd look on his face.

'Everything okay?' she'd asked, drained and fractious from another broken night.

'Her eyes are very dark,' Rohan had said simply, but in a way that sounded like things were not okay at all. Kim was too tired to try to work out what he meant.

'Yeah,' she said. Her caesarean wound was aching. 'I suppose so. It's nice, though. She's so pretty.'

Rohan hadn't said anything more.

A few weeks later, he'd got up in the night to give Zoe her formula and Kim, grateful to him as her body struggled to recover in a way it never had with Zara, had staggered to the bathroom. On the way back, she'd paused at the lounge room door. Rohan was sitting on the couch, lit by the dim glow of the side lamp, his chin coarse with stubble and his t-shirt soft and wrinkled from sleep as he cradled their daughter in the crook of his arm.

Formula finished, he was gazing down at her, gently running tendrils of her baby hair between his finger and thumb. Zoe's hair looked dark and fine in the low light. Over and over again, Rohan ran his thumb over the wispy strands. And even through the foggy cloud of her own exhaustion, Kim felt an uncomfortable realisation coursing through her. Because all of a sudden, she could tell what he was thinking.

It was absolutely ridiculous. For so many reasons. Not least, Kim realised when she looked back, because Rohan always knew where she was, pretty much every minute of every day. He had access to her phone. They had sold her car after she'd stopped working, agreeing to hold off getting a new one until after the baby arrived, when they would invest in something bigger and more suitable. For more than a year, Kim had either been at work or she'd been at home or she'd been with Rohan. And when she'd stopped working, those options had narrowed neatly from three to two. What Kim had decidedly not been doing in that time was sleeping with Charlie.

Kim forced herself to wait it out. She waited and waited, but in the end she was the one who broke first.

'What is it you want, Rohan?' she demanded. Frustration and a fear of waking Zoe turned her voice tight and shrill in a way she hated. 'Do you want to take a test or something?'

'Kim.' Her husband leaned against the lounge room doorway, arms folded, his gaze steady. 'Why would you even suggest that?'

Jesus, he knew exactly why, Kim thought as she lowered herself carefully onto the sofa. It was so late in the evening and she was so *tired*. Zoe had been screaming all day and finally, after literal hours of rocking and cajoling, had finally cried herself to sleep on Kim's chest. Kim held her now, barely daring to move.

Outside in the driveway, the car was partially packed up. They were due to drive to Marralee the next day. Rohan's dad was ill and his parents wanted to see the baby. Rohan had been worried about his dad's recent tests, Kim knew that. And she wanted to be understanding. But seriously? *Enough*. Her energy was sapped, her baby was relentless, her husband was behaving as though she'd done something she simply would never do, and sitting there, shaking with exhaustion, Kim had suddenly had it with this shit.

'You're right,' she snapped in a harsh whisper. 'Why would I even suggest that?'

'I have absolutely no idea.'

Kim looked at Rohan and in that moment she hated him. His calm stillness – the very quality that she had once absolutely loved about him – had eroded since Zoe's birth into something so brooding and distant. He would disappear into himself, thinking about – what? Kim couldn't guess.

It hadn't been like this with Charlie. When they fell out, it was robust, but it was fair. They made their points, tussled a little on the finer details, then they got on with things. It wasn't ideal, granted, but it was a lot better than this hard glinting silence.

She stared at Rohan, daring him to be honest with her.

'Rohan.' Kim gave in first. 'I'm only going to say this once. Ever. Zoe is your daughter.'

His face flickered. A fresh cold thread slid straight down Kim's spine. *Oh my God*. He didn't believe her. This wasn't silly troublemaking, brought on by new-parent jealousy or fatigue. He truly *did not* believe her. Rohan actually thought this baby could be Charlie's.

'*Rohan –*' Kim tried, with urgency this time. She hadn't taken this anywhere near seriously enough, she was realising too late.

'Why would you feel the need to say that, Kim?' He cut her off, outwardly unruffled in a way that instantly set her further on edge.

She shifted and Zoe stirred. Kim froze and held her breath, letting it out in a whisper. 'Because you –'

'I what? Kim?' Rohan's own voice was oddly light. 'Why are you saying this? I trust you. It's not like you're the type to get black-out drunk and go off with some bloke you can't remember.'

Sitting in her comfortable living room, holding her warm baby, Kim felt it. Right then, without warning but so brutally familiar. Her heart pounding, the adrenalin prickling. She stared at her husband.

'What are you talking about?'

He shrugged. Picked up a baby blanket that they'd chosen together and folded it neatly into quarters. 'You know, Kim.'

She did. Of course she did. But it was so out of context she felt breathless, like she'd been slapped. 'Down at the reservoir, you mean? The party?'

Something in her voice alerted him then. Rohan didn't react, but Kim could feel it. He'd overstepped a line that until now hadn't even existed between them.

'Yeah.' His tone hovered somewhere around apologetic. 'I guess that's what I mean.'

'How do you even know about that?'

Rohan put the baby blanket down. He lifted his head until his eyes met hers. 'Charlie told me.'

She held his gaze. 'Charlie did?'

'Yeah. I'm really sorry, Kim. Look, obviously, he shouldn't have. But you know what he's like. Big mouth, can't keep it shut. You can't trust him with anything.'

Kim looked across the room at her husband, still watching her from the doorway. She breathed in through her nose, and then out. She leaned a little deeper into the sofa cushions. She felt the weight of her baby against her chest. She nodded her head, up and down. She swallowed lightly, and then drew together every thread of strength and focus and concentration she could find to form two words.

'That's true.'

But it wasn't true. And Charlie didn't know.

Kim stayed up on the couch all night, holding Zoe. Rohan had finally gone to bed, only to get up again at 2 am and come through.

'Do you want me to take over?' His voice was kind and conciliatory. She suspected he hadn't been asleep.

Kim shook her head. 'No. Thank you, though.' She hesitated. 'Can you please pass me my phone?'

It was charging on the bedside table in their room.

Rohan also hesitated. 'Sure. It's kind of late.'

'I want to text Zara before I forget. To arrange to drop off her birthday present.'

'Okay. Whatever you need.'

He'd gone to get the phone. Then he sat on the arm of the sofa and waited, rubbing his tired eyes and yawning. Able to see Kim's screen. Kim had faltered, her baby on her chest, her caesarean wound still knitting together, her husband sitting patiently at her side. Finally, she texted Zara. She and Zoe would like to come to the vineyard to drop off her birthday present that evening.

When she'd finished, Rohan held out his hand.

'It's not at full battery. I'll put it back on the charger for you.' He glanced at the message as she passed it over and said lightly: 'I'm not sure tonight's going to work. I'm meeting my parents.'

'That's okay.' Kim made her tone match his. 'I can go on my own.'

'I don't know.' He smiled at her. This was a version of Rohan that she knew well. Rohan the peacekeeper, the patient stepfather, the family man. 'We missed Zara's real birthday. I think I'd like to be there too.' Rohan the decision-maker.

Kim sat awake for the rest of the night. By the time morning dawned, her husband had been thinking.

'Maybe we should give Marralee a miss,' he said over breakfast. 'You're tired. I'm tired. The trip might be a bit much.'

'We have to go.' Kim looked him in the eye. God, this dance was excruciating. Her phone was no longer in the bedroom. She'd seen Rohan carry it outside along with an armful of baby supplies and she could picture it in the locked car, placed carefully in the central console along with a bottle of water and some snacks and spare nappies. 'What about your dad?' she tried. 'His test results?'

'Dad wouldn't want to make things difficult for you.'

'Rohan.' Kim played her best and last card. 'Everyone's expecting us. They all want to see Zoe. If we don't go, they'll be worried. They'll come to us.'

She was right, and he knew it. He took his time, though, cleaning out the fridge and taking out the rubbish and packing the final bags and securing the house and Kim just waited, holding her baby, until at last he had run out of jobs. He unlocked the car. It was time to drive home.

* * *

Charlie was calling her again. It was the second time in as many minutes. Kim sat in the passenger seat next to Rohan, Zoe fast asleep in the back. From the bushland surrounding them, she knew they were still at least half an hour from Marralee. Her phone rang from the centre console. Kim glanced over at Rohan. His eyes were on the road.

'Are you going to get that?' Rohan didn't look at her when he spoke.

Kim wasn't sure what the right answer was. The ringing continued.

'Get it.' Rohan's voice was as steady as ever. 'Don't want to keep Charlie waiting.'

Kim reached for her phone, and as her fingers closed around it, Rohan glanced in the rear-view mirror. It was fast, but she caught it, as she was meant to.

'Perhaps keep it short, though, yeah? Your baby's asleep in the back.'

Your baby. Kim's stomach lurched with a force that made her want to double over. *Your* baby. Not *our* baby.

Rohan nodded at the ringing phone. 'Charlie wants you.'

'I'll get rid of him.'

The words came readily. Kim's thoughts were spiralling but her response was automatic, and somewhere amid the noise she found herself clinging to a small solid truth. *I know how to keep my husband happy.* Consciously or not, she had perfected the art. Rohan had spent their marriage training her in it. So for better or worse, she possessed those skills. She knew what to do, and she could do it now. Kim concentrated, lifted a finger, and answered the call.

'Kim. Hey.' Charlie's face appeared on the phone. He sounded a little surprised, and Kim couldn't blame him. He rarely called these days. It was even rarer that she picked up.

'Hi, Charlie.' She swallowed. Her voice sounded strange to her own ears and she sensed Rohan glance over. Charlie didn't seem to notice. As he adjusted the angle of the phone, Kim caught a glimpse of the vineyard kitchen. She'd spent so much time there that it still felt like hers and a wave of homesickness washed over her. Greg and Rita were there too, she could see, and a tall man she didn't know. Her elder daughter edged her way onto the screen and Kim felt the familiar pang deep in her chest. 'Hello, Zara, sweetheart.'

'Where are you?' Charlie was saying. 'Still in the car?'

'Yeah. We're – ah –' She couldn't think. Still thirty long minutes from town. 'Near the eastern bridge now. Listen, Charlie, what's up? It's not a great time, Zoe's asleep in the back.'

She caught the swift flash of jealousy in Zara's eyes and had the overwhelming urge to reach through the screen and take her daughter's perfect troubled face in her hands. *Oh, Zara, you silly, beautiful girl. Zoe has never, ever replaced you. You must know that, don't you?*

But Zara was already looking away, and Charlie was wearing that odd fixed smile he had when he was trying to pretend he was fine, and suddenly it all felt so wrong that Kim could barely stand it.

See, Rohan? she wanted to scream at her husband, even as she pressed her lips tightly together. *Nothing for you to get all upset about. I chose you over them, didn't I? Look! Right here. Look at my broken relationships with my daughter and her father. What more could you want?*

Rohan knew her well enough to read her silence. 'Calm down, Kim,' he murmured. His face didn't even change.

'That Rohan there?' Charlie cleared his throat on the other end of the phone. He was trying, Kim could tell. He had always tried. 'Congratulations on the little one, mate.'

For a horrifying moment Kim felt completely, wholly blank. What was a normal reaction to that? She twisted the phone screen so Charlie could see her husband. Rohan nodded and raised a hand.

'Thanks, mate,' Rohan said, so pleasant and measured that it made Kim feel light-headed. 'Sorry, we had better keep it down, though, if that's all right.'

He glanced in the mirror again, for longer this time, and something about the way his eyes settled on Zoe sent a jolt of fear through Kim. Rohan wouldn't actually hurt them. Would he? *No.* Surely not. He was upset, but Kim really couldn't believe he would cross that line. *But, the reservoir –* Kim slammed that door shut. Later. She could not think about that now. Still, this conversation felt very wrong. She needed it to be over, so she could sit carefully in the car, not moving, not speaking, until they emerged from this dense empty bushland and were back in town, on solid and familiar ground.

'Charlie,' Kim aimed for brisk and cool, 'we'll talk later, okay? I'll see you and Zara soon anyway.'

'Hang on, Kim, it's actually about you coming by tonight. We're not going to be around, sorry.'

There was a pause in which Kim could hear only the blood rushing in her ears.

'Was that tonight?' Rohan said, and Kim simply stared at him.

'Yes. Remember?' Her own voice seemed odd. They would be able to tell. She put her hand over the phone to muffle the sound.

'But I can't,' Rohan said, still perfectly normal. 'I'm meeting my parents.'

Kim blinked at him, entirely unsure for once how he wanted her to react. 'I was going to stop in while you're at the restaurant,' she tried.

Zara had elbowed her way closer to the screen now, chattering fast about something. Going out with her friends, Kim guessed. She took her hand away so she could hear better.

'– and I've already said I'd meet them. So that's okay, isn't it?'

Kim didn't know how to answer. *No.* Jesus, it was not okay. Not at all. She wanted Zara and Charlie to be at the vineyard tonight. She wanted them to be waiting for her and her baby to ring their doorbell. She needed them to be worried if she was late, and to ask questions if she didn't show up. What she really needed was to step through that door like she used to, and lock it firmly behind her as she had so many times before, and feel safe, the way she always had when they were still a family.

'I mean . . .' Zara faltered. Kim saw her silent appeal to Charlie for support. 'Dad's got to cover the festival stall anyway.'

Kim couldn't think how to respond. Not a single appropriate word came to her. It felt like she was silent for a long time. Too long, she realised as Rohan shifted his hands on the steering wheel.

'So neither of you will be home tonight?' she managed. 'You're both going out to the festival?'

'Yeah,' Charlie said. 'Sorry.'

'What about Rita and Greg?'

'All of us are going.'

'Oh.' *Shit.* 'Okay –' Kim was still trying to work out how to object, but Zara was too quick.

'Okay? Great, thanks, Mum.'

Kim could see her daughter smiling. She made herself take a breath and focus. They were still a long way from town. No-one would be at the vineyard tonight. She tried to think.

'Charlie –?' She thought she sounded pretty close to normal, but maybe not, because she could sense her husband on high alert now. Had he sped up the car? It felt very fast around the bends. 'You and Zara can't wait for me?'

'Look, Kim, not really. I'm sorry, but we'll rearrange. I've got to do the stall. And Zara's sixteen, she wants to hang out with her mates tonight. You remember what –'

'Yes, of course, I –'

Rohan's hand darted out and took the phone from her. Kim wasn't sure what she'd been about to say, but Rohan seemed to know before she did that it wouldn't be the right thing. He held her phone screen pressed flat against his chest. He was breathing harder, Kim could see. So was she. She could barely hear the engine over the pounding in her head.

As she watched, Rohan slowly put his foot down on the accelerator. He glanced once at their baby sleeping in the back seat, then to her disbelief, lifted his remaining hand from the steering wheel. Kim's heart leapt in her throat so hard she nearly gagged.

'Please. Rohan –' She formed the words but not the sound as the road zipped past the window, her lungs squeezed tight.

'You still there?' Charlie's voice sounded far away on the other end of the line.

Painstakingly slowly, Rohan raised the hand that had been controlling the steering wheel and put his finger to his lips. He looked again in the rear-view mirror at Zoe then at Kim. The car skidded a little.

Kim nodded, her heart drumming, her pulse catching in her throat. Rohan held her gaze for a long moment. A sense of understanding passed between them, although Kim couldn't quite have said exactly what she was agreeing to. Finally, *so slowly*, Rohan placed his hand back on the wheel. He took the phone away from his chest and passed it back. Kim breathed out the air she had been holding in, the release itself burning and painful. Rohan was talking, sounding so disturbingly *ordinary* that Kim struggled to take in the words.

'Hello? Can you hear us now?' Rohan had raised his voice half a notch, then dropped it again. 'Sorry, guys, this is all a bit hard with Zoe right here. Look, could we just agree Zara should go tonight? Have fun. We'll work something out for another time.'

'Great. Okay,' Zara said quickly.

'I –' Kim took a breath before she could change her mind, but Charlie was already talking.

'Hey, listen, why don't you stop by the festival instead?' he was saying. 'We'll all be there.'

'Well –' Kim knew instinctively how Rohan wanted her to answer. Her palm was slick against the phone. *Forget what Rohan wants. What does Zoe need?* Her daughter needed to be somewhere very safe. The festival? It was always busy, not just with tourists but with locals too. Kim would know a lot of people there.

'Yes. Okay, then.' She found the words fast, before Rohan could stop her. 'We'll come to the festival.'

Her husband shot her a look she had never seen before.

'I'm catching up with my parents tonight.' For the first time, Kim thought Rohan sounded tense. 'But yeah, we could maybe swing by.'

'All right,' Charlie was saying. Did he sound a little – what? Suspicious? Uncertain? Kim wasn't sure. On the screen the fixed smile was back. 'Good. Well, we'll see you three there.'

'Okay. See you there.' Kim could feel Rohan's eyes on her. She lifted the edges of her mouth into as much of a smile as she could manage, and gently bit the tip of her tongue. Zoe was so small in the back seat. They were expected at the festival. The town was not far away. This was nearly over. She was nearly home.

'Great. Bye, Mum.' Zara sounded distracted. 'Love you.'

'Bye, Zara.' Kim wanted to look at her daughter's face, but instead she could see only the fabric of Zara's top as she leaned towards the screen. 'I love you –'

She was gone. The call went dead.

Kim looked at the silent phone in her hand. Rohan reached out fast and palmed it, placing it carefully back in the centre console where he could see it. Kim wiped her hands on her jeans and made herself concentrate.

They were only thirty minutes from Marralee. They would arrive. They would go to the festival. Kim could picture it. A fragile bud of relief unfurled. She would find Charlie there. She would ask if she and Zoe could come home with him, and Charlie would say yes, because of course he would, because

she and Charlie had always looked after each other. The bushland was thick around her. All that she needed was waiting at
the end of this very long stretch of road.

Then Rohan slowed, and put the indicator on.

Chapter 35

'Kim was never at the festival.'

Falk spoke as quietly as he could over the clamour of the rides and music. He waited then, as Sergeant Dwyer simply stared at him for a long moment. The officer slowly tilted his head and raised his eyes upwards to the ferris wheel. Next to him, Raco did the same. Falk didn't need to. He had seen enough. The ride creaked and groaned overhead. *Gone before she was gone.*

Falk said nothing else, giving Dwyer the same space and time he'd needed himself to let the implications fully wash over him.

Falk wasn't sure how many minutes he'd stood fixed in that spot, staring up at the wheel as his thoughts tumbled in a new unsettling direction, but it had been long enough for Raco to notice. He had left the others queueing for a children's ride further up the path and wandered back to Falk, concerned. They had talked then, urgent, distressing words passing between them. *This, here. This is what we were missing.* The two men had looked at each other, then Raco had pulled out his phone and called Dwyer. The sergeant had made his way over from across the festival grounds, then stood in the shadow of the ferris wheel himself, arms folded and face set, as he listened to what Falk had to say.

'There were sightings of Kim.' Dwyer dropped his gaze from the wheel now, his voice low. 'I'm not talking just one, either. I've got a string of people who reckon they spotted her.'

'No. Saw someone like her, maybe.' Falk shook his head. 'Medium height, medium build, dark hair. There'd have been a hundred women here that night who would match that description. But no-one who actually knew Kim saw her, or spoke to her.' He watched Dwyer closely. The sergeant wasn't disagreeing. 'You said it yourself, mate, something seemed off there and you were right. We all see what we expect to see. A dad holding two ice-creams, standing outside the women's toilets, chatting to friends going in and out. Of course his wife's inside. Why wouldn't she be?'

Dwyer didn't reply immediately, instead glancing pointedly once more to the top of the wheel and then back to Falk. 'And here?' he asked neutrally.

'Eva Raco made me wake up to it. Something she pointed out as obvious. This is a small-town festival. Strangers wave at strangers from rides. Because it's what they do. It's fun.' Falk held out his hands. He wished he could go back, do things differently, but he wasn't going to make the error worse by trying to dodge it. 'Okay, I didn't know Kim, but still. I shouldn't have taken what I saw at face value. That's my fault.'

Dwyer frowned now. 'So Rohan – what? Parks the pram with Zoe inside then wanders over here and finds a couple of tourists who have no idea what his wife looks like?'

'Yeah.' Falk nodded. 'I think so. If he picks someone who

wouldn't know Kim up close, they're always going to take his word for it at a distance in the dark. Rohan gets chatting to the Queensland family, looks up at the ride, finds a woman with a resemblance to Kim and rolls the dice and waves, because why not? If she doesn't wave back, no harm done. But how bloody handy if she does?'

Dwyer stroked his chin. His eyes slid from the ferris wheel, moving out across the grounds and settling a short distance away. Falk followed his line of sight. Through the throng of people, he could see the extended Raco family. They were all gathered beside a kids' rollercoaster, talking and laughing as they waited their turn.

Rohan was there too. Slightly on the periphery but still very much part of the group. He held his daughter on his hip, with a trace of a smile on his face as he listened to Charlie launch into a story. Rita murmured something and lightly touched Rohan's elbow, and Falk felt Raco flinch beside him. Raco was staring at the man like he'd never seen him before, his face dark.

'Hey. Listen. It wasn't just you, mate. All right?' Falk leaned in, his voice firm. 'To control one person, a whole lot of other people have to be manipulated, you know that. Family, friends, strangers, all of us. We all bought into it.'

Raco didn't reply, his eyes still on his family. He gave a single, tight nod.

Perhaps sensing their scrutiny, Rohan shifted his weight and looked up. His gaze flitted across the crowd, smooth and light, before snagging first on Dwyer, then Falk and Raco. He couldn't have known the nature of their conversation, but still. They were three police officers and they were looking his way. Falk braced himself for a range of possible reactions and he sensed Raco do the same.

Rohan didn't move. He simply held his daughter and gazed back, his expression settling into something both interested and hopeful. It was the perfect response, Falk thought. Respectful, deferential. Perfectly believable, almost.

'If Kim was never here at the festival,' Dwyer spoke so softly it was hard to hear him over the clamour. His eyes never left Kim's husband. 'Then where is she?'

It was the question Falk wished he could answer. Rohan's expression hadn't changed but as Falk looked away, he thought he caught a flicker of calculation. It was there, then immediately gone. But it gave him a jolt, like seeing a decent actor dropping character. Just a split second but still long enough for the damage to be done, leaving the audience frowning and thinking: *Wait. This isn't real.*

So what was real with this man? Falk's thoughts rattled backwards, rewinding the minutes and hours, trying to find something he knew he could rely on. He wasn't sure what he was looking for and when a single memory began to emerge from the tangled mess, it wasn't one he'd expected. He wasn't thinking about the festival, or the vineyard, or even the town itself.

Instead, Falk found himself reliving his solo drive from Melbourne to Marralee those few long days ago. Heading towards the valley town for the christening, for the Racos, for everything else waiting here for him. The road had been empty and the journey had been long and so he had stopped for a break. He had pulled off the road, and driven up a side track. He had parked in a clearing at a spectacular hidden lookout, and discovered he was not alone.

Rohan Gillespie had been there too, with his one-year-old daughter, Zoe. Falk felt a small part of the memory start to crystallise with a startling, vivid clarity. Not the view, or the child's sippy cup or the box of sultanas. Not the glance of recognition or the stilted small talk about the Racos' christening.

A moment before all of that.

Just a few short seconds. When Falk had pulled in and spotted Rohan standing in the deserted clearing. Alone and unguarded. His back to his daughter. Staring pensively at the view. Falk couldn't know for certain what had been going through the man's mind. But if he'd had to guess, both then and now, Falk would bet that Rohan Gillespie had been looking into the void and thinking about his missing wife, Kim.

Chapter 36

Rohan

The lookout was empty, as usual.

Still, Rohan felt a stab of relief as the car rumbled to the end of the tight bush track and he saw no-one else in the clearing. He parked, ignoring the breathtaking view and instead looked over at his restless wife. Kim sat in the passenger seat, her hands tightly clasped and her eyes determinedly anywhere but on her phone. It was still lying where Rohan had placed it in the centre console and she'd been glancing at it – tiny, secretive looks – ever since the call with Charlie and Zara had ended. They both knew he'd noticed, there was no point pretending, so Rohan simply reached out now and slipped her phone into his pocket as he got out of the car. Kim's shoulders sagged. Rohan ignored that too, as he walked around and pulled open the passenger door.

'Get out, please, Kim.'

She didn't move. She was staring at him, breath shallow and hands poised, fully focused.

'Get out now, Kim.' He took a single step towards Zoe's door.

Kim got out. Of course she did.

'Rohan.' She was pleading in a way he didn't like. She'd found her voice and it was a rolling urgent torrent. 'Rohan. *Listen* to me. Zoe is your daughter. Please. Not Charlie's. *Yours.* She is.'

He didn't reply, but as he stepped closer to his wife she instinctively raised both hands, palms out, which he hated because all he'd ever done was try to love her. He took another step, closer again, *just to talk*, but she stumbled back this time and he felt another burst of something unpleasant in his gut. Rohan had always found it interesting, over the years, when Kim had inadvertently done something that reminded him of that night as teenagers at the reservoir.

Rohan had never understood Kim at school. She was nice-looking and friendly enough and she could have had – well, maybe not *anyone*, but a decent choice. But all she'd seemed interested in was getting herself worked up over Charlie Raco. Charlie, who didn't get worked up about her in the same way. Charlie, who would bicker and argue with her over nothing. Who would talk bullshit and joke around with his mates at a bushland party while his girlfriend got so drunk she could barely stand long enough to walk off. The big love story of their year, and Charlie hadn't even noticed her leave.

Rohan had noticed, though. Kim had been sitting on her own for a while and he'd been nursing a beer and debating whether to go over when she'd risen unsteadily and staggered away from the campfire. She'd disappeared through the trees and into the dark and he'd watched the empty space left behind, waiting for her to come back. A minute passed, and then another, and so he'd stood and followed, because it probably wasn't too safe for Kim to be walking home in that state. He'd caught up with her easily, then immediately wondered why he'd bothered. Kim had been crying hard, mumbling nonstop about Charlie. Rambling, incoherent rubbish. To shut her up more than anything, Rohan had found a tissue and helped her wipe her eyes and she'd seemed so grateful that he'd done it again, running his thumbs over her flushed cheeks until they were completely dry.

They'd walked a little way together, Kim lurching and sloppy, and Rohan had put his arm around her to keep her steady. He'd half expected her to push it away, but she didn't seem to notice or care, so he'd left it there. Was it even possible, he'd wondered, that she was doing it on purpose? Letting her hip bounce off his as she staggered, gripping his hand in her own sweaty palm? Rohan had still been considering that, when Kim had suddenly stopped, freezing in a dead halt on the track. He'd been able to tell from her face what was coming.

'Quick, this way,' he'd said, and Kim had clamped her mouth shut and let him lead her off the track and deeper into the trees. She'd braced one hand against a trunk, and leaned over just in time as she retched and then vomited. Rohan had stepped back so it didn't splash on his shoes. He'd waited, and Kim's eyes had been bloodshot and watery when she straightened up. She'd taken a single swaying step back towards the path, before Rohan had reached out and caught her elbow.

'Take a minute,' he'd said, guiding Kim instead to the ground. 'There's no rush.'

He'd sat down next to her, her weight slumped against his shoulder and her skirt bunched right up around her thighs.

Rohan had looked at that hem for a full minute, waiting for her to pull it down. She didn't move.

'Do you want me to straighten your skirt for you, Kim?' he'd said finally. When he'd looked over, her eyes were closed. She didn't reply.

'Yes?' he'd asked.

Kim had murmured something.

'Okay.' Rohan leaned closer.

She'd been so floppy it had been impossible to keep her sitting upright, so he'd taken her by the shoulders and lain her on the ground.

'Relax.'

Her bare legs had been warm and smooth under his palms. He'd run his hands along them and as he'd moved, he'd gazed down at her. Eyes shut, vomit in her hair. Her top had twisted up, exposing a broad slice of smooth skin. He'd moved his hands again, tracing patterns with his fingers across her body. One way, then back again and – Rohan had stopped.

Someone was coming.

He'd listened closely. Footsteps were tramping along the path, a torch beam flashing all over the place. He'd heard a girl clear her throat and it had felt like a personal insult. Naomi. Of course it bloody was. Making sure her presence was acknowledged at every possible opportunity. Rohan had got to his feet as quietly as he could. He'd glanced down. Kim had looked terrible, lying there like that in her own vomit. If Naomi caught them, she'd get the wrong impression entirely. Rohan had hesitated, then hastily hauled Kim up into a seated position, propping her against the tree trunk. Her head lolled and her face was slack.

Naomi was closer now, so he'd taken a few fast steps, ducking behind a large eucalyptus tree. Rohan had pressed his shoulder tight against the trunk before peering around.

Naomi had come into sight, marching along the path, and for a moment it had seemed like she would pass right by. Then the torchlight swinging from her hand had gone still. The beam had doubled back. In the harsh white cone of light, Kim was slumped against the tree like a dead weight.

For a second, nothing moved. Then the torch beam slid away from Kim, shaking as it reluctantly tracked across the expanse of dark bushland. Rohan had held his breath. The rush of blood in his ears mingled with the distant thumping undercurrent of music. But the accusing, reproachful shout he'd been waiting for hadn't come.

When he'd worked up the nerve to peer out again, Naomi had still been frozen on the spot. The light from her torch had been almost bouncing in her unsteady hands. Okay. So she wasn't about to point the beam his way, stride into the trees and give him a piece of her mind, Rohan had realised. Not even close. He'd felt a bubble of amusement rise. Naomi was completely freaked out.

'Kim?' Naomi's voice had been barely more than a whisper. No response. She had glanced one way, then the other, fast and furtive.

Jesus, Rohan had held in a lungful of air, anticipation rising. *She's going to leave her here.* Righteous, bossy, judgemental Naomi wanted to run away.

'Kim?' The girl's voice had been almost swallowed by the bushland. 'Seriously. Can you get up?' Another fast glance down the path.

Do it, Naomi, Rohan had silently encouraged. *Run home. Go on. No-one will know.*

The night air had seemed to quiver with indecision, then suddenly Naomi made a low noise in her throat. She'd stepped swiftly off the path and started trampling fast and noisily through the undergrowth towards Kim.

Rohan had watched, with equal parts surprise and irritation. He hadn't thought Naomi had it in her. Neither had she, judging by the look on her face.

Naomi had been swearing, a rapid stream of whispered words as she'd grabbed Kim and pulled, her hands rough, using whatever leverage she could to drag her up.

'Move, Kim. Now. Or you're on your own. I swear to God. I'm sorry, but I'm not staying out here. Move now.'

The urgency seemed to stir Kim, and she had struggled to her feet at last, allowing herself to be pulled towards the track.

Clear of the bushland and back on firmer ground, Naomi had put her arm around Kim, then paused mid-movement. Still breathing heavily, she'd run the torchlight over the other girl again, more slowly this time. Lingering on the vomit in Kim's hair, her twisted top, her rucked-up skirt. Rohan had watched from behind the tree with an odd fascination as Naomi had for a moment become eerily calm. She had taken a breath, then reached out with gentle, careful hands and fixed Kim's clothes.

'It's okay,' she'd whispered. 'I've got you now. I'll take you home.'

Naomi's face had been tight and pinched as she'd propped a shoulder under Kim's arm and led her away. Kim had stumbled alongside, her limbs moving heavily. She was – the thought had popped into Rohan's head as a detached observation – really very drunk.

He'd waited until he was sure they were gone, then had

stepped out of the bushland, dusted off his jeans and made his way back towards the sounds of the party. He was a little disappointed, he'd been willing to admit, but also oddly exhilarated. It had been interesting, being able to elicit those responses from the girls. Okay, things hadn't panned out exactly as he'd hoped, but it'd been almost better to discover how little effort it had really taken to get Kim where he'd wanted for so long. And seeing Naomi spooked had been a definite unexpected bonus. Rohan had thoroughly enjoyed that.

Back at the clearing, the party had been kicking into high gear just as a dejected Charlie was realising that Kim was no longer around. Rohan had helped himself to another beer and leaned against a tree, watching.

If Rohan were to do something like that again – and, look, he had no plans to or anything – but if he *were* to, he'd reckoned with a little refinement he could make things go differently. He'd loved the sense that both girls had learned something about themselves that night. That Naomi had discovered that when the shit hit the fan she wasn't as rock-solid fearless as she liked to think. And Kim – Rohan had sipped his beer – well. She had no fight in her at all.

Rohan had stood at the fringes of the party, turning those thoughts over in his head as he'd savoured both his beer and the sight of Charlie searching unsuccessfully for his girlfriend. Jesus, the guy was a joke. He had never, ever deserved her.

Rohan had thought that back then, and twenty-five years on, he still thought it now. He looked at his wife, who was watching him closely, her lips slightly parted. Her weight was forward, over the balls of her feet. She had backed away from the car, her eyes still fixed on him. Drawing him away from her daughter? Rohan wondered. He felt another flash of fury. Why would she do that? She didn't need to do that.

'Jesus, Kim.' He reached out his hand to her. 'Relax.'

She flinched at the word, ducking as though he'd hit her. She had tears in her eyes. Rohan felt the hot, burning swell of anger again. For God's sake, he wasn't *that* kind of man. Instead, he took a fast step forward, grabbing at her as she tried to pull away, dragging her into a tight embrace. His arm gripped around her waist and his hand rested on the back of her head. Her hair was soft entwined in his fingers. Her palms were trapped flat against his chest, her face buried in his shoulder.

'Rohan, please.' Kim's voice was muffled against him, like she was trying to catch her breath. 'They're expecting me. Rohan? Please. Let go.'

Rohan stopped listening and simply held on to her, so tight and close, because there was nothing left to say now. This was the end of them, and she must know that as well. Charlie's baby, the party at the reservoir. There was no coming back from that. But at the same time, he didn't want this to be the end. He didn't want her to leave him. It couldn't be fixed, he knew that, but he felt a childish protective surge. *She's still mine*.

He loved her, he did, even if sometimes this didn't feel like love but something painful and twisted and dark. But it must be something worth holding on to, because Rohan couldn't seem to let Kim go.

So he held her, even as she struggled, finding a fight in herself that he hadn't really thought she had. He was almost proud of her, as he whispered in her ear – *butiloveyoukim-pleasestopjusttrustme* – and pressed her face deeper into the clean cotton of his shirt. His wife's back was against the wooden safety barrier and he could feel her bracing against it, still trying to push him away, so he applied a little pressure with his elbow to her neck. They stood there, locked in a macabre convulsing dance until finally, after what felt like a long time, Kim wasn't pushing him away anymore. Rohan held her for a minute more, and then released her.

Kim slumped slack and lifeless against the barrier and it really didn't take anything to tip the balance and there was a terrible short pocket of absolutely nothing and then far below, the sickening crack and smack of something heavy plummeting through the thick bushland canopy and hitting the hidden ground beneath.

There was a silence. No. Not silence. Zoe was bawling from the car. Rohan blinked. How long had that been going on? He didn't know. He stood there, unsure how much time was passing – a minute, ten? – then made himself lean over the barrier and look down.

Nothing.

A hundred metres below, there was only an impenetrable tangle of trees. He was alone, and Kim wasn't there anymore.

They're expecting me.

Rohan looked up, out at the valley.

When he faced a difficult problem at work – a crumbling bridge, a bend in a series of support beams, life or death stuff if left unchecked – he always did the same thing. He ran through each viable option. It was an instinctive response after all these years and he almost wasn't surprised to feel it kick in now, stuttering and stumbling a little in shock before whir-ring to life. Pros and cons, non-negotiables. It was all taken into account. And eventually, the best way forward tended to become clear. Even if Rohan suspected the solution from the start, he still went through the process. It helped him commit to the decision, then execute it well.

This situation – high up and alone at the lookout – was different. But also, a strange, tiny voice whispered, not that different.

Rohan stood there, following each path of thought until at last he had a plan. He had a suitcase of Kim's belongings in the car. Her white trainers with the scorch mark, her anti-depressant medication. It was not a perfect solution, not by a long way, but it was the one he felt gave him the best chance. Rohan closed his eyes and tested it again. He could do this. If he held it together, he could.

The baby was still screaming.

Kim's daughter, Charlie's daughter. Not his. And Rohan didn't owe that child anything.

Rohan stepped away from the lookout, took a final breath, then climbed into his car. The passenger seat was empty. He started the engine and turned the wheel towards Marralee, ready to face his wife's family and friends.

Chapter 37

The placid water glinted in the late-afternoon light as Falk gazed out over the reservoir. He was waiting for Joel to arrive, the supplies they needed stacked neatly at his feet. Falk closed his eyes and felt the heat from the sun on his shoulders. The day was pleasantly warm, hinting at what would be in store in a few months' time here, when spring turned into summer. Back at the vineyard, Falk's bag lay half packed on the guest-house bed. He was due in Melbourne the following morning. He should probably check what the weather was doing there.

'Hey.'

Falk opened his eyes. He saw Joel walking along the track towards the Drop and raised a hand. 'G'day.'

'Sorry I'm late,' Joel said as he got closer. 'Zara called.'

'No worries. She okay?'

Falk and Raco had spent a lot of time with Zara over the past two days. She couldn't bear to stay still so they'd gone with her on long angry walks, Zara pounding around the reservoir trail, striding out fast, her footsteps thudding against the packed earth. A lot of the time she hadn't wanted to talk, breaking the silence only to throw out a barbed query or accusation. Other times she couldn't seem to stop, diving into circular, meandering conversations in which she asked the same questions over and over in different ways. Falk knew he and Raco weren't giving her the answers she wanted to hear, but he wasn't sure what else they could offer.

'Zara, mate, I don't think there's anything I can tell you to make this okay,' Raco had said finally.

They'd been sitting on a fallen log on a part of the reservoir track Falk had never been to before, listening to the gentle lap of the water. Exhausted, Zara had allowed herself to stop walking at last and she'd looked up at her uncle's voice.

'If you can take in anything right now,' Raco had gone on, 'I just want to thank you for not letting us give up. We loved Kim, and I know you know that. But you're the one who fought for her.'

Zara had gazed beyond him, out across the shimmering body of water. Somewhere on the other side was the stretch of reservoir track that led to the festival's east exit. Falk pictured the rope clipped across it, still and slack. No-one coming in or going out.

'What's going to happen to Zoe?' she had asked suddenly. Falk and Raco had exchanged a look. This was a different question at least, and the first time Zara had talked about anyone other than Kim. 'I knew Mum wouldn't have left her alone, but Rohan still did.' She sounded almost dazed at the realisation. 'How could he do that?'

'I'm pretty sure that at the time Rohan thought Zoe was Charlie's baby,' Raco had said gently. 'Maybe that made it easier.'

'Is she?' Zara had sat a little straighter. 'Like Nan said at the christening?'

But Raco had shaken his head. 'She's not. We can check for sure, but you can tell by looking that she's not. And Rohan took care of her all year, so he must have worked that out for himself before too long.'

'So who's going to look after her now?'

'Honestly, I don't know yet,' Raco had said. 'But we'll make sure she's all right, Zara.'

'Yeah. Okay. Good.' Zara had looked relieved, then she'd shrugged. 'I actually don't think she looks too much like Rohan, you know. She reminds me more of Mum.'

It had taken nearly thirty-six hours to recover Kim's remains from the bushland below the lookout. The dense terrain had challenged even experienced searchers as a team had attempted to navigate a way through. When the first night had fallen with still no news, Falk had felt his own doubts start to creep in. But he'd think again about that drive from Melbourne to Marralee. Pulling up at the lookout beside another car, finding Rohan Gillespie there. What had Falk seen? A grieving husband and father, taking a break to care for his young daughter and stare at the view? A controlling and violent man, composing himself at the scene of his worst act, before pulling down his mask? Falk would picture that single moment, and feel sure that the team would uncover what they were all searching for.

Finally, they had. Kim Gillespie, lost for so long, was at last found. It was only then, Falk heard, that Rohan had started talking.

'Zara seemed okay, actually,' Joel said now. He turned his head and squinted out at the reservoir, the water bright with reflected light. 'Sort of better, even. Better than she's been for a while, at least. She said the visit this morning went well.'

'Yeah, it did,' Falk said. 'It was needed, I think.'

In the early pre-dawn chill, every present member of the Raco family had gathered on the driveway outside Charlie's house. Falk had joined them as they'd driven in convoy up to the lookout, the darkness close around them. They'd arrived in time for first light, getting out of their cars at the end of the thin track and standing together in the clearing. Falk had seen Raco reach out, as always, for Rita.

Charlie had walked over to the edge of the lookout alone. He'd stared down at the dense bushland below, then covered his face and cried. His brothers had joined him, standing on either side, their heads close and their hands on his back as they spoke in soft, low voices. Eventually, Charlie had straightened and wiped his face.

'Hey, do you remember that terrible old bike Kim used to ride?' he'd said suddenly. 'The one she had that first day we saw her?'

'I remember it still took you bloody long enough to catch her on it,' Raco had said, and Ben had grinned.

'Yeah. That's true.' Charlie had smiled too. 'Worth it, though.'

They'd stayed up on the lookout and swapped stories as the sky lightened around them. Charlie had taken the lead, his memories spilling out. What he'd said to Kim when he'd finally caught up with her all those years ago, how she'd quickly become his favourite person, their happiness when their daughter was born, the way Kim used to sing made-up songs to Zara as a toddler. Zara had laughed in unexpected delight at that, brushing away her own tears as she nodded. She remembered that, and other things as well. So they'd all taken turns, standing in the clearing and reliving their favourite times with Kim, while the little kids had played on a picnic rug at their feet and the sun rose over the hills behind them.

Falk, who hadn't known Kim, had simply listened. When invited, he'd spoken briefly and from the heart about how lucky he thought Kim had been to have had all these people in her life. Lots of good people, who cared about her and each other.

'Yeah, Zara reckons it was really nice in the end,' Joel said now as he leaned against the barrier, his back to the Drop.

'It was,' Falk said. 'They're working out the funeral details, but it was good to do something like that just for –'

He stopped, a little unsure how to finish.

'Yeah, just for family,' Joel said, like it was obvious.

Falk started to correct him, but then stopped. Maybe that was right. 'Anyway,' he said. 'Let's get started, hey?'

He handed Joel a screwdriver and they crouched to open the paint can at Falk's feet. Falk pulled a couple of brushes out of a bag and together they set to work. They painted side by side as the sun grew heavier in the sky. The shadows of the graffiti marks were still there, despite their earlier cleaning efforts, and there was something deeply satisfying about seeing them disappear as the paint restored the barrier to a clear smooth white. After a while, Falk stopped and found a cloth to wipe a stray speck from the plaque.

In memory of Dean Tozer. Loved and missed.

Falk looked over at Joel.

'I'm sorry none of this gave you any more answers about your dad, mate.'

Joel shrugged, but his paintbrush slowed against the surface. 'It's okay.'

'It's not,' Falk said. 'It's still shit.'

Joel smiled at that, despite himself. 'Yeah. It is, a bit.'

'Sometimes things are. For what it's worth, I always think

no-one really gets away with something like this.' Falk nodded at the memorial. 'Not really.'

'They have, though.'

'I dunno. Having to live with it, knowing what you did. Worse than facing up to it, I reckon. But still,' Falk said, 'I get it. It's hard, not knowing.'

They worked together in silence for another minute, then Joel took a breath.

'What if I never find out?' His voice was quiet, and Falk shook his head.

'I'm not sure. Realistically, that might be the case now. I think all you can do is try to focus on what's ahead. Try not to let it hold you back from all the good stuff waiting for you. Because, honestly –' Falk stopped until the boy looked up. He wanted Joel to know he meant this. '– there's a lot of good stuff ahead for you, mate.'

Joel didn't reply but at least seemed to be considering that as he carefully painted around the plaque itself, his face relaxing for once as he concentrated on the immediate task in front of him.

They worked on, listening to the rustle and call of the bush-land and the gentle wash of the water below as the warm air helped dry the paint. It had been a while since Falk had done something like this, but he was enjoying the task. It reminded him of painting fences around the farm in Kiewarra with his dad as a kid. Whatever bad times there had been over the years, he found he was remembering the good times a lot more lately.

Amid everything, it seemed Charlie had gone straight home after their conversation in the main street earlier that week and, true to his word, had emailed Falk some figures. What it might look like if he came on board at the vineyard with Charlie and Shane. Falk had looked at the numbers, then closed the email. He'd thought about it for a while, then opened it up and looked at them more closely. He had done some sums on a piece of paper. Tried again. Got the same answer each time. He had closed the email once more. He hadn't opened it since.

'Hey, here they come,' Joel said now, glancing back along the track.

Falk wiped his paintbrush and turned at the sound of barking. Luna was racing down the path towards them with Gemma following some distance behind, her hair catching the light. She raised a hand and broke into a smile as she saw them.

'So, this is what you're both up to?' When she reached them, she ran her eyes over the clean, fresh barrier. 'Wow. Great job. I've honestly never seen this look better.' She flashed a smile at Falk. 'You know this is technically private property. Owners' permission pending, I'm guessing?'

'Something like that.' He smiled back. 'I thought, what's the worst that can happen? They send someone along later to do a better job than us?'

'Strategic rebellion. I like it.' Gemma ran a hand over the plaque, careful not to touch the paint. She turned to Joel. 'And what do you reckon? Do you think your dad would be happy?'

'Yeah.' Joel shrugged. 'Probably. But . . .' He paused, concentrating on wiping away a stray drip. 'I dunno. I've been kind of thinking about what you said a while ago.'

'Really?' Gemma looked up, surprised. 'What was that?'

'Just about how Dad'd be happy if I was happy.' Joel still didn't look at her, focusing hard on his brush. 'I was thinking maybe you've got a point about that.'

'Right.' Gemma looked at Falk over the boy's bowed head,

and her eyebrows lifted towards her hairline. She mostly managed to suppress the delight in her voice. 'Well. Yes. I mean, it's a thought to mull over, I suppose.'

She watched Joel for a moment longer, then put her arms around his angular frame and squeezed. A quick, tight hug that Joel returned, smiling a little to himself as she let him go.

Gemma turned back to Falk, her hand reaching out instinctively for his. He could feel her palm warm and dry against his own and hear the soft in–out of her breath. She stood close to him, her shoulder solid against his own.

'So,' she said. Falk's eyes met hers. 'What now?'

Chapter 38

Six Months Later

Falk stared at the computer screen and scanned the report in front of him, frowning at a couple of the numbers. He clicked open a second spreadsheet to see the corresponding figures, then did a quick calculation in the margin of the notebook in front of him.

Check this, he wrote, circling the results. The office was quiet around him and he glanced at the time. It was later than he'd thought. Falk rubbed his eyes, switched off the computer and stood, stretching. He gathered up his keys and stepped out from behind the desk.

'Luna,' he whistled softly, and she followed him out of the office, waiting at Falk's feet while he locked the door behind them.

The autumn afternoon sun was still bright in the sky as Falk and Luna headed down to the vines in search of Charlie. Falk had enjoyed watching the seasonal change in the vineyards over the past months. The harvest had gone well, both Charlie and Shane agreed. It had been a good year. Falk found Charlie fixing a length of snapped wire on one of the rows.

'Those invoices all look fine,' Falk said, holding the line taut while Charlie wrapped it around. 'I've marked a couple of items from last month that need reconciling, but I'll chase them down on Monday.'

'Great, thanks.' Charlie checked the wire, happy. 'You heading off?'

'Yeah.'

'I'm finishing up too. Time for a quick one?'

'Can't tonight. Joel's back for the weekend. Girlfriend too, this time.'

'Oh, yeah.' Charlie grinned as they started back up towards the house. 'Zara said something about that. The four of them are going for drinks tomorrow.'

'Four of them, as in Zara's bringing the vet?'

'She is. The vet is still going strong.'

He was a veterinary student intern, technically. On the advice of her therapist, Zara had decided to defer any plans and take some time out, which Falk thought was probably a wise move. She'd got a part-time job at the local animal shelter and kept bringing her work home with her, to Charlie's ongoing frustration. He never said no, though, and their back hallway now sported a line of food bowls. Zara had slowly grown friendly with the student vet, who Falk and Gemma had found to be both kind and competent when he'd checked Luna's teeth. For the young bloke's part, he seemed thoroughly thrilled to have Zara keeping him company during his year-long placement.

Zoe, now eighteen months old, was living with a local foster family who took her to playgroup and the park and dressed her in clean clothes in Kim's favourite colours. They brought

Zoe to visit the vineyard every other day. Charlie and Zara had sat down and discussed things carefully and had both been of the same mind, and Charlie was now working his way through a long and complex family court process. Gemma, who'd had to jump through a few custody hoops for Joel after Dean's death, had put Charlie in touch with her lawyer, who seemed quietly confident.

'All right, mate, have a good weekend,' Charlie said to Falk now as they reached the drive. 'See you guys on Sunday night?'

Falk nodded. The family barbecues at the vineyard had become a regular six-weekly event, when Raco and Rita would pack up the kids and drive over from Victoria for a few days. The schedule was dictated by Raco's rostered time off and marked in pen in everyone's diaries.

'Yep, see you then,' Falk said, and raised a hand goodbye to Charlie before setting off with Luna down the drive. He walked to and from work these days.

Falk had returned to Melbourne last spring, given it two weeks to see if he still felt the same, then handed in his notice at the AFP. The response from his superiors had been mild disbelief followed by genuine surprise. There had been a series of conversations encouraging him to reconsider. He'd appreciated it, but hadn't changed his mind. In the end, still incredulous, they had proposed an option of a year's unpaid sabbatical leave.

'That sounds pretty fair,' Gemma had said. 'Maybe take it, if they're offering.'

'It feels a bit one foot in, one foot out,' Falk said.

'Well, you don't have to look at it like that.' She'd smiled on the phone screen. She'd propped it up near the couch in her living room and through the door behind her, Falk had been able to see Joel studying at the kitchen table and the leftovers from dinner on the counter. Falk had been alone in his flat, the room so silent he could hear the cars passing on the road outside. The urge to be in Marralee instead was like a steady dull ache.

'I miss you,' he'd said.

'Yeah, me too. Looking forward to seeing you.' She'd glanced over her shoulder. 'Joel'll be happy to have you around, as well. So thank you again, by the way, for –' She laughed. 'You know, upending your whole life to give this a shot.'

He'd smiled at her. 'I'm happy to.' He meant it.

'I know,' Gemma said. 'But there's no point pretending this isn't a really big change.'

'So, take the sabbatical?'

She'd shrugged, then nodded. 'I think it depends on what feels right to you. But there's no harm in keeping your bridges intact. Just in case.'

So that door remained open, for now, but Falk found he never even glanced at it.

Instead, he went for long walks, wandering hand in hand with Gemma, Luna at their heels. Every day at the vineyard was different, and absorbing the layered operations that wove together to form the business was challenging and engaging. There was plenty to be done, both indoors and out, and Falk had always been a fast learner. Shane had not had to touch a spreadsheet for months and remained deeply grateful. Falk often stayed for a drink with him and Charlie before heading home; beer for them, iced water for Shane.

Falk had lived in the guesthouse on the vineyard at first, he and Gemma both agreeing it was better to take things slowly. She'd helped him unpack, sitting on the bed and leafing through his favourite novels. She'd borrowed a couple he'd recommended and invited him back to her place for dinner. Falk had turned up, then barely left. After two months, they'd given up the pretence and he'd packed up his belongings and books once more, driven to the cottage, parked under the shade of the eucalyptus trees and moved in for good.

Falk had learned his way around her kitchen, and he and Gemma spent early evenings opening and shutting drawers and passing each other sieves and pans and wooden spoons. He found out her favourite things to cook and had a crack at them himself with increasing success. They listened to music and opened good bottles of local wine and ate together at the table with the doors open to let in the warm night air. Afterwards, they'd sit on the verandah tackling the cryptic crossword online and watching the summer evening glow turn into night. Sex was regular and enthusiastic. He wore jeans to work. He shaved once a week.

Falk walked home now with Luna along the back roads, pausing as he passed the park and the oval. Shane had been on holiday from the vineyard for the past fortnight and Falk could see him kicking a football around with Naomi's three kids. She was lounging on a nearby bench, beautiful in her autumn jacket and dark jeans, half watching, half scrolling idly through her phone. She smiled and raised a hand as she spotted Falk, and he wandered over to join her.

'Hey.' She shifted up to make room. 'You've reminded me, I've got Joel's sleeping bag to return. I'll drop it by this weekend.'

'I don't think there's any rush,' Falk said. 'How was the big camping trip?'

'It was good, thanks.' Naomi smiled as her eyes followed

Shane across the oval. 'I mean, not the camping itself, obviously. That was bloody hideous. But the trip was fun. Kids enjoyed it. Shane and I had a nice time.'

'Great. Glad it's going well,' Falk said.

'Yeah.' Naomi certainly looked happy these days. 'I'm sure Shane'll have a few choice stories about camping to fill you all in on at the Sunday barbe–'

'Hey!' Shane slowed as he ran past, three kids trailing him. He pointed at Falk. 'You. Don't forget, training starts Monday.'

'Yep, mate. I remember,' Falk called back, but Shane had already gone.

'Looking forward to it?' Naomi said.

'I'm not sure.'

'Are you worried your footy skills won't be up to scratch and the other boys will make fun of you?'

Falk laughed. 'Yes, obviously, Naomi. That's exactly what I'm worried about.'

'It's a team of middle-aged men raised on wine and cheese. Trust me.' She patted his arm. 'You'll be more than fine.'

Joel was out in the back garden when Falk got home, swinging gently in the hammock with his arm around a girl. They were barefoot and lying on their backs, her long hair splayed out, talking softly together and gazing at the clouds. Gemma was absently stirring something on the stove while looking up the answers to yesterday's crossword.

'That ten-letter one was *antipodean*, by the way,' she said, leaning over to kiss him as he put his keys on the counter. 'Which is so annoying. We should have got that.'

'We really should.' Falk looked over her shoulder to see for himself, then nodded at the stove. 'You need help here?'

'No, all good. Go out and meet Molly.' She nodded towards

the teenagers outside. 'She's very nice. And it'll put Joel out of his misery. He's desperate for you two to hit it off.'

Falk laughed. 'I'm sure we will. Not that it'll matter. He obviously likes her, he's not going to care what I think.'

'You don't think so?' Gemma said mildly as she stirred and continued to scroll through the crossword answers.

So Falk made sure Joel knew he did like Molly, which was true. He liked the fact she obviously cared about Joel, for a start. They discovered they were currently reading the same book, and Falk lent her the author's previous one. She was a little shy at first, but clearly very smart, studying a technology subject that hadn't even existed when Falk was at uni.

'See, this is why I'm glad I'm not still battling it out in California,' Gemma whispered after dinner as they loaded the dishwasher. 'I slept in the office for two nights once trying to get something to work that Molly has literally just done on her phone. She said she learned that code in high school. Unbelievable. I feel a thousand years old.'

'But can she run a hugely popular and successful festival?'

'Maybe.' Gemma smiled. 'Probably, even?'

'I'm not so sure about that. But Joel seems really happy, hey?'

'Doesn't he?'

'Good to see.'

'God, yes. So good.'

After the kitchen was clean, they all watched a movie together. Falk sat with Gemma on the couch, Luna's head resting on his lap. When it was over, Joel and Molly went to bed and Falk wandered through the house, turning off the lights. He could hear Gemma moving around in their bedroom and the soft murmur of the kids talking in Joel's room. He let

Luna out one last time, waiting for her to come back and settle before locking the front door. He brushed his teeth, took off his clothes and got into bed, and he and Gemma reached for each other across the sheets.

'I love you.'

'I love you, too.'

Afterwards, Falk lay in the deep cool darkness and listened to the steady rise and fall of her breathing. He closed his eyes and slept well, as he did most nights. Because it was only very occasionally these days that Falk found himself lying awake, trying to work out exactly what was bothering him.

On Saturday mornings, Falk slept in while Gemma went to hot yoga. The house felt still when he got up, the sunlight bright in the windows as he dressed in his running gear. The door to Joel's room was still shut, with no sign of movement from either him or Molly.

This was the first time Joel had brought anyone home to stay and Falk had been sitting out on the verandah with Gemma a few days earlier when her phone had rung. It had been Joel calling from uni in a mild panic, asking if she would please tidy up his bedroom before he brought Molly back. Not even ten minutes later, he'd texted Falk, the state of panic now elevated to high, with the locations of a couple of harmless personal items he would really appreciate being quietly disappeared before Gemma got started in there.

Falk had found nothing he felt would elicit much more than a raised eyebrow from Gemma but had nevertheless covertly sanitised the scene. That done, he'd later given Gemma a hand bagging up the obvious rubbish, straightening up the stuff that wasn't and running most of what was left covering the floor through the washing machine.

Falk had come back from the laundry balancing an armful of folded clothes, and paused at the open door. Gemma had been sitting very still on the stripped bed, the swirling dust in the air carving out sharp beams of light across the room. A half-filled rubbish bag lay open in one hand and she was holding a small object in the other. It was the jar, Falk had realised with a jolt as she turned it over. The fragments of the broken barrier that Joel had collected from Dean's accident scene rattled inside. Falk had felt instantly both annoyed and surprised with himself for not having thought to remove the jar as well. He was too relaxed these days.

Sensing him there, Gemma had looked up, then immediately down at the open rubbish bag and the jar in her hand. Guilt had flashed across her face.

'He'd never forgive me.' She'd tried to smile.

'Are you okay?'

'Yeah. I am. I –' She'd put the jar down, out of sight. 'I just can't believe he still has this.'

The room was good enough, they'd decided, and had taken Luna for a long walk instead.

Gemma was back from yoga and the kids were up when Falk got home from his run. He showered and changed and they all had breakfast and coffee around the table, then put on their shoes and jackets and walked together into town. Joel took Molly off to show her around, and Falk and Gemma strolled a little further before he kissed her goodbye outside a café, waved through the window at Naomi and a couple of her other friends, and left them to it.

Alone again, Falk wandered back up the main street with

Luna, stopping for a while to browse in the bookshop. The street was busier when he re-emerged and he noticed Charlie's truck now parked up ahead. It was locked and empty, Falk could tell as he approached, but he slowed down anyway and looked around just in case. No sign of Charlie.

Falk called to Luna and kept moving. He passed the office block where Kim Gillespie and Dean Tozer had worked as next-door neighbours, and glanced over, as he sometimes found himself doing. The businesses lay closed for the weekend, their darkened windows overlooking the passers-by and the police station across the road. Falk caught his reflection in the glass. It felt like more than six months since the day he'd been standing there on the pavement and run into Charlie. When Charlie had first offered him work at the vineyard and a glimpse of the life he led now.

Falk quite often found his thoughts drifting back to that afternoon, perhaps because when he looked back now, the moment felt like a true fork in the road. Sometimes he thought he'd made his decision then, even if he hadn't realised it at the time. It had been a good decision. As he walked on now, with Luna beside him and the sun on his face, Falk knew that if he could go back, he would make exactly the same choice again. No question. Because whenever he thought back to –

Falk stopped abruptly.

A woman behind bumped into him and he apologised, stepping to the side of the pavement and out of the way. Luna followed, staring up at him as patient as ever, but Falk ignored her for once. Instead he simply stood there, with the Saturday morning foot traffic bustling past him and his thoughts some-where else entirely. Eventually, he felt Luna shift at his feet, curious as to what they were waiting for.

'Sorry,' he said to her, but still didn't move. Instead, he glanced onwards, the way they had been heading, towards home. Then he turned and looked back down the street. Falk's eyes fell to Luna's and he crouched down.

'We'll be quick,' he said, rubbing her ears. She didn't react. 'I just want to check.'

If Luna could have sighed, Falk felt she would have as she followed him back the way they'd come, walking faster this time. Charlie's truck was gone now, but Falk slowed as he neared the spot anyway. Thinking – yet again, but more carefully now – about that day six months earlier. He stopped outside the office spaces – 31A and 31B. Now a print shop and a law firm, formerly Kim's and Dean's places of work. *Small-town coincidence.* Sergeant Dwyer had told Falk that.

Falk turned and looked at the police station over the road. He hadn't fully believed Dwyer then, as he'd sat in the sergeant's office, distracted by a hundred other things. But the man had been right. Falk thought for a moment longer, then whistled to Luna and they crossed the street.

He tied her leash to the railings outside the police station, then climbed the steps and opened the door. In the reception area, he paused for another long minute, debating silently with himself while the officer behind the desk regarded him warily.

'Is Sergeant Dwyer here?' Falk said, finally. He wasn't quite sure what he wanted the answer to be.

'Back in an hour or so if you want to try then. Or you can leave a message?'

'No.' Falk was already moving to leave. 'It's fine. Thanks –'

He stopped again, though, one hand on the door as the thought lingered. Falk looked back at the reception area as he turned a question over again in his mind. It was definitely possible, he thought, but he wouldn't be able to guess. He needed someone who had been around at the time. Someone who would remember. Falk's eyes locked on the officer behind the desk, who was watching him now with mounting suspicion.

'Actually.' Falk walked back to the desk and asked the one thing he was suddenly very keen to know the answer to. The officer frowned, clearly baffled as to why this was of any interest at all. He had to think about it, cast his mind back a few years. But in the end he looked at Falk and nodded. *Yeah*. He'd been here then. And that sounded about right.

Falk had suspected it would, but he still felt a jolt at hearing the answer. 'Okay. Thanks.'

Luna seemed to be able to sense something was very wrong as she followed him home, and she had to scurry fast to match his pace. Falk felt bad and slowed a little, but he didn't stop.

The front door of the cottage was shaded by the trees and Falk caught the familiar tang of eucalyptus as he took out his key and let himself in. The house was empty and silent, as he'd expected it to be, but he was still glad. He walked straight down the hallway to Joel's bedroom. Not as neat as Falk and Gemma had left it, but a lot tidier than it had been.

Falk stood alone in the middle of the boy's room and looked around. He pictured Gemma, sitting on the bed, the dusty light slicing in from the window. Rubbish bag forgotten in one hand as she concentrated on what was in the other. He made himself focus and remember. *Where had she put it?* He turned and began scrabbling through the desk, working fast while he was still able to cling to the image he was holding in his head.

He found the small jar rattling around at the very back of the middle drawer.

Falk held it for a long minute, turning it over in his fingers.

Then he left the bedroom, moving through the quiet house to the kitchen. He opened the back door and stepped outside. He sat down in his favourite chair on the verandah and looked out at the view, the jar feeling oddly heavy in his palm. The bushland could be a thousand different colours, Falk had learned as he'd gazed out so many times now with Gemma beside him. Today, as he sat there alone, the green was full and dark.

Falk dragged his gaze away and looked down. He really was too relaxed these days, walking around with his bloody eyes closed when they should have been open. But he felt wide awake now. He turned the jar over in his hand once, then unscrewed the lid and carefully tipped the broken splinters of wood into his palm. He held them like that for what felt like a long time, making sure he was really seeing what he'd expected to see. Only when he was completely certain did he put the pieces back. One by one, tightening the lid. He lost track of how much longer he sat there, thinking about all kinds of things. The past six months. The past six years. The jar in his hand. What people will do for someone they love.

Then at last, he stood. Because he was sure, so he wanted to do this now. Before anyone came home, and he had to explain.

Falk walked back through the house. He crouched and stroked Luna's ears gently, leaving her bleating after him in the hallway as he pulled the front door closed behind him. He stepped out once more into the shade of the eucalyptus trees, got into his car and started the engine. Falk drove back into town, through the main street, and parked right outside the police station.

Chapter 39

Falk had had no reason to see the inside of Dwyer's office in the past six months, but it was exactly as he remembered it. Tidy and functional, with a single family photo on the desk.

The officer at reception looked mildly exasperated to see Falk return, but at least this time he'd been able to summon Dwyer. The sergeant had come out to find Falk in the waiting area.

'Come through, mate,' Dwyer had said, pressing the buzzer to allow access. Falk had started to follow, then paused. A collection tin for the family charity that Dwyer and his wife supported stood on the reception desk, and Falk fished around in his pockets before dropping some coins in.

'Thanks,' Dwyer said, but Falk shook his head.

'No need to thank me.'

Falk settled into the visitor's chair as Dwyer sat down at his desk. The light shone bright through the window behind him, and Falk looked beyond to the main street outside. He could see Kim's and Dean's former offices over the road, unremarkable among all the other shops and cars and people. All the commonplace, everyday sights that came together to make up this town that now felt to him like so much more than the sum of the parts. The Marralee Valley had come to feel like home. Falk took a breath. Time to get this over with. It wasn't going to get any easier.

'I think I know who was driving the car that killed Dean Tozer.'

Dwyer looked at Falk in the silent office. Backlit by the glare, his features were indistinct. He shifted and his desk chair creaked. 'Okay.'

'But if I'm right,' Falk said, 'then you know, too.'

Dwyer didn't say anything to that.

Falk waited. 'So am I right?' he said, finally. 'You do know?'

Dwyer's head moved, a tiny involuntary shake. 'You're going to have to give me a bit more than that.'

'Yeah. Okay, then.' Falk nodded. He reached into his pocket and took out Joel's small battered jar. The lid was slightly loose from having been opened and closed so many times over the past six years, the sides scratched from handling. Falk leaned over the desk, holding out the container so Dwyer could see the shards of broken wood inside. 'Do you know what these are?'

The officer put his glasses on and leaned in to look, quiet and still for a moment, then sat back. He knew, Falk felt sure. Or could guess.

'Where'd you get them?' When Dwyer took his glasses off again, his expression had altered a fraction. There was something in his face Falk couldn't read.

'Joel's kept them in a jar in his room for the past six and a half years. Chipped the wood off the barrier before it was cleared up.'

No reply.

'It's got some of the paint from the accident on it. See that, right here?' Falk opened the jar and shook a few of the larger pieces into his palm, then laid them out carefully on the desk. 'Blue paint from a blue car.'

'That's right,' Dwyer said.

'Unusual shade, though. Don't you reckon? Industrial. Lot of grey in it as well. Not all that common, when you think about car colours.' Falk looked up. 'But it was strange because as soon as I saw it, I felt like I'd seen it before. Couldn't remember where, though. I decided the festival car park, probably. Because there are a lot of cars at the festival.'

He waited.

'There are,' Dwyer said, finally.

Falk stayed quiet. The seconds ticked on. He'd really hoped Dwyer would meet him halfway on this, but the officer remained still, his face closed but his eyes alert. Fine. Falk looked down at Joel's collection lined up on the desk. They could do it this way.

'But here's the thing,' Falk said, his voice soft. 'I have remembered where I saw it. And I don't think this paint is even from a car. You know what I think it is?'

He reached out and sorted through the fragments of wood until he found the largest piece. He stood and held it up to the light, then walked a couple of paces across Dwyer's office.

At the wall, he stopped. It was still painted the same dull shade of formal office blue as it had been last year. The same as the reception area. The same shade Falk had found so oppressive both times he'd previously been at the station. Falk took Joel's sliver of broken barrier between his fingers and held it against the wall. He looked back at Dwyer. He didn't need to say it. It was obvious. The paint on the wall and the paint on the wood chip. The colours matched.

Dwyer didn't react. He didn't even blink.

'If I sent Joel's sample off to be analysed, is it going to come back as car paint?' Falk said. He tapped the wall with his knuckle. 'Or is it going to come back as this? Because according to your bloke on reception out there, around six and a half years ago, this station was being refurbished. So here's what I reckon: some of the paint used for this wall was splashed around Dean Tozer's accident scene to cover up the real colour of the car that hit him.'

'Righto. And you think that was me who killed Dean, do you?' Dwyer made a noise that sounded like a laugh, but didn't even come close. 'No. Not me, mate. I was here at the station bright and bloody early that morning. Organising the breath tests on the highway.'

'No. Actually, I don't think it was you.' Falk walked back across the office and paused at the desk. He sat down again, then leaned in and nodded at the framed family photo. 'But I think it was your daughter.'

There was a deep, heavy silence. Dwyer breathed in, his chest rising and then falling. He didn't say anything. Instead, he gently swung his chair around, angling it away from Falk and towards the window. The daylight fell bright and harsh on Dwyer's face as he gazed out towards the loose parade of locals strolling through the town that he himself watched over. The sound of Saturday afternoon laughter and conversation was muffled through the glass. Even to Falk, they somehow seemed a long way away.

'Caitlin was twenty-two when she died,' Falk said at last, when Dwyer still hadn't moved. 'Which would make her seventeen when Dean Tozer was killed. Early morning, the day after the kids' big opening night party for the festival. What happened? She was still over the limit trying to drive home?'

'She had a job.'

Falk blinked. He hadn't really expected an answer. Dwyer's voice was thick.

'She'd found herself a little part-time job working in one of the breakfast vans on the festival site. Me and her mum had made her take it because she'd been slacking off a bit at school. We'd stopped giving her money, were trying to teach her some responsibility.'

Dwyer turned his chair back, his face twisting as he ran a hand over his eyes. 'Christ. I hate that bloody party.'

He exhaled sharply, then dropped his arm. 'Caitlin wasn't supposed to go, wasn't supposed to drink. But she did it anyway, of course, because that's what they all do at that age. And most people around here think it's fine. But it's not always fine, is it? She woke up next morning, hungover, going to be late for work. Knew I'd be setting up breath tests on the highway. Knew we'd catch her if she went that way.'

Dwyer's eyes had fallen on the photo of his wife and daughter, but Falk suspected he was seeing something else.

'She called me first. Afterwards. I was already at the station, about to head out to the test site. She was a mess. The scene at the reservoir was –' He shook his head. 'Well, you saw it on that video. There was broken glass, by the way. As much as you'd expect. I swept it into the water so we couldn't test the fragments later.'

Falk looked at him. 'What colour was her car?'

'Black.' Dwyer shook his head. 'Left streaks all over that barrier.'

412

'So you covered it up?'

A tiny pause, and then Dwyer nodded. 'I already had the leftovers of a can from the station in my own boot. I was going to paint our dog kennel. So I splashed it on. Blue over black. Wasn't a great fix, to be honest, but it was my job to look closer than anyone else so . . .' He gave a heavy shrug. 'Caitlin's car was still drivable. I told her to get it home, hide it in the back garage. Told her not to let Cathy catch her.' Dwyer slumped a little at the mention of his wife.

'Does Cathy know?' Falk asked.

'No.' Dwyer was emphatic. 'She doesn't. I couldn't tell her. Couldn't do it. Still haven't. I never told anyone, told Caitlin she couldn't either.' He shook his head at the memory. 'After I did as much as I could do at the reservoir, I came back to the station. Waited for someone else to find it and the call to come in.'

Falk nodded. Dwyer attempted to meet his gaze but gave up. He rested his elbows on the desk, his head down and his face buried in his palms. Falk watched him silently, noticing with some surprise that the anger and disappointment he'd dragged in with him was beginning to soften. It was diluted with an understanding that felt almost new to him as he sat there and thought about Gemma and Joel. Raco, Rita, Eva. His godson Henry. How far would he go for these people he loved? Falk wondered. He hoped he never had to find out.

'I know how hard the last six years have been for Gemma and Joel.' Dwyer lifted his head now. 'The questions, the pain, all of it. You wouldn't be telling me anything that doesn't already keep me awake at night.'

Falk sensed that was probably true. There had been a lot

he'd planned to say, but the urgency wasn't there now. Instead, he listened.

'Caitlin wanted to tell them. She argued with me, said that we should.' Dwyer met his eyes now, steady and direct. It seemed crucial to him that Falk understood that. 'I scared her out of it. Told her not to, told her what she might be facing if she did. Jesus, she was *seventeen*. She was a confused kid and it was a stupid, unlucky accident. I did what I honestly believed was best for her.'

Misguided, Falk thought. A decision warped by love. But also probably true. Dwyer leaned back in his chair. His face was grey and his shoulders sagged. He looked ten years older.

'Guilt, though. I'll tell you, it's a dreadful thing. It eats you up. You've got no idea until . . .' Dwyer didn't finish the thought as his eyes locked on his daughter's photo. Caitlin Dwyer gazed back at them, with a smile that had been captured briefly years ago and was gone forever now. 'Some people can find a way to live with it. Some just can't.'

Chapter 40

Raco and Rita had brought Falk a rosemary and olive sourdough loaf from Kiewarra.

'It's this new thing McMurdo's trialling in The Fleece,' Raco said, unbuckling his children from their car seats. Eva and Henry greeted Falk with delight as Rita reached up and kissed his cheek. 'He read something about regional gastropubs luring out the cashed-up daytrippers from Melbourne, so he's got a new chef stocking all this local artisan gourmet stuff.'

'I bought a tub of honest-to-God tahini in there the other day.' Rita stretched her shoulders and looked out over the vineyard, raising her face to the late-afternoon light before turning back to Falk. 'I know we're always saying it, but you really should come and see this for yourself.'

'You know what?' Falk said. 'I think I actually do need to see this. Let me check with Gemma. We'll put something in the diary.'

And so they had done, then they all sat down together at the outside table, looking out over the vineyard and tearing off hunks of sourdough to pass between them as Charlie fired up the barbecue beside the barn. He and Shane fussed over the meat, while the others refilled their glasses and swapped stories as the orange sun sank lower in the sky. Eva ran through the harvested rows with Naomi's kids, chasing and hiding from each other, while Luna lay patiently nearby and let Henry stroke her ears. Falk could see Joel and Molly up on the verandah, laughing at some elaborate story Zara and the vet were telling that seemed to require a lot of mimed actions. Possibly involving a cow, he guessed.

Falk sat beside Gemma, and they held hands under the table. They had both been a little quiet, but Falk thought so far only Rita had noticed.

Gemma had listened, her back straight and her eyes dry and hard, as he'd told her about Dwyer. Falk had come straight home from the police station, taken Gemma to their bedroom, shut the door and explained the conversation he had just had. She had remained very still as he'd spoken, the frozen rigidity of the initial shock slowly beginning to pulse with a silent, controlled fury. She had said nothing for a long time and then finally: 'What happens next?'

Falk had looked her in the eye. 'What do you want to happen next?'

Gemma had sat for a long moment, then covered her face with her hands. Falk had handed her a tissue, put his arms around her and held her, quiet and close.

'Hey.' Naomi was frowning at her phone as she came out of the vineyard house, a cold bottle of sparkling tucked under one arm and a chilled water for Shane in her other hand. 'What's going on with Rob Dwyer? Are you guys hearing about this too?'

'I dunno. What?' Charlie said, turning over a steak.

'There's been something going on at the station all afternoon. Apparently he's out.'

'Out how? He's leaving Marralee?'

'No, out of the police completely.' Naomi's frown deepened as she flicked through her messages. 'That's what they're saying. Some senior people came up from Adelaide today. He's gone back with them. Not in a good way, by the sound of it.'

'Seriously?' Charlie checked his own phone. 'Can't see that staying under wraps for too long.'

Falk ran his fingers over Gemma's hand and felt the gentle pressure returned.

They had talked about it at length, together in the bedroom, Gemma swinging from rage and betrayal to something approaching compassion, and then back again.

'We need to tell Joel,' she'd insisted at one point, leaping to her feet. 'Right now.'

'We do.' Falk had put out a steadying hand. He could hear Joel and Molly outside, their relaxed words and hushed laughter floating across the garden. 'But not right now. Very soon, yes. Listen to them, though. He's happy, she's happy. We could let them have the weekend.'

Gemma had wavered, then eventually sat back down. 'What would you do?' she'd asked quietly. 'About Dwyer?'

'It doesn't matter,' Falk had said. 'It has to be your choice.'

'Yes.' She'd leaned against him. 'I'd still like to know, though.'

And so he'd told her. He'd do nothing. Gemma had looked up at that in surprise, but Falk had realised something while sitting in Dwyer's office, seeing the guilt on the man's face and the photo of his family in front of them and the charity collection tin on the counter. Neither he nor Gemma needed to do anything more, Falk felt as sure as he could be. Dwyer would make this right on his own.

Naomi was still scrolling through her phone as she put the bottle of wine down on the outdoor table. Raco opened it up and began to pour and Falk caught Gemma's eye. She gave him a smile, small but real, and a mutual understanding passed between them. They would tell the others tonight, but later, when the teenagers had wandered off and the little kids had fallen asleep in front of a movie. When the evening had settled and the talk and food and company would blunt the shock.

'I guess if Dwyer's really going there'll be a gap at the cop shop. Hope you're not planning to up and leave us,' Charlie called over. 'Shane's barely recovered from the spreadsheets.'

Falk realised Charlie was talking to him. 'Who, leave? Me?'

'Yes, mate. You.'

Raco laughed. 'Seriously? He's still AFP, if anything. That's not even close to how the national structure works.'

'Whatever. Bet they wouldn't say no, though.' Charlie grinned at Falk. 'If you were keen.'

'I'm not,' Falk said.

'No?'

Falk shook his head. He sat at the table with his friends, the sun low and the food nearly ready. The day done and the vineyard stretching out beyond. He could feel Gemma's hand in his, Luna at their feet.

'Never say never, I suppose. But no. Not now.'

This was good, now, and it was enough. He had all he wanted.

Acknowledgements

Sometimes researching a book involves huge amounts of patience, frustration and eye-watering detail, and sometimes it involves long, glorious days basking in the lush beauty of South Australia's wine regions. *Exiles* was an absolute joy to write, not least because of the setting. My sincere thanks to the many winemakers and vineyard owners, particularly in the McLaren Vale and Barossa Valley regions, who kept my glass filled so well as they offered me valuable insights into their businesses and lives in this truly gorgeous part of Australia.

My gratitude once again to the vast teams of people who have worked so hard to bring this book to readers, including Claire Craig, Clare Keighery, Ingrid Ohlsson, Cate Paterson, Charlotte Ree and Danielle Walker at Pan Macmillan Australia; Christine Kopprasch, Amelia Possanza, Nancy Trypuc and Maxine Charles at Flatiron Books; and Vicki Mellor and Lucy Hale at Pan Macmillan UK.

A huge thank you to my agents: Fiona Inglis and Benjamin Paz at Curtis Brown Australia; Gordon Wise, Liz Dennis and

Caoimhe White at Curtis Brown UK, Daniel Lazar at Writers House and Jerry Kalajian at the Intellectual Property Group.

My love and appreciation as always to my family Mike Harper, Helen Harper, Ellie Harper, Michael Harper, Susan Davenport and her parents Keith and Diane Davenport, who read and supported my books from the very start, and to Ivy, Ava and Isabel Harper.

To my beautiful children, Charlotte and Ted Strachan, who inspired all the best parts of Eva and Henry Raco, and to my husband Peter Strachan, who inspires all the best parts of everything, thank you for what you do to make these books possible. I love you very much.